White Trash & Recycled Nightmares

Rebecca Rowland

DEAD
SKY
PUBLISHING

White Trash & Recycled Nightmares
Copyright © 2023 by Rebecca Rowland
All rights reserved.

Published by Dead Sky Publishing, LLC
Miami Beach, Florida

www.deadskypublishing.com

Edited by Shawn Macomber
Cover Art: Anthony Galatis

ISBN 9781639511204 (paperback)
ISBN 9781639511228 (ebook)

Appreciation is made by the author to the editors of the following magazines and anthologies, where many of these stories first appeared, for permission to reprint.

"Layover" appeared in *Full Metal Horror III: The Unknown* (Zombie Pirate Publishing), "Extinguishing Fireflies" appeared in *Strange Girls* (Twisted Wing Productions), "Thug" appeared in *Curiouser* magazine, Summer 2021, "New and Perfect" appeared in *After the Kool-Aid is Gone* (D&T Publishing), "White Trash" appeared in *Totally Tubular Terrors* (charity anthology of the New England Horror Writers and Boston Horror Society), "Dora Mat" appeared in *Waxing & Waning*, issue 05, "Neighborhood Watch" appeared in *Coffin Bell*, issue 3.1, "Trip Trap" appeared in *Demonic Vacations* (4Horsemen Publications), "It's All Fun and Games Until" appeared in *Let the Bodies Hit the Floor*, Vol 2 (Sinister Smile Press), "The Found Boys" appeared in *In Time* (Transmundane Press), "The Thickening" appeared in *Strange Stories* (Forty-two Books), "Wendigo" appeared (as "The Thing That Goes Bump in the Night") in *Movie Monsters* (Thurston Howl Publications), "The Cave" appeared in *Little Demon Digest*, "Haunt" appeared in *Book of Bones* (J. Ellington Ashton Press)

Grateful acknowledgment is made for use in epigraph of excerpt from "The Collector" under copyright by Trent Reznor, 2005. All reasonable efforts have been made to obtain permission for use through Hal Leonard Permissions. Any inquiry about these efforts should be directed to the publisher.

Advance praise for *White Trash & Recycled Nightmares*

"Rowland's confident and poetic prose slices its way under your skin and lifts the veil on visceral, disturbing, and shocking terrors residing just beneath the norm."
—Tim Lebbon, bestselling author of *The Last Storm*

"There's nobody out there like Rebecca Rowland. These stories are razor-sharp, clever, and horrifying in all the best ways. Read everything she's written, starting with this collection."
—Gwendolyn Kiste, Three-time Bram Stoker Award-winning author of *The Rust Maidens* and *Reluctant Immortals*

"A powerfully evocative collection—packed with beautiful writing and deeply unsettling stories."
—Brian Keene

"Rebecca Rowland is a dangerous lady. She is cynical, lascivious, ironic, blood-thirsty, ice-cold, but also warmly feminist (unless the gals aren't worth it), a guy-lover (until the boys get a little too much toxic masculinity), and at any moment, she's ready to throw old snow beasts, walls of giant bugs, and...well, what's *your* nightmare? She will hand it to you freshly minted and explode your mind. You've been warned. Now read this book."
—Felice Picano

"These are some nasty stories with brutal, heartbreaking endings and shocking revelations. Rowland's characters feel like real people, so much so that you won't necessarily want those stories to end."
—Paula D. Ashe, Shirley Jackson Award-winning author of *We Are Here to Hurt Each Other*

"Sometimes shocking, sometimes mean, but always darkly entertaining, Rowland's WHITE TRASH & RECYCLED NIGHTMARES makes the dread tangible in each story."
—Kevin Kangas, director of *Fear of Clowns*

"Rebecca Rowland comes with all guns blazing. WHITE TRASH & RECYCLED NIGHTMARES is a top-tier collection of stories that fans of horror fiction will devour. The writing and characters are strong, and the concepts are both sinister and memorable. Make some space on your shelf for this one."
—Rio Youers

Contents

For Daniel Rowland,
who taught his daughter that if she could read,
she could do anything

I pick things up
I am a collector
And things, well, things
They tend to accumulate

I have this net
It drags behind me
It picks up feelings
For me to feed upon...

They will make me stay
They won't let me leave
There are so goddamned many of them
It gets hard to breathe

-Nine Inch Nails, "The Collector" (2005)

THERE WILL BE BALANCE

Sometimes, the hard, glittering truths of the world flirt with the almost ephemeral mysteries of it. For readers like me, who enjoy the thrill of horror as much as the allure of fantasy, those moments where cold reality and cooler mystery meet are some of the most exciting–and the most terrifying.

This book is full of those moments–instances of terrifying balance.

Now, Rebecca Rowland knows something about the art of capturing such moments in short fiction. This book you hold in your hands is testimony enough to that, but there's more. Counting among her extensive editorial experiences are seven horror anthologies, including the award-winning *American Cannibal*. She has clearly studied the art form of short stories, and delivers delightful throat-punches that often, only the best of short horror fiction can. Like her inspirations, particularly Chuck Palahniuk and Joyce Carol Oates, she knows when to be subtle and when to be violent, and best of all, she understands the sweet spot for horror readers that exists when violence and subtlety meet. She understands balance.

There is a mastery of image here, a deftness of language that presents a very real and insightful look into human thoughts and behaviors...as well as flaws and aberrations. There's a blend of the currently relevant with the universally and timelessly relevant, the combination of which is the human experience at its core. I believe there's a fine line, sometimes, between the uncanny valley and the everyday, and Rowland deftly darts back and forth across that line before finally plunging writers straight into the place where weird and tragic meet, that strange place of terrifying balance.

See, we understand treasure because we recognize trash, even with the subjectivity of value. And of course, we know dreams. Our greatest treasure sometimes is the ability to escape, if even only in our minds. And we value dreams all the more because we know nightmares as well. We know how quickly all that is good can be yanked away. We see that happening here, in this book, from story to story–how safety, security, sense of self, sense of the world around us, life, love, and health can be suddenly stripped away, and we can find our lives, our very selves, reduced from treasure to trash, from dreams to nightmares. Maybe that's the way of the universe, that nature (and supernature) rights things out again, that what goes around comes around, and what is given is eventually taken away. That's the horror, I think, of that place where reality and mystery meet–the idea, as is often reflected in this book, that true balance is a violent, frightening thing sometimes.

The trash in this book are the people for whom cruelty is second nature, and self-centered preservation of a way of life, however damaging, trumps the well-being of all around them. I know the phrase "white trash" has certain social connotations, but in this book, I feel it represents the idea that purity is an illusion, that innocence is never without an underlying ancient and terrible understanding. Bones, ostensibly the whitest part of any of us, are, essentially, nature's trash in the end. Balance, remember. In Rowland's worlds, we are nothing, and then, for a brief and shining moment, something (albeit sometimes something terrible), and then we return to nothing again–simply recycled nightmares.

And what is recycled in these stories? Most definitely it is the senselessness of tragedy, the horror of sudden and random acts of violence, that seem to permeate the world out there as much as the world in here, in this book.

Each story Rowland has crafted is one of balance–sometimes odd, sometimes teetering, and always unnerving. You'll find the recognizable, the familiar, and the normal, balanced out by the unusual, the alien, and the unthinkable. The magic of the writing, though, is that which parts you identify with and which you shrink away from might surprise you. They might well upset the balance in you, the reader, as good horror fiction does. And maybe that's the way of things. Maybe balance can only be found once it has been upended. Only then can the pendulum swing, its tumult and turmoil an attempt at righting the world again. That leaves a lot of exposed places, in the meantime, where truly terrifying things can surface...and often do. Things like what you'll find in the pages that follow.

In the meantime, the white trash and recycled nightmares you carry with you beyond this book, back to the cold reality of everyday life, waiting for its opportunity to flirt with mystery again, stay with you. You can try to fight them, and for a while, you might even win.

For a while.

But there will be balance.

Mary SanGiovanni
Edge of Another Dimension
July 10, 2023

LAYOVER

ADAM DIDN'T KNOW WHICH purchase it had been—the hand-carved whiskey cup that required monthly polishing with a thin coating of paraffin wax, the wine-scented bath soaps that he stuffed into Diane's stocking last winter, or perhaps the fancy night light that beamed rainbows of constellations along his daughter's bedroom ceiling each night—but someone sure as shit sold his name and address.

As if the hipster crap weren't profitable enough, now the companies earned additional income selling their mailing lists, flooding first his mailbox and then his recycling bin with a deluge of wasted paper.

Adam slid the strap of his overnight bag onto his shoulder, shifted his weight to rebalance himself, and pulled the pile of slippery catalogs and assorted envelopes from the mailbox. Diane had left the kitchen door unlocked, which was fortunate, considering Adam didn't have the grace to shuffle the stack in his arms while fishing for his house keys.

He dumped the duffle onto the linoleum and began sorting through the mail. He made three piles: one, bills and what appeared to be important correspondence; two, magazines and flyers he or Diane might want to peruse; and three, items to go directly into the trash.

The third pile was always the largest.

He didn't notice the postcard at first. In fact, if he hadn't stopped to look at the sealed envelope from a bank he didn't recognize, it might have slipped silently into the discard pile, never to be discovered. No one but his mother sent postcards anymore—and he doubted there was an event *Wish You Were Here*-able at the assisted living condo where she now resided forty-five minutes north along the New Hampshire border.

Besides, the location on the front of the card looked nothing like the green hills and valleys of New England.

Rather, the photo was of an area with flat earth and pallid grass and a cloudless blue sky, and no water in sight. Dominating the landscape was a single monstrous rock, a long, massive outcropping, narrower at the base but spreading slightly wider as it stretched toward the sky, jutting from the earth like a ship buoying above waterline, its front end slim and tapered from centuries of wind and weather. As he looked more closely, Adam spotted a figure—a plain woman in a black windbreaker standing at the helm of the pale white structure, leaning her arm against its hull, her palm spread wide along the rocky surface. With the contrast in size, Adam estimated the monolith to be about thirty-five feet high and another thirty in length. Along the bottom corner of the picture in simple, small lettering were the words *Monument Rocks National Natural Landmark, Gove County, Kansas.*

He didn't know anyone in Kansas. They must have gotten a neighbor's mail by mistake. He flipped the postcard over. Sure enough, it was addressed to him; his name, house number, street and city carefully lettered in neat block handwriting in the right margin.

In stark contrast, however, was the handwriting on the left side.

It was jagged, rushed, and only four words long.

It was your fault.

Adam flipped the card back to the photo. The woman in black leaning on the monument wasn't smiling. *More useless junk*, he thought, and tossed the postcard into the third pile, gathered the pile of trash into his arms, and brought it out to the garage for disposal.

· · · · ● · ● · · ·

Adam and Diane sat on opposite ends of the couch. The television played a show from the DVR, a new episode from a series they both enjoyed, but neither of them were really watching. She fingered the edge of her reading glasses and window-shopped on her iPad while he thumbed through social media posts on his phone. He didn't know why he looked. Everyone he knew seemed to morph into pod-people mannequins once they knew their moments were being captured for Facebook posterity. His finger pushed photos of frozen smiles...of pets in various stages of activity: sleeping, snuggling, running with their mouths open, rolling on a living room carpet...of carefully arranged dinner plates.

Adam didn't know when everyone had turned into commercial food photographers, but he had yet to log onto a social media medium without being bombarded by people's suppers.

Neither he nor his wife had spoken for at least a half hour.

"Do we know anyone from Kansas?" Adam asked at last, his voice sounding strangely foreign over the electronic hum of the television dialogue.

Diane looked up and pulled her glasses from her face. "Mike's wife is from Oklahoma, I think," she said after a moment.

Adam's eyes didn't move from his screen. "You know that's a different state, right?"

Diane snorted. "Shit. I guess Bush was right. I've been left behind." She stretched her leg and kicked her husband's hip softly. "Why? What's in Kansas?"

Adam drained the last of his vodka martini and stood up, sliding his phone into his front pocket. "Nothing. Just wondering." He began to walk toward the kitchen for a refill. "Need anything?"

Diane had already replaced her glasses and answered with a dismissive wave of her arm.

As he reached into the freezer for a handful of ice, his hip vibrated. Adam dumped the ice into the shaker and free-poured the alcohol as he checked his screen with his open hand.

You free to chat?

Adam wiped his other hand on his pants, then texted a response.

Maybe in an hour or so.

It was Marie, the woman he'd met in the San Diego airport two months earlier. They'd hit it off immediately, which wasn't such a stretch, since both of them were a bit loopy from a red-eye flight and had promptly hit the only open bar in the terminal at 10 a.m.—a tapas fusion place with beer and wine.

By noon, they were on their way to her apartment in La Jolla to take a catnap.

By four, Adam was hastily washing his face and junk in her bathroom sink and hoping that the cab arrived in time to get him to his next flight.

Marie wasn't the only woman he'd met on the road. There were many—so many, he'd have to sit down and count. Truth be told, most were now only fuzzy faces without names or even exact locations. Yet Marie had grown into a girlfriend of sorts, as much as a single woman a good decade and a half younger than him could be. Though Adam knew he had no right to ask her to wait around, to pine after him like a schoolgirl, he was convinced she was dating a stable of men. And he felt the jealousy rise in his throat like hot bile each time he considered this.

When he'd been in her apartment the previous week, he swore he could smell them, and his back stiffened like a tomcat.

She didn't reply, not right away, and then, *I'm headed out for the night in 30. Drop me a note this week when you're free maybe. Xx*

Adam swirled the ice cubes around the vodka.

What's the big plan? he typed.

He was trying to sound nonchalant.

He was failing miserably.

He strained the liquid into his glass and without thinking, gulped down half the amount immediately. The screen on his phone had gone to sleep, and he wordlessly willed it to vibrate without success.

He constructed her response in his head. *Gonna trust-fall into a big pile of cock!*

Wincing at his own imagination, he shoved the phone back into his pocket and walked back toward the living room.

· · · · · • · • · · ·

When his cell phone's piercing ring jarred him from deep sleep that evening, Adam was at first disoriented. He squinted at the digital clock nearby, then pawed in the direction of the sound in a scramble to mute it. He kept his ringer off nearly constantly, switching to audible alerts only when sleeping away during a layover as a countermeasure to assuage his anxiety at the hotel's wake up service. After silencing the sound, he glanced over at Diane, a barely visible shape motionless two feet away.

The screen on his phone read *Unknown Caller*.

He tapped the green button, pressed the receiver to his ear, and whispered, "Hello?"

There was silence on the other end and Adam assumed the party had hung up—a misdial realized too late to un-ring the nocturnal disturbance. He was beginning to pull the phone from his ear when he heard it: a quick breath, like a gasp of surprise, and then a piercing wail screamed from the earpiece: a long, unending shriek of terror, primal and desperate.

The sound stabbed Adam's eardrum like a sharp blade twisting into his brain. Startled, Adam dropped the phone. It bounced off the mattress, against the edge of the nightstand, and onto the hardwood floor.

Shaken and still disorientated, Adam jumped out of bed, snatched the phone from the ground, ran to the bathroom, and flicked the light switch. The stark white radiance was as jarring as the scream had been. Adam looked at the screen again. The caller had hung up. In its place was his regular wallpaper, the photo of him and Diane with Janie between them, the three sitting on a bench overlooking Wells Beach, watching the tide come in.

But the eerie scream still echoed in his ear.

Adam rubbed the stubble on his face and looked at himself in the mirror. His face seemed hollower than usual. Dark circles punctuated his blood-shot eyes. He was due back to work in six hours and he'd only slept for three. He placed the phone on the sink and opened the medicine cabinet, rustling through the arsenal of face creams and pain relievers the couple hoarded, finally discovering an expired but nearly full bottle of Xanax. He shook two tablets into his palm and then onto his tongue, dry swallowing them even though the crystal holder nearby overflowed with disposable cups. He'd be groggy in the morning, but at least he'd get some sleep.

· · • · • • · • · ·

The next evening, Adam lay stretched out on top of the scratchy blue quilt of the hotel room, a pile of obstinate pillows lodged between him and the headboard and a battalion of tiny vodka bottles he'd smuggled from the plane standing guard at the room service menu on the nearby desk. He'd hovered at the bar near the lobby for over an hour with no prospects for evening company and finally resigned himself to a few hours of bad television alone. He thought about calling Marie, but he was in Los Angeles. What would be the point? To talk? Were they high school sweethearts?

He picked up his cell three times but stopped himself before dialing, imagining her laughter tinkling through the receiver.

Oh, Adam, you're so funny. But why don't you call when you're in San Diego, yeah?

The honeyed voice drizzled over the barely audible push to get him off the line so that she could get ready for a date, for a night out with the girls, for a quick tumble with another traveler waiting for her in bed in the next room.

Adam selected a bottle from the congregation and twisted its tiny cap. He didn't bother to pour the liquid into a glass but drank right from its tiny top, feeling a bit like he always did at one of Janie's tea parties, the cups and plates three sizes too small for his hands. He realized he'd forgotten to eat dinner and leafed through the menu but found nothing appetizing and instead, used the nearby remote to turn on the television. Immediately, the screen buzzed to life, an available channel lineup with current show listings cascading downward.

His phone vibrated beside him. This time, it wasn't a call but a text alert from a number he did not recognize. He tapped the screen to open the message. It contained no words, only a photograph. Adam dropped the empty bottle onto the carpet beside the bed and spread his fingers on the screen to magnify what he was seeing.

At first, Adam thought it must be a crime scene photo, one of those fuzzy reproductions that forensic documentaries flashed across the screen for shock value, the victims' faces, and sometimes, exposed genitals, strategically blurred to appease the ratings police. But the photograph wasn't grainy. It wasn't a screenshot of a web image or a captured shot from the television. It showed no sign of pixelation.

It had been taken first-hand—and nothing on the subject had been censored.

The boy looked about seventeen—perhaps eighteen—years old. He was tall and thin in that late-adolescence awkward sort of way. Even as his body lay lifeless on its side, the boy's shoulders curved forward as if still self-conscious about his height. His lips were slightly parted in a small *o* and a maroonish stain had dried into a crusty blotch along the patches of hormonal acne dotting one side of his face. His hair was deep brown and slightly disheveled, as if someone had recently tousled it or removed a baseball cap too quickly.

And his eyes...?

Adam looked closer.

His eyes were entirely black, the pupils having swallowed the irises whole.

The boy was wearing a bright red t-shirt and as Adam let his fingers move the screen downward, he realized that was all he was wearing.

Which is to say, the boy—or what remained of him—ended at the torso.

His legs appeared to be missing or crushed beyond recognition, the area below his waist dissolving into a charred tangle of metallic debris and meaty pulp.

Adam turned the phone onto the quilt, facedown. He felt his stomach buckle and a sheen of sweat bead along his face. He closed his eyes and took a deep breath, then opened them and began unscrewing another of the vodka nips.

He was bringing the bottle to his lips as he picked up the cell again and dialed Marie's number.

Hey there, her voice purred after one ring. *It's Marie. You know what to do.*

A beep.

He clicked the red End Call button, then dialed another number. This time, a live person picked up and greeted him.

"I was just thinking of you," Diane said sleepily. "How's your day? What is it there? Nine o'clock?"

Adam swallowed, felt the alcohol burn a path down his esophagus and into his stomach.

"Yeah, about that," he said finally. "Is everything okay? Are you and Janie okay?" he asked nervously.

"Wha—?" Diane's concern reverberated through the receiver. "Yes, we're fine, everyone's fine. What's the matter?"

Adam paused, collected himself. "Yes, yes, everything is good. I just wanted to hear your voice, Dee," he said. "How is Janie? Did the weather cooperate for practice?"

Diane breathed a small sigh. "Oh, yeah. Rain held off the whole time. She is loving it so far. Exhausted, though. Out like a light right after dinner." She was quiet for a beat. "Have you been drinking? You're slurring your words a bit."

Adam's eyes drifted to the room service menu beside his hip. "Just a little. I forgot to eat supper. I'm ordering something now, I promise."

He picked up the booklet and opened it once more. He'd force himself to eat something, anything, just as soon as he got off the phone. He silently scolded himself for drinking too much on an empty stomach.

"Okay, well, I was just about to get into bed," Diane said, her voice still concerned. "Are you sure you're okay, Addy?"

Adam pressed his fingers into his eyebrows and kneaded slightly. "I'm good. I'll be home on Tuesday. Long day is all."

They exchanged goodnights and Adam held the phone in his hand for a moment after hanging up. He took a deep breath and opened his text messages, scrolling up and down the list of senders again and again.

The message containing the photograph of the mangled boy was gone.

· · · · ● · ● · · ·

Adam awoke on the sofa to his daughter staring at him blankly from the doorway.

"Can you read me a story, Daddy?" She was dressed in her raggedy, long-sleeved pajamas, the ones she'd outgrown at least a year earlier but still insisted on wearing, even as the hems of the pants legs crept further toward her knees.

Adam blinked and looked around the room. Christ, how long had he been asleep? Fifteen minutes? A half hour? The last thing he remembered was sitting on the couch next to Janie, watching a comedy program featuring home movie clips. Adam never saw what was so amusing about these types of shows, but they made his daughter laugh. Diane had left for her Book Club meeting an hour earlier, leaving him the reins, and he couldn't even stay conscious. What kind of parent was he?

"You're all ready for bed?" Adam asked. He tried his best to fake authority and stability, but he could see in his daughter's face that she wasn't fooled. "Teeth brushed?" She nodded her head. He tried to remember what else comprised the evening routine. He was home so infrequently at night, it was hard to recall. "You didn't take a bath, did you?"

An image of his daughter floating lifelessly in the tub, her face blue, flashed in his mind.

"No, Daddy," Janie sighed. "I took a bath yesterday, silly." She shifted from one foot to the other. "Can we read the one about the pigeon? I can read it to you."

Adam smiled. "Sounds good to me," he said and heard his knees crack as he stood up to follow her upstairs.

Janie was already climbing under the covers when he arrived at her room. She held a small, flat children's book on her lap. Adam sat on the edge of the bed and leaned down toward his daughter's pillow.

"Now what's this story about, again?" he asked her.

Janie smiled. "There is this pigeon, and he keeps saying, 'whatever you do, don't let the pigeon drive the bus!' but the pigeon really wants to drive the bus, so he tries to be sneaky and drive it anyway."

Adam watched the excitement build on his daughter's face and tried to control his own amused smile. "So, why is he warning you not to let him drive if he's going to drive anyway?"

Janie pondered the question, then opened the book to the first page. Without looking at her father, she replied, "I don't know, Daddy. Maybe he's telling us to get ready." She paused. "So, it's funny!"

She laughed, high-pitched and hurriedly, the way small children do before they learn to temper their emotions. Then she commenced with reading, Adam following along to help her sound out words that gave her difficulty.

When the story was done, Janie curled up deep into the blanket and closed her eyes, leaving the book askew next to her pillow. Adam kissed his daughter goodnight, replaced the book on her shelf, and switched on the star-pattern lamp. When he turned off the ceiling light on his way out into the hallway, the room was awash with pink and blue and yellow stars, an iridescent galaxy of dreams.

He was halfway down the stairs when the landline phone rang. It had to be Diane, or someone looking for Diane, although people rarely used the number unless they feared poor cell reception like sometimes occurred during a bad storm. He glanced at the clock. Half past eight. Diane wasn't expected home for another two hours, at least. The phone rang again, and Adam half-jogged into the kitchen to catch it before it woke Janie.

"Hello?"

There was no one on the line, just dead air.

"Hello?" Adam repeated. "I'm hanging up," he warned and listened carefully for any clue of who was calling.

It was the scream again.

This time, however, Adam heard not one voice screaming, but a symphony of them: deep, guttural cries intertwined with high-pitched wails. Barbaric, primal screams of agony screeched through the lines and into his ear. As fast as he could, he hung the receiver back onto the hook.

The house was silent. Adam felt his heart leaping in his chest. He thought of pouring himself a drink to calm down, then placed the idea high on a shelf. He'd been drinking himself into oblivion nearly every night since the postcard arrived, sometimes nursing the resulting hangovers with more alcohol. He'd gotten into the habit of chewing cinnamon gum at work nearly constantly to mask any odor leftover from his indulgence. It was a dangerous routine he'd created, and he needed to put a firm stop to it.

Adam picked up the receiver and slowly pressed the asterisk, the six, and the nine buttons. His hand shaking, he pressed the receiver to his ear again and waited. The phone rang once, then picked up, and a recording sounded.

The number you have reached is not in service. Please check the number and dial again.

He replaced the receiver and leaned his head against the wall. A minute passed, and the phone rang out again, startling him. He picked up the phone once more and listened with guarded anticipation, preparing for the cacophony.

Again, the caller was silent at first, but no scream followed. Instead, a very small voice, a voice from somewhere very far away, whispered from the receiver into his ear.

"You did this," it hissed.

And the line went dead.

· · · • · • · • · ·

Adam overslept the next morning. When he finally stumbled downstairs to the kitchen, the midmorning sun streamed square spotlights along the floors of the east-facing rooms. His head shrieked with pain, flashes of the previous evening only stubs of comprehension.

Adam remembered putting Janie to bed.

He remembered the phone call and the screams. The whisper. And he vaguely remembered calling the police station, the officer on duty at first patronizing and then quickly turning irritated, insisting Adam call back when he wasn't so intoxicated. He didn't remember drinking anything. Or, he didn't remember drinking very much. If he was honest, he didn't remember very much, period, after the conversation with the police except Diane coming home to find him sobbing on the floor, his head resting on one of the kitchen chairs.

"I'm so sorry," he said, as she helped him up the stairs and into bed. "I'm so very sorry, Diane," he repeated. "Please forgive me."

He continued to cry until the sinuses in his face swelled with pain and he passed out cold.

Adam slumped into a kitchen chair. His wife had left Janie's box of cereal on the counter nearby, within arm's reach, and he wondered if she'd done that on purpose, knowing he would be sitting there. She'd also left him a note and a sealed envelope, and as he shoveled fistfuls of sugary Os into his mouth with one hand, he held the paper with the other.

Sorry we missed you. Call me tonight. Hope you're feeling better.

PS: Janie said she drew you a photo at breakfast.
She put it in the envelope and said to take it with you.
Love you.

Adam brushed the sticky crumbs from his palm onto his knee and opened the envelope.

At first glance, the drawing appeared to be some sort of absurdist collage. Harsh, black marker lines dominated the image, outlining a long, cylindrical object, something that resembled a toilet paper roll more than anything else, with a wide, flat fin protruding from its back. It might have been a shark, but a shark broken in thirds, its head lopped off and missing from view. An inch away, another cylinder, the shark's back, perhaps; this one tapering off like a bullet.

Surrounding the broken obelisks were sticks and swirls of dark red and sandy brown crayon, a sprinkling of black marker x's mingling about the debris inexplicably. Even more strangely, a round, golden orb hovered in the top left corner, though not in the sky. Around the sun was more brown crayon and, with its close proximity, the bright yellow ball appeared to be on the same horizontal plane as everything else in the picture.

Janie had drawn him a photo of a sky fallen, floating in a sea of blood-thirsty predators. She knew the kid was creative and weird, but not this brooding.

How dark could the world of a seven-year-old be?

His phone vibrated in his pocket, and as he shoved a hand to retrieve it, he tilted the drawing in his other slightly. Still staring at the image, he lifted the phone to his face and answered it.

"Adam, it's Jed," boomed the voice into his ear. "Listen, I know you're off in three days, but can you pick up a shift? Just a day's worth, premium pay…it shouldn't put you over the cap. We're having some trouble shuffling a few coverages," he explained.

Adam could hear him gnawing on something thick, a cigar or maybe a sock, like Janie used to do when she was a toddler.

"Yeah, sure, Jed," Adam said, turning the drawing 180 degrees. Now the golden orb was on the bottom right of the frame. The gestalt was no clearer. "Where's the shift?"

More chewing. "Houston, this Sunday."

Adam's eyes drifted from his daughter's drawing to the empty alcohol bottle peeking out from the bin under the sink. He needed to clear his head. A change of scenery, more work—it was exactly what the doctor ordered.

And yet...

His eyes snapped back to the picture in his hand. There was something nagging at him from the back of his mind, a trickle of fear sliding over his brain and dripping onto his spine, sending a small shiver. He couldn't put his finger on what that something was, but he swore it was right there in front of him. He—

"Adam." Jed's voice sounded exasperated. Adam suspected he'd called a number of other people before asking him. "Sunday?"

Adam wiped his mouth with the side of his finger. "Yeah, Jed, sure," he said, "Sign me up."

Jed hung up.

Adam pushed back his chair from the table, poured himself a proper bowl of cereal, and washed back three ibuprofen tablets. In under thirty minutes, he was showered, dressed, and in his car, heading into work.

· · · · · · · · · ·

It was the jarring turbulence that woke him.

Adam felt the cold stainless steel against his cheek and opened his eyes. He had fallen asleep on the toilet and was staring at the swan neck of the faucet. He didn't know how much time had passed. He shoved the empty bottle of Xanax into his pant pocket and rubbed the right side of his face, trying to even out the red mark from the countertop nap. Someone was knocking softly on the door.

"Yeah," he answered hurriedly, "I'm coming. Just a sec."

He felt around in his jacket pocket; there were still two nips in there from lunch. He'd drink one now and save the other for his coffee with dinner, perhaps.

When he pulled the door open, the flight attendant was standing immediately outside.

"You feeling alright, Adam?" she asked. "You looked a little green at takeoff. Can I bring you a ginger ale? Maybe some Alka-Seltzer?"

Adam flashed her his wide grin, the one he'd practiced and honed into a perfect countenance—not too much tooth, not too much lip—that worked its magic to put nervous flyers at ease each time he and the crew introduced themselves to the passengers. He snatched a quick glance at the woman's nameplate.

"I'm right as rain, Annie. Just a little indigestion," he said cheerfully. "Not used to a hearty Texas breakfast, I suppose."

She eyed him with a sliver of suspicion but maintained her wide-eyed expression. "Well, you let me know if I can bring anything by, alright?"

He squeezed by her, holding his breath—he'd run out of cinnamon gum—then opened the door to the cockpit and walked inside. Jim, the white-haired co-pilot with the thick mustache, was laughing with another attendant; this one, a tall, dark-haired man. Adam slipped into the second pilot seat and strapped himself in.

"I was just saying to George here," the co-pilot said, "that I wondered if you got lost on your way back."

George chuckled and patted Jim on the arm. "I'm going to bring some coffee. Can I get you anything to go with it?" He looked at Adam expectantly.

"Coffee would be great; thanks," said Adam. His own voice sounded muted, like he was talking underwater. The instrument panel blurred, then shifted into focus. He rubbed his temples.

Jim unbuckled his seatbelt. "Looks clear for the moment," he said. "Before any more coffee, I'm going to hit the head." He stood up and walked toward the door to leave. "You got this?" he asked Adam, who nodded his head, feeling the heaviness in his brain slush back and forth as he did so.

"You missed a great view of Oklahoma City," George said when they were alone. "The Gold Dome is gorgeous this time of day. The sun's at just the right height. Glowing like a giant yellow star."

Adam nodded again, then focused his eyes on the control wheel. He gripped each side. Squeeze and release. Squeeze and release. A giant stress ball. He was feeling better already. Lighter.

At the front of the economy class cabin, Annie grabbed the handset from the wall.

"Ladies and gentlemen," she spoke into the microphone, "we are about forty-five minutes from Denver, and there's nothing but clear skies for the rest of our journey." She cleared her throat. "Those passengers on the right side of the airplane will be treated to a beautiful view of one of the Midwest's most dazzling landmarks, the chalk pyramids."

Two rows down, a teenager in a bright red t-shirt leaned his face on the window, keeping his eyes closed. At first, Annie thought he might be asleep, but he began to bob his head to the music streaming through his earbuds as a middle-aged woman in a black windbreaker leaned over him, pressing her iPhone against the glass and snapping photos.

In the cockpit, Adam squeezed the control wheel as hard as he could, felt the wet snow shift forward into a big pile at the front of his mind, and let himself fall into it. He thought of the previous winter, making snow angels with Janie, the dense silence of their empty backyard.

Perfect and unblemished.

It was Annie who was the first one to scream, and then the passengers began to join her, one by one, as the plane lurched forward, buckled, and folded into a tailspin, rocketing toward the Kansas prairie, a sculpture garden of massive white rocks stretching their hands wide to catch it.

The Perfect Costume

Mommy-lite.

That was what being a childless aunt was like.

Or, at least, that was what being a *responsible* childless aunt was like. I maintained the established rules, but did it with more smiles—more flexibility, I suppose.

And, if I were honest, I'd have to admit I was more fun to be around because I wasn't on the job twenty-four hours a day like my niece's mother.

I could afford to buy the most frivolous gifts because I didn't have to budget for school lunches and sensible children's clothes.

I could shovel candy and pizza and Popeye's chicken sandwiches down my niece's throat with abandon and avoid the next day's Pepto Bismol aftermath.

I was Auntie, and that's what aunties did.

Even responsible ones.

Elizabeth was my only niece, my sister's kid, the product of a one night stand following a particularly festive holiday party at Tara's work. *Sex on the copy machine*, Tara confessed to me, *Could I be any more pathetic?* After she said this, she licked the last scoop of strawberry yogurt from her plastic spoon then tossed the empty cup and the utensil in the garbage bin under the sink, not bothering to inquire if I recycled. We agreed not to check the pregnancy test stick until the prescribed amount of time had passed, but we both knew the answer before the alarm on my phone trilled.

Surprisingly everyone, Tara adjusted. She took a leave of absence from her job for the first year and stayed home with Elizabeth—*Lizzie*, Tara insisted, like that Hilary Duff television character she'd watched incessantly during the first few awkward years of high school—and moved into a tidy three-bedroom, two-bath home in a suburban neighborhood just east of Worcester. The rent and utilities were paid annually in full a year in advance. As it turned out, Lizzie's father was already financing a home and family, and he didn't plan on turning in that lease anytime soon. The domestic bill-paying-cum-hush money had been a bargain Tara couldn't refuse. Besides, Tara pointed out, she hadn't signed on for the whole 'til-death-do-we-part commitment when she climbed onto the office copier.

Eighteen years is enough, she chuckled, rubbing her ballooning belly a week before her scheduled C-section. *One lifestyle adjustment at a time, please.*

Tara enrolled Lizzie in daycare when she returned to work and I volunteered to keep her overnight at my apartment just north of Boston every other weekend. For the next six years, on the fortnight, Lizzie adjusted from life in a multi-floored home on a tree-lined street bursting with children her own age to one in a fourth-floor walk-up with three rooms and a galley kitchen and no trace of a human being under the age of twenty-one anywhere, not even a nearby playground.

Children are still malleable when they are little, I suppose.

On a cold early evening in mid-October, as I followed two steps behind my niece, I watched Lizzie run her hands along the natural woodwork banister of the wide staircase. She had been there a million times, but each time she entered my apartment, Lizzie craned her neck backwards in an exaggerated position to stare upwards at the tall, vaulted ceilings. Children were easily awed, I guessed, as well.

That morning, Tara had called me at work. "Think you can bring Lizzie to get a Halloween costume?" she asked—more as an instruction than a request.

I glanced at the weather app pinned to my desktop screen. The season's first snowfall—just a dusting, but still—was due on Sunday. Downtown

Crossing would be jammed with shoppers all weekend, but the subway, at least at the above ground line stretching through Malden, might be delayed if the tracks iced.

"Halloween is two weeks away," I replied, my voice hushed to keep co-workers at neighboring desks from hearing. "You're just figuring this out now?"

I was genuinely surprised. Despite the occasional spontaneous rendezvous, Tara was nothing but a ferocious planner. Before giving birth, she'd compiled a spreadsheet of every children's drink on the market, along with their sugar and net carb content. She'd insisted that nothing with the suffix *-ose*, no sucrose, lactose, fructose, or maltose, would ever be allowed in her daughter's body, as the last thing she wanted was to be the mom of a *fat kid*. "I mean," she explained, "maltose is just glucose on steroids, and sucrose is glucose *and* fructose, and—*Jesus!*—add a glass of lactose, and here I am with the fat kid with IBS from milk intolerance to boot? No thank you."

Tara worked for a food distribution warehouse. And thus, it was unsweetened almond milk and water for Lizzie from day one, with an ever-present shadow of an eating disorder looming in the not-so-distant future. As long as it kept the weight off her daughter, Tara would take it in stride.

"Don't you think I've asked her what she wants to be a million times already?" Tara said. "I even tried asking her friends' parents; you know: to see if there's some sort of character trend I'm not privy to. No dice. And every time I ask Lizzie, she tells me, 'it's a surprise.'"

"A surprise?" I echoed. "Well, maybe she's making her own costume. We did that a few years, remember?"

The phone line was silent for a moment. Finally, "I don't think my kid's the type. You know, the creative planner. That was more your jam, if I recall." I could hear my sister chewing on something: a straw or maybe a pen. There was a wet, sucking sound, then, "Come on, Carrie. You're her favorite aunt."

"I'm her *only* aunt," I corrected. I glanced at the time. "And yeah, sure, I'll bring her tomorrow. Maybe I'll get a head start on figuring out Christmas presents, too."

· · · ● ● ● ● ● · · ·

As soon as Lizzie tossed her small overnight bag into the bedroom and peeled off her heavy coat, I ordered a pizza and the two of us settled in on the couch for the evening, pushing aside the pile of linens that were stacked at one end every other Friday.

When Lizzie was smaller, we shared the queen-sized bed, but once she turned four or five, she started kicking and pushing violently in her sleep. "REM sleep behavior disorder," was Tara's immediate response after she picked up her daughter to find me nursing a black eye. "It's pretty rare in women and children, actually. Just the luck of the draw, I guess." She shrugged, then stared at Lizzie, who remained sitting on my couch even as her mother shook her jacket in the air expectantly.

I rustled my niece's hair. "We continuing our game in two weeks?" I nodded at the open Chutes and Ladders game board, its pieces frozen in a time out, balancing on the lip of the pass-through window to the kitchen.

In response, Lizzie smiled and stood up but still walked at a snail's pace toward her mother. As she wrestled her daughter's second arm into her tiny windbreaker, Tara said, "Look at poor Auntie's bruise. What do you say to your auntie, Lizzie?"

Lizzie looked shamefully at the floor. Before she could respond, I broke in. "It was just an accident, Tara. She can't help it."

However, I, a light sleeper as it was, did not want to risk further injury, and so I began sacking it out on the couch on the weekends I played hostess.

That Friday, as we took turns spinning the ticking wheel to maneuver our car-shaped game pieces around The Game of Life board, Lizzie and I ate pizza from the neighborhood delivery shop, the grease dripping from our slices and onto our chins and hands.

I moved my game piece forward. Lizzie read aloud the instructions printed on the tiny square and immediately began laughing, her mouth open and still full of masticated dough and red sauce.

"Auntie, you're getting married!" she exclaimed, then handed me the baggie of extra pegs we'd left in the box.

"I guess that means I get a nice wedding gift from you, missy!"

I selected a pink peg from the bag and placed it next to my own in the car.

"You're going to marry a girl?" Lizzie asked, taking another bite of pizza.

"Sure, why not?"

My dating life had never come up in front of my niece before, mostly because I was a bit of a commitment phobe. Despite the looming U-Haul stereotype, not one of my girlfriends—or fortuitously unplanned hook-ups—had stuck around for more than a month. It was the one trait I shared with my sister. In fifty years, I'd probably be living with Tara, Grey Gardens-style, two reclusive old women in babushkas and brocade house jackets.

Lizzie suddenly clamped a hand over her mouth.

"What's the matter?" I asked.

"I forgot: I'm not supposed to talk when I'm eating," Lizzie mumbled in a mushy voice, her tiny fingers pressed tightly together like a wall, obscuring her lips and nostrils. She swallowed, then pulled her hand away. "Mom says only pigs do that."

I playfully snatched the slice from my niece's hand and took an exaggerated bite of pizza, chewed it quickly, then opened my own mouth.

Lizzie gasped. "Gross, Auntie!" she exclaimed, then collapsed onto her side in a fit of giggles.

• • • • ● • ● • • • •

I balanced on the edge of the bed, reading the last paragraphs in the second book, my niece's eyes rapt to the pages as I turned them.

"Alright, kiddo," I yawned and waved the closed book in the air. "Looks like we'd better hit the library and get some fresh stock. Maybe tomorrow after shopping, yeah?"

"Okay, Auntie," Lizzie responded, her eyes suddenly heavy.

As I stood up, I pulled the blanket closer to my niece's neck. "Listen," I began. "Your mom is just making sure you grow up to be a polite young lady—that's why she doesn't want you to chew with your mouth full and makes you say *please* and *thank you*."

"Why?" asked Lizzie, her eyes full again.

"Why what?"

"Why do people have to be polite?"

I thought for a moment. I remembered the pink hat protest I'd attended a few years back, the women pushing tiny daughters in strollers and lugging tottering toddlers with feminist signs taped to their backs. *This is why you'd never be a good mother*, I thought. *You pretend to dish out these wise snippets of advice, but when it comes down to it, you're all surface.*

I cleared my throat. "Someone once told me that manners are important because they help make everyone feel comfortable. But that shouldn't be your reason for doing things all the time, Lizzie. You should always make certain you're comfortable, too. Okay?"

Lizzie smiled, the satin trim of the blanket tracing an underline along her bottom lip. "So I can chew with my mouth open?"

"Are you kidding? You think I want to smell that breath across the table?" I leaned down and tickled my niece's forehead, then kissed her cheek. "Night, stinky."

I awoke hours later, slightly disoriented. I grabbed my phone from the coffee table and willed my eyes to focus on the digital numbers. *3:08.* The apartment was silent, but I swore I'd heard a thump, some noise that had roused me.

Quietly padding across the hardwood floors, I pushed the door to the bedroom open and peeked inside. The window shades were open—I never closed them: it seemed pointless when living on an upper floor—and the illumination from the full moon bathed the whole room in an eerie, pale blue glow.

Lizzie was not asleep in bed.

She was not in bed, period.

Instead, she stood in front of the wide wall of windows, looking out, her disheveled hair on the back of her head a fuzzy haze framed by moonlight.

"Lizzie?" I called out quietly. "Lizzie, what's going on?"

My niece did not move. She did not acknowledge my presence at all.

I moved next to her. Lizzie was standing perfectly still, her eyes open, staring out at the dim courtyard below. *She's sleepwalking*, I thought. *Now that she is older, the kicking has progressed into wandering*. I made a mental note to double chain the door at night, then placed my hands on Lizzie's shoulders and gently guided her back into bed. My niece's eyes did not move, but in the quick glint of the light, I could see the pupils were dilated: wet, black pools of stillness, and I admit: I shivered a little, sickened by their deadness.

The next morning, I caught Lizzie staring at me over the pile of pancakes steaming between us. "Hey, did your mom tell you that you sometimes walk around in your sleep?" I asked, silently cursing Tara for not filling me in on this development. The kid could've hurt herself, for Christ's sake.

Lizzie stabbed a pancake with her fork and pulled it over to her plate, drowned it in maple syrup. "I wasn't asleep," she said. "I just like looking outside." She smiled, then shoved a mound of amber-glazed cake between her teeth and chewed happily.

"Oh, okay," I replied, confused.

The small courtyard was nearly barren, just a few unkempt bushes and patchy, brown grass. Clusters of rotting maple leaves and debris from the nearby street had blown themselves into indiscriminate piles around the property. It was nothing to gaze lovingly at, but I supposed I'd gotten used to the view in my decade of residence. Perhaps I no longer saw the forest for the autumn-barren trees.

· · · • · • · · ·

As the orange line train lurched to a jagged stop in the Downtown Crossing station, a man wearing a dirty brown leather jacket and a red-and-white striped knitted cap pushed angrily by us, nearly knocking me down. I steadied myself and without thinking, shielded my arm in front of my niece like a jersey barrier. As we disembarked into the bustling crowd of the underground, I held tight to Lizzie's hand, my niece's diminutive fingers almost imperceptible under layers of wool mitten and leather glove.

The seasonal Halloween warehouse had sprung up in a recently abandoned department store space like a tent revival, selling decorations, party supplies, and costumes for all ages and proclivities. I stood guard at the top of the aisle as my niece walked slowly down the children's display, running her hand along the polyester princess and fairy garb like she had along the banister the evening before. Soon, a handful of other children joined her, and I could see Lizzie exchange pleasantries with her peers, but over the cacophony of the store crowd, I could not make out what they were saying.

One child, a girl a bit older than Lizzie carrying a costume intended to scare—a witch? a zombie? a ghoul? something dark-colored and with sharp teeth, anyway: they poked out from atop the flowing garments—sidled up to Lizzie and began fingering a plastic scythe hanging just above their eye level. In response to this invasion of personal space, Lizzie frowned and turned her upper body so that she could face the Grim Reaper girl head-on. I stepped forward, unsure of what the girl planned to do. I could see Lizzie's mouth moving, but I could not make out what she was saying.

Just then, the Grim Reaper girl smiled broadly and leaned in to whisper something in Lizzie's ear. Lizzie pulled her head back and frowned, then responded. The Grim Reaper's face drained of color and, for a moment, I thought she might be getting ready to vomit or pass out. Before I reached the two of them, the girl turned around and scurried down the aisle and out of sight.

"What was that all about?" I asked. "Do you know that girl?"

Lizzie shrugged and turned back to the wall of accessories. "No. Just some girl."

I looked nervously down the aisle to where the child had absconded; new children began to file in, snatching randomly at the shiny clothing and knocking hats and canes and broomsticks from their hangers with their awkward perusal.

"Do you want me to help you find anything?" I asked.

The temperature in the store seemed to have risen ten to twenty degrees in the short time since we'd arrived.

Lizzie spun to face me. "I can't find what I want," she said. "Can we go to the library now?"

I frowned, imagining my sister's consternation when she picked up her child the next day sans costume. "Is your outfit a surprise? Is that why you're not telling me what it is? Because you can still surprise Mom. We can hide the costume at my place until you come for trick-or-treating in two weeks."

"My teacher said the perfect costumes are the ones that surprise people. I have an idea for my costume," Lizzie paused for a moment, then smiled. "And I want to surprise you, too, Auntie."

The man in the leather jacket and red and white cap appeared in the same car on our ride back to Malden. *Does he just ride the T back and forth all day?* I wondered. I'd heard of people doing that, especially if they were homeless or jobless, or both. Pay one fare and ride the same train as it crisscrossed Boston over and over, transferring lines to change the angle of the rotation, a spirograph around the city. In his endless Möbius strip, the man had obviously forgotten his earlier shove, or he simply gave it no mind, as when he met my eyes, he smiled—a warm smile, I thought, a genuine one that betrayed his otherwise appearance. He had the kind of face I expected to see plastered across my television set in a news story about escaped convicts people shouldn't approach.

I looked down at Lizzie. She was staring out the window, even though the train had entered a tunnel and there was nothing to look at but soot-covered walls and the occasional flashing signal. I could see my own face reflected in the glass. My niece's just below it, her eyes blank and unblinking.

"In the store, what did you and that girl talk about that made her run like that?" I asked.

The car flooded with light and the train entered the Malden station.

"This is our stop, Auntie," Lizzie said excitedly.

She stood up but held tight to the handrail in front of her as the car squealed to a stop. We stepped onto Commercial Street and I paused to zip up Lizzie's jacket and readjust her scarf. It was unnaturally cold, even for the New England coastline in late autumn. I could see our breath in the air as I leaned close to my niece, two wisps of smoke mixing together, then dissolving into nothing.

· · ●·●·● · ·

"Are you sure you don't want to just switch weekends?" I asked, turning the empty Reece's cup wrapper over and over in my hand, the sugary smell of peanut butter wafting around my desk like a tiny air freshener. "I mean, we'll have to walk a bit to get to a neighborhood with houses giving out candy."

I moved the receiver to my other ear.

"No, silly. This will be fun. It'll be like a sleepover. You'll see. Besides, spending Halloween at Auntie's house is all Lizzie has been talking about the past two weeks," Tara responded, her mouth making a sucking sound at the end.

I was suddenly irritated. I wondered if it was due to all of the sugar I'd shoveled into my mouth that afternoon. Everyone's desk seemed to be overflowing with tiny candy bars.

"What are you chewing on?" I asked. "The sound is driving me a little nuts."

I know it can't be actual food, I wanted to add. My sister drank Slim-Fast shakes even while she was pregnant.

Whatever it was, Tara removed it from her mouth, her voice suddenly clearer. She ignored the question. "We'll be there, regular time. I'll pick up Chinese for dinner on the way, ok?"

Tara kept her promise, arriving just after six-thirty carrying a large fragrant paper bag and her overnight suitcase. Lizzie trailed behind her, an oversized backpack strapped to her shoulders. The evening was especially chilly, so when our bellies were full, the three of us piled into the bed together and turned on the room's television set. Tara lay on the left side, I on the right, and before long, Lizzie was snoring happily between us.

When I awoke, the first slivers of daylight were just beginning to peek into the horizon. Lizzie had buried her face in my shoulder, one arm draped across my stomach. I turned my head to look at my sister. Tara was a foot away from us, turned on her side, her back slowly rising and falling beneath the comforter. Lizzie's head smelled faintly of cinnamon, my shampoo—she had taken a shower as soon as they arrived the night before. I leaned my face down and buried my nose in my niece's hair; I didn't wake again until my bedmates had arisen.

· · • • • • • • · ·

Despite the cold weather, most of the exhibits at the Boston Aquarium were mobbed with families; children, many of them dressed in colorful costumes, pressed their faces and hands against the glass of the three-story tank, their eyes peeled for shark sightings. At the shallow touch tank, Lizzie dipped her hands hesitantly into the warm water and allowed her hand to glide along the top of a silvery gray cownose ray. "Auntie!" she called. "It feels so smooth!"

I smiled at her from the crowd of adults standing guard a few feet away. "Hey, you should get a pic," I said, nudging my sister. Tara was pawing at her phone and chewing her bottom lip. "Do you want me to take the photo?" I pressed, pulling my own phone from my jeans pocket.

Tara tapped quickly on her screen. "Yeah, would you?" she answered without looking up. "I'm trying to solidify plans with Robert. He wants to come over tomorrow and celebrate All Saints Day with us, whatever that entails."

"Like a religious thing?" I asked. "How do you celebrate that?" I held my phone steady and snapped a few shots of Lizzie touching the stingrays.

Tara continued to text. "I don't know...he's Spanish. Like, from Spain. He says it's this whole thing where he goes to the cemetery and leaves flowers on his mom's gravestone and then has a big dinner."

"You're bringing Lizzie to visit his dead mom?"

Tara rolled her eyes and sighed, already exasperated with my inquiry. "No, dummy. He's going to the cemetery and then wants to have the big dinner with us."

I continued to watch my niece who was now petting a small shark as it swam beneath her grasp. "Celebrating death holidays with him. Sounds like this is getting serious," I said dryly.

Tara tucked her phone into the inside of her jacket. "Meh. It's an amusement, at least. Give me a break: I'm thirty-five. I'm just going to be a mother for the rest of my life?" She looked over at her daughter. "We have to find a bathroom right away and wash her hands. I don't even want to know what's on them now."

· · · · • · • · · ·

After we were certain we'd visited every inch of the aquarium, the three of us perused the gift shop, then walked slowly back to the subway station. The sun was low in the sky, and families had begun their journeys home in preparation for the evening's trick-or-treating.

At the State Street station, we disembarked and walked hand-in-hand along the long transfer corridor to the orange line. Despite the cheery rainbow painted on the hallway wall, the area smelled damp and fetid, the stench of old urine seeping into our nostrils like an obnoxious party guest whose volume only increased as an evening groaned on.

Lizzie seemed not to notice. She swung her arms blithely forward and back as we emerged from the hallway, pulling Tara's and my hands with her while she double-stepped to keep pace between us. There were only a handful of people waiting on the platform, but I could hear many more behind me, their voices echoing along the long chamber.

With her free hand, Tara thumbed the screen of her phone. "Lizzie, Robert is coming for dinner tomorrow. Are you going to show him your costume, or do you want me to take pictures tonight?"

Lizzie let go of our hands and pretended to study the giant subway map on a nearby wall.

"Did you finish your costume?" I asked, trying to keep my eyes on both my sister, who was walking obliviously close to the edge of the platform, her focus locked on her screen, and my niece, who in stark contrast, appeared to be looking everywhere at once, trying to digest everything about the station.

"Almost," said Lizzie, spinning around in a circle, her arms spread wide.

"She said it's in her backpack," Tara added. She pressed her phone against her stomach as if to hide the screen from view. "Are you excited to go trick-or-treating with Auntie tonight?" she asked.

Lizzie smiled and nodded fervently but said nothing in return. She stopped spinning and faced her mother, her face suddenly blank and focused. A gaggle of teenage boys spilled from the connecting hallway and bounded boisterously onto the platform.

The faint rumble of an incoming train echoed from the tunnel as its headlights' illumination peeked timidly into the open cavern of the station.

And with this, Lizzie ran quickly behind her mother and violently shoved her, spilling Tara, her phone still clutched in one glued hand, face-first onto the tracks.

Before I could react, before anyone could react, the approaching express train sailed around the corner and over Tara with a sickening crack, her body a surreal magician's trick as it vanished beneath the train cars. As the squeal of the emergency brakes applied a moment too late waned, the crunch of ribs and spine and skull under metal wheels slowly morphed into a wet splotching, like a lemon half being pressed inside a manual juicer.

As everything moved in slow motion around me, I turned to my niece in horror. "Lizzie?" was all I could say. "Lizzie?" again. "Lizzie..."

The seven-year-old stepped back from the tracks and slipped her hand inside of mine. "Let's go home, Auntie. We can go trick-or-treating now."

The crowd swelled, alternately gasping and sighing, and I felt the air around me soften; everything muted and melted like the aural glow of a 1970s television program.

"Oh my God, Lizzie—"

"Come on," my niece said, pulling on my hand in a buoyant attempt to drag me toward the subway stairs. "I told you I had the perfect costume."

She blinked and smiled wide.

"I'm your daughter."

Extinguishing Fireflies

I.

Lea rinsed the soap suds from the dish in her purple-gloved hand and gazed aimlessly out of the picture window in front of the sink.

A group of neighborhood children, all about nine to twelve years of age, were gathered in a loose huddle by the large oak tree at the bottom of the hill on the corner, all dipping their heads as if in shared prayer. Her daughter, Arielle, squatted down as if to study the ground a little more closely, her strawberry blonde hair glinting in the sun like slivers of pure gold had been surreptitiously woven into her locks.

Everyone had told Lea to avoid cats when she was pregnant with Arielle.

"Toxoplasmosis," Barbie said, actually pointing her finger in the air, dictator-style, to solidify her solemnity at the advice. Barbie, too, was pregnant, two months ahead of Lea, her belly rounding like a strange mushroom top on her stumpy torso. "It's serious shit, my friend. 'Causing all sorts of dementia and birth defects and God knows what else," Barbie continued. "Remember the movie *Trainspotting*? That guy died, and from a kitten, no less."

Lea rubbed her tummy. She'd taken to running her hand along the uterine outline pushing urgently between her belly button and topmost tuft of pubic hair as of late. It soothed her somehow, feeling the taut, hard musculature hardening in preparation for what she knew would be a difficult labor. All of the women in her family had spent multiple days in the delivery ward, chewing ice chips and sweating like cattle dressed in ill-fitting pastel hospital gowns. "Try to convince your doctor you need a scheduled C-section," her aunt had warned. "It will save you hours of agony and frustration." But Lea welcomed the challenge. She'd pay her dues just as all of the women before her had done.

"I think that character was supposed to be severely immunosuppressed," Lea explained calmly. "And there was cat poop all over his apartment. It's fine, Barb. Really. I wash my hands all the time."

Barbie's cat elimination crusade was inspired by her success at forcing her own wife to permanently relocate their feline ward to her mother's house two years earlier. Barbie had never liked cats, or animals in general, and her first pregnancy had been the perfect opportunity to rid her world of her partner's odious remnant from college apartment life.

Lea didn't formally own a cat, but she often fed and cared for the sparse local feral colony, leaving a few cardboard boxes with discarded bath towels next to her garage in the winter months and even brushing and feeding a few of the friendlier strays when they ventured onto her porch on quiet summer evenings. After she gave birth, she'd have a cat in the house: she was certain of it.

Barbie rolled her eyes and clicked her tongue. "Alright," she said with an audible sigh, "but when your kid comes out with four legs or extra fingers or whatever, don't say I didn't warn you."

Four and a half months later, Arielle was born with bright pink skin and a swirl of downy hair on her head.

A year later, her blue eyes darkened to a hazel-green and her forehead crinkled into a tiny M-shape when she cried.

And as a bonus, Maleeshka, an orange tabby kitten, joined Lea's household as a permanent resident.

II.

It was a cloudless Sunday morning in late May. Lea had made pancakes for breakfast, and after wolfing down at least five of them, barely registering the sweetness of the maple syrup, Arielle bounded from her chair and out the back door of the small Cape Cod home she shared with her mother. Lydia, her best friend who lived just three houses away, was already at the end of their deserted side street, drawing a hopscotch grid on the blacktop. Arielle stopped just inches from the edge of the court, then bent slightly to catch her breath.

"Hey," nodded Lydia, pushing herself to her feet and brushing the pavement dust from her knees.

"Hey," answered Arielle. She lifted a hand to her forehead and pushed away a strand of hair that had fallen loose from her barrette. She held her fingers together like a tiny fist. As her best friend one-two footed her way along the hastily drawn court she'd constructed, Arielle looked up into the dusty incline of new homes that sprawled languidly up the steeply paved hill that intersected their street. "Let's go up there," she said, pointing to the road that seemed to lead directly into the sun.

"Why?" Lydia asked. "Kelly and Lisa will be coming soon. Shouldn't we wait?"

"I don't know. I just want to see," Arielle explained. She picked up the hopscotch marker, brushed the dirt off of it, and carefully placed it in her pocket. Lea would be irritated if she got dirt on her clean clothes so early in the day.

Lydia shrugged. "Alright."

They bounced, side by side, up the hill. The girls weren't worried about oncoming traffic. Hardly anyone traveled the winding suburban side streets in their neighborhood—certainly not on a weekend morning. Arielle played the balance beam game she sometimes did when walking from one place to another and not in any hurry to get somewhere, placing the heel of her shoe directly in front of the toe of her other shoe, forming an unbroken line, then repeated the process with the back foot, walking like this as fast as she could without breaking the line or toppling sideways.

Arielle was so focused on keeping her foot alignment straight that she didn't see the boy on the bicycle barreling toward them from up the hill. He stopped short when he reached the two girls.

"Hey," he said. "Who are you?"

"Who are YOU?" answered Lydia without missing a beat, her hands on her hips. "We live down there." She pointed to the bottom of the hill, just a few houses away.

"I'm Robin. We just moved over there." He pointed across the street to a greenish-gray bungalow with redwood trim. A botanical garden appeared to be spilling over the side of one of the balconies. A set of brick steps that led to the front door was crumbling, some of the stones askew.

The two girls sized him up. He was about Lydia's height, but he was definitely older. His skin was very pale, and the exertion of riding in the morning summer sun had ruddied his cheeks. His hair was shaved military-style: painfully short on the sides and less than an inch long on top. What hair could be seen was light brown but showed carrot orange in direct sun. His eyes were squinty and brown and were framed by pale blonde, almost white, eyebrows.

"I'm Lydia," the more brazen of the two girls finally replied. "I'm ten. Arielle here is nine." She thrust a thumb in her companion's direction, then replaced her hands on her hips. "How old are you?"

"Twelve," answered their new alabaster neighbor.

Just then, Lydia leaped backwards as if stung and grabbed Arielle's arm. She stared at the edge of the curbing next to their feet. "Did you see it? The thing that just ran by?"

Arielle and Robin turned in unison and looked in the direction Lydia was pointing. Three feet in the distance, a small, brown ball with black stripes scurried away from them, toward Arielle's backyard.

"Duh. It's just a chipmunk. You guys are chickens," Robin rolled his eyes. "Girls." Arielle said nothing but stared at him for a long minute.

"Want to walk up the hill with us?" asked Lydia.

Robin hopped off his bike and smiled. Only one side of his mouth moved upward, giving him a Wile E. Coyote appearance. "Okay." He held onto the silver handlebars of his bike and walked it beside him.

The three children sauntered in silence until they reached a broad driveway flanking a wide expanse of lush green lawn, and the two girls watched in horror as Robin's front tire ventured onto the blacktop an inch.

"Don't let your bike touch their driveway!" Arielle yelled. "Get off! Get off!"

Robin, startled by the outburst, pulled his bike away like an alligator had suddenly appeared and was hungrily snapping by the foot of the road. "What? What do you mean? Why?" he asked.

Lydia looked carefully around, then lowered her voice. "Werewolves live there." She pointed up to the house at the end of the driveway, her eyes wide. "We're not even supposed to walk this close to their grass."

"Aw, you guys are stupid," Robin said, his sideways grin making another appearance. "There's no such thing." Robin swung a leg over the seat of his bike and positioned his feet on the pedals and laughed a little, but he backed the bike's wheels away from the driveway at the same time.

The girls glanced at one another. "All I know is, a few months back, like maybe two or three, a kid went missing," Lydia explained in a hushed tone. "They put flyers in everyone's mailboxes about it. I mean, not about them being werewolves, but about being careful about playing after dark and stuff."

"We're not supposed to be outside alone," Arielle added. She looked down at her feet. There was a black smudge on her right sneaker. She licked her index finger and bent down to rub away the blemish.

Robin kicked his pedal defiantly and jerked his head backward. "So what? So a kid went missing? And?"

Lydia looked quickly at her friend for confirmation, but as Arielle was too busy wiping the grime from her shoe, she continued alone. "So they found the kid two days later, right here on this lawn. His body was all cut up...like, sliced. Blood everywhere. And—and here's the creepiest part—his chest was ripped open and his heart was missing."

Robin swallowed. "Sliced, like with a big knife or something?"

"No," Lydia said. "Rows of cuts, four or five of them, over and over. Claw marks, they say. And his chest had bite marks where the heart was torn out, but not human teeth marks: deep pricks, like fangs had made them."

Arielle straightened and put her hands in the pockets of her shorts. "They found pieces of fur in the blood. That's why they think whatever killed him wasn't human. Probably a dog, but a big one. Or at least a really scary one."

Robin edged his bike further away from the driveway, bent down, and wiped the sides of his tires, as if removing the invisible murder cooties from their treads.

"It's a good thing I met you," he said finally.

The girls nodded at him solemnly.

Then the three turned around and made their way back to the corner hopscotch court where Kelly and Lisa were waiting for them.

III.

Lea squinted at the window. The girls remained in their loose circle. *What's so fascinating*, she wondered. She peeled the gloves from her hands and draped them gingerly on the edge of the sink, then shoved her feet into the old clogs that lived nearly year-round by the entrance to her three-season porch.

At first, Lea thought the rodent must be sleeping, playing possum for the audience of little girls, but after she slid her body, hips-first, into a small opening in the cluster, she saw the inch-wide half-moon circle missing from the back of the tiny animal's head, its gooey insides moist and shiny. Her daughter was still crouched, staring at the carcass.

"I bet Robin did this," said Lydia finally, not acknowledging Lea's arrival.

"You don't know that," said Arielle without looking up. She stood up then, stretching her arms downward toward the pavement and shaking her hands like a gymnast preparing to mount parallel bars. "It was probably an owl or a fox or something. Besides, you don't even like chipmunks. You scream when we see them run by."

"It looks like someone bit it," added Lisa. "You think Robin bit a chipmunk? Gross."

Lydia crossed her arms in front of her chest. "He's weird. So maybe." She looked around nervously as if to check that the topic of their discussion wasn't standing right behind her. "I don't like him," she added.

The other girls shifted visibly in their sneakers, the small crowd teetering side to side slightly.

"Yeah," punctuated Lisa, but she said nothing else.

Kelly, a tall girl with brown hair and eyes, looked at Lea. "Miss Bastille, could you get rid of it? I don't want to look at it anymore."

Lea turned to her daughter.

Arielle stared back at her but said nothing.

Finally, Lea smiled and turned back toward her house. "I'll get a garbage bag," she said. Before she began to walk, she added, "Don't touch it."

In unison, the girls' mouths drooped downward in disgust.

They didn't need to be told.

· · • • · • • · • • ·

Later that night, Lea sat on her three-season porch in the moonlight, listening to the incessant chirping of the crickets in the rhododendron bushes outside.

If she tilted her head just right, she could gaze at the faint stars in the sky. There hadn't been many fireflies that season, which saddened Lea, as she loved to watch them dance around the rows of tiger lilies that lined her property line. It was mid-July, late in the season to catch a beautiful light display, but still, she watched hopefully in the dark from her vantage point in the worn chair behind the screen.

When Arielle was small, about four years old, Lea handed her an old jelly jar and led her quietly to the blinking insects hovering along the back edge of their property one late, sticky evening. As they reached the faint outline of the flowers, Arielle dropped the jar. Lea leaned down to feel around in the dark grass and retrieve it. Her fingers caressed smooth glass and she looked up just in time to see Arielle pounce violently forward onto the congregation. Her daughter began to slap the dancing lights to the ground with ferocity, one by one. Arielle cackled with delight as each of the lights were extinguished until mother and daughter stood in the stark darkness, cold grass tickling the sides of their sandaled feet.

Lea did not bring Arielle to see the fireflies again after that.

A warm wind whispered through the window, bringing with it the summer fragrances of honeysuckle and fresh mown lawn, and Lea heard a soft scratching at the screen door. She rose to open it and, as she did, Maleeshka bounded inside and immediately onto Lea's chair.

"Oh no you don't, you seat hog, you," Lea said, picking up the orange cat and sitting back onto the chair.

Maleeshka balanced herself on Lea's lap and rubbed her face on the woman's chin. Lea stroked the soft back of her feline companion, now fully grown. Her cat had become somewhat aloof in her adult stage and Lea had to remind herself that this was all part of life: you nurtured a living thing in order to prepare it to thrive in the world independently. She ran her palms along the thick muscles on Maleeshka's wide torso and felt the cat's body vibrate with happiness.

"My Maleeshka," Lea cooed softly. The cat ducked her head into Lea's arm and purred even louder, her whole body shaking. "Did you kill that poor little chipmunk?"

Maleeshka said nothing, only pushed her head into Lea again, then dropped to her side and exposed the stripes on her stomach, her white fur luminescent in the pale light. Lea leaned closer and gently stroked her soft belly.

"What am I to do with you, my little killer?"

She continued to pet the cat softly as she looked out at the backyard again.

A lonely firefly blinked weakly along the fence.

IV.

Robin's father had bought him a vintage Schwinn American bike when they first moved to the neighborhood. It had a navy-blue seat, silver handlebars, and white hand grips, but the rest of the body was a deep apple red. Robin rode it everywhere, sometimes pedaling all the way to the top of the steep hill where he lived just to sail dangerously back down, gaining speed as he swerved along the curves of the suburban road. He rarely had to worry about obstacles. The street was traveled by residents only—even joggers avoided it due to the treacherous incline.

Robin lived alone with his father; no one knew what had happened to his mother. Robin never volunteered an explanation and he was an only child, so the secret remained carefully hidden. The only thing the neighborhood children learned was that Robin's dad loved to frontload emotions onto his son, lavishing him with marathon bonding sessions, barrages of hugs, and games of catch for a full weekend then forget Robin existed for the remainder of the week. He was a primary caregiver dressed in a divorced dad suit.

On a late weekday morning at the end of August, just before school was set to resume, Robin rang the doorbell of the white shingled Cape and shifted nervously on black rubber mat, waiting for a response. After a moment, the door opened and Lea appeared in front of him. She was wearing a red kerchief on her head, something his father's mother used to call a *babushka*, and she wiped her hands on the front of her t-shirt.

"Hi, Miss Bastille," said Robin. "Is Arielle home?"

He looked at Lea's right breast where a white smudge of whatever had been on her hands highlighted the outline of her nipple.

Lea saw his eyes and smiled but kept her lips pressed firmly together. "No, Robin," she said, "she left hours ago. I think she went to Lydia's house. You're welcome to come in and help me with the rest of the pies, though."

Robin forced himself to look at the ground, at anywhere except Lea's nipple beaming at him through the screen door.

"No," he said finally, "no, that's okay. I'll see her later, then."

He walked quickly down the three cement steps and righted his bike, which he'd left carelessly on the front lawn, and wheeled it back into the street. He was out of Lea's sight before she could shut the door.

Robin didn't want to go to Lydia's house, but he didn't want to go back to his house either. He was certain that the girls would be out to play soon. The sun was hot and high in the sky, the perfect weather for savoring the last hours of freedom before they'd be trapped in a claustrophobic classroom again.

He pedaled his routine climb up his street, passing his own house and continuing up the hill.

He passed the werewolves' home, the front of their small, tidy house guarded by large, green shrubbery—the kind of bush arrangement his father said only funeral homes should sport.

Robin saw that they had planted marigolds along the margin of their walkway. The flowers' strong scent kept tomcats from spraying, he'd heard once.

Makes sense, if they really are wolves, Robin thought. He chuckled to himself. *Stupid girls.*

It was a good half mile to the top, and the street ended in a patch of woods that disappeared suddenly into a steep ravine that hid a small stream. The neighborhood had settled into a droning hush, the late summer heat causing the homes' central air units to work overtime to neutralize the humidity. He edged his bike backwards so that his back tire touched the mossy edge of the undeveloped land and mounted his Schwinn once more. Determined to reach maximum velocity this trip, Robin began the adrenaline flight downhill.

He sailed past a woman pulling rakes and other garden tools out of her garage; whooshed past a mail carrier stuffing a small package into a street-side mailbox.

As he raced around a sharp curve, he tilted his body so severely, he knew that if he hadn't been going so fast, he certainly would have fallen over.

Might want to chart that move using a protractor when I get back to school, he thought.

He was straightening himself out of another curve just as his house came into view when, seemingly out of nowhere, a large orange cat appeared in his path.

It must have been a suicide mission on behalf of the feline interloper, as it sauntered part of the way across the road, then stopped, sat, and looked directly up at Robin as his shape grew larger and larger. The bike had picked up such momentum, a split-second decision had to be made.

Choosing to spare the wayward pet an unpleasant demise, Robin cut his handlebars sharply to the left to swerve around it. The bike lurched sideways and the front wheel struck the curbing with such force, Robin was thrown forward, off the bike, and onto the grass in front of his house. He managed a half-hearted somersault but struck his head on the bottom of the brick stairway his father had recently repaired. The cat, for its part, turned around and walked back to where it had come without a hint of apology.

Stunned by the suddenness of the whole incident, Robin remained on the ground for a moment. He felt something warm and sticky on the back of his neck and was horrified to see gobs of bright red blood on his palm after he touched his hair with his hand. He felt nauseous and curled up into a fetal position on the front lawn, closing his eyes against the midday sun.

He fell asleep— undoubtedly the worst thing to do with a probable concussion— and remained on the lawn, bleeding from his head wound, until the sun began to dip low in the sky. It was only then that his father, who had been working at home all day, wandered outside, not to check on Robin, but to check the mailbox. He ran immediately to the abandoned bike and inspected it for damage, then returned to his son's bewildered face, which was caked with dried, brown blood and sunburned a deep crimson on only his right ear, right cheek, and right side of his nose, so that he resembled some deranged villain from a comic book.

"What happened?" he asked Robin incredulously.

"I swerved so I wouldn't hit a cat," Robin explained. "My head hurts."

His father pursed his lips like he always did when he was thinking. Then he said, "Come on inside and wash up for dinner. I'll take a look at the bike in the morning. I have to finish one more thing and we'll eat."

Robin's dad returned to the house, shutting the door tightly behind him so as not to allow any more of the cold air to escape. Robin pushed himself to a sitting position and blinked, his eyes stinging. Seeing a movement out of the corner of his eye, he turned sharply to the right, the taut and injured skin on his face and neck screaming in response. There, just a foot away, sat Maleeshka, thumping her tail against the grass and staring at Robin.

"Thanks a lot," Robin said to the cat. He scowled and waited as if expecting the animal to respond with an explanation. "Why'd ya go and do that?" he asked.

Maleeshka continued to stare at him silently, but her tail's slapping accelerated its rapid rhythm.

"Idiot," he added.

Robin picked up a stray rock from the grass near his leg and threw it at the cat's head. He missed his mark, but not because he had bad aim. He missed because at that same moment, Maleeshka folded herself back on her hind legs, then sprang full-force at Robin's head, landing on his face and immediately digging her razor claws into his blistering, tender skin. She screeched and moved in a wild frenzy, tearing the damaged skin in strips from his skull, piercing his eyeball and pulling it from its socket, clamping her jaw on his nose and jerking her head back and forth until she'd ripped a hunk of flesh and cartilage from bone.

Robin's arms flailed in an attempt to bat the animal away, but they were useless. His scream was immediately muffled by a choking of matted fur over his mouth as the cat continued to bite and claw his face and neck. He could see nothing but felt himself falling backwards, back onto the grass that had begun to cool in the absence of direct sunlight. He heard the hum of the neighborhood air conditioners join together in a united requiem, and then nothing.

V.

Lea pulled the shades of her daughter's window against the blackness outside. The lamp on Arielle's nightstand cast a pinkish glow around the room, making the air feel even warmer. She sat on the edge of the twin bed and smiled. "Are you excited for school next week?" she asked, already knowing the answer.

Arielle rolled her eyes. "No, but it's getting boring here anyway. And soon it will be Halloween!" She opened her mouth in a wide grin.

Lea poked the bottom of Arielle's left incisor with her finger. "Are you ever going to lose this one?" she asked.

"Maybe I already did and it grew back overnight," laughed Arielle. "Did-ja ever think of that?" She smiled again, then closed her eyes. The two were silent for a moment, then Arielle spoke again. "Are you glad it's just the two of us, Mommy?" She opened one eye and waited cautiously for her mother's response.

Arielle had asked this question many times before, and Lea always responded the same way.

It was their special, secret game.

"I am," Lea said. "You're my sweet pussycat girl."

Arielle smiled and closed her eyes again. "And are you always proud of me?" Her lids stayed shut this time.

Lea stroked her daughter's forehead, pushing the stray locks of hair back onto her head. Then, she took Arielle's hand in hers and gently tickled her fingertips along her daughter's palm. She traced the tiny lines that ran from her wrist to the base of her fingers, then angled Arielle's hand downward and looked at the child's nails. They were still caked with dried blood and bits of skin. Lea delicately ran her own nail under each ridge to pull the debris away.

"Always, my Maleeshka," she said, and turned off the light. "*Always.*"

THUG

You can't trust a thug.

Everybody knows that.

My daddy always said, *They'll just as soon stab their companion as continue on their merry way.*

You can't blame them, really.

Every choice we make as humans is dictated by the instinct to survive.

I had this science teacher back in high school. He dressed in three-piece suits every day, even when it was hot, and he wore a series of rotating bow ties—a different one for each day of the week.

The red one was for Tuesday.

It's funny, the things you store away.

He kept my attention the whole year, even though Biology was never my jam. He once said, "When it comes down to it, everything we do in life is for just one goal: to procreate, continue the species."

Although that statement got a lot of low chuckles from my classmates—especially the boys—it's true.

It's our instinct to exist—to *continue* to exist—that rallies us forward.

Of course, that doesn't mean you have to be easy pickings for predators.

The thugs at the truck stops, they're easy to spot. Most of the time they walk with a swagger no driver can pull off after an exhausting fourteen-hour stretch. Their eyes shine everywhere at once, like the lights on a pinball machine. Their hair hangs slightly limp from running their hands through it all the time. When I spot one buying a credit for the showers, I duck out of line and force myself to eat before washing up and wait until he's retreated back into the shadows, out of the fluorescent spotlight, hair damp and ready for more palm grease.

Some of the other drivers, they seek out the thugs. Some of the shiftier ones are looking for speed or other contraband. A few might partner up to make a little extra cash under the table, hauling stolen goods or trafficked women. In the mid-nineteenth century, the Brits termed a professional criminal or a murderer for hire a *thug*, and the term stuck. Nowadays, it can mean any seedy, lawless individual—violent or otherwise.

The thugs on the roadways, they aren't so easy to spot.

There are always more people on the highways in the daytime, but I prefer driving at night.

I don't break road-time parameters. I just sleep when the sun is out.

What does it matter, so long as I make my delivery deadlines?

My cab is shaded from the daylight and the lizards don't rap on my windows so much when it's high noon.

They're probably sleeping, too.

Besides, I'm tired of the looks I get once they see I'm not a man, though sometimes the gals look relieved.

They're tired of worrying what some crazed male loner might do to them under the yellow glow of the lot lights, cracked and crazed through the dirt on the windshield.

I'm a woman who operates an 18-wheeler. I've been driving for over half my life now. I know to park my truck in the front line, closer to the building entrance, when I'm stopped for my ten-hour stretch time. I don't walk between rigs if I can help it, even in the daytime. I loop my seat belts through the door handles for extra security. And when I'm walking through a diner or a convenience store, a leather slap jack is steeled in my back pocket.

When I'm sleeping in the back of the cab, my hunting knife is by my arm. The faded flier, the one shoved into my hand that week following the night I was first pulled over, remains tacked to my wall next to my tiny microwave. It warns truckers to beware of hitchhikers, features prominently the badly drawn sketch of a mysterious figure with a sweatshirt hood pulled tightly over their face.

Sometimes that fuzzy face is the last thing I see before I drift off to sleep.

I ignore the sexual innuendo that crackles across the CB.

I am only desirable over radio waves; in person, I become invisible.

I have reached the age—or the size or shape; it doesn't matter, really—where I no longer exist to men.

It's a strange sensation, to be present one day and absent the next, even as you hold your hand in front of your face and see it's remained corporeal.

One day, it no longer matters if you're his Miss Forever or his Miss Right Now.

Then you're Miss-ed Entirely.

I admit that, when it happened—when I first disappeared—it was somewhat jarring. As much as I loathed the cat calls, the unsolicited criticism I'd glean from drivers of the Y chromosome, instructing me to return to the kitchen and care for my non-existent children, I felt somehow naked without my feminine mystique. Then I walked into a ladies' room and shut myself into a stall where, on the back of the door, I saw that someone had scribbled in clean blue ink, *A sex symbol becomes a thing, and I hate to be a thing - MM* and I got it.

Being invisible is an advantage.

No one looks twice at any embarrassing wares you might plop onto the counter at the drugstore.

No one in the next booth raises an eyebrow when you shovel heaping spoonfuls of gravy-soaked potatoes into your mouth.

My daddy took me hunting for the first time when I was twelve. I never really took to it—never got used to watching the last vestige of life evaporate from an innocent animal's eyes. Still, his knife was the first item I packed when I began long-hauling. If you've never been hunting, you might not realize the importance of a carefully selected knife. You should always go with a fixed blade. The folding ones might be more compact, but the fixed ones are stronger, more durable.

Bigger isn't always better—my classmates in that science class would have gotten a hoot out of that—but it's more important to have control over the weapon.

A clip-point blade with a sharper point is preferable over a drop-point design, but a short, serrated section at the tip makes easier work of dressing your kill. And, although stainless steel is easier to clean—a point to consider when you don't have a sink at the ready—carbon steel remains sharper for longer.

I am an independent contractor.

A sister doing it for myself, as the song goes.

When my daddy got sick, I tried sticking to short hauls, ones that would allow me to return home every night so that I could feed and care for him as best I could.

When he died, I switched to OTR driving.

Long-haul freight pay is much better and, while Daddy had dissolved into nothing, his medical bills had not. Every now and then, I supplement my income with a few underground jobs. I've built enough bridges over the years that those who find themselves in a jam know how to find me. More often than not, if I can swing it, I'll do the work off the books...and ask no questions.

I won't take a transport job from a thug, though.

That just goes without saying.

Two years into my long-haul career, I was pulled over by a Statie. At least, I thought he was state police when I saw the red flasher in my rear-view. Local cops have no jurisdiction on the interstate. I may have been going over the speed limit by a hair or two, but I had to make my clock and I didn't think the slight increase would register on a radar gun. I was still a kid then, still learning the ropes, the unspoken rules of surviving alone on the road for weeks at a time. I thought nothing of it when the man I thought was a trooper made me climb out of my rig and into the back seat of his unmarked car.

Not long after that is when I disappeared.

The showers are the hardest part to get used to, I think.

At least they were for me.

I've never been a high-maintenance kind of gal, but I did like to linger in a long, hot shower after a ten-hour day behind the wheel. For my first month sleeping in my cab, I was wary of truck stop showers and relied on the surplus of bathing wipes Daddy left behind. When I finally ventured into the line to purchase a bath credit, I steeled my back and put on my best poker face.

I didn't want anybody to smell my fear.

Once inside the stall, I locked the door and dropped my duffle in front of it, believing in that fanciful way vulnerable women sometimes do to create an additional barrier against trespassers. I kept my eyes on the doorknob the whole time, rubbing my hands over the glass enclosure to clear the condensation as the water beat down on my fetid hair and shoulders. I stepped into the clean clothes so quickly, my skin was still damp, and the fabric clung to my spine and legs, making me feel shrink-wrapped.

Just a few years later, it wasn't until the manager was beating furiously on the door to remind me my time had expired that I peeled myself up from the tiles. I just couldn't wash the dark brown moons from under my nails.

They're still there today, if you look really close.

When the fliers started appearing at rest stops and weigh stations along the interstate, I added each updated version to a rapidly growing pile under my bunk. Details of the seemingly random attacks along the highways emerged slowly, the police apparently anxious to keep their evidence close to the vest.

The victims varied in age and physical characteristics, but all had been transients in one form or another.

Travelers by car, by SUV, by semi-tractor-trailer...their abandoned vehicles discovered by law enforcement or good Samaritans only hours after their deaths, bodies slumped over the steering wheels, still dripping.

The most gruesome detail was the calling card the perpetrator left.

A signature mutilation of sorts.

During or soon after each man was killed—the fliers never specified which—the killer sliced open the victim's torso from neck to crotch as well as horizontally, to form a sort of T-shape or perhaps a plus sign then pushed hard on the sides of the abdomen to force sinew and cavity pieces to spill from the gash.

My daddy taught me to eat a baked potato that way: crisscross along the crisp skin and a gingerly smoosh from the hot bottom to ready it for butter and sour cream.

In one or two of the cases, the abdomen cuts had been too deep, severing a portion of the transverse colon so that it snaked from the upright victim's belly like a broken hose.

I think about that detail a lot when I lie in bed and look at the sketch artist's rendering.

My science teacher with the bowties went on for weeks about animal survival skills.

Most creatures aren't tremendously strong or all that large, and those that aren't find other ways to compensate for their shortcomings, like the poison dart frog with its beautiful but toxic skin or the graceful bald eagle with razor sharp talons as long as human fingers. The slyest of mammals establish a territory and defend it by marking it as their home in some significant way to let competing predators know that they won't give it up without a fight.

If the animal isn't able to properly manage its territory, it will die.

The longer it holds the fort, the stronger it becomes.

Add in the ability to camouflage, and the creature is nearly indestructible.

Fliers still appear at stops today, but they're updated less frequently.

Life moves on, I suppose.

The world is wary of bigger and meaner things, and like my science teacher said, it's all about continuation. I keep pulling my sweatshirt hood tight over my head as I scan the dark roads of the interstate each night.

The thugs who adapt to their environment are the most dangerous ones of all.

TOM MORELLO IS IN THE BACKSEAT

IT WAS SUPPOSED TO be a joke.

On an exceptionally warm spring afternoon, twenty-five years before #metoo, #TimesUp, and #YesAllWomen and nearly fifteen before hashtags, period, the men of the Alpha Beta Pi—or Pi Alpha Beta, or Beta Pi Alpha; did it matter, really?—fraternity sat around the expansive living room, staring at the image on the big-screen television one of their fathers had lugged up to the house after winter break.

It was supposed to be a joke.

And it *was* a joke—at least to the senior members of the male organization, the ones who claimed the most comfortable chairs in the room, the velour recliners and tufted sofas, while the newest recruits leaned against door frames and hunkered cross legged on the Berber carpet stiff with dried beer spills and vomit stains.

It was supposed to be a joke.

Yet, as they watched the screen, no one was laughing.

The television was one of those all-in-one units—arm-span in width, the base built into the screen so that it weighed more than a man's chest of drawers but had the stability quotient of a drunk freshman girl on a balance beam. The behemoth could not be in a home with children under the age of ten, as one energetic shake would likely send it toppling forward to mercilessly crush tiny arm bones and ribs and skulls in its wake. The picture it cast did not make up for this safety glitch, either; there was a narrow arc within which one could sit and view the screen clearly. From the side, the images were dark and fuzzy, and anyone watching from an angle had to squint to decipher the content.

Scott and Logan were hunched on the right end of the couch directly in front of the TV. Jack, the fraternity president, sat upright on the left, his shaggy brown hair placed purposefully disheveled around his face and his bare arms spread wide so that he resembled a crucified messiah. Derek, his right-hand man, stretched comfortably in the plush blue recliner next to him, clutching the remote control.

"What'd I miss?" Brad, another senior, stumbled into the room, stepping over the juniors on the floor, carelessly kicking a few of them with his Doc Martens as he plopped into the small space between Logan and Jack. Brad was more often referred to as Bread because looked a little too much like the Guy Smiley puppet on the children's show they all remembered watching as a kid, the way his feathery black hair stood staticky aloft and his eyes leered open and alert under stick-straight caterpillar eyebrows. One night at dinner, he opened his mouth to show how far he could unhinge his jaw, and Derek and Logan—the three of them high as kites all afternoon after acing the Organic Chemistry midterm—traded fuzzy snippets of an episode on the show where the puppet traced the life of a sandwich. *It's your old pal, Mr. Bread!* they screamed, over and over, irritating the rest of the brothers, who hid the house bong for more than a week after.

Scoops, the youngest of the residents at the house and the only sophomore living at the fraternity house, hovered just outside of the door frame between rooms, his sneakered feet planted firmly in the kitchen. Scoops' real name was Scott, but the frat already had a Scott. Besides, his mother worked at the Kellogg's plant and sent him weekly care packages packed tightly with boxes of Raisin Bran, something he tried to keep to himself until the brothers pestered him about why he kept a tiny refrigerator stocked with milk cartons pilfered from the cafeteria, and he reluctantly pulled out the plastic bin of cereal containers shoved under his bed for them to view.

From then on, he was Two Scoops.

Scoops for short.

Technically, the brothers argued, it was because of Scoops they were congregated in the living room.

Technically, it was Scoops' fault.

It was supposed to be a joke.

Yet now, someone—four people, to be exact—were dead.

It had been a tradition.

A ritual, really.

And rituals, after all, were sacred by definition.

Each new member of the brotherhood had to place a personal ad, run it for at least two months, and keep photographic records. The Pioneer Valley spouted a plethora of indie newspapers flooding the congregation of college towns in the Amherst area: the UMASS flagship campus was so large, it was practically a city all on its own from September to May, so there was certainly no lack of readership. *The Manor*, an alternative publication focusing chiefly on the experimental area music scene, onslaught of microbrew pubs and piercing parlors, and whiffs of avant-garde productions wafting from the Berkshires' theater scene, hosted a broad personals ad section. It was the mid-nineties, pre-Patriot Act and post-condom normalization, and anyone wishing to bypass the singles bar scene could place an anonymous ad and collect the responses with just a few taps of a push button telephone.

Except, of course, that it *was supposed to be a joke.*

The brothers weren't actually looking for companionship.

They wanted something else.

"Dude, they are crazy for it," Derek had said, slapping Scoops on the back a little too enthusiastically. "These married chicks...they've been cooped up with dirty dishes and screaming kids, and their husbands are at work all day, coming home too exhausted to give a fuck."

Bread wriggled his furry stick-brows. "Seriously, it's like the fat girls in high school. They aren't the hottest, but they make the extra effort because they know they gotta even the playing field."

He placed his mouth over the top of the long glass tube and pulled with his lungs.

The bong water gurgled and slurped as a thick fog of smoke built up in the chamber.

"We've all done it," Scott added.

And they had.

Scoops had seen the evidence: volumes and volumes of picture albums filled with Polaroids and glossy 3x5s of fraternity brothers posing with older women, some just a few years their senior, others at least a decade or more. More often than not, the women were not clothed. Or, if they were, their dresses and underwear had been pushed purposely askew for the camera by the hosting brother, making the models appear even more slovenly than they already seemed with their smudged mascara and friction-rawed lips.

Scoops noticed that nearly all of the women looked unconscious, or at least too intoxicated to notice the camera lens. He touched the edge of the photo spread with his index finger.

"I take her out on a date?" he asked timidly. "I don't even have a car."

Jack leaned his head back and laughed. His hair fell perfectly back into place as he tilted his face forward again. "First of all, we have the wagon if you need it." He was referring, of course, to the station wagon nestled quietly in the single garage of the fraternity house, another oversized parent donation that came in handy whenever the house had an event planned. "And second, most of the time, the chicks want to come here, relive their lost college years or some shit."

He pulled the neck of the bong toward his face.

"It doesn't matter where you meet them," explained Scott. "The point is, you gotta craft a romantic ad—"

"Something about appreciating older women," interjected Derek. "Fine wine, experience is sexy, blah blah, all that crap."

"Get them to meet up with you. The sluttier the outfit, the better," said Scott. "Jack and Derek can take the photos, unless you're some sort of budding Ansel Adams."

Scoops looked back down at the album. The woman in the photo at the top right corner of the page wore nothing but a plain white bra, the kind he remembered seeing in the fat Sears catalog his parents received every year before Christmas.

"Ansel Adams shot landscapes."

The woman's eyes were half-closed, as if she were being roused from surgery sedation.

"Yeah...well, whatever, you know what I mean," Scott said. "The rules are clear: she's gotta be married—living together or engaged doesn't count. She's gotta take her clothes off. And there's gotta be a picture of it." He leaned over to reminisce at the pages of photos open on the table. "Pic or it doesn't count. Dig?"

"For the album."

Scoops looked at the brothers. "For the album," he repeated.

Jack smiled, exhaling a stream of white smoke between his teeth. "Well, one copy is for the album. The other is for the cuck."

Scoops frowned.

Seeing his reaction, Jack explained. "For the husband she's fucking around on."

"We check her purse, get her address, then send the photo anonymously to the guy, give him a head's up about what his pig wife's been doing while the rooster's sleeping on the job," said Derek.

"Can't let a fellow man look like an ass just because his wife gets a little...antsy," said Scott. "Bros before hoes, my man." He held his hand up, palm facing forward, and Jack reached up and slapped it with his own. "You got this, Scoops," Scott added, slapping the sophomore's back again.

And he had—at least, initially.

Scoops, with his hangdog eyes and freckles, instantly put the women at ease when they showed up at the fraternity house that winter. The rules stated that he had to lure, undress, and snap photos of three separate married women.

The first two had been so easy, he breathed a sigh of relief when the photos came back from the lab, even felt a smile of pride tickle his face as he looked through the pictures. The women, both of them smiling—at least in the first shots in their series—holding plastic cups of vodka soaked fruit punch...then sitting on the couch in the living room...then lying on the same couch.

As the pile of photographs progressed, the women's eyelids sunk a little bit lower, creating a flipbook of their setting consciousness.

It was the third woman that inspired the joke.

She'd forgotten her purse as she stumbled off to the bathroom and Bread rifled quickly through her belongings to retrieve her wallet. Inside was a billfold displaying a rainbow of snapshots.

"Here's the lucky guy," Bread said, holding up the miniature book of pictures open to a head and shoulders shot of the woman in her bridal gown and veil cutting a tall wedding cake with a broad-shouldered tuxe-doed man.

"Aww," the brothers cooed sarcastically in unison.

Bread flipped to the next photo, then began to chuckle. "Hey, looks like Pauline here is married to a cop."

He held up the billfold again.

The man from the previous photo was clothed in dress blues.

Scott leaned closer and squinted. "Sergeant, looks like. Good for old Pauline."

Scoops looked nervously toward the hallway. "Come on, guys, hurry up," he whispered.

Bread handed the wallet to Scott, who aimed his camera at the driver's license inside. "I think we'll have to arrange a very special photograph session for the pig wife of a pig," Bread said. He raised his brows up and down conspiratorially, his big puppet mouth toothy and wide.

The brothers shoved the contents back into the purse just as Pauline walked, stumbling only slightly, into the room, holding the side of her head with one long, manicured hand. "I'm so sorry," she said. "I'm not much of a drinker. It's gone right to my head."

Her words slid greasily around her mouth, oozing like music from a record on a speed just a hair too slow.

She was captured for posterity just a half hour later.

Scoops was thinking about this, about the half-smile that had been on Pauline's face as the brothers removed all of her clothes from her unconscious body and took turns posing next to her, their arms first wrapped tightly around her bare torso then other bare body parts strategically placed for the most damning dioramas.

"That's it, That's it," Jack said excitedly, leaning forward and resting his forearms onto his knees. "Turn it up, D."

Derek pointed the controller at the television and tapped the volume button.

On the wide screen, though dotted in shadows for most of the junior brothers, teams of workers wearing navy and yellow coroner uniforms carried long, black bags on silver stretchers, gingerly stepping out of a tall brick home, down tidy cement stairs, and along a geranium-lined walkway. The camera panned sideways, revealing rows of police vehicles, radio cars and forensics vans, as well as unmarked sedans so obviously belonging to law enforcement that they might as well have government plates, then reversed direction, stopping on a crowd of looky-loos gathered transfixed by the commotion.

"Who do they bring in to investigate a cop who wipes out his whole family?" Scott asked. "More cops?"

"*Who watches the Watchmen*?" snickered Bread.

"Internal Affairs or some shit, I'd guess," said Derek.

"Would you guys shut up already?" Jack said, his eyes fixed on the continuing coverage.

A thin woman with straight brown hair, likely a neighbor, stared at a point to the right of the camera and spoke into the fat microphone being held in front of her.

"Here's the media whore, running to every network," said Bread. His voice rose into a mock soprano. *"They were such a lovely family. We'd see them at block parties and barbecues, and our kids played with—"*

"I said *shut up*," snapped Jack.

There was a low groan among the brothers as the screen changed to commercial. Jack stood up quickly, nearly knocking someone's Styrofoam coffee cup off of the table in front of him.

"I didn't hear any mention of our photos, did you?"

Jack looked around quickly, making eye contact with each of the men.

Everyone shook their heads.

"No one just ups and shoots their family out of the blue, guys," Scott said. "Even if he got the pictures." He scratched the side of his unshaven face. "No one is going to bother tracing 'em, even if they find them."

"Scott's right," chimed Logan. "Dude just wigged out or whatever. Probably a fucking ticking time bomb. All of those boys in blue, they're just itchin' to go all Rodney King on people. Just give them an excuse. Right?"

"No wonder he offed himself after," added Derek. "He was probably fucked up way before ol' Pauline got the wandering panties."

Jack stepped over the brothers on the ground and over to the sophomore, who still remained silent.

"You alright, Scoops?" he asked, slapping him on the upper arm.

Scoops smiled weakly and nodded his head.

"Good." Jack ran his hand through his hair and stepped around him. "Some people can't take a fucking joke," he said, more to the air than to any of the brothers.

Then he opened the refrigerator and looked for something to make himself a sandwich.

· · · · ● · ● · · ·

Nora leaned on the rail attached to the bar and watched her friends as they jumped and laughed on the dance floor.

"You do know this isn't a funeral, right?" Sabrina teased the woman next to her. She held up a fistful of bills to wave down the bartender. After ordering her drink, she added, "I mean, the excessive liquor alone should have clued you in."

Nora laughed. "Apparently, you haven't been to an Irish funeral." She ran her fingers through her hair and smoothed the torso of her shirt self-consciously. "Some bachelorette party. I'm the only one without a present. I feel like a jerk."

Sabrina sipped her drink. "First of all, that's not true. And secondly, don't be. There's plenty of time." She elbowed Nora. "Speaking of gifts. Want to place bets on who drops a cheesy pick-up line first?" She jutted her chin toward the gaggle of young men pushing their way through the crowded club to the bar. "My money is on the tall one with the metro hair. Any guy who spends more time grooming in the mirror than I do is definitely digging his heels deep into the Alpha spot."

Nora squinted at the approaching herd. "I say the weird-looking one with the dark hair. Certain to overcompensate for those crazy eyebrows. The comic relief." She pulled her money out of her front pocket and singled out a large bill. "Winner gets next round?"

Sabrina smiled and forced her shoulders back to accentuate her cleavage. "You're on, sucka. My money says your guy can't stand still long enough to come up with a coherent sentence."

The brothers shuffled as close to the bar as they could, angling between patrons to get the bartender's attention. Catching Sabrina's eye, Jack moved closer to the two women and leaned his hip against a barstool.

"Well, hi there," he said, flashing his best game show host grin. "I'm Jack. Can I get you two ladies a refill?"

Nora clinked her nearly full glass against Sabrina's for him to see. "I think we're good, Jack."

"...but perhaps you could stay close," added Sabrina. "We don't plan to nurse these all night." She held out her empty hand. "Sabrina."

Jack took her hand and held it for a few beats too long. "Like the 'teenage witch,' eh?" He continued to grin. "I'd better watch out—is this the coven's night out?"

Sabrina glanced at Nora and laughed. "Well, you know how it is, Jack. Even sorceresses need a little R&R."

Nora smiled brightly and held out her hand. "I'm Nora. No television reference included." She nodded toward Bread. "Who's your friend?"

Jack reached back and pulled his fraternity brother closer to the women. "Ladies, this is Brad."

Bread, for his part, smiled distractedly but turned and looked over to the dance floor. He leaned toward Scott and whispered something into his ear, and the two chuckled conspiratorially. Derek passed bottles of beer around to the group. Bread and Scott walked away without bothering to say anything further to the women.

Sabrina formed a fake pouting expression with her mouth but leaned closer to Nora to whisper in her ear.

"Told ya."

Nora kept her countenance neutral and sipped her drink.

It was true: Sabrina always knew how to read men from a mile away.

Jack's face did not change. "Seems like the party's on the dance floor. How about you accompany me, show me a few spells on the way?"

Sabrina smiled, but Nora could tell the college boy was trying her patience already.

"Sounds like a plan," Sabrina said brightly. "Meet up again at the party?" she asked Nora, winking.

Without waiting for a response, she grabbed hold of Jack's upper arm and disappeared into the growing cacophony.

All but one of the fraternity brothers dispersed, a baby-faced kid who looked barely old enough to be in college, never mind in a bar legally. The freckled-faced loner leaned his back against the spot Sabrina had vacated and tilted his bottle of beer to his lips. He wasn't what Nora had in mind, but he would do in a pinch, she thought.

"So," she said loud enough to get his attention. "Alpha Beta Omega Gamma?"

Scoops turned to look at her and quickly swallowed. "How did you know I was in a fraternity?"

Nora smiled and tilted her head to indicate the crowd. "Most of the people here are from the college, but I didn't mean a fraternity. I mean, are you an Alpha, Beta, Omega, or Gamma man?"

Scoops frowned good-naturedly. "I've heard of being an Alpha male, but not the others," he said. "And no, I'm definitely not an Alpha male." He laughed. "Despite my obvious physical prowess."

Nora smiled again. She liked his self-deprecation. She let her eyes travel up and down his body, then rested on his face. "Not the Beta either," she said, pretending to think. "Betas lack male energy. You definitely have plenty of that."

Scoops felt his face flush and he swallowed a mouthful of beer to conceal it. Clearing his throat, he asked, "So what's an Omega man, besides a Charlton Heston classic?"

Nora laughed. "You stole my punch line!" She watched Scoops look out into the crowd, scanning the dancers jumping around the main floor. "It means you pull back from power struggles, that you have no interest in being the Alpha in a group nor just one of the pack."

Scoops turned his body to face Nora. "Let me guess. You were a Sociology major?"

Nora laughed again. "It's been a very long time since I was in college."

She finished the rest of the liquid in her glass and laid the empty receptacle on the bar top.

"Maybe I'm a Gamma," Scoops volunteered flirtatiously.

"A man always on the lookout for new experiences," Nora said. "That's the best kind of man there is." She nodded toward the two women approaching them. "Here come my friends."

Tien and Leah looked similar in age to Nora and Sabrina: no older than their mid-twenties, but somehow much too old to still be in school.

Tien, the taller of the two, eyed Scoops suspiciously, then turned to Nora. "We're leaving. Anyone need a ride to the party?"

Nora glanced at Scoops. "I have the Pinto. I still have to pick up a present, so I'll meet you guys there."

An intoxicated but jubilant woman appeared next to them; a short veil attached to a laurel wreath of white satin encircled her head. She wrapped one arm around Leah and smiled broadly.

"Did someone say present?"

As if just noticing the man standing next to Nora, she widened her eyes and placed a hand delicately on her own collarbone. "Why, don't *you* look promising?"

Nora laughed. "Why don't you guys take Elizabeth with you, and I'll catch up in a minute?"

Leah stared at the fraternity brother, making him shift a bit in discomfort. "Sounds like a plan," she said, her eyes still on Scoops. "See you there, Nora."

As the three women were reabsorbed by the crowd, Scoops said, "Looks like you're running late to something, er...Nora?"

"I'm fine," she reassured him. "They were just checking on my well-being. You know how it is: girl alone in a bar swarming with testosterone. The lame pick-up lines alone are enough to cause alarm." Her eyes twinkled. "What's the best line you've ever used to get a girl to come home with you?"

The Polaroid snapshots of the naked Pauline posed in various positions flashed across his mind, and he shook his head as if to jostle them loose.

"I'm not much of a ladies' man, I have to admit."

He looked around the crowd again. None of his fraternity brothers were readily in sight.

"How about you? Any foolproof one-liners?"

Nora leaned closer to him. He could smell her perfume, a clean musky scent mingling with the sweetness of her breath. "I tell the guys that Tom Morello is in the backseat."

Scoops laughed. "Wait—what?"

She looked around dramatically and lowered her voice as if revealing a top-secret mission.

"Say I'm in the front seat of the car, and things get...romantic. I tell the guy, *Tom Morello is in the back seat.*"

"The guitarist from Rage Against the Machine?"

"That's the one. But what you call a mere guitarist, I call a musical god, thank you."

"And that moves things along, does it?"

Nora raised an eyebrow. "You have to admit, if Tom Morello were in the back seat, you'd jump back there in a heartbeat whether you found me attractive or not. The coolness factor is irresistible."

Scoops smiled into his beer. "You got me there, I guess." He leaned back onto the bar. "I suppose a better question would be, has Tom Morello ever been there when you've climbed into the back?"

Nora thought for a moment. "Not yet. But like Schrödinger's cat, until you check each time, you can never really know for sure, right?"

Scoops emptied the rest of his beer into his mouth and shoved the bottle onto the bar. He held out his hand.

"I'm Scott," he said.

Nora accepted his hand and shook it lightly.

"It's very nice to meet you, Scott. How'd you like to be my last-minute date to a party this evening?"

· · · • · • • · ·

The air outside felt cleaner, thinner, than it had inside of the club. All of the warm bodies writhing like intertwined snakes about a swamp pit had made the bar smell almost inhuman.

A dying smell, Scoops thought.

Again, his mind flashed back to the afternoon, the image of the smallest body bag being wheeled out of the suburban Colonial.

"This is me," said Nora, pointing to a rusting beige two-door parked under a streetlamp.

Scoops opened the passenger door and climbed inside, the back of his jeans sliding a bit on the vinyl seat.

"Pinto hatchback," he said, looking around the dimly lit interior. "I didn't think any of these were on the road anymore. Didn't they all blow up?"

Nora put the key in the ignition and paused. "I did toss out that recall notice last week," she said, suddenly mock serious. "Well, cross your fingers."

She smiled and turned the key forward.

The engine stuttered for a beat then roared to life.

The after-market cassette player illuminated and music—much louder than Scoops had anticipated—filled the car, Zack de la Rocha screaming that he didn't need a key, he'd break in.

"'Know Your Enemy.' Nice choice," said Scoops.

He watched the sleeping businesses and silenced houses flash by as Nora's car sailed along the main road, then turned onto a side street.

"I couldn't agree more," said Nora, who took her eyes from the road only to wink at Scoops before resuming her focus forward.

The two were silent for a while, listening to the music. Finally, Nora took a sharp right onto an unpaved road that led into an expanse of thickly foliaged woods. The car bounced and shifted as it maneuvered the uneven terrain.

When Scoops turned to look out of the car's back window, he saw nothing but a gaping maw of shadow. Any hint of civilization had been swallowed whole by the forest.

"What sort of party is this?" asked Scoops. "A pagan sacrifice ritual?"

Nora laughed. "Somebody once told me that horror movies are the best movies to take a date," she said.

Nora squinted at the darkness that hovered just beyond the reach of the headlamps' faint incandescence. The car slowed to a stop, and Nora pushed the shifter into park. She turned to face Scoops, her face barely visible in the glow of the dashboard.

"Something about the adrenaline rush, how it heightens the nervous excitement of attraction."

Scoops let his eyes wander along the faint outline of her neck and shoulders, the firm roundness of her breasts. "You ever see the *Twilight Zone* movie?" he asked. "The one with Dan Akroyd in the car at the beginning?"

"Of course," she said. After a beat, she leaned forward and kissed him. Her mouth was wet, hungry. When she finally pulled away, she tilted her head and whispered, "Why? *Do you want to see something really scary?* Because...well, I—"

"—think Tom Morello might be in the backseat?" finished Scoops.

He grabbed the back of her neck and pulled her back to him. They moved closer to one another, their hands running over each other's bodies, then under their clothes, pushing them upward, open. Without further discussion, they climbed between the front bucket seats and slid into the back of the car.

"Take your clothes off," Nora whispered.

Her soft, warm hand cupped his face, then slowly stroked his ear. The height of the front seat blocked much of the dashboard. It was so much darker now, he could barely make out her shape in the darkness.

Shivering, he slipped off his t-shirt, pushed his sneakers from his feet, and arched his back to slide off his jeans and boxer shorts. When even his socks had been removed, he reached in the direction of Nora's voice to pull her bare body to his.

Except, when his hand met her shoulder, it was still clothed. "Hey, I—"

There was a sudden flash of light in the window and he *sensed* rather than *saw* Nora's arm as it moved quickly through the air toward his face.

The excruciation of the leather slapjack on his temple blinded him all over again.

Scoops felt a rush of nausea roll over his body and, as the door behind Nora opened with a long, loud creak, he felt himself falling sideways, his cheek meeting the tacky vinyl with a muffled thud.

Sticks and gravel tore into the skin of his heels. He was floating backwards, elevated like a struggling magician's trick, his head nearly four feet in the air and his feet diagonally dragging along the ground. Strong hands gripped him under his arms and around his naked thighs. His erection, softened but still struggling for closure, bobbed weakly in the air like a deflated rubber flagpole. Above him, the sky was dotted with a million stars.

Gradually, the trees on either side of him sharpened, a soft yellow glow illuminating their trunks and surrounding shrubbery. His captors let go of him in unison, but before he could react, someone yanked his arms behind his back and tied his wrists.

Scoops tried to turn his head to see what was happening, but his skull screamed in agony.

The now familiar smell of clean musk wafted over his face.

"Scott," Nora said, placing her hands gently on his cheeks. "I'm going to help you sit up. How does that sound?"

Before he could respond, Nora grabbed him by the shoulders and pulled him to a seated position, and rough pine needles jabbed into the back of his bare thighs. Someone else grabbed his wrists again and pulled them tight against the hard bark of a tree pressed against his spine. He wriggled his fingers and discovered that they were nearly immobile. Scoops blinked and tried to focus his vision as Nora backed away.

In front of him, perhaps ten feet away, was a small campfire. A large dark sack sat partially open next to the burning wood. His eyes drifted sideways. Around the fire, equidistant and firmly yoked to the surrounding conifers were Jack, Derek, Scott, Logan, and Bread. None of the seniors looked to be conscious. More concerning, Jack seemed to be bleeding from his mouth. His eyelids drooped partially open, the whites behind them unmoving.

Sabrina sidled next to Nora and draped an arm around her shoulder. "See? You had plenty of time to get a present after all," she said. "But you still owe me that drink."

One by one, the women filed next to them and stretched their arms toward the night sky.

When they were assembled, Elizabeth detached the veil from her laurel wreath, threw it into the blaze, and began to laugh. The flames devoured the tulle greedily, and Elizabeth raised the satin ring from her head and held it up to the moon. In unison, the women began to chant the incantation—a ritual, really, and rituals, after all, were sacred by definition.

It was supposed to be a joke, Scoops thought, his head throbbing, and the bride-to-be was laughing.

He squeezed his eyes shut as the women removed the carving knives from the sack and began to dress their offerings.

It was supposed to be a joke.

New and Perfect

Despite years of harsh New England weathering, the words on the dilapidated green and silver road sign could be seen clear as day:

Welcome to Mansfield: Where Life is New and Perfect.

The irony of the carefully lettered town motto snaking around speckles of rust and dull streaks where the reflective paint had worn thin was never lost on Rachel.

At twenty-two years old, Rachel was at the age where most of the girls she'd grown up with in Mansfield had fled the isolated suburb for dorm life at a big-city college. If they had resolved to stay, it was only to storm the market for a spouse—some big, strapping young man with a shadow of forgotten puberty hidden beneath a neatly-trimmed beard, a husband who could provide her with both the freedom to quit her entry-level job and the imprisonment of caring for household and children.

Rachel had neither an interest in pursuing a career, nor a strong urge to couple with anyone, and so, she spent most of her weekdays as a mail clerk at the factory—Sealing's, a domestic goods manufacturer and Mansfield's chief employer—and most of her evenings alone in her two-room apartment on the edge of town.

She had a few friends, all girls from work who fell squarely in the second category of young Mansfield women, and she liked being around people, but she was perfectly content to go to work, walk the hour-long commute home to an empty abode, and fall asleep each evening with a book on her chest.

Mansfield's main street was three blocks in length and boasted a town hall and post office, a library whose annex housed the parks and recreation department, a health and safety complex complete with police and fire stations, and one long building with three small stores: a grocery with a built-in pharmacy, a hair salon, and a hardware store. On the edge of the main drag sat Sal's, a family restaurant that doubled as the town's only bar. There were no clothing stores in Mansfield. Residents could travel a few towns over to peruse the department or discount superstores, but most simply ordered their necessities online.

It was easy for any girl to do when she knew her measurements.

Her parents had always taught Rachel that a lady watches her figure, and Rachel's hadn't changed in six years.

Nothing had changed in six years, really, and Rachel was content with that as well.

On a Friday evening in late January, two girls from Sealing's persuaded Rachel to accompany them to Sal's after work. Rachel knew one of the women vaguely—Tina was her name, Rachel thought—but the other was new. She'd graduated from high school only seven months before, and she'd befriended Tina in the secretarial pool where they both worked.

"Hi, I'm Nancy," the new girl said brightly, holding out a tiny manicured hand toward Rachel as the three walked briskly to Tina's car in the Sealing's employee lot.

When she held Nancy's tiny hand in hers, Rachel felt its feminine softness nearly melt in her grasp.

"Rachel," she replied, doing her best to watch where she was walking while still looking at her companions.

Both of the women wore fitted overcoats over soft, fuzzy sweaters; sheer black stockings peeked out from beneath tight black skirts and above curvy, high-heeled shoes.

Rachel glanced at her own attire, a simple navy dress hidden under the well-worn pea coat she'd owned since freshman year. She shoved her hands back into her coat pockets.

On the short ride to Sal's, Rachel learned that Tina and Nancy frequented the bar on Friday nights.

"It's payday, so the guys are in good moods," Nancy explained.

She added that she hoped a man she'd met there weeks ago—Tad, or Ted, or possibly Tom; it was hard for Rachel to hear clearly over the rush of hot air screaming through every vent, making the windows fog slightly—would return. He was a broad-chested man with a quickly rising position at city hall, Nancy pointed out, and he was twenty-five, a prime age for settling down. She said this and smiled conspiratorially, then turned her body back to the front and pulled down the visor to inspect her face. Rachel ran her finger slowly along the wet condensation of the narrow back window. Her cuticles were dry and ragged.

As the car came to a stop and the heater abruptly silenced, slivers of rain began to dot the windshield. Almost in unison, Nancy and Tina pulled their hoods over their heads and opened the doors. The three women ran to the door of the bar just as the sky opened and sheets of icy water poured down behind them.

It was warm in Sal's, almost oppressively so, Rachel thought. The cacophony of happy voices amplified by liquor ricocheted off the walls. A jukebox in the corner shuffled through pop songs from the late twentieth century. Dale McLauren, the high school's new football coach, appeared behind Tina. He was the type of person who introduced himself using his full name, and in turn, when others referred to him, they did so as well. Tina and Dale McLauren had been dating for a few months and Tina had confided in Rachel that she hoped he'd propose commitment soon.

"Dale McLauren is the kind of man who takes care of things," Tina had said. "He will take care of me."

Dale kept his arm wrapped tightly around Tina for most of the evening, unclenching it only to pay the waitress who brought him another beer. Three other men that Rachel recognized as ex-football darlings from her time in school soon joined the group, and the conversation vacillated between NFL draft predictions and the upcoming Super Bowl.

Bored, Rachel focused most of her attention on manipulating the jukebox playlist using an app on her smartphone.

It wasn't until the voices quieted around her that she looked up again.

The crowd had thinned, Nancy was nowhere to be seen, and Tina was sliding her hand into the arm of her jacket.

"Dale is taking me home," she said as Dale helped her the rest of the way into her coat. "Nancy took my car to follow Todd. Dale's house is just two blocks from your building. Do you need a ride?"

Tina looked deliberately at the two men who remained at the table then let her eyes snap back to Rachel's.

"It's okay," Rachel answered, awkwardly pulling her pea coat from the back of the chair and wrangling it about her shoulders. "I'm used to walking."

Before anyone had a chance to argue, Rachel had pushed open the exit door and was walking briskly toward home.

The cold rain had evolved into sleet, and although there was no wind, Rachel felt the weather pierce the exposed skin of her cheeks and ears. Thin rivers of icy water trickled down the nape of her neck and wriggled down her spine. It was at least two miles to the apartment building. She regretted declining Tina's half-hearted offer.

A long-hooded car slowed alongside her, the passenger window lowering as it did so.

"Hey," the man's voice called. "Hey, Rachel. It's really coming down. Get in. We'll give you a ride."

Rachel looked up. The football darlings. The two who had remained at the table as Dale and Tina prepared to depart peered out at her from the front seat of a dark-colored sedan, one of the expensive, American models Rachel had seen advertised in a magazine once. Watery mucous dripped from her nose, mingling with the sleet on her face. Without another moment of hesitation, she walked to the car, opened the back door, and climbed inside. In the interior light's dim illumination, the upholstery resembled red velvet cake. She pulled the door closed. The air smelled like dry cleaning and fresh dollar bills.

"Thank you," she whispered, her lips shaking from the cold.

Rachel raced to remember the two men's names. The driver was *Henry?* *Harvey?* The other, *Jeff. Yes.* And *Harvey.* She was sure of it now. *Jeff and Harvey.*

The three rode in silence for a long minute as the wipers waved back and forth, parting clumps of slush like spindly Moseses.

Harvey glanced at Rachel in the rearview mirror. "You never dated much in high school, did you?" he asked suddenly.

Rachel considered his question. No, she couldn't remember ever going out on a date. Come to think of it, she couldn't remember if she had attended prom, which seemed odd, since it had only been five years ago.

Doesn't she like men? the men asked, more as a criticism than an actual question.

She answered without hesitation.

I like them fine.

Why do you ask?

The two men chuckled and glanced at one another. And then Rachel spied the edge of her building two blocks ahead of them on the left and she asked Harvey if he wouldn't mind pulling the car onto the side street beside it.

As the car hugged the curbing, Jeff turned his body to face Rachel. "Hey, mind if we use your bathroom?"

There was something in the way his words lilted that made Rachel's back stiffen. She paused, her hand on the door handle.

Sensing her hesitation, Harvey chimed in. "It's the least you could do, I mean, after we saved you from this awful weather."

"Sure," said Rachel slowly.

All she wanted was to strip the damp clothes from body and get into a hot shower to warm up, but Harvey had a point.

She owed them.

• • • • • • • • • •

As sheets of frozen rain again poured from the sky, the three ran toward the main entrance, clutching their jackets close to their bodies to keep the wind from forcing them open. Once they had made it inside the foyer, a warm blanket of air immediately enveloped them. Rachel led the way up the stairs. Her apartment was on the third floor—the top floor. The men said nothing as they followed immediately behind her.

With every step, the relief she felt after escaping the weather was gradually replaced with prickles of unease.

Something wasn't right, but she shook off the anxiety, attributing her misfiring intuition to exhaustion and paranoia.

Her parents had always taught Rachel that a lady makes everyone feel at ease.

As she slid the key into her lock, Rachel tried to fill the awkward silence with innocuous chit-chat.

"The weatherman said the precipitation would stop before morning. I hope the sidewalks won't be too slippery tomorrow."

But her hand hadn't even grazed the light switch before Harvey grabbed her from behind and wrestled her to the ground, knocking her head hard on the shiny oak floor.

Rachel was stunned and speechless.

What was happening?

What did she do?

What was *he* doing?

As she tried to speak, a wave of shimmering dizziness flooded her mind. Jeffrey's hazy silhouette hovered in the doorway above. When she felt Harvey's hand reach roughly up inside her dress, she clawed instinctively at his face.

If she made him angry, a voice deep inside warned, he might kill her. She stopped clawing and squeezed her eyes shut.

Stop it stop it stop it stop it please please please please stop

Although she said nothing, uttered not a word besides a terrible whimper, Harvey clamped his hand over her mouth. When he was done, Harvey grabbed Rachel's neck and squeezed, only for a moment. But in her panic, Rachel twisted her head and looked around.

Only then did she see the tiny light on the phone's camera, the one Jeffrey was holding, pointing in her direction, capturing her nightmare for posterity.

She closed her eyes again. She felt Harvey's body lift from hers, the fetid breeze as he swung his leg over her torso, and, finally, the clumsy rumble of boot stomps as the men exited without a word.

They didn't even bother to shut the door behind them, just *stomp-stomp-stomp* along the thinly carpeted hallway, down the fluorescent-lit stairway, and they were gone.

Rachel's body, framed by the awkward triangle of light streaming in from the hallway, felt alien to her.

Detached.

Betrayed.

After a moment, she pushed herself to a standing position.

Statistics from PSAs, numbers written in fat red lettering splattered like blood trails along the headlines of articles in the fashion magazines she sometimes apathetically perused blinked in her brain.

1 in 6 women.

Every 75 seconds.

She pawed the wall for the light switch, closed the door, and turned the lock, feeling the weight of this ironic action heavy on her shoulders.

In the unforgiving brightness of the bathroom mirror, a distorted face stared back at her. It was puffy and red, the skin on her left cheek and neck pink from where Harvey's beard rubbed it raw. Rachel could still smell him on her. Fresh dollar bills, an oddly astringent scent considering how unclean she felt. When she returned to the front room, the apartment closed in around her like a coffin. She rebuttoned her coat and left, not bothering to lock the door behind her.

The Cadillac was gone. So was most of the sleet. In their place, a thin icing of clear slickness coated everything, a snail's secretion. Rachel walked carefully down the block. She passed a bright yellow fire hydrant glazed and scintillating in the streetlight and felt an overwhelming desire to smash the ice with her fists, to crackle and craze its perfectly smooth coating.

Dale McLauren's house was blue. She knew this from Tina's descriptions. It stood near the end of the second side street, the last structure before a large open lot yet to be developed.

When she reached it, Rachel could see lights in the windows, so she did not hesitate before ringing the doorbell. It was one of those camera bells and in the silent second following her push, she felt eyes size her up.

Dale McLauren is the kind of man who takes care of things. Rachel heard Tina's voice in her head. *He will take care of me.*

A moment later, Dale was in the doorway, and a recount of the event poured from Rachel's mouth, spilling onto the porch and splashing Dale's face, turning it flat as stone.

When she finally stopped speaking, Dale McLauren inhaled a long, heavy breath.

"Rachel," he said finally, "I need to take care of this right away." He stared at her, his expression unchanged. "Come with me."

She followed him to the curb and climbed into Dale's truck—one of those oversized-cab models that made Rachel feel small as the passenger seat swallowed her whole; a toddler in a rocking chair. After letting the defroster run a moment to melt and clear the windows, the truck pulled away from the house and onto the main street. No other motorists were on the road. The town, most of its residents safe asleep in their warm homes, appeared as abandoned as a child's playground in winter.

They passed the town hall that housed the parks and recreation department.

They passed the grocery with the built-in pharmacy, the beauty salon, and the hardware store.

They passed Sal's, its parking lot empty and its American beer neons dark.

Finally, they passed the health and safety complex.

Dale McLauren did not slow the truck down.

In fact, he turned off the main drag and into the industrial park.

When Dale pulled into the parking lot of Sealing's, he passed the turn for employee parking and pulled into a spot for VIPs.

Dale was a very important person, at least at close to three in the morning.

What were they doing at the factory?

"Relax," he said, turning off the engine. "I told you: I am taking care of this."

Her parents had always taught Rachel that a lady did not argue with authority.

She followed Dale McLauren through the doors of the main entrance and down a series of hallways Rachel had never seen before, each one broken into segments by shiny sliding doors.

As she waited patiently next to a tall green plant, examining its leaves in the hopes of determining if it were real, Dale ducked into a small side foyer and spoke with the security guard behind a desk. Rachel wondered how the plant had managed to flourish so far from any natural light, but then she remembered having read that fluorescent lamps gave off a kind of luminescence that, if focused correctly, kept sheltered greenery contentedly thriving.

The security guard glanced over at Rachel then picked up a telephone receiver and spoke quietly into the mouthpiece.

Dale turned and walked briskly further down the long hallway.

Without a word, Rachel trailed behind. She followed him into an elevator and stood obedient as he pressed a button and the car dropped gracefully downward. When the doors opened again, Dale emerged and marched efficiently down the long, dark hallway to a big silver door. He paused only once to ensure Rachel was still behind him then opened the door.

Inside of the room was a wide metal desk manned by two bearded employees wearing white overcoats. Behind them were two doors, each clearly marked with its purpose.

Dale approached the desk, his hand resting lightly on Rachel's shoulder.

"Exchange," Dale told the men, escorting his ward forward.

The man on the right grabbed Rachel by the arm and led her into a lightless container behind the door on the left.

"Reason?" asked the other man.

Rachel stood silent as the door marked *Returns* closed behind her, sealing her away in the darkness.

"This one is broken," Dale said.

Then he crossed his arms over his chest and waited for the right door to open.

MONSTERS

Just a few yards away from us, two brown bunnies hop around in the grass. It's green but patchy with weeds. Because the wild creatures have become acclimated to suburban life, the sizzle of the grill and Tommy's incessant humming are innocuous background music.

Dawn and I sit at the table, under the umbrella, the sun hot and constant in the early July afternoon. We do this now every week: one night at Dawn and Tommy's sprawling condo, one day at my small bungalow, Tommy always manning the grill. It gets no use otherwise—not since Sam and Sadie lived here—so I am grateful my old college pal has taken the reins.

The humming, however, I could do without.

Tommy shakes his hips a bit as he pushes something around on the rack, AirPods shoved deep in his ears. It's something by Motley Crue. "On With the Show," it sounds like, from Tommy's Mick Mars muzak rendition.

Dawn chain smokes and flicks her ashes in an old coffee can I've filled with leftover sandbox sand.

"The yard looks great," Dawn says.

I can't tell if she's being snide or sincere.

I watch one of the rabbits nibble on a patch of clover.

"Thanks," I say. "I pay a guy to come over and mow, trim the trees and everything once a week. It just got to be too much." I nod at the fenced-in rectangle jutting out behind my garage. "The garden is all me, though."

I have over-planted. I have more tomatoes than I know what to do with. Acid teeming with tiny yellow seeds gurgles in my stomach. Even from our distant vantage point, I can see clumps of bright red heckling me from their vines. Dawn notices them, too.

"Hope you like tomatoes," she says, lighting another thin white cancer stick.

I snort. "Last week, I brought in a basket of them and left it in the office break room with a handwritten sign, encouraging people to take them home," I admit. "I've become *that* person."

"You could always take the fencing down, let the bunnies take a nibble," Dawn says.

"I thought of that, but the leaves are toxic, actually," I say, pleased that my late-night Google wanderings are finally relevant to real, human conversation. "And I like watching them."

I nod at the two creatures just as one hops furiously around the side of the garden and out of view.

Dawn takes a long drag on her cigarette then holds it just a few inches from her mouth, like she needs constant reassurance that her next dose of nicotine isn't too far away. Her eyes stare straight ahead and her lips are still curled into a small *O* like a plastic sex doll. After a long pause, she glances back at Tommy at the grill, then turns her head and blows a long white billow of smoke away from my direction.

"I don't know who he thinks he's fooling," she says, and for a moment, I am unsure who she is talking about. "Tommy," Dawn adds, reading my mind. "He's fucking someone at the office. Has been for a few years now."

I frown. "What makes you say that?"

The disbelief feels synthetic in my mouth, like a piece of paper surreptitiously stuck to a piece of hard candy, rolling around on my tongue. Everyone knows Tommy is a ladies' man— *Dawn* knew it when she met him. It was one of the reasons they never agreed to marry.

Somehow, Dawn worked out in her mind that by keeping Tommy uncaged, he'd never wander.

Dawn blows another plume of smoke, then crushes the half-burned butt into sandbox filler. "I can smell it on him. When he comes home. Twice, maybe three times a week."

"Busy guy." It's all I can think to say.

"You don't know the half of it," Dawn says. "He got her pregnant." She glances at me, then looks down at the coffee can. The tiny wisp of smoke from her extinguished cigarette has died away. "I only know because a few months ago, I happened to be checking some transactions on our bank account before bed and I saw he'd withdrawn four hundred dollars that afternoon. Late, like five or six o'clock, and come right home. Never mentioned it."

I say nothing but nod. Sam, my husband, had done the very same thing, except he'd liquidated most of the savings account. Never said a word when he got home. The police showed me the bank's security video of him, his broad grin toothy and white, his face happy and relaxed, even from a distance. Readying for a permanent vacation.

"So I followed him the next day," Dawn continues. "Planned Parenthood." She replaces the plastic cover on the can and a whiff of dirty ashtray leaks into the air when the seal clicks.

I wrinkle my nose. "You catch a glimpse at what she looked like?"

"Nah," Dawn says. "But I heard him crying that night. Late. He thought I was asleep." She runs her hands over her knees, like she is brushing invisible dirt from them. Then, she utters a small laugh. "I mean, what did the girl think? He was going to leave me and run away with her and the kid?" She catches herself, looks quickly at me in apology, but I shake my head. She rubs her knees again. "All I mean is, I pay the mortgage. I pay all of the bills. He couldn't afford to start over. More than half of his damn paycheck goes to student loan payments. Hell, I probably paid for the fucking abortion."

The remaining rabbit creeps cautiously toward the ceramic birdbath by my back bushes and hunkers down, a brown loaf of fur baking in the sun. I think of telling Dawn how I've named the bunnies—there are three who frequent the yard and I've figured out ways of telling them apart—but the small piece of embarrassing trivia seems woefully out of place.

I then consider telling Dawn about the night Tommy made a pass at me. That, too, was only a few months ago.

Dawn lowers her voice, even though it's obvious that the volume of Tommy's music is too loud for him to overhear. "Some nights, I fantasize what it would have been like if the girl had died during the procedure. I know that's rare, but I think of how Tommy would have had to keep that from me, too. How hard it would have been for him." She stares at me blankly. "Every time I think about it, it makes me happy. Do you think I'm a monster?"

I pretend to mull over the question. "No. But I'm not the best person to ask." I look back at the garden. "I think I'm going to pull some of those tomato plants out. Plant pumpkins for the fall. What do you think?"

"You ever hear from him?" she asks, ignoring my question. "Sam?" she adds.

I knew who she meant.

"I mean, it's been almost a year," she adds. "No leads, nothing?"

I shake my head and look over at the birdbath. The bunny appears to be sleeping, even though his eyes are wide open, two black marbles glazed with water, staring like the dead. Two robins are splashing, carefree above him, their orange breasts bright as the sun.

"No," I say. "No leads."

Tommy wanders over to the table, snapping a pair of large silver tongs. "Dinner is ready," he announces too loudly. "Come, bring a plate."

The next morning when I am backing my car down my driveway I see a bloodied brown rabbit lying still along the double yellow line of the road, its entire front half flattened like a pancake, the fuzzy white tail untouched, sticking straight up in the air like a surrender flag.

I cry so hard on the drive to work, I have to lock myself in the bathroom when I arrive and stay there, holding a paper towel soaked in cold water to my face until the redness disappears.

· · · ·•·•· · ·

At six o'clock, the carcass is still in the street.

Surprisingly, it has not sustained further damage. Drivers must have swerved around its tiny body throughout the day, not wanting to muss their tires with roadkill remnants. The white fluff of tail sways a bit in the breeze, giving the remains an unnerving, zombie-like quality. I exit my car in the garage and walk directly into the breezeway, not wanting to look.

From my kitchen window, I see my other two regular visitors hopping about the backyard, sniffing here and there at the green ground, looking for food.

I wonder if they are looking for their missing friend.

I balance an open box of crackers, a sleeve of cheese slices, and a glass of Portuguese wine in my arms and trudge toward the living room, collapsing backwards onto the sofa. There are no lamps in this room save for a slim torchère I've slid against the recliner in the corner. With Sam and Sadie gone, there's no one to look at. In winter, I bathe in the gray-green glow of the television, but the sun sets so late these days, the light from the naked windows suffices.

I am three crackers in, a chunk of honey-colored cheddar in my mouth, when I hear them.

"Do it!" The small but gravelly voice commands loudly. "Stop being a pussy!"

I stand far enough back from the window that I am shrouded from outside eyes but can view the street clearly. Standing on either side of the dead rabbit are two boys, eight or nine years old, oblivious to the possibility of oncoming traffic. I think I recognize the smaller of the two; I've seen him walk a fluffy golden retriever past my house on occasion, so he must live nearby. He's short but wiry with black hair that sticks out in odd angles, mirroring his pointy nose and sharp eyebrows. In my head, I name him Max because he vaguely resembles a character in the Maurice Sendak picture book that frightened me a child. When someone gave Sadie a copy as a birthday present years ago, I tossed it into the recycling bin as soon as the last of the party-goers departed.

The other child is larger, much larger than Max, with hair slightly lighter on a head at least twice as wide. Two fat arms squeeze out from the armholes of a dirty t-shirt, but this boy, the obvious alpha of the pair, doesn't seem the least bit uncomfortable, and the wild, furry eyebrows that he raises conspiratorially as he smirks at his friend only add to the boy's beast-like appearance. I spy a bike lying askew on the tree belt behind him and I wonder how the Beast was able to maneuver it while still managing to carry the large tree branch he's wielding in both hands.

"*Ewww*," Max yells, but it's punctuated with a trill of laughter.

The Beast is poking at the carcass with the stick, resting one end of the massive implement on his shoulder and dragging the point back and forth over the dead bunny like an ogre scribbling uncoordinatedly with an oversized pen.

"Step on it," demands the Beast. Again, his voice is raspy but forceful, like he's spent years sucking on fat cigars and slapping disrespectful underlings around.

Max reels backward as if preparing to stomp on the small lump of brown fur, then resumes his stance, still laughing. "*You* do it," he says. "Stab him in the ass!"

The Beast lifts the branch off the ground and my hand goes to my face, ready to cover my eyes, when the scene is interrupted by an unintelligible screeching call echoing from somewhere nearby.

Max turns to his left and looks up the street. He mutters something and turns around, walking toward my front lawn. I retreat, thinking he has seen me, but he stoops down to snatch a backpack that had been lying on the tree-belt.

I hadn't noticed it earlier.

Apparently, the camouflage-print on the bag's front side is doing its job.

Max begins to walk away from his friend but turns to look back, saying something too soft for me to hear.

The Beast nods, his mischievous grin wide. "Bring a shovel," he says, then hurls the branch a few feet down in the road, adding to the makeshift obstacle course for oncoming drivers. He throws himself, rather than climbs, onto his bike, and pedals away in the opposite direction.

The bunny's white tail waves ever so slightly in the wind of his wake.

· · · ● · ● · · ·

I don't want to keep a strange boy's backpack in my house, I don't want it in my possession at all. The camouflage-print sack is on the tree-belt again when I back my car out of the garage the next morning. It is still there when I return after work that evening. I resolve to find the boy's mother and hand it to her. I don't bother rifling through its contents; the zipper is filthy, a splatter of something sticky and dark cakes the back side, and it smells ripe. *Mean boy*-ripe, the stink of hormones quickly churning and empathy slowly decaying.

I am not sure where Max lives and I'm only familiar with a few of my neighbors, so I start with the tall white box Colonial five houses down. It has a tidy lawn and lush patches of sunny daisies huddled on either side of the front steps.

I hold the backpack by the black loop on its top, sandwiching a wad of tissue between the fabric and my skin.

I don't want to touch it.

A moment after I ring the doorbell, an elderly woman appears on the other side of the screen. Her skin is so thin, it's nearly translucent, ropes of blue veins wrapping like vines around her hands and forearms.

"You're the one whose husband took off with your kid, right? A little girl?"

The woman squints her eyes at me as if trying to read my expression, but I keep it blank.

She mashes her teeth together and utters an odd sigh, a trill like hissing, and for a split second, I think of Sadie and Sam, cuddling tightly together on the sofa while I sit miles away in the recliner. It was always how we watched television together. Sam and Sadie, Sadie and Sam, their heads bobbing together, perpetually entwined, like charmed snakes.

"I live in the yellow house on the corner," I say. "I found the bag on my lawn this morning."

Another memory flashes by: Sadie tumbling sideways on the grass, trying in earnest to complete a cartwheel, unable to keep her feet pointed toward the sky. Sam pushing the lawnmower down the tree belt abutting the road, the cacophonous whirr drowning out all other sounds, including my daughter's pleas.

Watch me, Mommy. *Watch me. Watch me.*

The woman continues to squint, and I wonder if she is visually impaired or just snooty.

"Might be the Brownings," she says finally and juts her chin forward, indicating the house across the street. "Moved in just after Christmas. They have a son. Pale with dark shaggy hair, skinny." Her mouth turns down into a snarl. "A bit of a devil, that one."

Before I can thank her, she steps backwards, into the darkness, and shuts the door.

The house opposite hers is a plain brick Cape with ragged evergreen bushes smothering the windowsills. A bright pink geranium slithers from a hanging pot near the front door. As I step onto the cement stairs, I can see the back of the plant is brown, wilted, the hearty side turned purposefully forward so that no one but those belonging inside know of the rot. I pause before ringing the bell, then simply leave the backpack leaning against the railing and walk home.

When I am leaving my house later that night, on my way to spend dinner at Dawn and Tommy's, I stop to collect the mail that's been lingering in my box all day. Out of the corner of my eye, I spy the Beast riding his bike furiously toward my section of the street, his corpulent legs pumping the pedals so hard, I can hear the growling hum of metal gears. I turn to face him just in time to see him cut suddenly to the left and ride his vehicle over the bunny's corpse. He laughs, a fat guffaw that echoes in the staid, humid air, then he twists his path into a figure eight, returning to the carcass to squash it again. The white tail no longer sticks upward. I think I see brown and red splotches along the Beast's back tire as he circles back again to his target, chortling like a sinister brute.

My hands are still gripping tightly the jumble of white paper envelopes and glossy postcard ads when I climb into the driver's seat and shove my key into the ignition. I back the car into the street, barely checking for any oncoming traffic before finally unclenching my left hand, letting the pile tumble awkwardly to the floor beneath my feet. My hands are so clammy, the sweat has soaked through a few of the bills, which gum together in a disorganized clump beneath my seat.

· · ● · ● · · ·

In the morning, I am nearly at the end of an early run, the sun already bobbing hot on the horizon, when my phone rings through my headphones. It's louder than I remember the ringtone being and I quickly yank one of the plugs from my ear for relief before checking my screen.

"I did it." Dawn's voice screams into my skull as soon as I click the ANSWER button, and I frantically tap the volume control. She doesn't wait for my reply. "After you left. I confronted him about the girl."

There is the distinct ticking noise of her lighter; an audible inhalation of breath.

I stop and lean forward, resting my hands on my thighs. "Why?"

There's more I want to say, but it seems pointless in the moment.

"*Why?*" Dawn echoes incredulously. "I needed him to know that I knew. That he wasn't pulling off some perfect crime undetected." There's a whistling sound of breath in my earpiece, the exhale of her smoke. She continues, her voice growing more manic. "I couldn't take it any longer, seeing that smug look on his face, thinking he was getting away with it, right under my nose."

I stand up straight and begin to walk. A thick drizzle of sweat slides down from my forehead. I lift up the bottom of my shirt to my face to wipe it away.

Sam.

I think of him sitting there, on the edge of the bathtub, holding an orange plastic boat in his hand. Sadie splashing away below, obliviously happy, one of her many toys taking flight in the commotion and landing next to my husband's thigh. My glancing at the vanity, seeing the small, neat cluster of toiletries suspiciously pulled from cabinets and drawers: shaving cream, deodorant, hair gel, the travel container for toothbrushes, Sadie's hair detangling spray, her favorite comb, and...

Dawn's voice evens, drops to a conversational tone. "He told me I was crazy," she says. She is doing her best to sound even-keeled, but I can hear the twang of desperation in her voice. The self-doubt. "Looked me straight in the eye and said I was imagining things."

I replace the other headphone in my ear and turn right, walking up the hill. I am only a block from my house, but the street winds like a serpent. It isn't until I reach the last curve that I see the gathering. Two police cars, blue light blenders twisting on their roofs, everything silent above the steady murmuring of neighbors who huddle together on the sidewalk. An ambulance is parked further down the road, almost at the corner, the back doors wide open, a gaping maw.

"I gotta call you back," I tell Dawn, and pull the headphones from my neck and shove them in my pocket, not bothering to check if she has hung up the call.

There's something in the road, a dark lump.

At first, I think it is a large dog, something gray and black.

When I am almost to the crowd, I realize, it's a boy. A child, about eight or nine years old, wearing a dirty gray t-shirt soiled with satiny brown puddles. He is facing away from me, straddled halfway between a face-plant and a fetal position, but still, it's obvious that his silhouette is altered in some way. The curvature of his spine is twisted; his shoulder, dented. I squint and hold my palm up to my forehead to shield the sun's glare, and I think I see a wide, dark mark running across his back, across his ear, across the dark brown hair matted red with blood.

I see it again: Sadie splashing, laughing so hard, she begins to hiccup; Sam, sitting on the edge, rolling his tongue—something I could never do, no matter how many years of Spanish I took—to imitate a whirring motor as he leans down with the orange toy boat, running it over the water. I stand with my hands on my hips, silently watching my husband and daughter. Sadie shrieks so loud with delight, I think it will shatter glass.

A woman wearing a green terry cloth bathrobe sidles up beside me. "Oh my God," she says, her tone bleeding schadenfreude, "what happened? Is that Jeannie's boy?"

I lean forward again, pretend to retie the laces on my sneaker. I'm trying not to look at the Beast, lying there, crushed motionless as the bunny, but I can't avert my eyes.

I have to see his face.

I have to know if his eyes are open, if they have grown wide and bulbous, the pupils huge, swollen, as the last vestiges of fear leaked away.

Like Sadie's looked, underneath the bathwater.

Sadie.

Expressionless. Eyes open and round. Sam's voice behind me, from the hall, calling. The look of confusion, then horror and surprise.

Then, nothing.

The woman in the green bathrobe turns to another neighbor and I back away slowly until I am at the edge of the crowd again, a 16mm film reel looping backwards through the projector.

When the Beast is out of sight, I spin my body and run as fast as I can, cutting back down the main artery and up my street, my lungs stinging like I've inhaled gasoline. The corner of my yellow siding is visible, then the remnants of my bunny, now more road than fur and bones.

From my front lawn, there comes a high-pitched, frantic shrieking. A grackle, its black feathers shining iridescent in the morning light, lands on the grass adjacent to the sidewalk, carrying something in its mouth. Two robins dive-bomb him from either side, pecking at his wings, screaming. In response to their attack, the dark bird drops its treasure onto the grass and begins to stab it with its beak. It continues to pummel the small, featherless hatchling mercilessly as its parents clamor helplessly, and within seconds, it is nothing but a bright pink pile of sinew and fragile bone.

I slow my pace and trot without pausing, directly to the side gate, to the garden. The heavy shovel is still leaning against the back of my garage where I left it.

The sun grows hotter, brighter, and sweat stings my eyes. My hair is drenched, but I don't stop. I begin to dig a shallow hole in the only remaining spot behind the bountiful, verdant vegetable plants.

I will give bunny—what remains of him—a proper burial.

His body will slowly decay into fertilizer. In the autumn, bright orange pumpkins will grow above him, atop of everything else rotting beside him, the secrets I've hidden deep within the soil. My harvest will be fat and healthy.

In the fall, I will pluck orange happiness from the ground, scoop out its insides, and carve terrifying faces in its flesh.

I will grow monsters.

MOUNTAIN OF THE DEAD

DAY 1

Weather: Sunny but cold

"Have you looked at a calendar lately?"

The woman at the front desk bent her head down slightly to stare at them over her glasses disapprovingly like an ancient librarian shaming a group of incessant talkers.

James flashed her his best all-American-boy smile, the one he usually reserved for nosy neighbors and professors who questioned his integrity on a take-home exam.

"I can see you have one right there, ma'am." He pointed to the one standing next to the computer, a word-of-the-day, flip-style like the type his mom always gave him for Christmas in his stocking. *"January 27, inauspicious,"* he said, as if she couldn't read it herself.

The owner of the bed and breakfast was not amused. She sighed and turned to look at her screen.

"What name did you say this was under?"

Pete popped his head in front of James' body. "Dubinina. Pieter," he said, then added, "We have a reservation for seven."

The rest of the group teetered behind him in the dark sitting room. No one had bothered to bring the gear inside. The game plan was to leave before the sun rose so that they could begin the trail first thing in the morning.

The woman removed her glasses. "Hiking in the dead of winter. I can't understand it." Her eyes wandered over the group. Two women and five men. "We only have four rooms."

"That's fine," Pete said quickly. "To be honest, we've been in an SUV for eight hours together already and we'll be sharing a tent for the next week. I don't think we'll mind squeezing into anything you can spare."

Caridad removed her hat and squeezed it with both hands. "Do you have any—"

"We'll be gone by sunrise. You won't even know we were here," Pete broke in. "We're just starving and exhausted. We'll be out of your hair after dinner."

Once the formalities were settled, the seven trudged slowly up the stairs to remove their jackets and winter layers.

"I don't know what the problem was. It's not like travelers are beating down her door to stay here this time of year," said Marie, once the two were in the room she was to share with Caridad. "I mean, we saw, what, two cars in the last three hours?"

Caridad sat on their double bed and bounced slightly. "Do you think she has anything to drink, like something for a cocktail?" She rubbed her left palm with her right hand.

"Is that what you were going to ask her?" Marie laughed.

Caridad smiled. "I'm really wound up, you know? This is no joke. We're going to be out of all radio contact for at least a week. That doesn't make you at least a little uneasy?"

James pushed the door to their room open. "Knock knock," he called but continued to enter. "I hear someone is feeling wound up. I have just the solution—"

Caridad through a pillow at him. "I'm serious. I wish Pete would tell us exactly what he thinks we'll find up there. The suspense is killing—"

"According to Pete, we could be the first ones to solve one of the 'twentieth-century's biggest mysteries.' That's all I know," Marie said. "I trust him. He wouldn't drag us to a desolate hiking trail in the middle of winter unless it was something really big."

"Zoinks, mystery solved," James turned to see Paul join them. "Hey Fred, I was just being reminded by Velma and Daphne here that we are on the brink of greatness."

Paul rolled his eyes. "Anyone in the mood?" He produced a kaleidoscopic glass pipe from his pocket.

"We can't smoke in here," Marie said.

Paul began to break up the small stash of weed from a plastic baggie on top of the dresser.

"You say that now, but who the hell knows what she has for food? She didn't even remember we were coming. You think she's prepared to feed eight people on a whim?" He began to pack the bowl. "I'd drum up some munchies now, my friend. We need sustenance."

He brought the flame of his lighter to the pipe to punctuate this statement just as the rest of the group filed in.

"Should you be doing that here?" asked Thomas.

Paul motioned to him to shut the door. Louis, Thomas, and Pete climbed onto the bed and stretched their legs.

Caridad playfully punched Louis in the calf. "Enjoy the space now, boys. It's going to be cramped as hell in that tent."

She took the pipe from Paul and Marie opened the only window. A gust of frigid wind instantly filled the room.

Paul squeezed his body next to Louis' and hugged him. "It's the best way to keep warm." Louis turned onto his side and kissed him.

Caridad exhaled a long stream of white smoke. "That reminds me of that episode of *Taxi*. You know, the one where Latka gets trapped in his cab with a woman in the blizzard?"

Pete folded his arms behind his head on the pillow. "I remember that one. The woman says they have to have sex or they will freeze to death. But Latka's married to Carol Kane, right? So he doesn't want to. He keeps mulling over the choices: *Sex, death? Sex, death?*"

He stretched out one arm to retrieve the pipe from James.

James began to laugh. "What did he choose?"

"I don't remember an episode where Latka dies," said Marie.

"Andy Kaufman died."

"Yeah, but not on the show."

Thomas sat up. "How was I not aware of this lively, underground *Taxi* fan club?"

He climbed over Pete and walked to the dresser to refill the bowl.

After taking a long drag, he offered it to Louis, who shook his head. "It smells like a skunk popsicle in here."

Pete sat up. His eyes were glassy. "In all seriousness," he said, "I asked you guys specifically because you're my best friends, and I want to share this with you." He paused to take another pull. "Plus," he added, his voice halted from holding the smoke in his lungs. "All of you are kick ass hikers. It's going to be brutal—no doubt—and we can't afford any dead weight."

Paul and Louis glanced at each other, a motion that was not lost on the group cramped in the small space.

"What is it?" asked Marie.

Paul sighed. "Louis wrenched his knee last weekend, and I can tell it's still bothering him."

Louis held his hand up. "I'm fine, it's fine," he said, but he looked down in avoidance.

"It's a shitload of hiking and skiing," Pete said. "I mean, it'll be hard enough walking ourselves, never mind carrying your gimpy ass if you get sore," he joked.

"Honestly, it's fine," Louis protested. "That's not it." He took a deep breath. "I know you are going to think this is stupid, but I've been having these nightmares."

"More like night terrors," corrected Paul. "He's woken me up, screaming."

Marie frowned. "How long has this been happening?"

Louis shrugged. "Ever since Pete asked us to go on this trip," he said. "I never remember what they are about." He smiled weakly. "I guess it's best I told you, just in case it happens tonight."

"Way to establish a cover for the brutal murder of your boyfriend, Paul," James said. *"Don't be alarmed, people: that's just Louis having another bad dream again. Disregard the bloody handprints on the bed post in the background."*

Caridad shook her arms. "Fuck, guys, cut it out. I'm wound up enough. I don't need to get paranoid, too."

Thomas wrapped his arm around her shoulder. "Cari's right. Enough of this bad juju. We are going to have the best story to tell our grandkids someday." He made a fist with his hand and pointed it toward the group. "To adventure."

The remaining six made fists and bumped them together in an imaginary toast.

"Adventure."

Night 1

Weather: Cold, with partly cloudy skies

Caridad held her phone in front of her as a flashlight. The house was completely silent: so quiet, she thought she could hear some of the men snoring behind their closed doors. She had managed to creep soundlessly down the stairs and into the kitchen and crossed her fingers that the cabinets didn't squeak when she opened them. As soon as she wrapped her hand around one of the door handles, there was a whisper behind her.

"What are you doing?"

She jumped, then spun around to see Thomas standing in his stocking feet and wrinkled boxer shorts. She removed her hand and placed it on her chest.

"You scared the bejesus out of me," she whispered. "What are you doing down here?"

Thomas moved toward the refrigerator and opened it. "Same thing as you, likely. I'm hungry."

The bluish light of the interior shone on his pale skin, giving it an alien glow.

"That's the first place I looked. Nothing good."

She began opening and shining her light into each cabinet.

Thomas took out a carton of orange juice just as Caridad opened the last upper cabinet.

"No, we can't. She'll see the dirty glass."

Thomas raised an eyebrow. "Who needs a glass?" He brought the container to his lips and drank a long gulp.

Caridad squatted to inspect the lower shelves.

"No one puts food in the lower cabinets," Thomas said.

Caridad carefully opened a door. "Why not?"

Thomas thought for a moment. "I don't know, mice?" he offered.

"In every apartment I've had, the mice have traveled up inside the walls. How else do you think they get to attics?" Caridad closed the doors, then shimmied sideways and opened the next set, still balancing on her haunches.

"Jackpot," she whispered excitedly.

Inside the lower corner cabinet was a box filled with identical jars. She grabbed one and held it in front of her light. The gelatinous amber-yellow substance inside moved ever so slightly when she tipped the glass.

"How about some honey bread?" Before Thomas could answer, she snatched two more jars and stood up. "There's bread in the box on top of the fridge."

The two of them sat quietly in the kitchen, Caridad's phone on the table between them to offer some light. Thomas pulled the slices of bread from the package while Cari unscrewed the top of the jar.

"We need a knife. No way around it," she said.

Thomas leaned back and pawed blindly inside the dish drain. "How's this?" His hand returned with a steak knife.

"Did you just feel your way around a stack of sharp utensils?" Caridad asked. "We need something to spread it, not kill it."

Thomas took the open jar from her and stuck the knife inside. "This is fine," he said, slathering the bread with a large glob of honey. He did the same on a second slice, and the two ate them without speaking. He repeated the routine, then held the empty jar above the light.

"Why isn't there a label?"

The words came out slightly garbled behind a mouthful of bread.

Caridad waited to swallow. "Probably homemade. My mom used to buy honey from a farm stand every summer."

Thomas put down the jar, and picking up the cap, ran his finger along it. He felt with his thumb the debris it left.

"Think she forgot they were there?"

Caridad shrugged, her mouth full again.

"We should make a bunch of sandwiches to take with us on the road," he suggested. "How many jars are left after these?"

"Four, I think. Three or four."

Thomas unscrewed the top from the second jar. "She'll never miss them."

Day 2

Weather: Cold with partial sun

"It's not okay," Paul insisted. "And I'm staying behind, too."

Louis sat on the edge of the bed. "Absolutely not. I feel like enough of a jerk having to stay behind. I just know there's no way my knee is going to be okay trekking through snow uphill, never mind cross-country skiing. It was stupid of me to come." He put his hand on his boyfriend's upper arm. "But you are not missing your chance to do this. You'll be kicking yourself forever."

Paul sighed. "So what are you going to do for the next week? You didn't pack your laptop."

Louis laughed. "I don't need technology to write, babe. I'm sure she has a few pens and some paper kicking about." He stood up. "I'll have no excuse not to write. Think of it this way: when you get back, you'll have a great story to tell, and I'll have the first draft of a new novel." He placed his hand on the back of Paul's head and pulled him closer, so that their two foreheads were touching. "The bigger problem is, how to tell Pete?"

"How to tell me what?" Pete's head poked out from behind the open door.

Paul pulled away. "Louis's knee isn't going to make it. He's going to stay here." He leaned over and kissed his partner quickly. "I'll never forgive you for leaving me to deal with James by myself, you know."

Pete seemed lost in thought for a moment; then he said, "We'll miss you. I'll leave my credit card with a note on the desk." He ducked out of the room then reemerged. "No raiding the mini-bar," he teased, shaking his finger at Louis.

"We'll just pick him up on the way back," Paul said. "Yeah?"

Pete paused a beat before resuming his smile. "Absolutely."

The first tickles of pink and orange were just beginning to poke out from the horizon when the SUV pulled away from the bed and breakfast and toward the mountain in the distance. Paul craned his neck and watched Louis as he shrank to a smaller and smaller figure behind them. A thought tumbled across his mind.

"Shit! I hope the owner doesn't blame the missing jars on him," he said, reaching back to rifle under the packs stuffed in the storage area.

"Missing jars?" echoed Marie.

Thomas pushed Paul's hand out of the way and replaced it with his own. It reemerged, grasping a grocery bag of sandwiches and tossed it to Marie in the row in front of him.

"I'll have you know, I walked outside in my shorts in the pitch black to hide this contraband."

James rummaged through the bag. "What are these?"

"Honey sandwiches," said Paul. "I can't believe—"

"And," Thomas interrupted, "as a bonus, we have two more unopened jars and another weapon." He pulled the steak knife from his coat pocket and held it out for everyone to see.

"You stole one of her knives?" Marie asked.

"What was I going to do, leave evidence?" Thomas said. "All of you need to become better food burglars. No way I go on a season of *Survivor* with any of you now."

"Won't the jars freeze in the cold?" James asked.

He took out a sandwich and inspected it, then passed the rest of the bag to Marie.

Thomas ignored him. "Lesson one, leave no trace."

"He's knows what he's talking about," Paul said. "He emptied our dorm fridge on a regular basis junior and senior year."

Thomas laughed. "Lesson two: deny everything." He motioned at Paul jokingly with the steak knife. "And if you know what's good for you, buddy, you'll keep your trap shut next time."

Marie leaned forward. "What do mean, another weapon? What weapons are we carrying?"

She offered the bag to Caridad in the front seat.

Cari shook her head. "I feel a little off. What was that dinner she served?"

Pete kept his eyes on the road except to glance once at the bag in Marie's outstretched hand and shake his head.

"Some kind of stroganoff. When's the last time you ate beef? Your stomach's probably rebelling."

Caridad said nothing to this and Marie passed the bag back to Thomas. "The rifle, under the packs. I saw it when I was shoving this out of sight."

"A rifle?" James repeated. "Why do we have a rifle? Are we going big game hunting for Yeti? Is that our big adventure, General Zaroff?"

"I'm sure you didn't see a gun," Marie said, readjusting her seatbelt.

"The hatch light was dim, but I know what I saw," insisted Thomas. "Pete?"

Pete cleared his throat. "We're going to be in the middle of nowhere. I brought it just in case. It isn't even loaded. The cartridges are in my pack if we do need them, but really: it's just for an emergency."

· · · ●·●·· ●· ● ·

By the time they pulled into the small lot at the base of the mountain, the morning sky was veiled with a scattering of thin, white clouds.

Marie pointed at the sun. "See the halo? Snow's coming. We better boogie and get as far as possible before we have to set up camp."

They took turns strapping their packs to their backs, the cross-country skis sticking out from the tops so that the group resembled a gathering of old-fashioned bumper cars. They walked in relative silence for a few minutes until Caridad, walking next to Pete at the front of the procession, stopped and leaned against a nearby pine tree.

"Hold up, I just need a second," she said, bending slightly forward.

Marie grabbed the water bottle from the back of her pack and handed it to Cari. "Drink this."

"Thanks," Caridad said and unscrewed the top of the bottle. She lifted the canister to her lips, intending to only take a few small sips but instead began gulping the liquid as fast as she could.

"Whoa, whoa," said James, pulling the bottle away. "You're going to make yourself—"

As he said it, Cari turned back toward the tree and vomited, spraying the trunk and foliage in the immediate vicinity with a yellowish soup.

"Fuck," she spat, still looking toward the ground. "Sorry, guys."

Pete rubbed her back. "You probably just needed to get it out. You'll feel better now. We'll go slower," he said.

She snatched the bottle back from James and took a small drink, swished it around her mouth, spat again.

"Okay, no, I'm good now. Really," she said. "Sorry about that."

Just as Marie had predicted, the first flakes began to fall by the middle of the day. They continued to trek on foot until the sprinkling of white doubled and tripled in size, the sky quickly dumping inches of accumulation on the ground in front of them. When the trail evened off, they stopped to strap on their skis and slid over the untouched blanket of snow single-file, leaving only a double line of twin ravines in the whiteness behind. The snowfall began to taper, but they didn't stop until they reached a broad clearing.

"This is it. This is where we need to set up camp," Pete said suddenly and waved his arm in a wide, sweeping motion.

The group looked around. The ground had begun to slope steeply upward and there were only a few trees in a hundred-foot radius. If they were going to push forward that afternoon, the incline alone would make for an onerous journey.

Paul pointed to the cropping of trees they'd passed a short while back. "How about there? The ground is more even and we'll get the additional shelter from the branches."

Pete shrugged off his pack. "That would be backtracking. No, this is the place."

James jabbed his pole into the snow. "We're setting up our tent on a hill? I'm all for upping the degree of difficulty, man, but that's ridiculous."

Pete unstrapped his skis and set them vertically in the snow in front of him. "There's a shallow crater right here. We'll line up our skis around it, in a semicircle, and pitch the tent in the middle."

Thomas shook off his pack and began unstrapping his skis. "I'm with Pete. Let's just get some shelter set and take a break. I'm exhausted."

His speech sounded slightly off, like he'd been sipping strong liquor and was trying to overcompensate for the resulting slurring.

Marie glanced sideways at him, then unfastened her skis and held them in front of her.

"Where should I stick these?"

Pete shimmied along the outside of the designated campsite dragging his feet in order to carve out a clear line in the snow. Marie placed her skis a few feet from Pete's and then turned to Thomas. He was stumbling forward, unsteady on his feet.

"What is the matter with you?" Marie called to him, concerned, but Thomas only stumbled one more step then collapsed onto his knees.

Marie crouched next to him. "Are you okay? What is going on?"

She brushed the dusting of snow from Thomas's pink face, then took off her glove and held the back of her hand to his forehead.

"You mommying me now, Marie?"

The words came out thick and heavy, like mashed potatoes.

"Guys?" Marie yelled to the rest of the group.

They stopped their unpacking and trudged over to Thomas.

Marie turned to Caridad. "How are you feeling? Any better?"

Cari adjusted her hat. "A little. I don't feel like I'm going to puke anymore, but my back and arms are killing me. I just feel wiped."

Marie looked back at Thomas. His eyes were closed, but he remained sitting up on his heels. "Where did you say you got that honey?"

Caridad paused, then responded. "In a cabinet in the kitchen. She had a half dozen jars. None of them were open."

"When you opened them, did they make a popping sound?"

"No. Why?"

"What do you mean, 'pop'?" James asked. "Jars don't pop when you open them."

"No, no, you're right. Jarring honey isn't like home canning," said Marie. "There isn't the same degree of danger of food poisoning, but if the honey isn't heated or pasteurized, it can cause some problems..."

"Problems?" James' voice cracked. "You mean food poisoning—botulism, don't you?"

Thomas leaned slowly, finally lying down onto his side, his cheek in the snow. "I'm just going to rest for a bit," he mumbled.

James took two steps backward. "This is from the sandwiches? Shit. Shit." He put his hand on his head.

"How many did you eat?" Paul asked.

"I don't know... four, five, maybe? How many did you eat?"

Paul thought. "Three... I think. Marie?"

She stood up. "I ate maybe half. I didn't care for them. Too sweet."

"Then make that three and a half. I ate the rest of yours," said Paul.

James took off his hat. He pointed at Caridad, then at Thomas. "So this is what we have to look forward to tonight?" He ran his gloved fingers through his hair, making it stand up in all directions. "Thanks for the poison picnic, guys. Real nice."

Marie rolled her eyes. "I'm sure if that's what caused the sickness, it was only in the jar they ate last night. It's pretty rare for honey to be that infected, never mind a whole batch." She pulled Thomas back to a sitting position. "Just hold tight. Once we get the tent up, you can lie down. Okay? You don't want frostbite."

She pulled on James' arm and the two of them walked back inside the circle of skis. Paul followed them, and finally, Caridad.

Pete stayed staring at Thomas for a long time.

Night 2

Weather: Frigid, Light to moderate snowfall

Five hikers waited together in the dimly lit tent, listening to the soft caress of the falling snow above their heads.

"Pete," Marie began, "we're turning back in the morning. The mountain isn't going anywhere. We can come back, and—"

"No." Pete's voice was gruff and louder than it needed to be in such an enclosed space.

Caridad groaned and hugged her arms to her chest. She had been lying in a fetal position for the past hour, weak with exhaustion. Even breathing seemed a chore. She concentrated on her inhales and exhales, hoping the monotony would lull her to sleep. Beside her, Thomas lay on his back. The sweat on his brow had soaked through his woolen hat and trickled down to leave a growing dark stain on the makeshift pillow behind his head.

"What is wrong with you?" Paul asked weakly. He squinted his eyes to focus on their leader, his vision alternately blurring and doubling. "We're sick, man. What in God's name could be so important?"

Pete took a breath, then fumbled through his front coat pocket. He pulled out an object wrapped in a faded maroon cloth.

"This," he said softly.

Paul waited for Pete to continue. When he didn't, he yelled, "Look, none of us are in the mood to play a guessing game. And quite frankly, unless it's a magical cure to make me feel less like garbage, I don't think I care what you're holding."

Pete smiled. "I told all of you about my dissertation topic, right?"

"The Dyatlov Pass, yeah," Marie said. "So?"

"So this—" Pete gingerly unwrapped the cloth to reveal a folding knife, its edges slightly tarnished with age. "Is the knife owned by one of the victims, Lyudmila." He methodically unfurled each of the implements attached to the handle: tin and bottle openers, awl, fork, corkscrew, and finally, a blade. "She was my great aunt. It's how I selected my study."

Paul snorted. "And? You couldn't have shown this to us in a nice, warm hotel room with room service that didn't include a breakfast of misery?"

"The hikers, all of them died on the pass. Their bodies were found strewn all over the half mile area, some with crushed rib cages or pieces missing from their flesh..." Marie recounted. She looked hard at Pete. "Your aunt, your aunt was found with parts of her lips ripped away, her eyes and tongue missing..."

Pete's voice stayed even. "I had to recreate the same conditions as closely as I could. If we—"

James unzipped the entrance and ducked back inside. His hat and coat were covered with a dusting of white. He wiped a yellowish dribble from his chin with the back of his glove.

"To whoever's skis are at 11 o'clock, I sincerely apologize for the Jackson Pollock paint job." He sat down next to Paul, then turned to face Pete. "Are we going for our Swiss Army knife badge, Pieter?"

"There were no other footprints but theirs," Marie continued, speaking more to herself than to anyone in the room. "No one else was there. And they all died."

"James, you can help me explain," Pete answered. "What did you finally get your degree in?"

"Japanese language and culture," James said. "Boy, were my parents pissed. They wanted another surgeon. Maybe if I can convince Dr. Marie here to marry me, that will make up for it?" He shook his head. "Whoa...a little dizzy."

Thomas cleared his throat. It was the first they'd heard from him since helping him into the tent that afternoon. "You are writing your dissertation on Dyatlov Pass," he said weakly, slurring each word. "You managed to get an item that belongs to one of the victims, your relative, and you drag us into a blizzard to do what?"

"That's not all I have of hers," Pete said.

He removed from his other pocket a small, oblong box and opened it. Inside was a lock of dark blonde hair.

"Why do you have her hair?" Paul asked. "Why would anyone have someone's hair?"

Caridad's voice was soft. "Women used to do that, cut off a lock of their hair and give it to their sweetheart if they were going to be separated for a while. My grandmother showed me hers, the piece she cut for my grandfather when he was in the war."

James was puzzled. "*Tsukumogami*," he said. "What are you trying to evoke?" He reached over to the box, replaced the cover, and turned to the others. "*Susu-harai* was the tradition in Japanese culture to discard objects after they reached ninety-nine years of age because at year one hundred, they would attract a spirit, a *yōkai*, which then turned the tool into a sort of honing device for the apparition, a *tsukumogami*."

"Exactly," said Pete. He carefully closed the knife and rested the lock's box on the ground in front of him. "Don't you get it? This is my chance—our chance—to find out what happened on that mountain. Lyudmila's spirit will show me."

"Wait. I thought Dyatlov happened in the fifties," said Marie. "You're a couple of decades short."

"The numbers are metaphorical," Pete said, "like those in the Book of Revelation. What's important are the conditions...and the object."

James shrugged. "He's right. Most scholars believe the time is irrelevant. As long as the object is considered to be old, it's fair game for the *yōkai*."

Pete's voice became louder. "We are going to evoke her, Lyudmila, and we are going to find out, finally know, what happened on that mountain."

His eyes darted furiously around the group, like those of a rabid animal. Before anyone could question him further, he opened the box with the lock of hair again, placed the folded knife on top, and recovered the container. He lay down in his sleeping bag and pulled the box inside with him, where he slept with both of his hands curled around it the rest of the night.

Day 3

Weather: Partly cloudy skies, overnight snow accumulation:12-16 inches

"It's been over three hours. Where could he be?" James asked, more as a rhetorical question than anything else, and no one offered a response.

He sat on his pack in front of the fire.

Paul, Marie, Caridad, and Thomas did the same.

The group had awoken to find Pete's bed empty, the box with the hair and the knife still tucked inside.

"He's doing this out of spite, you know," said Paul. "He knows that we won't leave without him, and if we don't leave soon, we'll never make it all the way down the mountain before dark." He coughed, trying to clear his throat. His tongue felt swollen and dry, and he still saw doubling when he tried to focus his vision. "Passive aggressive: that's what it is."

As he said this, all five of the hikers looked over at the smooth snow surrounding the tent. No footprints could be seen except those leading a few feet away from the shelter, punctuated only by small circles of urine. Outside of a two-yard radius, the snow was undisturbed in all directions.

Marie tilted her head toward the sky. "The good news is, I don't think we'll be seeing more snow for a bit." She looked at the rest of the group. Everyone looked exhausted. Thomas was bent over, his head propped in his hands. "Anyone feeling better?"

Thomas mumbled weakly without looking up. "Remember Sit 'n Spins? The amusement of pulling yourself around and around and then letting yourself fall sideways and onto the floor? The whole room spinning until you thought you were going to puke your brains out? This is that. Without the amusement part."

Each word sounded smothered, like his tongue was wrapped in cotton batting.

"I'd take one of those preschool torture devices any day over this," said Caridad. "They never made me feel like my lungs were stuffed with cotton candy." She consciously inhaled and exhaled for the group. "Think it's the elevation?"

Marie kept her face blank. "Could be. Just try to take it easy. Stay in front of the fire and keep warm."

"I haven't thrown up today," offered James weakly. "Yay me."

Paul said nothing but pulled the hood of his jacket over his head.

The five listened to the wind shake clumps of snow from tree branches in the distance.

"If he's not back by—" James began, but Paul cut him off, sharply.

"He'll be back. At least by dinnertime. He didn't take his pack, his skis, or any supplies. What's he going to do? Eat tree bark? Sleep in the pitch black in the cold without shelter?" He picked up a handful of snow and threw it at the fire. It sizzled slightly. "*Tsukumogami*, my ass."

Everyone was silent as their eyes searched the landscape beyond the camp.

"The *yōkai*: are they friendly spirits?" Caridad asked, her breath catching.

"The depictions range from those that cause mischief to those that..." James paused. "Well, those that do quite a bit more damage." His expression was serious, a rare occurrence.

Marie mirrored his countenance. "You don't think he's evoking Lyudmila, do you? You think he's going to bring something else back."

James looked straight ahead, toward the closest copse of pine trees. "It's said that the one that becomes a *yōkai* before its time is the angriest spirit of them all."

"If he did transform that knife into a *tsukumogami*, where does that leave us?" asked Paul.

"*Montaña de los Muertos*," said Caridad. "That's where we are. I checked the map before we got out of the car."

All of them looked at her, silent.

She smiled weakly. "The Mountain of the Dead."

Night 3
Weather: Frigid, clear skies

An hour after sundown, Pete still hadn't returned. The group lay huddled together in the tent, the emergency lantern turned to its lowest point, just bright enough for the tent to be illuminated should their friend try to find his way back in the dark.

"Tomorrow, we pack up the gear, including Pete's things, and we double time it down to the road. As soon as we have cell service, we'll call the police," said Caridad.

She coughed. She didn't know if her lungs would allow her to descend the mountain at top speed, but at least there wouldn't be the weather to worry about. She could do it. She just had to focus on keeping her breath steady.

Marie blinked back tears. "Something must have happened to him. He wouldn't have done this just to make a point. We know Pete. He's stubborn and single-minded, but he's not suicidal."

At that, a rustling sound crackled from outside the tent.

"Pete?" Thomas called. "Pete!"

The rustling stopped, replaced with a scratching sound—not outside of the tent, but on it.

Something sharp was dragging along the nylon wall.

Back and forth, back and forth.

It drifted along the right wall and over to the front, where the zippered entrance was secured shut.

"Pete, you made your point," James called out. "It's a scary story, and it's cool that you've taken the responsibility to solve the mystery. Now come inside and eat something. We all know you must be starving."

The scratching stopped.

Paul looked at the others. "I have reached the end of my patience for bullshit." He crawled over to the tent's exit to unzip it, but when he attempted to bring the pull upwards, it wouldn't budge. "It's jammed," he said, still yanking on the zipper to try and open the door.

"Let me see," Marie said. "Maybe there's a bent tooth or something." She removed her gloves and ran her hands along the length of the zipper, then pulled them away quickly. Her fingertips were covered with a black ooze. She examined the substance, looked at the zipper, and back at her hands. "What the—"

"Hey. It's me. Let me in." Pete's voice drifted eerily to them from outside the tent.

Marie grabbed the zipper from Paul's hands and tried to pull it upward. "Pete? We're trying, but the zipper is stuck."

Thomas felt around the ground of the tent. "Hold on. I took this out of my coat last night so I wouldn't accidentally roll over and stab myself in my delusional state." His hands found what they were searching for, and he held up the steak knife in triumph. "Ah ha. See? 'Told you it would come in handy."

He began to crawl over to the doorway but James reached out his arm to stop him.

"Don't," he whispered. James' eyes were wide, his mouth fixed in a flat line. "I don't think it's Pete."

"What?" yelled Paul. "What do you mean, it's not him? Who the hell else would it be?"

Pete's voice did not change its volume or tone. "It's me. Let me in."

"That's not Pete," whispered James.

"Pete?" Marie called to him and continued to fidget with the pull. "Pete, I'm trying, but the zipper is stuck."

James tapped Thomas on the shoulder and pointed. A black, greasy substance was oozing from between the teeth of the door's closure. It continued to emerge until the entire zipper was covered in a dark, gelatinous film.

"Marie," James hissed. "Marie, get away. Get—"

The zipper split, the door halves falling open like a stage curtain.

Marie wiped her hands on her knees and stuck her head outside. "Pete? Where are you?" she called, her voice becoming smaller.

There was an agonizing beat of silence. Then, almost inaudibly, they heard something growl.

Marie pushed to her feet and ducked outside of the tent. "Pete?"

It all happened so quickly that they barely registered the motion. One minute, Marie's legs were visible from their vantage point on the floor of the tent. The next, they were pulled upwards, into the air and out of sight.

Then, from somewhere above them, Marie screamed.

"Holy fuck," Paul muttered as he crab-walked backwards toward Thomas and James.

Caridad plastered herself against the back wall of the tent but reached one arm out to feel along the ground in front of her.

Something heavy bounced against the top of the tent and rolled down to the snow and did not move.

The growling was louder, much louder this time.

It was Pete.

At least, it was *once* Pete.

Something else had put on a Pete skin and was walking around in it, like a master puppeteer. Once-Pete ducked its head into the tent and positioned its face so that it was facing them.

It was impossible to know where it was looking. Its eyes were missing.

In their place were wet, black sockets.

Once-Pete opened its mouth but did not move its lips. Instead, a Pete voice played from somewhere inside of the ghoul, a record player on permanent skip.

"Let me in. It's me," it said again.

Once-Pete did not walk or crawl but simply glided over towards Paul, who was huddling in a crouch in front of the other two men.

Caridad, finally finding the object she sought, lifted the rifle but turned it so that the butt of the gun faced forward. Just as Once-Pete leaned forward to grab Paul, Cari threw the rifle, javelin-style, in an attempt to strike the attacker. Her faltering strength, however, caused her to miss her mark, and instead, the butt of the gun struck Paul in the temple, leaving a deep gash. He collapsed forward, unconscious.

James pushed himself to his feet and ran forward, out of the tent and toward the dying fire. Marie was standing in front of it, her back to him.

"Marie? Marie? What happened? What—"

The woman turned to face him, and the Once-Marie opened its mouth. Black ooze poured from between its lips, the eyeless sockets glinting in the moonlight. It pounced onto James, pushing him onto his back, and dug its knees deep into his chest.

"No!" James cried out in pain. "Please, no!" Once-Marie knelt harder, and James felt his ribs crack and fold inward, then a sharp, stabbing pain as one impaled his lung.

Once-Pete grabbed Paul's shoulders and dragged him effortlessly out of the tent. As it did so, Thomas drove the steak knife into the nylon wall behind them and pulled downward as hard as he could. The barrier tore open with a satisfying ripping sound.

"Come on," he said, pulling on Caridad's arm. The two leaped from the shelter and ran out into the snow.

They ran as fast as they could, realizing too late that their damaged lung muscles would not allow them to go far. They both fell to their knees, gasping for air.

"Tree," Thomas wheezed. "Climb tree," he said.

In the bright moonlight, Caridad could make out the outline of the copse of trees James had been staring at earlier. She pushed herself to her feet and walked slowly, the air barely circulating in and out of her lungs in short, jagged breaths.

Once again, she concentrated on her inhales and exhales.

Thomas did not follow behind her.

She glanced backwards and could see nothing but the dim glow of the abandoned tent and shadows on the snowy field.

Finally, she felt the bark of a tree in front of her.

Climb tree.

Thomas's words echoed in her mind. She would climb as high as she could and hide there until the morning.

Surely this was only a bad dream. She would hide until morning and they would find her, here in the tree, having sleep-walked in her feverish state.

Cari concentrated on her breath, aligned it with each move of her feet and hands higher. Breathe in, step; breathe out, reach and pull. When she could go no further, she balanced herself onto a branch and straddled the trunk, holding onto it in a bear hug. She pressed her ear against the trunk. Her heart beat against her chest, echoed into the heart of the tree and into her ear. She closed her eyes and exhaled.

It wasn't until she felt the warm fluid oozing down the trunk and over her arms that she opened her eyes, but she already knew what she would see.

There, hovering in front of her in the shadows, was Once-Thomas.

White Trash

We watched as Judy's mother's eyes darted nervously about the camera's frame, alternately squinting and welling with tears, sometimes looking straight into the lens, seemingly right at us: Elaine, Carrie, and I, folded like origami animals on the stiff sofa in Carrie's living room.

A disembodied microphone shoved itself into the frame and Judy's mother's gaze drifted off camera, toward some unseen target in the distance as she spoke.

Elaine and I were silent, transfixed by the brief interview. Carrie scraped at the pink polish on her fingernails, spilling a dusting of glitter on the gray wall-to-wall carpet that was soiled here and there by muddy shoes and dropped dinner plates. The room was stifling, even warmer than it should have been on an early July day, but then again, the big picture window—a staple of all of the tiny ranch-style homes that lined the street like candlepins, ready for strike—didn't open, and the only air conditioner was in Carrie's mother's bedroom, and we certainly weren't going to hang out in there. No one was allowed, anyway: not since Carrie had turned sixteen three months earlier.

The news clip ended and a Burger King commercial appeared in its place, the voiceover belting out a song about "doubling my way," and Carrie pawed around the flotsam on the glass coffee table in search of the remote. She found it and clicked the channel button just as giant metal tongs placed two strips of bacon on melted cheese.

"So gross," she muttered.

Brightly colored images and snippets of sound flashed by before finally settling on a music video by RUN DMC. Carrie tossed the controller onto the carpet and padded over to the round dining table at the opposite corner of the L-shaped room, her bare feet soundless under the music.

"Billy and Skandar will be here soon," she said to no one in particular, then fished a small mirror from under the pile of dishes and discarded newspapers.

I turned my attention back to the television. There was a close-up of the rappers' Adidas sneakers, then Steven Tyler was pressing his cheek against a wall.

"They're not going to blame us, right?" Elaine asked, pulling up her long legs and stuffing her ankles beneath her, her mind still on the news report. "I mean, we weren't even there."

Her bony knee brushed up against my thigh and I flinched in response.

Carrie ran a dark pencil around her gray eyes, pulling the bottom lids down slightly and filling the waterlines with black kohl. She pulled her hand away and blinked three times.

"Of course not, stupid," she said, looking into the hand mirror, then grabbing a Q-tip and smudging the color slightly. She turned to look at Elaine. "Why would they blame *us*?"

I opened my mouth to speak, but the sharp rap on the picture window cut me off. Without waiting for someone to answer him, Bill Sayus opened the front door and strutted inside. Bill strutted everywhere. It might have been the black steel-toed boots that he wore every day, even in the middle of summer. I didn't think I'd ever seen his legs. I imagined they were as freckled as the rest of him.

"Shut the door," Carrie yelled immediately. "It's hot outside."

Bill did as he was told and walked further into the room.

He glanced at the tv and snorted. "What the hell is this shit?"

Elaine unfurled herself and stood up, readjusting the large black belt with shiny metal medallions that encircled her narrow hips. Without a word, she shimmied past Bill and toward the short hallway that led to the bathroom. I heard the door creak shut.

Bill fiddled with the tape deck on the portable radio on the ledge of the window. Aerosmith's "Same Old Song and Dance" began to play mid-song. Bill collapsed backwards onto the couch next to me, not bothering to turn off the television, and the two songs clashed against one another in my ears. Steven Tyler battled with himself to gain control of the air.

"Jude's mom..." he began, trailing off in thought. "I mean, what the absolute fuck, right? Yammering on. Yeah, your daughter wasn't such an angel, you know."

He looked at me and laughed. I could smell a sweet musk, a man's deodorant, and under that, the sourness of old beer, not leaking from his pores but from somewhere on his clothing, like someone had spilled it on him days earlier.

"Right, Gigi?"

He elbowed me like we were a vaudeville comedy duo.

"I guess," I said, reaching down and grabbing the remote. I clicked the mute button instead of shutting the set off; I wanted something to look at besides Bill. A British pop band's video had begun; the pale singer with a mop of shocking orange hair stuffed under a scally cap brooded against a dismal landscape. On the boombox, the faint rubber band opening riff of "Sweet Emotion" twanged.

"You saw her, right?" Bill continued.

"Yeah, I—"

It had been a rhetorical question. "She just stared off into space. Didn't even bother to apologize." He snorted a laugh. "Poser. Fucking white trash."

It took me a moment to realize he wasn't talking about Judy's mom; he was talking about Judy, about the last time we had all been together. I crossed my ankles and pulled my hands out from under my legs. I had forgotten I was sitting on them. The stitches of my jeans left imprints on my skin, puffy red slashes along my wrists.

Carrie returned to our side of the room, drinking a sweaty bottle of key lime wine cooler.

"No way," she said as Bill stuffed a Marlboro Red between his lips and dug his hand into the front pocket of his faded jeans for a lighter. "You know the rules. My mom will kill me if she smells smoke in here."

He leaped from the couch and sauntered into the tiny kitchenette, the only square of floor besides the bathroom not covered in the endless carpet, stopping at the back door.

"When are you gonna move this stuff?"

He nodded toward the jumble of items stacked in the doorway. I could see the handle of a snow shovel peeking out from behind a broken metal chair from the dining set, both of them leaning against the peeling white paint of the rickety door jam. The previously straight spine of the chair's back had been crushed. I thought I could see the outline of a boot toe at an angle. My mouth felt dry.

I looked at Carrie. She was looking at the pile, too, but her expression hadn't changed.

"Just go out the front," she said, motioning with her bottle.

I stood up. "I'll go with you," I said.

I fumbled for my purse where I had stored it beside the sofa and fished out my pack.

I caught Carrie rolling her eyes. "Don't let any more hot air in, please," she commanded.

The temperature seemed to have risen steadily over the course of the day, and the setting sun still beat mercilessly on our faces. I held my hand up to my forehead like a visor but felt my cheeks begin to sweat. I turned my back to the glare and felt the rays sizzle against the back of my neck.

Somehow, in the years between splashing around a neighbor's pool as a carefree ten-year-old and then, I'd become a vampire.

The front lawn wasn't much to look at. There was grass, but the ratio of brown dirt, still moist from the weekend's rainstorm, to green was definitely in the former's favor. I pinched a cigarette between my lips and Bill immediately brought the lighter in front of my face. The air was so still, he didn't need to cup the flame. A small white dog wandered aimlessly by the lot, not bothering to acknowledge us. The fur around its mouth and feet was yellowed.

I looked past the dog and down the road to the right. Carrie lived on a side street, one of many branching from a four-lane thoroughfare. Kids used the busy road to drag race at night, and it was known to be a last tragic stop for wayward neighborhood pets, especially at sunset, when westbound drivers white-knuckled their steering wheels and squinted their way home.

I pulled a long drag and with my free hand, pulled my t-shirt away from my chest over and over, trying to let some air inside. The dog stopped at the edge of the neighbor's yard and sniffed.

Bill squatted down and balanced his elbow on his knee. "The police came to my house last night. Scared the fuck outta my mom," he said, his eyes on the dog. "I told her, *Ma, it's nothing, don't worry about it*. But you know how Moms are."

I stopped fanning my shirt. "What did they ask you?" I said.

Bill stood up again, took a drag of his cigarette, then flicked the butt toward the street using his thumb and forefinger, the way I always wished I'd been able to do. I watched a slim curl of smoke drift from the mound of dirt where it had landed. "I mean, I guess because of that stupid report she made, they wanted to know if I had *run into her* or if I knew where she was going Friday night." He shook each of his legs, one by one, like he was shaking sand after a day at the beach. "I mean, it was definitely a fishing expedition. If they knew anything, they would have just straight-out asked what happened...or maybe hauled me in."

The matter-of-fact manner with which he explained this made me uncomfortable, but I concentrated on keeping my expression blank.

"Yeah," I agreed. "Probably just trying to cover their bases."

We were silent for a beat. I wanted to ask Bill about the afternoon he and Skandar walked Judy home from school. I never heard the whole story, just bits and pieces from the rumor mill. On the day in question, Carrie and Elaine and I had ditched the last two periods and taken the city bus to the mall, but before we returned home, Judy called each of our houses, panicking and crying to our parents. She nearly blew our cover. When we saw her the next day, she was still upset, but Carrie shut her up pretty quickly.

Privately, Carrie confided that Bill said that Judy had seduced him—and Skandar—and now she was just blowing smoke because they didn't want to be her boyfriends.

But then Judy spoke with the guidance counselor. And things got complicated.

A screen door slammed across the street, its sound crisp and clear in the still air. Skandar loped across the lawn, along the road, and up Carrie's driveway. Beads of sweat were already pooling on his forehead.

Many paces behind him, Little Bob slowly approached. Everyone called him Little Bob because his father was Big Bob, but I never understood why there needed to be a distinction. Bob's father was retired, much older than our fathers, and he rarely left the house anymore except to frequent the nearby pool hall. Little Bob stopped going to school after the tenth grade and spent most of the day playing Zelda on Nintendo. With his round torso, six-two frame, and puffy cheeks, Little seemed an awkward moniker, especially since he likely doubled his dad in weight. The Bobs lived in the house across the street, a mirror image of Carrie's except gray instead of ivory.

I wondered if the wall-to-wall carpet inside was ivory.

I didn't know where Mrs. Bob was and no one ever asked. For all I knew, she was trapped in the house along with them.

"'Sup, Ginny," Skandar nodded at me and wiped his brow.

Skandar lived at the other end of the street, far to the left. His house abutted the baseball diamond at the neighborhood park. On more than one Saturday during the spring, a fly ball came sailing over the fence while we sat around his backyard. Each time, Skandar snatched it from his lawn and tossed it into his shed, adding, "Finders, keepers, bitch."

"Hey," I answered coolly.

Skandar nodded to Bill. "Cops go to your house?" he asked. He motioned with his hand in a come-hither movement, indicating he wanted to bum a smoke. I never understood how someone who seemed to be buying new music every weekend never had enough money to buy a pack of his own.

Bill threw his red and white pack at him. "Yup. You too?"

Skandar shoved a cigarette in the corner of his mouth and fished the lighter out of its makeshift holder in the clear cellophane wrapper.

"Yeah. No one was home but me, so I let them in. I told them I hadn't seen her in weeks, not since we walked her home, you know?" He inhaled deeply and exhaled out of his nose, the smoke coming out in two white streams like a dragon. "They kept asking where my parents were. I'm like, 'They both work nights, officer.' After the third time I said it, they just got up and left."

"I don't think they can question you without your parents being there. You're a minor," I volunteered, suddenly the group's legal guide. When the two boys just stared at me, I shrugged. "I think," I added, less certain. "I don't know. My parents watch a lot of *Hill Street Blues* and I think that was on one of the episodes."

"What show are you talking about?" Little Bob asked, finally joining the group.

Bill smirked and looked away. "Nothing. Don't worry about it."

He turned back to me and shot me a warning look, not wanting to continue the conversation.

On Friday, Carrie had the same expression on her face when the four of us—me, Carrie, Elaine, and Judy—walked back to Carrie's house from the park and I suggested taking a detour to the Cumberland Farms convenience store three blocks down so I could buy a soda.

That night, Carrie had called Judy and asked her to meet us at the picnic tables at dusk so that we could watch the Independence Day fireworks together.

"My mom's gone for the weekend. She won't be home until Tuesday morning. We can party afterwards at the house," she said and grinned at Elaine, who covered her mouth with her hand to stifle a laugh.

Bill and Skandar arrived only a few moments after we did. When Judy saw them enter, her face blanched and her lips curled into a small snarl, like she had swallowed something rotten.

Skandar stepped daintily on the tip of his burning cigarette, then lifted it to his face to inspect that the fire had been extinguished. He shoved the slightly flat butt behind his ear, presumably to revisit later.

"What does Carrie have to drink? It's hot as hell out here," he said.

When the four of us slipped into the relative cool of the living room, taking great pains to close the door quickly, I noticed Elaine had resumed her folded perch on the sofa. Her hair had doubled in size, likely a result of furious underbrushing and a quarter can of the Aquanett in Carrie's bathroom. I made a beeline to sit next to her. Available seating at Carrie's house was never a guarantee, and I always staked my claim when any more than the four of us—now, three of us—were there. Carrie wandered closer to the boys, still holding the wine cooler. She tipped the bottle to her lips and swallowed the remaining pale green liquid.

On the silent television screen, David Lee Roth pinwheeled around a stage wearing an assortment of sparkling outfits. Someone had flipped the tape over, and Steven Tyler was screaming that he was back in the saddle again. Bill grabbed the empty wine cooler bottle from Carrie's hand and held it horizontally in front of his jeans zipper.

"That's right: I'm talking about a *Yankee rose*," he said, smirking at his girlfriend.

"Waaah-wah," Skandar added, mimicking Steve Vai's guitar.

Carrie offered a half smile and walked into Bill's embrace. He tilted his head down to hers so that his long hair spilled over his face, covering their kiss like a shroud.

Elaine stretched her body up and turned toward the framed watercolor print hanging on the wall behind us. She rubbed her index finger along her lip gloss, trying to dissemble her reflection in the glass. The picture was one of those useless pink and lilac landscapes with a location no one had ever heard of written in matching lettering along the bottom. I thought my dentist had a similar piece in his waiting room, and when I mentioned that to Carrie once, she confessed that her mother had swiped it from a dumpster behind a medical office building.

Steven Tyler's voice was finally given a rest as Skandar fiddled with the boombox. He pulled a plastic cassette box out of his back pocket and slid its contents into the player.

"*Under Lock and Key*: got it this morning at Strawberries. I only played through the first side."

After a beat, the eerie dissonance of George Lynch's guitar echoed the opening bars of "It's Not Love." The television show broke for a commercial and Mitch Gaylord began to spin over and over on a gymnastic bar on the screen. Everyone silently watched as a clip featuring Janet Jones stretching her naked leg around Gaylord in a dimly lit room flickered by.

Incongruously, Little Bob said, "You guys going to see *Labyrinth*? Bowie looks crazy in it."

"Fuck that," Bill answered sharply. "Puppets creep the hell outta me."

We all silently agreed.

The boys walked over to the dinette set, each claiming a seat. I saw Little Bob glance over at the fourth chair. It seemed to scream at us from its forced ostracism in the debris pile. Elaine was looking at the chair, as well. Bill looked from Bob to Elaine to me.

I swallowed hard.

Everyone's thoughts were talking at once.

"Just keep your traps shut and no one is the wiser, got it?" Bill said to no one in particular.

Skandar fingered the filter of the clipped cigarette behind his ear.

· · · • · • · • · ·

Friday night, Judy had been sitting in that chair at the dining table. Bill and Skandar flanked either side of her. Carrie and Elaine stood across from her on the other side of the table. I hung back, near Little Bob on the couch.

Carrie swirled the diet Coke in her glass and took a sip.

"You guys," Judy looked over to me, then back and forth between Elaine and Carrie, her eyes wide and pleading. "Why aren't you helping me? Please?"

Carrie slammed the glass on the table. A splash of soda escaped along the side. "You try to steal my boyfriend, and now you want me to help you?"

She rolled her eyes dramatically. "You've got to be kidding. You deserve everything you get."

Tears began to slide down Judy's cheeks and she wiped them away, embarrassed. "I didn't try to steal anything. They asked to walk me home, and I let them, and—"

"You invited them inside," interrupted Elaine. "Why would you invite them inside?"

She raised her eyebrow, proud of herself for solving the case with her sly interrogation.

Judy sniffed hard, the snot sounding wet and heavy in her nose. "It was hot and I asked if they wanted some iced-tea or something. I didn't ask for—"

Carrie held her hand up. I wasn't sure if it was to stop Judy from talking or to prepare to strike her. "Shut up. Just shut up. You're a liar and a slut."

Judy stood up from the chair with such force, the chair fell backwards onto the floor behind her.

"I am not a slut! Your boyfriend is a fucking rapist! He—"

Carrie slapped her so hard across the face that she had to shake her hand afterward, trying to obliterate the sting. Behind Judy, Bill stomped his foot onto the chair, then began to trample and kick it, over and over. Judy covered her head with her hands and bent forward, trying to protect herself, but Bill grabbed her by the throat and pulled her to the ground. He pushed her shoulders into the mangled chair back.

"Do you know what they do in prison to guys convicted of rape?!" Bill was screaming. His voice reverberated in my chest. "They become someone's bitch. Is that what you want to happen to Skandar and me? Is it?!"

Little Bob's stomach growled audibly. Judy blinked rapidly but said nothing. Her hands had moved to the sides of her head, over her ears. The left side of her face was red and starting to swell.

"You think you're better than me? Better than us?" Bill continued.

Carrie leaned sideways and rested her head against Elaine's. "I didn't think it would go this far," she stage-whispered and clamped her still-ringing hand over her mouth, but the edges of her broad grin leaked out from either side. Elaine giggled nervously in response.

Judy remained silent and slowly let her hands fall to her sides. She was staring ahead without expression, like a moment of clarity had settled upon her. She transported herself somewhere else.

"Please..." said a voice so small, I almost didn't recognize it as Judy's. "Please. I just want to go home. Can I just go home?"

Bill leaned his head closer to Judy's, his hair falling over his eyes and his mouth slightly open so that a thin dribble of saliva dripped onto her face. "Of course you can go home. Me and Skan will walk you." He said this so coolly, so evenly, that I had to look around at everyone else in the room to remind myself what had just transpired. He pulled his head back but maintained his predatory stare. "Sound okay to you?"

Skandar reached down and ran his hand through Judy's hair, then along the side of her cheek, like a parent might do in a gesture of love.

Judy closed her eyes.

Just say yes, I thought. *Just say yes, and walk home, and forget any of this happened, and everything will be fine tomorrow.*

Judy's house was only a half mile away, on the other side of the park.

The rain was just beginning to fall as the three of them left Carrie's house.

It was a Little League team who found her body, pale and bloated from lying in the flooded dugout all weekend.

• • • • • • • • • •

Just as Don Dokken finished asking *Why, baby, why?* for the hundredth time, the phone on the wall of the kitchen clamored loudly, and Carrie bounded over to answer it.

After listening for a moment, she placed the receiver on her shoulder. "It's for you, Ginny."

I looked up in surprise.

"It's your mom."

I walked slowly to the kitchen. Carrie lingered after I took the phone from her, so I nonchalantly wandered away toward the heap in front of the door.

I cleared my throat. "Hello?"

My mother's voice was sharp in my ear. "Virginia, your father is coming to pick you up."

"What? No, I'm sleeping over Carrie's tonight," I said, without thinking. "Why?"

My mother was silent for a moment. "The police are here," she said flatly. "They want to ask you some questions about Judy."

"I don't...I mean, what—like what?" I stammered.

I realized the room had gone completely silent.

Even the music had stopped.

I turned around. Not only was everyone staring at me, but Bill had somehow made his way into the kitchen without my hearing. He was so close, I could have reached out and touched him. His hard, blue eyes were fixed on my face.

"Where were you on Friday night?" my mother asked.

"I—I told you. We went to see a movie, and then we slept at Elaine's," I said, looking away.

My face felt hot. I wondered if I had gotten a sunburn in the little time I had been in the front yard.

"What movie?" she asked quickly.

"*Ferris Bueller's Day Off*," I said. "I *told* you. We went to see it again."

In truth, I hadn't seen the movie, not even once. None of us had. But there had been so much buzz about it, so many details spilled and lines repeated when we'd been at school that it was easy to claim to have seen it. We practically knew the damn film by heart and we'd never seen anything but the trailer. Over the previous three weeks, we used the alibi when we snuck into cars with older boys, when we drank stolen liquor with Bill and Skandar and Little Bob in the woods behind the park, even on the night we spent at a seedy country-western bar we managed to be served at, discovering only later that it doubled as a den for prostitutes and johns.

The *Ferris Bueller* attendance became a running joke between the three of us, but at that moment, I was far from laughing.

Again, there was silence.

Silence on the line, silence in the house.

Finally, after an audible breath, my mother's voice needled curtly over the line. "Your father is already in the car. Be outside when he arrives, Virginia." She hung up the phone without saying goodbye—something she'd never done to me, no matter how angry she'd gotten.

I replaced the receiver on the hook and walked over to my bag and shoved the Marlboro Lights into the bottom, under a camouflage of makeup and refuse. I slung the strap over my shoulder and headed toward the bathroom to wash my hands and douse myself with perfume to mask the smell of cigarettes.

When I returned to the room, someone had turned on the radio. Rock 102, the only station we listened to with any regularity, was playing The Firm's "Radioactive."

The group was gathered tightly together, and everyone turned to look at me.

"My dad's coming to get me," I said. "I'm supposed to meet him outside."

Carrie crossed her arms in front of her chest. "What's going on, Ginny?" Her voice sounded pleasant enough, but her mouth was tight and she was frowning.

I shrugged, trying to appear relaxed. "I guess the police stopped by my house. My parents just want me to come home. That's all. No big deal."

"The police came to your house *today*?" Elaine clarified. "Why did they come today? Didn't you talk to them on Saturday?"

"Of course," I said.

We all had. Judy's parents had spent Friday at a neighbor's cookout, and by the time they got home, Judy was gone. When she didn't come home at all, they'd called all of our houses, asking if we had seen her, and then they'd called the police.

Bill walked closer to me. He tapped the end of his plastic lighter on his hip.

"Why do they want to talk to *you* again? I mean, you and Judy weren't even that close." He tapped his hip harder. "Why didn't they come here, talk to Carrie?"

My face was definitely red. Neck, too. My skin prickled. "I don't know." My voice sounded small, far away. "I really don't."

I looked at Carrie. She was still frowning. Elaine caught my eyes and immediately stared at the floor.

Paul Rodger's voice crooned from the speakers, filling the uncomfortable silence, singing that he was not my captive.

Finally, Little Bob spoke. "You're not going to tell them. Are you, Ginny?"

I swallowed hard. I saw Judy's mother sobbing on the television, the big microphone pointed at her face like a bank robber holding a teller at gunpoint.

"No," I whispered. "I won't."

Outside, a car horn honked just as Bill clamped his hand around my upper arm. I shook him off of me and ran to the door and pulled it open wide. I didn't care how much hot air I was letting in. The gray outline of my father loomed motionless behind the wheel of the station wagon in the driveway, details swallowed up in the glare of his headlights pointed at the house. Instead of running toward the car, I ran in the opposite direction, to the right and down the street as fast as I could.

I kept running, even as my lungs seized with pain and the shapes of cars and trucks whizzing by on the main road grew clearer. There would be no break in traffic, no window to sprint to the other side of the street, but I ran. I ran.

The front grill of the first car pummeled my abdomen. I felt something pop, explode inside my gut. Searing agony flooded my body, mixing with the sick sensation of weightlessness as my body sailed onto the hood and rolled over the windshield.

My purse bounced away from me, spilling its contents over the pavement. My package of cigarettes, the hard pack chosen for its durability, crushed under the wheel of another car whizzing by.

Poser. Fucking white trash.

My body ricocheted off fiberglass and chrome and rolled, topsy-turvy...

Puppets creep the hell outta me

...into a half somersault...

David Lee Roth rolling around the stage

...landed in a heap...

the chair's back a twist of metal in the debris in front of the door

...on the asphalt...

Joe Perry on the guitar Steve Vai on the guitar George Lynch on the guitar Jimmy Page on the guitar

...and the next car's brakes' squeal was so very loud that—

Dora Mat

Dora Matthews wiped the droplets of water and debris—as well as the sprinkling of thick black body hairs her husband Mark had carelessly shed—from the edge of the white porcelain tub.

Mark's girlfriend would be visiting today.

Dora didn't want the woman to think her a poor housekeeper.

She already must believe Dora was a poor wife. Why else would she be sleeping with her husband?

Mark didn't know that Dora knew of his indiscretions, but his wife's suspicions were piqued one early evening the previous spring when he arrived home and she could smell the evidence. She knew another woman had been there—the way you know when someone has burned dinner the evening before or that your great aunt who promised to quit smoking has pilfered a cigarette a few hours before your quick kiss to her on the cheek.

It wasn't a perfume that she smelled, either.

No, it was the odor of something larger: the scent of secrecy, of newness, and of rediscovered youth.

It was the same scent she had been smelling on Mark a few times a week for the past year, especially after she arrived home following her evening shift at the city library. He had seemed happier over the last twelve months, too, sometimes whistling while he did his domestic chores like a stock character in a Thornton Wilder play. One Saturday that September, she watched him from the kitchen window as he raked the oak leaves into a rust-colored pile in the backyard. He seemed lost in his own thoughts, earbuds securely fixed in his ears, and Dora could have sworn she saw him sway a bit like he was dancing dreamily in time to the music.

Yes, Mark was happy again.

And Dora understood that it was not because of her, but despite her.

She had given him everything he could have wanted: a clean home, a warm meal every evening, a travel and leisure partner. He had wanted children—*they* had wanted children—but it hadn't quite worked out despite both their best efforts. It was only three years previous when she'd left the white pregnancy test stick next to the coffeemaker for him to find, certain that the bright pink "+" sign was a predictor of happy times to come. Then, two months later, she'd found herself fidgeting in the scratchy plastic chair of the hospital laboratory waiting area, blinking quickly in an attempt to adjust her eyes to the harsh fluorescent lighting, the kind of incandescence that made everyone, even supermodels, look somewhat mummified.

She'd glanced at the bloodwork order her doctor had handed her wordlessly after she'd slid from the ultrasound table and back into her loafers, the remnants of warm lubricant greasy on the button of her jeans.

Spontaneous abortion, the order for blood work read.

It was a term that seemed woefully incongruous to the situation. When Dora read the diagnosis, she expected a flash mob to appear from behind the corner of the phlebotomy office, jazz hands raised in unison to the tinny boombox blare of a 1980s Michael Jackson or Debbie Gibson song. After that day, there were no more pink "+" signs, no more visits to the gynecologist for ultrasounds.

It would be only Mark and Dora, Dora and Mark only, from that point further.

Except it *wasn't* just the two of them.

Not anymore.

Now, it was Dora and Mark and the *girlfriend*. This interloper was the concubine, the side dish, the "*other* woman," as if to imply that Dora and the girl were on equal grounds: here stood one woman, there stood the other. Dora imagined herself as a piece of apple pie at a dessert buffet, Mark leaning over to savor the offerings with his eyes. *Would you like a slice of chocolate cake, sir? Perhaps a dish of orange sherbet?* She imagined her husband crossing his arms over his chest and pretending to ponder his options before opening his mouth to display every sweet tooth in a broad, pearly grin.

He'd have a slice of each, of course.

Life was just too darn short.

Dora pushed herself up from the edge of the tub and brushed her hands on the front of her thighs. She'd worn her old jeans, the ones with the frayed hemlines and splatters of blue paint from when they'd redone the bedroom five years ago. She was proud to still fit into the clothes she'd purchased a decade earlier. She had tamed her figure's growling thrusts at expansion, even though it had gotten more difficult to stave off the creeping roundness in her belly and hips as she approached her mid-thirties.

Dora caught a flash of her image reflected in the vanity mirror. She placed the sponge on the edge of the sink and ran a moist hand through the tendrils escaping from her wide headband. She was still pretty, she thought. Not in that bouncy, twenty-something way, but attractive, certainly. When they went to dinner at the posh Delaney House or to The Chandler, the steakhouse that opened in the casino downtown, Mark always appeared proud to be seen with her hanging onto his arm.

"You clean up nice, Dorey," he'd said to her just last Saturday, eyeing her slim calves that tapered into the three-inch heels in which she'd pirouette for the rest of the evening.

As he said it, Dora imagined herself rubbing a big bar of Ivory soap over her face, drawing streaks of pale skin into inch-high layers of marital dirt and grime.

Clean up nice.

She stared at her reflection for a moment longer, pulled the rubber gloves from her hands, and dumped them into the trash barrel next to the toilet along with the sponge. Then she carted the barrel away into the garage to empty it.

As she pushed the pile of soiled paper towels and discarded bathroom remnants further into the larger brown barrel, compacting the waste as best she could, Dora thought of the time she'd gone to a local bar at the meek but disillusioned age of nineteen, fake ID in hand though her youthful beauty made it inconsequential. It was there that she spotted a boy she recognized from high school, a senior when she'd been a sophomore with whom she'd never exchanged a word. It was karaoke night, and when he ran up to the microphone and began to wail "New York, New York" like Frank Sinatra had climbed into his abdomen and was slowly ripping his way out, she felt her stomach quiver and flip.

The boy's name was Jeremy. He had striking orange hair and pale cerulean eyes. And in that moment, she had a crush on him the way young girls had crushes on rock stars or movie idols. As he slithered drunkenly along the mic stand, alternately removing and replacing his Irish hat, he was completely oblivious to any voyeurs. It was his confidence that Dora found sexy. Mark had been the same way when Dora first spotted him, his shoulders straight and back, his cool, sideways glances that indicated indifference, and one eyebrow always slightly raised as if to say, "Yeah, what of it?" The confidence had been ephemeral, though, and after a year or two of home cooking and general domestic bliss, the shoulders began to slump and the eyebrow rested. Until the previous year, that is.

Soon after their eighth anniversary, Mark began making himself a bone-dry martini each afternoon when he arrived home from work, a habit Dora at first found quirky and fun. She'd even contributed to the mid-century modern diorama, donning an apron as she served tuna noodle casseroles and Jell-O salads, planning elaborate cocktail parties where their friends could mingle about their home, chewing on toothpick-ed appetizers.

Marriage is not a frozen tableau, however.

It is always moving, even if the participants don't sense its motion.

One sunny afternoon the previous March, Dora's world didn't just shake; the ground split open from under her and swallowed her whole.

Mark arrived home as usual, walking straight to the liquor cabinet and removing a half-empty bottle of Grey Goose and the silver shaker in one seamless motion. Dora had stayed home sick with the flu and still donned a pair of ratty flannel pajamas, her hair a haphazard top knot stuffed into a satin elastic.

Running a finger delicately along her upper lip, red and raw from blowing it all day, she spoke to her husband. "Hey you," she said, "how was work?"

With one hand, Mark slid a long-stemmed glass from the rack beneath a kitchen cabinet; with the other, he pushed the lip of the cocktail shaker into the ice maker handle on the front of the refrigerator. An avalanche of crushed cubes tumbled out, filling the room with a cacophony Dora had never acclimated to: she had grown up in a home where no one raised their voice, even in anger. Disagreements were solved with quiet discussion or, more often, complete silence.

"Great," Mark answered. "You know, busy, but good." He poured a healthy splash of vodka over the ice. "How are you feeling? Any better?"

Dora stopped rubbing her chafed skin. "A little. I'm sure I'll be back tomorrow. My fever broke this afternoon." She paused, then walked towards her husband. "I'm not contagious anymore, I don't think."

She leaned forward and kissed his cheek. The grit of five o'clock shadow was rough, abrasive against her lips. She pulled away again, and he turned away from her and placed the cap on the container before shaking it violently.

It was then that she smelled it: a foreign odor, one that made her nose wrinkle instinctively. It wafted from his body like heat escaping asphalt on a summer day. It wasn't unpleasant, per se, but it definitely did not belong to their home, their marriage...their *life*. Dora had caught trails of it here and there over the previous few weeks but she had dismissed the alien scent as an aromatic hallucination.

That afternoon, she thought momentarily of those 1950s B-movies with alien invaders who inhabited unsuspecting human hosts.

Mark was no longer Mark; at least, he didn't smell like Mark.

She brushed off the feeling, attributing it to an alteration in her olfactory senses brought on by her illness.

"I can put a frozen casserole in the oven," she offered. "Or we could order in. What would you like?"

Mark lifted the martini to his mouth and poured the clear liquid down his throat, emptying the glass. He glugged more of the bottle into the shaker. "Yeah, either one. Whatever is easier." He glanced at Dora for a moment, then looked sheepishly away. "I'm gonna jump in the shower."

A moment later, he was carrying the newly full glass into the bathroom and turning on the exhaust fan.

Two hours later, Dora scraped the food remnants into the garbage and stacked the soiled plates into the dishwasher. As the machine began its soft hum, she padded into the living room to join her husband but found Mark sprawled along the sofa, his eyes closed and one of his arms folded across his chest. His other hand still held his cell phone and stretched awkwardly toward the carpet like a tree branch bending somberly with the weight of snow and ice.

Dora listened.

His breathing was long and steady.

He was definitely asleep.

She carefully placed his errant arm on his stomach and removed the phone from his grasp. It awoke from the movement and the screen lit up, prompting Dora for a pin code to unlock it. Dora and Mark had an unspoken agreement: they knew each other's passcodes, not just for their phones but for their laptops, their social media accounts, and their bank accounts. But they'd never used them—at least, Dora hadn't used Mark's. What reason would she have for opening her husband's phone when she had her own? She didn't know why she did it. It wasn't like in the movies—she didn't have a premonition or a vision or even a suspicion. But she tapped in his four digits just the same without a moment of hesitation.

The text exchange was still on the screen.

I miss you, it read.

She glanced at her husband's response.

I can still feel your mouth on my skin.

Dora blinked. She looked away, tried to focus on the droning television in the corner. She looked at her husband. His face was blank, slack. She returned her eyes to the screen.

This is the beginning of something special, Mark wrote.

Dora scrolled upward.

I know I should feel guilty, but I don't, the other person wrote. *I need you.*

Dora looked at the owner's name at the top of the screen. *Nicole*. She frowned. She didn't know a Nicole. Mark had never mentioned a Nicole. She wondered if Nicole was someone he worked with or if he had met her somewhere else, some place he had visited without Dora. Somehow, this thought stung worse than the lascivious exchange.

I need you too, Mark wrote. *More than you can imagine. You are my only thread in this world tying me to sanity. At times I feel like it's going to snap. I can't take this prison much longer.*

Prison? Dora flinched at this portrayal.

Oh, baby, Nicole wrote back. *Can I come to your place Friday?*

Of course.

Good. I can't wait. I miss you.

I can still feel your mouth on my skin.

Nicole responded with an emoji of a blushing smiley face.

This is the beginning of something special.

Mark hadn't pressed the SEND button after finishing this sentence. It wavered in his text box, the sliver of cursor blinking expectantly alongside it.

Dora clicked the power button and the screen went black. She placed the phone on the end table and walked back into the kitchen. She grabbed her car keys from the hook beside the door and walked through the breezeway and into the garage. She climbed into the driver's seat of her sedan. The car was cold, having sat in the garage all day. Without thinking, she placed the key in the ignition and swiveled her wrist forward, and the engine roared, the sound echoing against the enclosed space.

She sat with her slippered feet resting under the brake pedal for a moment, looking around at the contents of the garage. The half-empty can of Rust-Oleum paint thinner tilted sideways against the bottles of engine oil and gas-line cleaner on the back shelf, a large green recycling can, the somnolent gas grill cloaked by a waterproof cover—a forgotten ghost of summer. A green canvas camping chair, folded tightly like a sleeping bat, leaned against the far corner, draped in spider webs. She reached her hand up to turn her key back and shut off the car's engine, and then stopped.

How easy it would be to watch the exhaust fill the dim space until the air became hazy and simply fall asleep.

Dora leaned her head against the back of her seat and closed her eyes. She thought for a moment. With one quick flick of her wrist, she silenced the motor. When she walked back into the living room, she saw that Mark had switched positions, lying on his side, his knees pulled up slightly toward his chest like a toddler. His head balanced precariously on the edge of a throw pillow.

He's going to have a nasty stitch in his neck when he wakes up, Dora thought.

Then she turned and retired to their bedroom for the evening.

· · · ● · ● · ● · · ·

The following Friday, Dora sat hunched behind the large evergreen bush that flanked their back fence.

She was half-sitting, half-squatting in the green camping chair now relatively free of cobwebs. She wore a dark brown sweatshirt with the hood pulled tight around her head and a pair of wide sunglasses digging into the tops of her cheeks. Within the span of one week, she had become Ted Kaczynski.

Dora had signed up for an extra shift at the library Friday afternoons, but she'd called in sick that morning after Mark had left for work. She exited the house her expected time, but instead of turning left onto Main Street, she made a quick right and nestled her car in the back of a bank parking lot then walked nonchalantly home, bypassing the screen door and walking straight through the backyard and to the rickety chair she'd set up the day before. She had tested the view from her home's windows—the chair was invisible from every angle—but even so, when Mark bounded onto the breezeway three hours earlier than his work scheduled him to leave, she flinched a bit, tilting her head in the fear she'd been discovered.

Less than an hour later, she watched a petite brunette open the screen porch door, hesitantly slip inside, and rap softly on the window.

She looks like me, Dora thought. *Or, me, before we got married.*

Dora, a decade younger.

Her husband appeared in the doorway and quickly ushered his visitor inside, not bothering to look around for witnesses.

Dora stayed at her station and watched the door as hours passed. When Nicole finally left, Dora waited until her shift was due to expire, then creeped stealthily along her neighbor's property and onto a side street. She changed her clothing in her car, drove home, and made dinner for her husband like nothing had happened.

She repeated this cycle for weeks, then months. Pinterest surfing, cookie baking, and adulterer stalking: those became her pastimes.

Although Mark didn't know it, she had given up her Friday hours at the library for good.

Her shift was in the backyard.

By August, the girlfriend rarely bothered to knock; more often than not, she'd tap softly on the window, then walk right into the house without hesitation.

Please: make yourself at home, thought Dora as she watched the darkness of the kitchen swallow Nicole whole. *Come on in. It's open.*

In the hours following the woman's arrival, Dora dug. She kept a sharp, new garden spade in the dirt behind her vantage point and spent Friday afternoons digging, then refilling holes.

As the hazily sunny days of summer evolved into the cinnamon-spiced overcast afternoons of fall, Dora continued going to work.

She continued to shop for the groceries, make the dinners, and clean the house.

She continued to spend her Friday afternoons watching.

Wash, rinse, repeat.

Dig and fill, dig and fill.

• • • • • • • • • •

Now, it was the Friday afternoon following Halloween, nearly seven months since Dora had first read her husband's text exchanges. She walked from the garage onto the cement front steps, picked up the heavy doormat, and shook it violently. A cloud of dust and pollen surrounded her, dissipating as suddenly as it had arrived. Dora spotted a few stray candy wrappers on the walkway and picked them up. Soon, it would be time to remove the earthy autumnal decorations and replace them with sparkly Christmas ones.

There was something about the winter, with its barren tree limbs, hoary skies, and icy carpets of snow that made Dora think of cleanliness, immaculacy. It was pure and perfect, the crisp air of coldness. Everything would be silent or smothered.

Mother Nature cleaned up nice.

Dora returned to the kitchen, rinsed her husband's martini glass in the sink and placed it gingerly in the dishwasher. She opened the cabinet beneath the sink and pushed the empty can of paint-thinner aside. She would have to put dishwashing detergent on the shopping list: they were almost out. She still couldn't believe that after so many years of daily martinis, her husband hadn't noticed that his vodka tasted different.

She shut the door to the machine and walked quickly to the bathroom. She knew she only had a few minutes left. Dora glanced about the room: nothing was out of the ordinary. Mark's body was safely hidden behind the curtain of the tub, and she'd cleaned up all of the vomit he'd sprayed during his shower. His lips and fingers were tinted a periwinkle blue. Dora certainly hadn't expected his body to thrash about the stall like it did. Now, he was curled up on his side, his knees pulled slightly up to his belly, his pale head lying motionless in a gelatinous puddle of dark red blood: an *amuse-bouche* of just desserts.

It was just as Dora slipped quietly behind the door of her dark bedroom, clutching the garden spade in her hand, that she heard the soft knock on the window of the breezeway.

Come on in, she thought. *It's open.*

NEIGHBORHOOD WATCH

THE LAST THING THE neighborhood needs is more children, she thought.

When Tracy bought the house ten years back, practically all of her neighbors were shoveling AARP informational mailers into their recycling bins like squirrels stowing nuts in their nests.

Now, at forty-two years old, she was the oldest resident on her street.

Over the past decade, she had watched eight new families move onto the block. Each one boasted at least two children under the age of ten. On sunny days, the street was awash with bicycles and skateboards, a rainbow of multicolored helmets sailing down the sidewalk.

The block seemed to be running out of space, and it made Tracy feel exhausted.

It was Memorial Day weekend when Curt pulled the large U-Haul truck onto the bottom of the driveway of their green shuttered bungalow. His wife Janis parked the maroon minivan in the street directly in front of the walkway to their new home, and before she could walk around to open the trunk's hatchback, three tow-headed children spilled from the sliding side door and raced up the front steps.

Tracy leaned forward on the sofa cushion and watched them, her body shielded by the darkness of her living room. Warm air wafted through the window screen, bringing with it the smell of fresh cut grass and lily of the valley. Above her neighbor's house stretched a bright blue sky without even the faintest wisp of a cloud. Tracy knew she should be outside. She should be yanking the weeds out of her rose garden. She should be trimming the overgrown forsythia bushes that lined the margin of her property. She should be brushing the dust off of her patio furniture and placing the pieces into an inviting arrangement. She should *not* be huddled on her couch, still wearing an old t-shirt and ratty pajama shorts in the middle of the afternoon, spying on her new neighbors and listening to an infomercial announcer's insistence that no, she could *not* go without a new set of kitchen knives.

"But wait! There's more!" the voice on the screen screamed excitedly.

She didn't wait.

Instead, she shoved her feet into the dog-eared flip-flops pushed halfway under the sofa and walked reluctantly into the kitchen. Her cat, Doodle, was balanced precariously on his back on the windowsill, his upside-down head lolling bizarrely to the side to face the incoming sunbeam. She absent-mindedly ruffled the long fur on his stomach as she passed, then opened the door to the cellar and walked carefully down the old wooden stairs. Her basement floor was unfinished, just a wide expanse of hard dirt, and the room smelled dank and earthy. Tracy padded over to the washing machine and mechanically transferred her wet clothes to the dryer. She felt along the inside of the washer's tub to make certain she hadn't left a wily sock behind then slammed the door to the dryer and started it.

She was careful as she made her way back to the stairs so that she didn't dig her feet into the ground. She didn't want to track the cellar into her home.

When she returned to the living room, carrying a rocks glass full of equal parts ice cubes and vodka, she could see that the conveyor belt transferring household items from the mini-van and truck to the house had started. She watched Janis maneuver the slightly overgrown lawn while balancing brown boxes in her arms. She watched Curt, with some effort, wrestle the dolly holding a large white refrigerator down the sidewalk that had buckled from frost heaves and time. The appliance wobbled slightly, and Tracy sipped her drink and wondered how it would fare up the dilapidated back steps. Curt looked to be relatively young, mid-thirties at most, and wore a thick beard and mirrored sunglasses. His arms bulged with strength, but his belly was round.

A dad bod, Tracy thought to herself. *That's what they call it these days.*

Even from across the street, she could see the sweat pooling on his face and soaking his hair. A thin girl, her blonde hair in two bobbing pigtails, tottered behind her father, carrying an empty fish tank.

Tracy tilted her head back and let the last dribble of vodka slide into her mouth. The ice cubes slapped against her teeth. She knew she should welcome the family to the neighborhood. Eight new neighbors and not once had she ventured over to introduce herself, and now, it was long past the point of making their acquaintance without significant awkwardness. Instead, her interactions with them were limited to half-hearted waves and the occasional nod when she passed one of them mowing the lawn or walking the dog.

Back on the television screen, the infomercial was replaced by a black and white *Twilight Zone*. Tracy knew this episode well: four odious relatives visit an elderly, dying man in anticipation of a large inheritance; since it's Mardi Gras, the benefactor insists that they each wear a mask he's selected for them. Tracy licked her teeth and glanced at the cable box. It was two in the afternoon. She debated pouring herself another drink when her cell phone jingled from the end table. She squinted at the caller's name, then hit the green ANSWER button.

"Hey, Caroline," Tracy said, the hoarse voice taking her by surprise. She tried to recall the last time she had spoken.

"What are you doing?" her sister's voice in the speaker was aggressive, overly awake. Tracy sometimes wondered if her sister had a closet amphetamine habit. "I'm driving and 95 is a shit show. Why is everyone traveling on a Saturday afternoon, for Christ's sakes?"

She was headed to her beach house in Ogunquit, Tracy knew, like she did every weekend after Easter.

The air from Caroline's open window screeched in the background.

Tracy cleared her throat. "*You're* traveling on a Saturday," she pointed out and walked closer to her window.

Curt and Janis were standing on the tree belt in front of their house, facing one another. The man was yelling something and waving his hands in the air; the woman stared at him, her hands gripped firmly to her hips.

Caroline ignored Tracy's comment. "And did Mom call you about the Fourth? Patrick's having a barbecue for the fireworks. Make sure you set aside the weekend and we can drive up together." Tracy heard a metallic clicking sound, then a deep inhale. How her sister managed to light a cigarette while driving on the highway with her windows open was a mystery. "It's not like you need to take vacation time, after all," she added.

Tracy swallowed. "Yep," she replied curtly.

"Did you call that lawyer I sent you? He's supposed to be the best, especially for your kind of case." A deep inhale in, then a quick exhale. "Did you call him?" she repeated.

"The review isn't until July," Tracy said, sitting on the sofa.

The new neighbors were still arguing, but she still couldn't make out what they were saying. Suddenly, Curt grabbed Janis by the shoulder and began to shake her violently. Caroline continued to talk in her ear, but Tracy let the phone slide down to her neck as she watched the scene continue.

"I have to run, Carrie," she said, half into the receiver and half into the collar of her t-shirt. "Call me tomorrow, ok?"

She clicked the END CALL button without taking her eyes off of her neighbors or waiting for an acknowledgment from her sister.

Curt released his hold on his wife and turned and stomped into the house like a petulant child. Janis, once alone on the sidewalk, rubbed her shoulder with her left hand and walked cautiously into the back of the moving truck. She reappeared a moment later carrying a pair of lamps as if nothing had happened.

On the television, the elderly man screamed at his heirs from his deathbed: "*Without your masks, you're caricatures!*"

Tracy watched the couple and their children continue their unpacking for another moment. Then she wandered back into the kitchen to make herself another drink.

·•·•••·•••·

That night, when Tracy awoke on the couch, the cable television's power-save function had turned the screen off, leaving her temporarily blind.

The green digital numbers read 10:30.

Tracy sat up and blinked quickly, slightly disoriented.

When had she fallen asleep? Her mouth felt tacky and dry, stuffed with cotton balls. A beam of light from the streetlamp outside her window cast a yellowish glow on the sill. The air smelled damp and green, like it had rained in the last few hours. She sat forward and patted the object sticking out of the back pocket of her shorts, then started to rise to walk to her bedroom. A movement outside of the window stopped her.

Curt was still milling about the moving truck, but his movements were slower; his sunglasses were off, and even from across the street, it was obvious from his face that he was exhausted. Tracy leaned forward. Curt was pushing a wide, flat broom across the floor of the cargo box; each time the bristles touched the air just behind the truck, a cloud of brown dust mushroomed. When he was done sweeping, Curt climbed down and disappeared up his driveway, holding the broom. The back of the truck gaped open.

Well, it's not like there's anything left to steal in there, Tracy thought.

She stood up and stretched. She'd had issues sleeping for nearly a year now, sometimes spending most of the night sitting up in bed, pawing her cell phone or watching reruns of *Criminal Minds* or *I Love Lucy* on the television.

A few months earlier, when the warm weather nudged away winter's chill, she began going for walks in the middle of the night, sometimes clocking two or even three miles as she ventured further and further from her house. She thought the exercise would make it easy to fall back asleep, but more often than not, she returned home even more awake than before.

She started showering at three in the morning and arriving at the office by five, sometimes startling the overnight security guards.

Her broken internal clock took a toll, though: before long, she was dozing off at her desk, often without warning. One minute she was wide awake, entering figures on a spreadsheet, and the next, she was trying to rub away the crease that had formed on her cheek after waking with her face pressed against the side of her leather blotter. One late afternoon, as she was peeling the edge of her mouth from the hardwood desk top, she lifted her head to see Kate, her co-worker in the next office, standing in the doorway, staring at her.

"Are you alright?" Kate asked in a tone that communicated faux concern intermingled with snide judgment, a manner often reserved for colleagues who were both semi-incompetent and painfully unaware of their stupidity.

Tracy blinked at her, her vision still slightly bleary. "Yes, yes," she said as quickly as possible. "I'm just fighting a migraine. You know how it is."

Kate smiled, her lips pressed together so firmly, they appeared to have been glued shut. "Yes, well, I hope you feel better. Your head was on your keyboard last week when I walked by." She fingered the three silver bangles encircling her left wrist. "Maybe you should see a doctor."

Tracy pasted across her face the broadest grin she could muster. "I'll do that: thanks." She assumed this would satisfy her co-worker, but the woman remained at the door, still looking at Tracy. "Did you need something?"

Kate loitered at the door a moment longer, then finally turned away. She left Tracy's office without another word.

And then, of course, the incident occurred.

Tracy walked to the other side of the room and had almost made it to the hallway when she heard a door slamming—faint—from outside. She turned to see Curt returning to the truck. He was carrying a long canvas sack, one of those industrial laundry bags. It was at least three feet across and Curt held it tight atop his forearms like a groom bringing his new bride across the threshold. When he reached the open cargo hold, he shifted the bag in his grasp, and it was this instance that made Tracy shuffle quickly over to the window to get a better look.

Before he tossed the sack into the cargo box, it appeared to wriggle. Tracy ducked backwards but kept her eyes on the bag. With horror, she thought she saw it buck slightly and roll on the floor of the empty freight area, even as Curt reached up and pulled the door shut. Then, her new neighbor climbed into the cab and drove the truck away.

· · · ● · ● · · · ·

The next morning, Tracy stared blankly at the coffeemaker as it gurgled its last brew breath. Her hair was still wet from the shower and she absent-mindedly tousled it with her left hand as she reached for a mug on the wall hook with her right. The headless voice of George Stephanopoulos drifted from the next room. Tracy had always liked George. He was from Massachusetts, a local boy, so that won some points with her. Of course, she'd been too young to vote when he had been Bill Clinton's campaign advisor, but there was something about his presence that made Tracy trust him. She never missed his Sunday talk show, even when she had not slept well the night before.

The night before.

She vaguely remembered waking up on the couch and watching the man across the street as he completed his unpacking, but there had been something odd about the sight that she could not remember now, something about a chest, or a bag, or a—

Her phone began to ring insistently from her back pocket.

"Morning, Caroline," she said into the receiver. She shook the confusion from her head and poured herself a cup of coffee.

Her sister's voice blared into her ear. "Trace. You'll never believe what my neighbors did last night. I mean, seriously—"

Tracy balanced the phone between her ear and her shoulder and brought the mug to her face. She breathed in the steam from the coffee, then lowered the cup to the sink and poured out half of its contents. As her sister's rapid chatter continued, she opened the cabinet nearest to her and fished the half-empty container of Jameson from the collection of tall bottles at eye level. She felt jittery, like she had popped a few too many No-Doze tablets on an empty stomach. As she poured the whiskey into her cup, she watched the deep chestnut coffee lighten to a hazy caramel color. She didn't feel much like baking, so after rifling through the other cabinets and discovering an unopened bag of cookies, she determined that these would make a fine welcoming gift for her new neighbors.

Caroline's hyperactive drone continued in her ear as she walked into the living room, sipping her makeshift Irish coffee and bringing with her the Jameson bottle under her arm. Across the street, Curt walked back and forth from the house to the garage, carrying an assortment of home improvement materials: a hammer, a large hand-saw, and a hatchet, up and down the empty driveway. Tracy sat on the couch and tried to listen to the news program while interjecting sincere *uh-huh*s into the phone at appropriate times, but her mind was racing and she desperately wanted to catch up with it. Her eyes ping-ponged from the screen to the window and back again.

Curt now carried a bulky black trash bag in each of his hands, and he walked with his legs spread wide and sailor-like, giving him the appearance of a human balance scale. He dropped the bags at the end of the driveway and Tracy could hear the thump of their weight as he did so.

"...so I said to Nancy, if that daughter of hers is getting married on a Caribbean beach, well, I just—" Caroline's voice blathered on.

Tracy looked back at the screen. A diplomat from some country Tracy wasn't familiar with was talking to a correspondent, explaining that if economic sanctions continued, the United States would be sorry.

Curt returned with another pair of heavy trash bags and plunked them next to the first ones.

"—And that's when *I* said, *you've got to be joking, right?* Then Ann jumped in and—"

Tracy couldn't take it anymore. It felt like the room had begun to spin. She was on a tilt-a-whirl and was trying desperately to jump off. "Caro? Caro?" she yelled. "You're breaking up. Can you call back when you have better service?" She'd used this act before, but usually it was with her mother, and she doubted her sister would fall for the trick. However, she didn't wait for her reaction and simply clicked the END CALL button and tossed the phone onto the cushion beside her.

George nodded solemnly into the camera.

Tracy gulped the rest of her drink and took a deep breath. The heat of the liquid carved a path down her throat and into her stomach, and she felt her cheeks flush with alcohol blossoms. She poured another healthy splash of the whiskey and tried to settle her thoughts.

Curt made a third trip down the driveway, bringing with him only one full bag this time. He dropped it next to the others, wiped his palms on his thighs, then walked into the house.

George moved onto another political hot button story, but Tracy did not take her eyes off of the bags.

How does someone who just moved in the day before acquire so much trash?

• • • • • • • • • •

This time when Tracy woke up the green numbers on the cable box read 7:13.

She was sitting straight up in her red wing-back chair, her head nestled firmly in the corner at the top. A coffee cup containing an inch of pale yellow liquid sat on a coaster on the side table nearby, and Doodle the cat was stretched out in a dusky sunbeam in the middle of the rug in front of her. Tracy leaned forward; her shoulders and upper arms ached, but she supposed that was stiffness from her awkward sleeping position. She could see through the window the edge of Curt and Janis' house, and while it was still light out, she resolved to bring the welcome treats over to their home and introduce herself.

She padded over to the front hallway and stuck her feet into the old flip-flops waiting conveniently by the doorway to the kitchen. As she packed the cookies into a plastic container left behind from Christmas baking, she noticed bits of dirt trailing across the linoleum. She checked the bottoms of her sandals; they were covered with the same dirt, likely remnants from the basement. She must not have been as careful walking back from the dryer as she thought. She grabbed a broom from behind the pantry door and swept up the debris, then checked her reflection in the hall mirror before clicking the container shut and walking across the street.

The barrage of trash bags was gone, but the maroon minivan was now parked in the driveway. Two of the three blonde children squatted behind it, scrutinizing the pavement. As Tracy moved closer, she saw that they were drawing with colored chalk: a tri-color rainbow, a tree, and block letters spelling out B-E-A-T-R-I-C-E dotted the small square of blacktop. As she climbed the steps onto the covered porch, the smaller of the two girls glanced up at her but said nothing and returned her focus to her sketching. Before Tracy could press the doorbell, the heavy green door opened and her new neighbor appeared at the screen.

"Hi... hi there," Tracy said, a bit taken off guard. "I'm Tracy. I live across the street." She tilted her head in the direction of her house. As she did, she glanced at her beige stucco bungalow. It seemed small and sad from this angle, a tiny doll house with overgrown flower bushes and a lawn in desperate need of fertilizer. She turned back to face the door and held out the container of store-baked goods. "I brought you some cookies. I hope you have a sweet tooth!"

The man peered down at the box in her hand, then looked back at Tracy. He pushed open the screen door an inch.

"I'm Curt. That's very nice of you, Tracy." He paused for a moment, then cleared his throat nervously and continued. "Would you like to come in?"

He backed away from the screen a few inches.

Tracy walked inside and was instantly swallowed by the coolness of the dimly-lit living room. She took a few steps forward on the hardwood floor and stopped. Curt shut the door behind her and stood awkwardly next to it. She held out the cookies again. "Dessert. For you," she said, smiling.

The third child, a boy whose hair was nearly white, appeared in the doorway at the far end of the room. "Dessert?" he echoed hopefully, then bounded excitedly over to Tracy like a puppy. He turned to his father. "Can I have some?"

Curt tousled the child's hair playfully. "Andy, this is our neighbor across the street, Tracy. What do you say?"

Andy turned back to Tracy. He threw his shoulders back and stuck his hand out robotically. "Nice to meet you, Tracy. My name is Andy."

Tracy grasped his hand quickly, then handed him the plastic container. "Welcome to the neighborhood," she said, more to the air than to Curt or Andy. The boy thanked her for the box and wandered back into the room at the far end of the house. The two adults stood silent in the room once more. Tracy glanced about, expecting Curt's wife to appear, but she did not. The house was still.

"So, anyway," Tracy started, as if Andy had interrupted a lively conversation, "There is a great Polish bakery about a mile and a half that way and there's a park two blocks over that way with a nice playground for kids." She motioned with her hands. "They have fireworks in July. You can spread out a blanket and watch the sky explode with color right above you."

She realized she was talking very loudly and fast.

This must be what it's like to be Caroline, she thought.

"I saw you moving things yesterday," she continued, then immediately regretted saying it. Curt's face shifted, and there was something in this new countenance that made her uneasy. "In the afternoon. With the kids. And a woman with auburn hair in a ponytail," she added quickly, placing her hand inside the back pocket of her shorts and feeling for the object inside.

"My wife," Curt said. "Janis." He stared at Tracy for a long moment. "She went out earlier in the day but hasn't returned yet. I'm sure she sends her appreciation for your welcome gift. That was very thoughtful of you."

Tracy shifted her weight from one foot to another. There was something wrong about the situation, but she couldn't put her finger on what it was. "Well, I'd better get going," she said, edging back toward the door. "Again, welcome, and I'm sure I'll see you... and Janis... soon." She turned her back to Curt and grasped the doorknob, half expecting a blow to the back of her head, but she exited without incident.

· · · · ●·●· · · ·

The next day was a holiday, but the network channels resumed their vapid schedule of both health talk shows that made Tracy feel like a bit of a hypochondriac and recycled game shows that made Tracy feel like a bit of a moron. She had curled herself into a ball on the sofa, her knees nudging her breasts, and Doodle poured himself into the space behind her legs and snored softly.

Her cell phone rang but she ignored it.

It was likely Caroline again and she didn't have the energy to manufacture an escape plan this time.

In the distance, she heard the soft buzz of her dryer timer, indicating that her sheets were done.

She reached her arm across to the coffee table, grabbed the remote control, tapped the channel button until the screen dissolved into black and white.

Another Twilight Zone, she thought. *They always do these marathons on holiday weekends.*

This episode told the story of a woman driving cross-country who keeps seeing the same hitch-hiker everywhere she goes. Tracy stretched her arm out to the coffee table again, trying in vain to grab the tequila sunrise she'd made herself promptly at noon. It was just out of reach, so she sat up, stretched, then snatched the glass from the table. The ice cubes were just starting to lose their jagged edges. She sat forward and patted her back pocket.

On the television, the woman driving cross-country had sought out a mechanic to change her flat tire, and the man was expressing surprise that the woman survived the accident that caused the repair. Doodle yawned and rolled over onto his side; his eyes remained closed. Tracy peeked outside. No one was in front of Curt and Janis's house, and their shades were drawn. Just as she was rising to bring her empty glass into the kitchen, Tracy heard a knock at her front door, a quick rap.

Tracy smoothed her hair with her hands and walked to the entryway. She certainly wasn't expecting anyone, and she would have simply pretended to not be home, except there weren't any strange cars parked near her house, and she was curious to see who was visiting. Surprised to see Curt standing on the other side of her screen, she glanced quickly at the latch on the door to double-check it was locked.

Curt squinted at her, flashing a lopsided grin. "Good morning, Tracy," he said. "I'm just dropping off your container. The kids sure appreciated the cookies: thanks again." He squinted again, and Tracy wondered if, between the sunglasses and dark house, Curt had an oversensitivity to light. She said nothing back to him, and he fidgeted a bit, then added, "Can I give you back the container?"

He waved the box in front of the screen.

"Oh, uh, of course," Tracy stammered. She unlatched the door, opened it, and accepted the plastic tin from her neighbor. "Thanks."

They were both silent, staring at one another. "Well," Tracy finally said, "I suppose I should go finish my laundry."

She backed away as she said this. Curt waved his hand in a half-hearted goodbye and Tracy shut the door.

"I believe you're going my way?"

On the television, the dazed woman did not respond, only stared into the vanity mirror of her car as the dead hitch-hiker grimaced menacingly at her from the hollow of her back seat. *The Twilight Zone* episode was ending.

Tracy walked through the kitchen, slid her feet into her flip-flops, and walked down the basement stairs. The dryer had contorted the pile of sheets into a tangled ball, and the sheets trapped inside were still damp. She pulled the pieces apart and placed them orderly back into the drum, then turned on the machine. It wasn't until the clothes began to tumble that she turned around and only then did she see him standing directly behind her.

"I know she's here," Curt said. His eyes were fixed, unmoving.

Tracy put her hand inside her back pocket and gripped the object inside. "Who's here?" she asked. She glanced at the shovel leaning against the furnace about ten feet away.

Curt started to walk to the right of Tracy, looking at the ground.

"Janis. My wife. She told me she was coming over here yesterday afternoon. She left, and then you showed up at the house two hours later."

He continued to walk the perimeter of the cellar, keeping his eyes on the dirt floor.

Tracy was so quiet in her movements, he didn't know she had crept up behind him until he felt the blade pierce his neck. His jugular vein erupted, spraying blood all over the nearby wall, as his hands clawed in vain at Tracy's fingers pushing the sharp edge of the box cutter deeper into his throat.

When at last he collapsed, Tracy wrestled the weapon from his body, then calmly brought it over to the laundry sink to clean.

The dryer purred and continued its soft thumping. Tracy retrieved the shovel and began to dig a fresh hole, but the tip hit something metal almost immediately. She bent down to inspect the culprit: three silver bangle bracelets still attached to a partially decomposed arm.

She recovered her missing co-worker and began to dig five feet away, next to Janis's makeshift grave.

The basement seemed to be running out of space, and it made Tracy feel exhausted.

TRIP TRAP

TRIP TRAP VACATION REVIEW
  Bay Breeze Beach Resort, Clearwater, FL
  Denise C.   (10 months ago)
  4/5 stars

My husband and I stayed here for the first time last week. The place is huge! Seven floors, two restaurants, an indoor and outdoor pool, and three bars, not to mention a gigantic stage and dance floor right on the water. We were never at a loss for something to do, and we didn't even leave the premises. That being said, if you're looking for a hotel where you can hit the hay before sunrise and/or sleep through the night, make sure you request a street-facing room. The dance club opens at 10 p.m. and we could hear every bass thump from our fourth floor room, even with the window closed and the a/c cranked. We'll likely return, but we'll be bringing ear plugs with us.

• • • ● • ● • • •

The overnight bag was small, but it was heavy. The strap seemed to dig deeper and deeper into Shannon's shoulder the longer they stood there.

In contrast, as soon as they had hit the lobby, Lily had dumped her bag—a worn-out duffel leftover from her college days—onto the white tiled floor and simply slid it forward with her foot, soccer-pass style, as the line to check in crept along.

At last, when it was their turn, Shannon blurted out her last name and handed over her credit card before the clerk's wooden smile could begin its practiced emergence from her lips.

"And we'd like a room on the street side of the hotel, please," Shannon added.

Lily groaned. "Are you serious? We paid for a hotel on the beach. I'd like to see the *beach* from our bed."

Shannon's eyes did not move from the clerk's. "Street side," she repeated. "And as far up as possible, please." Only then did she turn to look at her girlfriend. "I researched this place thoroughly, okay? And I didn't bring my sleeping pills."

"We're on vacation," argued Lily. "Not at a sleep study." She raised her hands above her head and made a motion like she was pushing the ceiling. "Three days, two nights, and this is the first time we've been away in over a year. We are partying, baby!"

She swung her hips around in a comedic manner, then stopped abruptly.

Shannon raised her eyebrow. "New beginning: remember?"

"Okay, well, then, at least get two keys. In case I want to stay out later than you."

The clerk handed Shannon two key cards, still not smiling. "Room 713. Take a left off the elevator and it's at the end of the hall on the right." She frowned at Lily. "Facing the street."

Shannon responded with a tight-lipped half smile, readjusted the torturing strap, and tucked the keys into a back pocket of her jeans. It was freezing in the lobby, and she was grateful she hadn't changed into shorts and a t-shirt at the airport as she first had planned.

The two women stood in the nearby hallway, staring wordlessly at the two elevator doors in front of them, the digital numbers above each gradually counting down. A sunburned college kid wearing aviator sunglasses and an old baseball shirt joined them. Almost immediately, a putrid haze of cheap whiskey and keto breath wafted through the air. The man leaned forward as if the two women's refusal to acknowledge him was simply due to his being out of range of their vision.

"Hey, girls," he said. "You just get here? My name's Tom."

He thrust his hand in front of Shannon's breasts, stopping only an inch from her sweatshirt zipper. Men were always ogling Shannon and Lily had learned to ignore the flickering gazes, but it still irked her at times, even after three years of living together.

Lily turned and positioned herself in front of Tom. She grabbed his hand and shook it hard.

"Hi there, Tim," she said, her voice taking on an exaggerated drawl Shannon only heard when she was talking down to someone. "I'm Daisy, and this here little lady is my sister Mae. We sure do appreciate the welcome wagon!"

Tom backed away a step. "Uh, it's *Tom*, actually. You're sisters, huh?" He paused, thinking for a moment before a mischievous grin angled up across one side of his face. "Vacationing together? Gonna let loose and have some fun?"

Lily let go of Tom's hand and instead, stepped back and wrapped her arm around Shannon, bringing their faces so close together, Shannon could smell the Chapstick on her lips.

"Nothing gets by you, Tim," Lily said. Then, in a move she often did when she wanted strangers to keep their distance, she stuck out her tongue and ran it from the bottom of Shannon's cheek to her temple, maintaining eye contact with Tom the entire time.

Tom's face raced through expressions like a deck of cards in the middle of a dealer's shuffle and finally resigned itself to one of confused repulsion. He turned to face the still-closed elevator doors and muttered under his breath.

"What was that, Tim?" Lily cocked her hand around her ear like she was listening for a far-away alarm bell. The silvery doors on the left slid open and the car emptied quickly, but Tom turned on his heel and walked quickly toward the door on the opposite end of the foyer marked Stairway.

Lily snatched her bag from the floor, and the two women got onto the elevator alone.

"You don't have to be so hostile all the time, you know," Shannon said, pushing the button marked 7. "He's just some stupid frat boy. There are a million down here. The South and Mid-West states might as well abbreviate themselves with Greek letters."

Lily rolled her eyes. "How sad is that? Poor Southern and Midwestern-ers: they have to make people in their college swear an oath to promise to be their friends forever. Like when you're a kid and your parents make you play with their friends' kids and you have to be nice to them or else. So pathetic."

The car rose one floor and stopped. When the doors opened, a small cleaning woman pushing a laundry cart wheeled into the car. Without acknowledging the women, she reached across and pressed 3. As she did, the sleeve on her right arm pushed up toward her elbow. Shannon couldn't help but stare. Her olive skin was covered in large red welts, raised blisters with pinprick dots in the centers like tremendous bug bites.

The woman caught Shannon's gaze and quickly pulled her cuff down to her wrist and tucked her hands behind the cart.

Oblivious to the exchange, Lily turned to face the woman. "Ma'am, do you know if there are Coke machines on the floors?" She ran her fingers through her hair and glanced at Shannon. "I'm super thirsty. We should've gotten something when we landed."

The elevator dinged, and when the doors opened, the woman wordlessly pushed her cart forward, turned left, and disappeared out of sight. Lily and Shannon looked at each other and couldn't help but laugh.

"Staff is super helpful here, I guess?" Lily said. "Chatty."

Shannon patted her on the shoulder softly, a move she found herself doing more and more often, like her mother did to her father. "How about we dump this stuff in the room, get changed, and go down to the pool bar?"

Lily once again wrapped her arm around her girlfriend, but this time, she pulled Shannon's head closer to hers and kissed her playfully on the forehead. "Now you're talking, sister."

• • • ● •• ● • •• ·

Trip Trap Vacation Review
Bay Breeze Beach Resort, Clearwater, FL
Reina L.   (7 months ago)
1/5 stars

Enjoyed the food, the pool (bar area with Todd) and even the club, but the room was so f***ing gross. (See photo) Yes, that is a pair of someone's UNDERWEAR hanging from the shower wall. We called the front desk to get a new room but they said they were booked and offered to re-clean it, but the lazy ass maid only removed the panties. She didn't wipe up the bristles of hair that were all over the tub. I mean, they were ten times nastier than regular stranger hair: thick, straight, and black, and like an inch long—did someone shampoo their pet boar in there?? Anyways, the only silver lining was that we scored a room facing the street so we didn't have to hear the constant beach noise like everyone seems to be complaining about on here. Boyfriend still had the TV blaring all night. He claimed could hear the people next door "rustling" around in their beds. I don't know. I slept okay. I didn't shower all weekend, though.

• • ● •• ● • •• ·

It was after four o'clock, and the beach had gotten progressively busier as the day wore on. Shannon was glad Lily had rented chaises for them, but she had been drinking vodka and grapefruit juice like water—or, more accurately, instead of water—and she was starting to feel a bit loopy.

It didn't help that they'd forgone renting an umbrella in the hope that they could infuse a week's worth of tan from just two days of prolonged sunbathing. Shannon's skin was beginning to feel like a fallen apple's after it's been left outside to blister in the sun for days. She sat up and patted her hand beneath the chair to feel for her shirt.

Lily turned her head and lifted her sunglasses. "Where are you going?"

"It's too hot," Shannon said. "I gotta cool off for a bit."

Lily sat up. "Want to go swimming?" As she said it, a pair of jetskiiers slid onto the edge of the shore, spraying a rush of water onto some nearby pre-teens playing in the sand. The children began to scream as if on fire.

"Nah," said Shannon, pulling the shirt down over her bikini top. "I just need to get out of the sun for a while. Plus, I have to pee. Need anything?"

Lily twisted her body around and relaxed onto her stomach. "Pee for me too," she said in a sleepy voice.

Shannon stepped into her shorts and then her flip-flops. She felt for the room key in her back pocket, just in case she wanted to buy something at the bar after all, and walked as gracefully as she could in the dense, white sand toward the hotel's outside pool.

The poolside bar was full. The bartender looked slightly overwhelmed as he juggled orders from people sitting on all sides. A pair of small children splashed around in the pool, but for the most part, it seemed to Shannon that the Bay Breeze catered to adults. Even the father of the two kids in the water seemed rather disinterested in their activity, but the mother walked back and forth along the side holding her iPhone sideways and pointed at the pool.

"Big smiles, guys," she yelled in a sing-song manner, "y'all are on Facebook now."

"Jesus, DeeDee," the father yelled from his vantage point in one of the blue-covered lounge chairs, "put the phone away and *play* with the kids for once. Why do you have to document and post every goddamn thing?"

He had said it too loudly for anyone in earshot to not feel uncomfortable, but it was too late to take it back.

His wife seemed unfazed and continued to snap her photographs. "People enjoy seeing our vacation, Kevin." She paused to wipe an errant spittle of pool water from her screen. "Didja see how many people 'liked' the mini-golf pictures? Did you!?"

Shannon pushed her sunglasses onto the top of her head and opened the glass door to the hotel lobby. A cold gasp of air slid past her and escaped into the world. There were two restrooms just inside to the left, and Shannon ducked into the one marked Ladies, catching her pink reflection in the mirror immediately inside. The lights weren't on, but there was plenty of natural light streaming in from the windows sidling the ceiling. The temperature was at least forty degrees cooler inside, but instead of feeling relief, her skin seemed to shrivel at the sudden drop. No one else was in the bathroom, so she chose the first stall out of convenience, wrestled her shorts and bathing suit bottom down to her knees, and sat on the toilet.

The stream of urine felt hot as she released it. She poked her finger at the skin on her right thigh, watching the place where she pressed turn white then fill with color again. She'd either have a decent base tan by the evening or a wicked burn: she couldn't tell. Her head still felt foggy, and she propped her chin in her fist and leaned forward, her elbow on her knee, and closed her eyes.

When she opened them again, her head was facing the floor, and that was when she saw the bug. No—*bug* was the wrong word for it. It could only be called a beetle. Or a *roach*. It was nearly two inches long; its body and spindly legs a deep, shiny black. Thin antennae wiggled at its head as it seemed to be considering Shannon's bright yellow flip-flop from a half foot away.

Palmetto bug, Shannon thought. She'd heard of these disgusting things from her aunt, who often vacationed in the Carolinas and had discovered one or two in the cabins where she'd stayed. *Christ, they're enormous.*

It's more afraid of you than you are of it.

This bizarre piece of advice, something she could not attribute to any one person but had definitely heard in more than one context, echoed in her head.

Keep your eye on it, her mind responded. *The only thing that's worse about seeing a creepy bug is not knowing where it goes.*

In one fell swoop, she yanked her suit and shorts back up to her hips and stood up. She stomped her foot hard on the tile floor, expecting the roach to scurry off somewhere into the dark recesses of the hotel bar's plumbing. Instead, the bug bolted forward and made a beeline toward Shannon. For a moment, Shannon thought of the raccoons she saw in her backyard each summer.

If they don't run away from you, they're probably rabid, Lily would say, *so just keep away from them.*

Could Palmetto bugs be rabid?

Shannon didn't know, and frankly, she didn't care. She pushed the stall door open and ran for the exit, not bothering to flush, wash her hands, or even button her shorts.

· · • • · • • · · ·

Trip Trap Vacation Review
Bay Breeze Beach Resort, Clearwater, FL
Jake B.   (5 months ago)
5/5 stars

Writing this as we chill in the Tampa airport on our way home to Philly. Me and my boys had a *kickin* bachelor party for my man Steve at the Bay Breeze! We got stuck with a boring ass room way up on the top floor with nothing to see on our side but the Sunoco and some pirate mini golf place across the street, but it's all *obama* cause we hooked up with some fresh girls with a room overlooking the dance floor. Only thing that sucked is someone must of brought a ferret or something. My duffel bag got golf ball sized holes all over the side with tiny teeth marks like something chewed on it all weekend.

• • • ● • ● • ● • •

"Want me to get you something and bring it up to the room?" Lily sat on the edge of the bed and stroked Shannon's hair. "You hardly ate any dinner."

Her girlfriend was lying on top of the quilt. Shannon's face and chest were a deep ferocious red; even her lips looked puffy and sore.

"It's okay," she answered. "I took a few Tylenol and drank a ton of water. I just want to nap for an hour. You go on down." Lily raised her eyebrow and looked dubious, but Shannon patted her hand. "I'll text you when I'm on my way. Really. Go."

Lily stood up. "Okay. I'll go down and scope out stuff while you're napping, and then we can decide what we want to do."

"Do me a favor and shut off the air conditioner before you go? Maybe open the window? It's freezing in here."

Lily complied, the wall unit shuttering to a wheezy stop, then sighing. The windows were the ancient, hand-crank style, and they hadn't been opened in quite some time, so it took a bit of wrestling, but finally, the smells of salt and sand tempered with car exhaust drifted into the room.

Shannon turned painfully onto her side and looked at the window. "It's so nice to see the sun and blue sky," she said.

Lily laughed. "We live in Massachusetts, not in a bunker. We have sun and sky."

"No...the air smells different here, you know?" said Shannon, closing her eyes. "The sun is different here, everything feels different. Softer. Like the whole state has been tumbling in a dryer with one of those anti-static sheets."

"Yeah, I don't know about the anti-static thing. You should have seen the hair on this chick that walked by me after you went to the bathroom," quipped Lily. "A walking Poison reunion poster."

When she looked at Shannon again, she was asleep.

• • • • • • • • • •

The slight murmur from the traffic and street activity had died down by the time Shannon woke up. The light outside was dim, but it wasn't quite fully dark. At first, she was confused; she patted the space on the bed beside her and the quilt was cool and empty. But then, as she sat up, the hot pulsing of her sunburn reminded her where she was, and she leaned over to turn on the light on the nightstand. Far below the window, somewhere on the street, a gaggle of people was laughing. Someone drinking too much, too early in the day. She couldn't throw stones.

As the group moved on down the street, their noise softened, and it was then that Shannon heard the other noise. A rustling, like leaves...and yet, not leaves exactly, but more like a thousand needles scratching against dry paper. She sat as still as she could, trying to pinpoint from where the sound was coming. It sounded like the headboard, but when she pressed her ear against the plain wood, she knew that wasn't the place, but it was close.

Shannon stood up next to the bed and faced it. The scratching was coming from the wall behind the headboard. And not from one area of the wall, but from the whole wall. Something within the wall, behind the wall, was scratching, tunneling, chewing; hissing and tearing at the air like a big white noise machine.

She walked over to the wall and pressed her cheek against the faded, an- tiquated wallpaper. Something was behind the wall, or maybe just behind the wallpaper. As she pressed her cheek harder, she thought she felt the wall shift and press back, an undulating wave like a rolling massage mat, gliding its tongue along the side of her face.

· · • • • • • • · ·

Trip Trap Vacation Review
Bay Breeze Beach Resort, Clearwater, FL
JAnna O.   (3 months ago)
5/5 stars

OMG my husband and I had such a great time at the Bay Breeze!! He's not really a beach person, so we drove into the city during the day and we found this AMAZING popsicle place that sells these things called Hyppo Pops, which were so delicious I actually cried a little when I finished my blackberry goat cheese one. At night, we went to the Iguana Bar next door to the hotel, and it's a hopping tiki-bar where you can sip Pina Coladas right on the beach! We went back to the Bay Breeze after and sat at the bar nearest to the hotel (my husband doesn't like loud noise) and met other couples there who were super nice! My husband says they were swingers and had been trying to get with us for the night, but I think he's just being silly. I took lots of pictures but Trip Trap only lets you upload ten so here are all the best ones.

· · • • • • • • · ·

The Iguana was packed with people, but it wasn't anything Shannon and Lily found unusual. They were still in their twenties, when bar-hopping and or a Tool concert were completely worth it even if they couldn't hear or eat solid food the following day.

Lily had explored the block while Shannon was asleep, and in addition to buying an obscene amount of ibuprofen ("to help your sunburn, and also, in the likely event I have a wicked hangover tomorrow morning"), she found the tiki-bar attached to the hotel next door to the Bay Breeze Resort.

"It's supposed to have a ton of great pub food," Lily said. "Plus, it's right on the beach."

They had eaten dinner, a large meal in comparison to what they usually ate, but somehow, Lily was slurring her words at eleven o'clock at night.

"Why can't I dance? I don't understand, Shanannarama." It was her pet name, the one she took out and presented as an offering when she really wanted something Shannon was hesitant to give.

"I think we can all agree, despite alcohol consumption, that uncoordinated twerking is never something friends let friends do: not in public or in private, my love," Shannon replied. She grasped Lily's face in her hands and kissed her long and hard.

Lily pulled away and smiled. "But I like dancing."

Her voice cartwheeled and somersaulted in the air.

"Besides," Shannon continued, "those guys kept rubbing up against us."

She took a long sip of her chocolate martini. Lily had been right: the Tylenol, plus some food and an Advil or too chased by a handful of sugary drinks made every pain disappear. It might make her kidneys disappear one of these days, too, but she would consider that point tomorrow.

Lily painted a somber countenance on her face. "You're afraid of cooties, aren't you? Be honest. All along, a closet hypochondriac."

Shannon laughed. The opening beat of Britney Spears' "Work Bitch" pounded insistently out of the speakers in the ceiling. "Hey, we can go back there if you want. *What happens in Florida, stays in Florida.*"

"No, I think the saying is, What happens in Florida...ends up a lead story on *The World's Dumbest Criminals*," Lily said, her face beaming with happiness. "Or on one of those weird *How Did They Die* shows on that crime station...you know the one?"

"Didn't you say you had to use the ladies' room?"

Shannon didn't mind when Lily drank too much. Although they scrubbed the bathroom weekly without exception, the unspoken rule was: whoever throws up in the toilet that week cleans it. And Lily was a happy drunk, at least. She hoped it would always be this way.

When Lily departed, Shannon continued to sip her drink and gaze about the room. Across the bar, a fidgety man wearing a coral-colored tank top two sizes too big was chatting up a petite woman by his side. She was likely his wife, Shannon thought; they both had that lived-in look to them. As he spoke, more into the woman's hair than into her ear, he kept readjusting the shirt, pulling it forward so that it nearly exposed a nipple. Finally, he reached a hairy arm over his shoulder and scratched the top of his back. The woman remained uninterested, concentrating her attention on a television set hanging from the ceiling. Big Tank stopped talking and began to scan the room with his eyes, his hand continuing to pick and burrow into hidden skin.

A gust of Gulf breeze stroked Shannon's back and tousled her hair. She was beginning to move her gaze onto another patron when Big Tank turned his body to face the tables behind him, giving Shannon a clear view of his back. The billowy shirt had fallen backwards, revealing the flesh on his upper shoulders. As he pulled his hand away, it was finally clear what had been causing his insatiable itch: the tanned, hairless skin was covered in bulbous welts at least an inch wide, pustules with tiny pinpricks exactly like the ones on the arm of the woman on the elevator. These eruptions, however, were crisscrossed with deep red lines where the man's fingernails had dug at the irritation.

She watched in horror as the man reached another hand to his back, raking it furiously until one of the pustules tore open, and deep, red blood began to pool at the break.

Shannon nearly knocked Lily down as she ran headfirst into her on her flight out of The Iguana and into the street.

• • • ● • ● • • •

Trip Trap Vacation Review
Bay Breeze Beach Resort, Clearwater, FL
Liz G.   (1 month ago)
3/5 stars

We usually stay in Key West, but this year, with the hurricane damage, we had to find a new place to go, so we looked at places on the Gulf Coast. Unfortunately, this resort just did not meet our expectations. The beach was super crowded during the day with jet skiers always blocking access to the water. The breakfast was nothing special, neither great nor awful, and the hotel room itself was clean but really old. The wallpaper looked kind of scratched up, and it was torn in a few places, and there was a big, dark brown stain on the carpet next to the bed. When we went to get ice from the bin at the end of the hall, we spotted a hole in the wall next to the cooler: a big hole, like someone had put a fist through it, and a few more dark brown stains around the edges.

• • • ● • ● • • •

Lily was drooling on her as they kissed, something that wasn't on its own a dealbreaker, but combined with her inability to shake the image of Big Tank's back, she knew her head was nowhere near where it should be for good sex.

She pushed Lily off of her and sat up.

"What's wrong?" her girlfriend asked, at a volume about two clicks too loud for a bustling nightclub, never mind a hotel at three in the morning.

"Shhh," Shannon whispered. "You're screaming."

Lily rolled onto her back and put her hands behind her head. "What? Are you afraid the neighbors will hear me? I doubt anyone's even next door. We haven't heard a peep, not even a toilet flush or a television."

Shannon was quiet for a minute, and then: "Have you ever seen a bed bug?" She glanced about the room, wondering what the signs of an infestation were.

Lily thought for a moment. "No, I haven't. They're supposed to be pretty nasty, though. Why? Do you have a rash or something? The man you saw in the bar: that's really bothering you?"

"No...I—"

Shannon ran her hands along the bed sheets. They were stiff, but the subtle pilling reminded her of how many other people had pressed their skin against them. She eyed her overnight bag on the floor of the open closet and thought of the cleaning woman's arm, of the man in the bar's back.

Should she move the bag to the top of the dresser?

Could bed bugs crawl up walls?

"I just think that—"

Shannon began to finish her thought, but when she turned to face Lily again, she could see her girlfriend had passed out cold.

Instead, she looked at the bed sheet. She imagined a million tiny beetles crawling inside of the mattress below her, burrowing through the stuffing and filling the springs. She got up from the bed and walked to the window. Lily had closed it when they returned home and had turned the air conditioner on low, but Shannon was cold again, so she shut it off.

Lily began to snore. Her mouth gaped open and Shannon imagined the big Palmetto bug, the one from the bathroom, crawling inside of it.

The air conditioning unit powered down slowly. The final fan whirred and rattled, then fell mute. There was a beat of complete silence, and then... the scratching in the wall began. It was the same sound Shannon had heard earlier, but this time, it seemed louder, amplified like Lily's voice became when it was soaked in alcohol.

The scratching, like a million tiny needles, was everywhere in the wall, a collective consciousness of sound, and she placed her hand on the area of the wall closest to her and felt the movement below: a million tiny fingers ticking and tapping a Morse code softly into her palm.

Shannon scanned the wall.

She could see where the strips of wallpaper met: it was right behind the bed, a foot or so behind Lily's head.

She climbed back onto the bed, then stood upright in front of her pillow and reached her hand to touch the seam. If she held her hand *just so*, she thought she could feel it: something was pushing against the seam, trying to break the seal. She looked toward the ceiling and spotted a small section where the old glue had finally given up, an edge that had broken free of the wall and was jutting slightly away. If she stretched her arm, really reached, she could touch it, and she did. Perhaps if she could pull the paper away, she could see what was hiding beneath it.

Shannon shifted onto her tip-toes but only managed to sink further into the mattress. She moved closer to Lily's snoring face and stepped on the pillow. Stretching her arm and lengthening her body as far as she could, she finally grasped the errant flap in between her thumb and fingers and pulled, but as she did so, she lost her balance and tumbled backwards onto the mattress, the edge of wallpaper still clutched in her fist.

The piece that ripped from the wall was about the size of Shannon's hand, but it revealed something extraordinary. The naked plaster was, indeed, moving, but it wasn't a wave looping over and over, as she had imagined. Just beneath the wall's skin was a bump slightly smaller than the size of her fist, running wildly back and forth. Was it another one of those Palmetto bugs? She shivered instinctively at the thought.

Shannon snatched one of her flip-flops. Without thinking, she began to slap the exposed plaster with it, but the action was woefully ineffective.

The movement continued, unfettered.

She dropped the shoe and glanced quickly around the room for something more substantial. There was a small iron, *for our guests' convenience,* sitting at the top of the closet. As fast as she could, Shannon leaped from the bed and retrieved it. She'd quiet the scratching, and then she and Lily could get a good night's sleep and relax the rest of the weekend.

It was okay if a few bangs woke up her girlfriend—neither of them could be expected to sleep with a giant beetle running back and forth behind their heads, could they?

She smashed the iron against the lump, but each time, the movement continued; the scratching, in fact, seemed to grow louder. Shannon struck the plaster over and over, a twisted game of Whack-a-mole gone horribly wrong.

Lily opened her eyes and looked around, confused. As she began to lift her head and sit up, the edge of the iron's metal plate hit the plaster just right and broke the surface. The wall stopped undulating, and the rustling abruptly silenced, like the breaking of a neck at the end of a hangman's noose.

Shannon walked awkwardly but triumphantly backwards on the bed, trying to maintain her balance. She smiled at Lily. Her girlfriend looked in horror at the baseball-sided hole Shannon had made.

Neither of them said anything for a long minute, and then, the wall spilled its secret.

A waterfall of black exoskeletons and legs and antennae erupted from the maw, spraying Lily's face with clicking, ticking roaches. The whole wall rippled, pushing its contents through the hole like a terrible birth, and Shannon dropped the iron squarely on her bare foot.

· · · · ●· ● · · ·

Trip Trap Vacation Review
Bay Breeze Beach Resort, Clearwater, FL
Jeannie M.   (1 week ago)
4/5 stars

Fun in the sun! Great drinks! Great location! Staff is kind of blah, though. I went to the front desk to ask for a band-aid, and the concierge just stared at me, saying nothing. Whatever! Cool water sports, and a fun dance floor right on the beach with a HUGE screen that displays light shows and video. Bring a sweatshirt for sure. They keep the lobby and restaurants super cold; everyone who worked there seemed to be wearing long pants and long sleeves like we were in Alaska in the winter or something. Also, we'll probably explore other places to eat when we return next break. We got a huge plate of nachos in the restaurant and I think they left our plate under the heat lamp too long ,'cause everything, even the black olives—and there were like, a million of them—were crunchy. Otherwise, totally awesome time!

It's All Fun and Games Until...

"Do you smoke cigarettes, er..." the pretty nurse looked down at her clipboard. "Kristin?"

The patient smiled. "It's Kristina, and no, not for a long time."

She remained pleasant, still smiling. The clinic wasn't one she'd used before, but it was nearly identical to all of the others she'd visited: urban, mobbed, understaffed. She wouldn't be remembered, and that was her goal. This nurse had forgotten her already.

The distracted woman's eyes remained glued to her clipboard. "Drink alcohol?"

Kristina pretended to check her watch. "Is it after twelve yet?"

There was no response, not even a wince. Kristina could see by her tag that the nurse's name was Deenie. Her scrubs were covered with tiny cartoon animals: dogs, cats, bunnies. She thought she might even have spied a snake among the menagerie. She was an attractive woman and might even be someone Kristina would approach in a bar if the situation were different.

When the patient said nothing more, Deenie looked up. "I'm sorry, I didn't catch that," she said.

Kristina smiled again. "Just kidding. Very rarely."

Kristina was lying. She meant *rarely* in the sense that rarely a day went by that she didn't have a vodka tonic in her hand before sundown. It was always five o'clock somewhere. She limited her drinking to one, however.

Any more than that, and things got sloppy. One was just enough to take the edge off, give her a bit of liquid courage to continue her hobby.

Deenie didn't ask her if she used street drugs. She didn't look the type, she supposed, and Kristina wondered if that was a compliment.

"How long have you been diabetic?" Deenie asked.

"I was diagnosed when I was twelve," the patient told her, "so almost twenty-one years."

She had her responses committed to memory, down to the subtlest detail of facial expression. In a pinch, she could always visit a needle exchange program, pick up a handful of syringes that way, but the staff would be more likely to commit her image to memory in those types of places. Junkies, it seemed, were less likely to be believed than those with broken pancreases.

"Do you test your sugar regularly?" Deenie finally looked up from her chart, her eyes skimming the young woman for just a moment before busying herself with fumbling with a lancet and test strip.

"Of course," Kristina lied.

Deenie held her hand out. "What's your most recent A1C number?"

"4.7," Kristina said. Confident, proud. She didn't respond to the hand yet. Sometimes, just saying this number allowed her to avoid the needle.

Deenie waved her palm toward the patient. "Let's have a finger."

Kristina was not so lucky today. She offered her left hand, and the nurse wiped a white wet pad over the top of her middle finger. The alcohol smell was crisp, anxious. Deenie held the lancet to the disinfected digit and pressed the button. It snapped, and a tiny bead of bright red appeared. Deenie scooped it onto the test strip and the two women waited for the countdown on the test machine to beep.

"Are you sexually active?" Deenie asked, returning to her clipboard. She was wasting no time. Minutes were at a premium.

"No," Kristina said.

"Are you interested in being tested for sexually transmitted infections today?"

Does chlamydia pass by osmosis these days? Kristina wanted to ask.

"No, I don't think that's necessary. I just need a refill." The patient was batting a thousand in the bullshit department this visit, bowling a perfect game. "Anything special on your request list for Santa this year?" she added, only recognizing afterward how creepy the attempt at small talk sounded.

If Deenie was repulsed, she didn't show it. The machine beeped and the nurse recorded the number on the chart. "4.9," she said. "Good work."

Kristina smiled, hiding her irritation at this patronizing statement.

Deenie dumped the needle and used test strip in the sharps container. "The doctor will be in shortly. Have a good holiday."

She did not look at the woman again before leaving.

Kristina removed her refuse from the bright orange bin marked with a *Caution!* warning, wrapped the pieces in a tissue, and shoved them in her purse. She was obsessive about keeping her DNA inside of her body; even one stray hair could be the end of her fun. She never knew what hypochondriac might be lurking at her family reunions, sending their saliva to 23andme.

It's all fun and games until someone gets handsy and scratches themselves a fat genetic sample for the police to test, she thought.

A half hour later, Kristina was on her way to the nearest pharmacy. On the rental car's radio, Bing Crosby crooned about silver bells. Kristina sang loudly along as she tossed the prescription onto the seat next to her and turned on the wipers to clear the softly falling snow. She would be restocked and back on the road by nightfall.

· · · ● · ● · · · ·

Though in truth, it began years before, the game truly took shape in the spring of 2006.

Kristina was a freshman in her second semester at Hofstra University, her big adventure to Long Island, the strip of land abutting the Big Apple, and her only friends on campus, three boys who shared a room at the other end of her dorm hall, invited her to join them on Spring Break. Edward, the oldest of the boys, borrowed his parents' Ford Taurus sedan, and the four took turns driving the long haul down Interstate 95, the landscape changing from browns and grays to sunny greens as they approached Florida.

Kristina hadn't minded sharing a room with the other three—they knew she favored other women and didn't bother trying to convince her otherwise—but after two nights, she was bored, antsy. There were only so many drunken pool gatherings and beach fires to keep her interest, so on the third evening of their stay, she bowed out from the festivities. Edward lent her the car, and she cruised the boardwalk before heading north, finally turning into the parking lot of an ancient IHOP when her stomach began to growl.

A middle-aged woman with reddish-brown hair, the kind that used to be fiery but had dinged and darkened after years of hard drugs, hot sun, and cheap motel shampoo, approached the passenger window just as Kristina turned off the motor. She motioned to the driver to roll down the window, but Kristina climbed out of the car instead.

"Hey," she called over the car roof to the woman who remained bent, staring inside at the cloth front seat. "Can I help you with something?"

The redhead straightened up but her shoulders slumped. "I was just wondering if you could help me out. I ran outta gas."

The woman's lip twitched a bit, a nervous tic.

Kristina raised her eyebrow. "Where's your car?" she asked. "I have a can in the trunk. I can drive you to the station to fill it up."

She didn't—and she wouldn't—but Kristina never missed an opportunity to call out a con game.

The woman hesitated, thinking. "You need any company tonight?" she eventually asked, but looked slightly apprehensive. It was the South, after all, and while prostitution might be casually tolerated, lesbianism very often was not.

Kristina glanced at the woman's clothes. It was clear she hadn't showered in days. Her hair hadn't been brushed in quite some time and her orange blouse billowed around a skeletal frame.

"You got a place?" Kristina asked. "I was just going to get some food here, but I'd be up for some pizza delivery."

She'd eaten pizza for the past four days and couldn't fathom smelling the sweet tang of tomato sauce and grease again, but it was clear this woman was desperate for a way to make quick cash. Kristina mentally counted the stack of bills in her back pocket.

The redhead looked around nervously. "Yeah...yeah," she stammered. "I got a place not far from here. It ain't on the beach or nothing, though."

Kristina laughed. "That's okay. I've had my fill of sand for the day." She climbed back into the car and unlatched the lock. "Get in," she said, loudly enough for the woman to hear her through the glass. When the woman obliged, Kristina stuck out her hand before turning the key again. "My name's Kristina," she said.

"Julie," the redhead offered, avoiding Kristina's eyes. She shook her hand limply. Her fingers were long and soft, her fingernails bitten down to the quick.

They drove a mile down the road until Julie pointed to an abandoned-looking motel abutting a tattoo parlor.

"Right there," she said. Her hand shook a little and she replaced it on her lap.

As the two women approached one of the room doors, Julie glanced sideways at her companion. "Wasn't expecting company. Sorry about the mess."

Kristina smiled, taking great care to show Julie all of her teeth. "I'm not a neat freak myself."

The room was dark. Heavy curtains were drawn across the picture window where a small, round table stood with two rickety chairs. Nearby, a queen-size bed, its sheets and coverlet a tangled mess and its two bed pillows pushed together against the headboard, appeared slightly damp, the mattress dented with shadows. The redhead raised her arm and turned on a hanging light above the table. An empty jar of peanut butter, a handful of dirty, wrinkled t-shirts, and two well-worn fashion magazines, their covers slightly frayed, jumbled themselves into a tall heap a few feet below the bulb.

Julie held her arm out. "You can sit anywhere," she said, and Kristina rested herself in one of the chairs abutting the pile.

They were both silent for a moment as Kristina surveyed the room. Julie remained standing and began to tap her foot slightly.

"So, what were you looking for?" she asked.

Business-like.

Impatient.

Kristina stretched her arms and folded them behind her head. "I thought we were getting pizza. I mean, if you have other plans, I don't want to keep you..." She reached one hand back down behind her jeans and pulled out her folded money. "But I'd like to buy you dinner, and maybe pay for a bit of your time."

She unfolded the bills and spread them out into a fan. She had close to three hundred dollars, more than half of her money left for the week.

Julie's eyes widened, and she sat down on the edge of the bed. "You really want pizza?"

Kristina shoved the money into her front pants pocket. "What I'd like is for both of us to relax. Not worry about the time for once. Catch my drift?" She smiled again, making her mouth as wide as she could manage. "Why don't you call and order, then hop in the shower while we wait. Put on some comfy clothes, some pajamas maybe. And I'll take off my shoes—if that's okay with you—and wait for the delivery guy."

Julie bit her lip and glanced at the pile of debris next to Kristina. "You sure?" she asked, hesitant, her eyes still on the pile.

Kristina nodded. "Yep." She crossed her legs.

The redhead picked up the beige telephone beside the bed and dialed, already knowing the number by heart. As she replaced the receiver on the base, she stood up.

"About thirty minutes, the guy said. Probably closer to forty-five, knowing them."

Kristina kicked off her shoes. "Great. I'll just hang out while you shower." When Julie looked around nervously at this, she added, "I promise: I'm not going to rob you. If it makes you feel better, I'll hang out in the bathroom."

Julie looked at the floor. "You really just want to hang around? Nothing else?"

Kristina cleared her throat. "Well, Julie, to be honest, I am hoping for a little more. But I'm also not a fan of making women do anything they don't want to do. I know you sleep with men for money. I have enough to pay you, too. But just kicking back and watching some tube is cool, if that's all you're comfortable with."

At this, Julie crossed her arms across her chest and peeled her blouse over her head. A carpet of orange freckles was splattered between the edges of her light green bra.

"Come join me in the shower," she said, and Kristina followed her into the bathroom without another word.

Forty minutes later, she was wiping the handles of the faucet with a corner of the wet bath towel and checking the drain for remnants of her hair when she heard Julie chatting with the pizza delivery person.

When the outside door shut again, Kristina emerged from the bathroom. She hadn't bothered to redress, and Julie paused to stare at her naked body as she walked uninhibited across the room.

Julie sat cross-legged on the bed in a ragged pink bathrobe, the unopened box of pizza in front of her. She reached her hand forward, pointed the remote control at the ancient television, and clicked a few of the buttons. The sound screamed to life, a newscaster covering a race at the local speedway.

"They never give me napkins," Julie yelled over the cacophony. "But I keep a stash of them over there, on the table." She nodded toward the pile of debris, then stopped, suddenly remembering something. "I'll get 'em," she said, starting to unfold herself.

Kristina held her hand up. "I got it." She walked toward the table and began to rifle through the mess until an unusual item revealed itself. "What's this?" Kristina asked, holding up the large black gun using a corner of one of the t-shirts.

Julie slid to the edge of the bed. Her eyes were wide. "I got it for protection. Two of my friends, they went...they disappeared over Christmas, you know." She swallowed, staring at the gun. "One turned up dead. Just thought this would maybe help."

Kristina turned the gun carefully so that the t-shirt fabric covered her finger as she aligned it against the trigger.

"You're a regular Annie Oakley, huh?" she asked, closing one eye dramatically and pretending to aim the muzzle at the lamp. Smiling.

Nothing to fear here.

Julie laughed nervously. "Annie Oakley used a shotgun," she said.

Kristina lowered her arm. "You wanna play cops and robbers?" she asked playfully. She smiled again, and Julie had to admit, the sight of the starkly nude woman holding the big gun seemed slightly comical. Kristina winked at her. "Well, ma'am, I'm gonna have to take you in," she said in a mock drawl. "You're too darn purty to be eatin' that here pizza all alone." She walked slowly toward the bed, then gestured gently with the gun. "Turn over and lie on your stomach so I can cuff ya."

Julie smiled nervously but didn't move. Surely, this woman was joking. She had expected the woman to get dressed, eat a slice of pizza or two, and be on her way. Perhaps she could be persuaded to stay longer, pay more money. She hadn't expected to be horsing around with a gun. The woman was close enough to touch her.

Kristina nudged Julie's knee with her own. "Go ahead. Turn over and lie down," she whispered.

Julie hesitated for a moment, then did as she was told. Immediately, she felt Kristina's weight shift onto the bed behind her, the visitor's knees on the back of her arms.

Kristina had never been a fan of strangling her prey. Though satisfying in its own right, the act was too time-consuming. She knew other killers confessed to wanting to savor the moment, to take their time watching the life drain from their victims' eyes, but Kristina knew the truth: Strangling caused a woman's vagina muscles to clench up. And most of her male brethren stuck their undersized cocks in their prey as they killed them because it gave them a sense of not being the woefully ineffectual lovers they actually were.

For Kristina, being gratefully absent of this problematic appendage meant strangling was nothing but a nuisance.

She was working on crafting a signature, injecting air into a target's vein—clean yet satisfying—but she hadn't quite perfected the move.

"Don't take this personally," she said softly then held the tip of the gun up to the back of Julie's head and fired.

Blood, skull, and gray matter blew everywhere, including onto Kristina's stomach, but she did not flinch. Where the muzzle had been, a deep red hole, almost black, wet and gooey, appeared in its place. A faint trail of smoke drifted up from between Julie's wet locks. Kristina rolled off of the limp body, rested the gun and t-shirt on Julie's terry clothed back, and pushed the pizza box open with her knuckle.

On the television, a lacquered-hair reporter squinted seriously at the camera as she walked sideways alongside a wooded area. "*This is the third body to turn up along LPGA Boulevard,*" the woman stated robotically. "*Police say the victim suffered a gunshot wound to the head and...*"

Kristina picked up a slice of pizza and took a generous bite. The pie had cooled significantly, but the chef had been generous with the tomato sauce, and a glob of it spilled from the side and dropped onto her thigh.

"*...There appears to be no connection between this recent murder and the string of bodies being discovered along...*"

Kristina shoved the rest of the piece into her mouth and chewed. She looked down at Julie's body, completely still.

"Well, I'll be darned," she said to it, her voice muffled through the mouthful of masticated cheese and dough. "You just gave me the best idea."

• • • • • • • • • •

No one expects a woman to attack them.

Unsurprisingly, men are statistically more likely than women to commit violent crimes, sexual crimes, even low-level, petty assaults. Even in innocuous social situations, men are more likely to trigger anxiety in others. Because of this, women are more likely to be on guard when in the presence of a strange man than with a strange woman.

Gynophobia, the specific fear of women, is a rare disorder and only develops years after the person suffers chronic abuse by women. And even then the sufferers tend to be male. Not female.

Not Kristina's victim of choice.

Kristina knew these facts. Christ, the College had financed her education with a full-ride scholarship for her to study them. After her graduation with a degree in criminal justice, Kristina stayed in Long Island, working as a process server. The pay was dismal, but the position allowed her little restrictions on her travel and time consumption. She was good at her job, able to blend in nonchalantly with just about any crowd and harmless looking so that no one hesitated to open their doors when she rang a doorbell. She saved up her vacation time, and each December, she traveled to a new part of the country, one she'd researched weeks in advance. One with a recent history of unresolved crime.

She perfected her syringe technique, but she was careful—even meticulous—to stage her bodies to match the victims of area predators.

In the Information Age, the internet—especially with its histrionically-headlined news-zines—was nothing but a geyser of details in which copycats could freely bathe.

December, 2009. *Remains of a twelfth victim appear near the Mouth Pleasant neighborhood of Cleveland.*

December, 2010. *Suffolk Police report four bodies along the north side of Ocean Parkway.*

December, 2011. *Discovery of a fourth body in the Matanuska Lake region, north of Anchorage.*

December, 2012. *Bodies unearthed in lot next to Kentucky homeless shelter.*

December, 2013. *Santa Clara authorities track the culprit behind fourth shooting in Sunnyvale.*

December, 2014. *Dismembered remains of four victims uncovered near Paris, Maine bed and breakfast.*

December, 2015. *Skeletons of four people found behind a Connecticut strip mall.*

December, 2016. *Seventh woman bound, gagged, and stabbed in Detroit neighborhood.*

December, 2017. *Dallas police "baffled" after nine residents found dead at same apartment complex.*

December, 2019. *The bodies of five sex workers located in field near Oklahoma City drug house.*

December, 2020. *New Orleans officials "disturbed" over missing women dragged from nearby swamp.*

• • • ● • ● • • •

December, 2021.

• • • ● • ● • • •

From the clinic, Kristina stopped into a chain pharmacy in northern Connecticut to refresh her supplies before heading toward Boston. Revere Beach, its shoreline mostly vacant in the brutal winter months of New England, was the recent recipient of three unidentified corpses, the flesh so water-logged that cause of death had yet to be determined, though initial reposts theorized the victims had been injected with something.

A predator after her own heart.

As she pulled onto the interstate, the snow intensified. Bing Crosby became Elvis Presley, crying about a blue Christmas. As the sign for the

Massachusetts Turnpike came into view, the white flakes doubled, then tripled in size and intensity. Just beyond the green placard, bright lights of consumerism illuminated the sky. Target. Bed Bath and Beyond. Barnes and Noble. Kristina glanced at the digital numbers on the dashboard. She had plenty of time to wait out the squall.

The mall's three-story garage was packed, and it took a bit of circling to secure the only open parking spot, one hidden from view inside a dark corner. As she slipped through the glass doors leading directly into the Christmas Tree Shops, Kristina stuffed a twenty-dollar bill into a bell ringer's red kettle.

The store was oppressively warm, and she wandered slowly along the aisles, maneuvering around overflowing shopping carts and screaming baby carriages. Her hands remained clenched in frustration at the traffic and storm.

She entered a nearly empty aisle full of housewares and table settings and pretended to scan the dinner plates in interest. A young woman wearing a gray winter hat, the only other shopper in sight, turned to look at her. Kristina felt her gaze and shifted her body away in discomfort.

The woman pointed a woolen gloved finger at her. "Kristin, no, Kristina, right?"

Kristina swallowed and turned slightly. The nurse from the clinic. "Yes, how did you—" she began, feigning confusion.

"Doctor's office," she said, smiling. "Earlier today." She glanced at the rows of unboxed glassware lining the shelves in front of them. "Holiday shopping?"

Kristina smiled but kept her lips tight. "Yes, just a few last-minute things. More of a once over for later purchase. I tend to work best as a last-minute shopper." She pretended to evaluate a frosted blue beer stein. "You?"

The nurse laughed, then, inexplicably, leaned close to Kristina and whispered conspiratorially. "To be honest. I'm just wasting some time before I jump on the Pike." She leaned back and smiled warmly. In the air between them lingered a flowery musk scent, a perfume Kristina recognized but could not quite identify. "I've been helping to care for my great aunt over the past few months. She lives on the shore, so I stay there on weekends to give my cousin a break. The snow kind of grounded me for a bit, but I'm glad for the postponement." Her eyes stared directly into Kristina's. "My name's Denise. Deenie, for short."

Kristina nodded. The piercing of her bubble of anonymity made her uncomfortable. She thought of her car in the parking garage, the clumps of snow already melted by the time she got out and began walking to the mall door.

"Hey," the nurse continued. "This is going to sound weird, but are you hungry? I was thinking of getting a drink and some dinner at one of the places inside. You feel like a bite?"

Kristina frowned but said nothing. An elderly woman in a pastel pink coat and hair scarf walked obliviously down the aisle and pushed past them, knocking Deenie forward again. Kristina felt the nurse's knee graze hers and smelled the subtle perfume again. The feeling, the smell, was pleasant. Comforting, somehow. She felt her hands relax.

Deenie waved her hand in front of Kristina's face. "Hello? Some food? What do you think?"

Kristina snapped back to attention. "Sure," she said. "That sounds good, actually. Lead the way."

Despite the mob of shoppers clogging the hallways, the pizzeria chain was relatively empty and sat the women right away. As she slid into the booth, Kristina pulled her jacket from her shoulders. A member of the young wait staff materialized beside their table with a pad and pen.

"Can I start you off with something to drink?" she asked brightly, handing each woman a thick, heavy menu.

Kristina laid hers on the table. "Vodka tonic. Tito's, if you have it," she said. "With lime."

The server looked at Deenie. "For you?"

Deenie glanced over the menu at Kristina, then turned to the girl. "I'll have the same. Thank you." When they were alone again, Deenie balanced the menu on the edge of the table and began to flip through the plastic-covered pages. "Do you need to test?" she asked, still looking down.

"What's that?" Kristina asked, folding her hands on top of her menu.

Deenie jutted her chin toward her companion's menu. "Test your blood sugar. Before you eat."

Kristina paused. The comment felt like a trap.

"No, no," she said, keeping her voice even. "I'm fine. I'm not hungry. My machine's in the car."

"I'm sorry," Deenie said, looking up and resting her menu on the table. "That was unintentional. Everyone says I need to learn to shut off 'the nurse voice.' My mom was the same way. Always offering unsolicited medical advice on diet and lifestyle."

Kristina smiled. "Your mom's a nurse, too?"

"Yeah," Deenie said. "Was. Pediatric, though." She pushed off her coat and unwrapped her scarf from her neck, revealing a plain white blouse unbuttoned down past her cleavage. Kristina wondered what had happened to the animal-print scrubs. "Up in Maine. Small town near the Canadian border no one's heard of." The server reappeared and placed their drinks in front of them. "Sucked being a kid," Deenie continued. "I practically had to be bleeding out my eyes to stay home sick from school." She laughed and took a sip. "This is good," she said, then to the server, "I think we'll just stick with drinks for now, if you don't mind."

The waitress forced a smile and retreated without a word, leaving the menus on the table.

Kristina swallowed a small mouthful of her drink. "So, *Deenie*. That's unusual. What made you choose it for a nickname?"

The nurse gulped her drink quickly. When she finally rested her glass on the table again, it was half gone.

"My mom named me Denise just so she could call me Deenie. You know, like the Judy Blume book."

Kristina ran her finger along the condensation on the edge of her glass. "I think I remember reading it as a kid. Doesn't the girl have scoliosis or something?"

She eyed Deenie's collarbone. The skin there was unblemished, smooth and soft-looking. When she looked up to Deenie's face, she realized the nurse had been watching her.

"Well, that makes sense," Deenie said, laughing. "Named after a character with a medical issue. Of course."

She looked over toward the bar and made a soft gesture with her hand to wave down their server before bringing the glass to her lips and hurriedly swallowing the rest.

As she ordered a refill, as if on cue, the restaurant was silent for a moment then resumed with its holiday soundtrack. Annie Lennox purred about a winter wonderland.

"Eurythmics," Deenie said when the server disappeared again. "One of the few holiday songs I'm not sick of hearing."

Kristina laughed. "I think that's the point: to play the shite out of Christmas songs until we can't stand the sound of them anymore. That way, come January, we won't feel so depressed that the holidays are over."

Deenie smiled. "You're probably right. It's all a ruse to try to psyche us out."

She reached over and squeezed Kristina's hand suddenly, then pulled it back. Her cheeks flushed slightly.

An hour later, as the two women walked out into the bustle of the mall thoroughfare, Deenie stumbled a bit, then put her hand over her face in embarrassment. "I know, I know," she said. "Don't worry: I'm not planning on driving for a while. I still have some things to do here before I head towards Boston." She wrapped her arm around Kristina's and leaned in closer. "Where are you parked? I'll walk you to your car."

Kristina felt her stomach jump.

She thought of the nurse's collarbone, how soft the skin looked.

The unbuttoned placket of her blouse.

"I'm way over in a dark corner," she said. "And it's freezing. I appreciate the offer, but you're not walking me all the way over there."

Deenie hugged her arm tighter, then leaned closer to whisper in Kristina's ear. "Tell you what. I'll walk you, and you can drive me over to the other end of the mall." Her breath was hot on Kristina's skin, making it feel as if a current had run through it. "I have to walk over there anyway. This way, I have some company." She leaned her head on Kristina's shoulder. "Besides, it's safer if there are two of us."

The two hurried, still clutching each other, across the parking garage to the furthest corner until Kristina unwrapped her arm to fish inside her jacket for her keys. She pressed the button on the fob twice to unlock both doors and the car's lights blinked softly in the dim light.

"Wow," said Deenie, giggling. "You weren't kidding. This *is* a dark corner."

She opened the passenger door and slid inside.

Kristina shut her door and put her key in the ignition. The radio sprang to life, Bruce Springsteen screaming that Santa Claus was coming to town. She turned to grab the seatbelt when she felt Deenie's hand on her shoulder. "Hey," the nurse's voice whispered. "Before you do that…"

Kristina turned her head, preparing to kiss the woman sitting beside her, when she felt a sharp sting on the side of her neck. Instinctively, she reached her hand up to touch it, and her fingers met Deenie's gloved hands. They were holding a syringe firm against her vein, the nurse's thumb pressing forward the plunger until the barrel's contents emptied themselves into Kristina's bloodstream.

Deenie leaned closer and whispered into her ear, her voice completely absent of any slur or joviality.

"Don't take this personally," she said, her tone measured.

Businesslike.

Patient.

"But you were the easiest one yet."

THE FOUND BOYS

MICHAEL WASN'T PREPARED FOR how cold the evening would be; he wore his tattered Irish flat cap that was more for the fashion of the thing than for actual warmth. He'd left his jacket at home as he'd assumed he and John would be catching a ride home from the bars, and since most of the night would be spent roaming around the city's new casino, excess layers would have been superfluous.

When John suggested that they walk home to their loft apartment in a far corner of the South End, a good fifteen blocks away, Michael had agreed enthusiastically—a steady intake of dirty martinis with little food to absorb them will do that—but after they crossed East Columbus Avenue, the wind picked up, and the chill crept up Michael's spine, taking hold of his torso and refusing to release.

He stopped on the edge of the curbing and took out his phone.

"I'm going to get a car. This is ridiculous." He pulled up the app on his screen. John walked faster down the sidewalk and disappeared down Union Street, behind the wall of the underpass.

Believing John had not heard him, Michael replaced the phone in his back pocket and half-jogged, half-skipped ahead to catch his boyfriend, who, for his part, had dissolved into the cement shadows.

"John— Hold up—" Michael's foot traced the outline of something heavy and damp, and the break in his stride caused Michael to hop twice to right his gait.

Don't be a dead body. Don't be a dead body.

He glanced at the ground and willed the offending obstacle to be something innocuous: a bag of trash partially covered by an old plaid shirt that had been ripped in half as neatly as if a surgeon had done it. Michael lightly touched his glasses, resumed his quick pace, and exited the tunnel.

John stood on the edge of the parking lot across the street. Just beyond him, the scintillating outline of the Basketball Hall of Fame building twinkled, a rippling LED display washing over the brick structure like an ocean wave. John's blonde hair glowed silver in the luminescence.

"Hey," he said over the traffic whizzing between them, "wanna go to Diane's Place? Or maybe get a burger at Last Option?"

Michael waited for a silver sedan to pass then hurried across the freeway access road; a tractor-trailer clamored noisily above him, making his shoulders hunch instinctively.

"Why did you run off?" he asked his partner when they were within polite speaking distance again. "And no, I don't want another drink. I'm freezing. Let's head home, okay?"

John put his hand on his hip.

"It's ten o'clock. It's Saturday. Are you kidding me?" Although the brisk autumn air had sobered Michael's tongue, the same could not be said of John's; his words were intelligible but ran inelegantly together like the legs of a newborn colt. "We were just talking about this."

Only a week ago, Michael and John had returned home from a friend's baby shower.

Michael was driving—one hand at 6:00, the other at 2:15 Scotland time: the stereo. He always told himself that once he was granted tenure, his first investment would be a new car with all the bells and whistles. For now, however, he would have to make do with a used two-door, a moderate monthly payment, and a sound system that was only impressive at the start of the millennium. He wasn't doing half-bad for himself, really. An assistant professorship in a prestigious local college's History department at the less than thirty years old, a full five years younger than the national average, was nothing to sneeze at. Besides, with John returning to graduate school, they had to be frugal investors.

As Michael tapped the button on the radio, trying to find the local jazz station, John dug in the map holder in his door.

"What are you looking for?" Michael asked, glancing sideways only for a split-second. The worst thing that could happen to him now was a distracted driving accident; with the fierce competition for a foothold in the department, he needed to keep his personal life spotless.

John's hand reemerged clutching three small glass bottles.

"I *knew* I left these in here." He unscrewed one of the caps. "About halfway through the gifts, I remembered they were here."

He tipped his head back and dumped the contents into his mouth and swallowed.

Michael smelled something sterile and fruity. "Are those vodka nips? What the hell are they doing in my car?"

John opened another bottle.

"This one is coconut. Smell it."

He waved the bottle under Michael's nose, who shooed it away with his stereo hand.

"Listen, Jim Morrison," he said, slightly annoyed. "We are five minutes from home. You couldn't wait?"

John took a small sip of the second bottle, leaned his head back, and shut his eyes.

"Janis Joplin, thank you. But I mean, seriously: if I had to feign excitement at one more fucking onesie, I would have made a bee-line right to the car stash." He paused. "The most engrossing conversation I had all afternoon was about how to make the best pistachio muffins. That is what our life has become, Michael."

Michael stopped at the red light. "This is adulthood, John. People get jobs, get married, have families—"

"And stagnate until death." John stretched his arms wide, folded them back toward his chest, and swallowed the rest of the alcohol in the bottle. "I'd rather leave a young and beautiful corpse."

"Stop. You're being morbid and weird. I don't like it."

They were silent for a long minute. John twisted to face his partner.

"How about this? I'll be thirty when I graduate this time, so why don't we make a concerted effort to seek out adventure these next two years? Then, I will settle down in a respectable job, and you and I will rest...er...I mean, nest, cocoon, whatever."

Michael raised an eyebrow, focusing on the road.

"Seek adventure, huh?" He laughed a little. "Nothing extreme, right?"

John smiled. "Of course not. Just try some new things. Take risks while we're still young enough to take them."

Michael was thinking of this conversation in the dim parking lot when John shivered.

"Shit, I really need to pee," John said, glancing around as if a toilet might pop up spontaneously from the pavement.

When one did not materialize, he turned his back and walked toward the rear of the lot. The strip of tourist attractions on this side of the freeway abutted a river, the banks of which housed a healthy amount of shrubbery and hiking paths. He could relieve himself there.

Michael followed, rubbing his hands together to stave off the icebox sensation growing in his fingers. A guardrail separated the edge of the lot from the makeshift bike path, and from there, the ground, dotted with scrub trees and overgrown bushes, sloped urgently to the water. The darkness swallowed his boyfriend again as John swung a leg over the chrome divider and hopped out of sight.

Michael trotted quickly after him. As he stepped carefully over the guardrail, his eyes scanned the debris on the ground: an open condom wrapper, a crushed can of Natural Light, a single large and silver hoop earring. Toward the river was cloaked in almost complete darkness.

"John?" he said nervously as he walked ahead, willing his eyes to adjust to the lack of streetlights. "*John.*"

Again, his toe caught on something, and this time, Michael fell forward, jutting his hands in front of him to cushion his landing. A sharp pain shot into his palms. Gravel. His knees ached. He had landed on something solid, something metal or wood, but it could have been worse: he felt bars of metal in front of him as well. He could have smashed his head on one of those.

He ran his already throbbing hand over the ground in front of him and squinted, trying to make out the shapes. Train tracks. He had forgotten that the train ran through here, along the river. He started to sense the shapes of trees in front of him. And he could have sworn he saw—

An arm hooked around his elbow and pulled him up.

"Are you all right?" asked John. "Why did you come down here? I just wanted to piss out of view of the highway and street."

Michael brushed his hands on his pants. He could feel the wet dirt caked on the tops of his knees.

"Yeah, okay, so let's climb back up, all right?" His voice sounded small. He didn't like being disorientated.

"Well, I didn't find a place yet. I heard you stumble and came back over here." John tugged on Michael's forearm lightly. "Let's walk a little bit down this way. If we can navigate the bike trail, we can follow it just about all the way home."

"Are you crazy? It's pitch black down here." Another tug on his sleeve.

"No, not completely. Look—over there." He pulled his arm toward the river.

Sure enough, in the distance, there was a soft, flickering glow. *Someone's campfire?*

His vision had adjusted enough, revealing the strip of grass separating the tracks from the narrow path of blacktop, then the overgrowth of wild shrubbery that hid from view the fire's origin. His hands were still terribly cold; a moment or two alongside a fire might warm them enough to sustain him for the walk home.

"All right, but could we at least walk slowly? I don't have your night vision, Batman," Michael said.

The two ambled toward the light, John doing his best not to rush Michael even though his bladder must have felt like it would explode. When they pushed aside the thick branches of a low evergreen bush, they discovered what was waiting at their destination: four men wearing long, heavy coats gathered near a small campfire only a few feet from the water's edge. Michael hadn't anticipated a group, and he absentmindedly patted the thin wallet tucked into his back pocket. He was about to pull John back behind the foliage and suggest they find another makeshift bathroom, but it was too late: they had already been spotted. He cleared his throat and walked slowly over to the foursome.

"Hello. My name's Michael, and this is John," he said, trying his best to keep his voice even and strong.

These men are just homeless, they aren't dangerous. Being down on your luck doesn't translate into being criminal.

Still, he believed his best course of action was to appear as robust and confident as possible; he had read somewhere that malefactors were less likely to attack someone who appeared able to defend himself.

"We didn't mean to startle you. We were on our way home and decided to take a detour along the river."

The tallest of the crew, a pale man dressed in a long, black overcoat, offered a leather-gloved hand.

"You can call me Peter, though some people still call me Jack." He nodded his head toward another member of the group, a serious-looking man with large, black-framed eyeglasses and a closely-cropped receding hairline. "That's Nibs. The guy next to him, we call Twins, and that's Toodles—though she likes to be called by her given name, Mary Parsons—over there."

It wasn't until Michael looked more closely that he realized the figure standing on the far edge of the fire was, in fact, a woman.

"Mary's from here originally: she's the one who suggested we stay in these parts for a while."

With this remark, the woman's eyes met Michael's.

"That's right. Me and my husband Hugh lived in Massachusetts for many years, 'til the bastard turned out to be a back-stabbing snitch."

She sneered involuntarily and coughed into her shoulder. She wore an incongruously new-looking pink pea coat that appeared to be a size or two too big for her small frame.

"New England weather doesn't bother me a bit. I'm from Rochester originally. It's cold as hell half of the months of the year. But this guy—"
The man Peter called Twins directed his thumb toward Nibs like he was

hitchhiking. "This guy—all he does is complain about it. Sally Sensitive would rather stay inside with his puzzles."

Nibs grumbled something under his breath, picked up a stray twig from the ground and traced designs in the dirt. Michael watched him for a long minute; when he raised his head to look about him again, Twins stood beside John. The strange man was staring wide-eyed at Michael's partner, like a small child examining a new and strange insect.

"What's your last name, John? Does it start with a J by any chance? You know, to give you a double initial?"

John shifted his weight from foot to foot.

"No, it's Darling. My last name is Darling." He scratched his neck nervously. "Hey—is there any place I can take a leak around here? I really gotta go."

Twins cocked his head slightly to the right, toward a gathering of scrub trees and overgrowth a few yards away. "Sure thing, *Darling*: right in that brush. Watch out for the twisted roots and sharp rocks. Damn near twisted my ankle the other night, walking through there in the dark."

John nodded and sprinted in the direction of the shrubbery. He stumbled up the embankment and disappeared behind a bush. As he did so, Nibs dropped his stick and followed him.

"So," Michael said, training his eyes on the bush, silently willing John to reappear. "You said Mary suggested that you stay around here. Does that mean none of you are from New England?"

Peter was busy picking up dried leaves from the ground and tossing them into the fire and did not respond.

A long, uncomfortable minute went by.

Finally, Nibs emerged from the brush; his hands were shoved deep in his pockets.

"I'm from the Bay area," Nibs said, as if a part of the conversation all along. "Presidio Heights, in particular, though I traveled a bit when I was younger: Napa Valley, Riverside...even down to Lake Tahoe for a short while. You could do that back in the 60s: hitchhike your way all over California."

The 60s?

Michael frowned. The man looked no older than thirty-five, forty at the most. It was his glasses—the thick, Mid-Century-modern frames—and the 1950s hairstyle that aged him. Michael doubted that Nibs had been alive in the 60s, never mind wandering about like a free love tourist, but he decided to play along, at least until John returned and the two of them could make their way back up to the lighted trail and toward home.

"That sounds exciting. I haven't traveled much. I'd like to—I just don't have the means right now. I did study abroad in college, spent some time in Barcelona."

He pronounced the city *Bar-theh-LOH-nah* in a perfect Castilian accent then immediately regretted it. He sounded like a snob.

"Europeans are so traditional," Peter said. "Stuck in their own circle of hell, never learning from their mistakes."

Peter's voice held a slight lilt, a hint of an accent not present before.

"As I'm sure you've surmised, I'm from London originally. East End, to be exact." He smiled, and his teeth glimmered slightly in the firelight. "Of course, I haven't been back in a very, very long while."

Nibs and Twins looked at each other and smiled.

Mary Parsons pushed a limp strand of hair behind her ear, exposing a large silver-colored hoop earring to glint in the firelight.

"Last time I was out in these parts, I was accused of consorting with the devil: can you believe that?"

A haggard cacophony spilled from her mouth, a wet mixture of cough and laughter.

"Imprisoned but beat the charge. Could you beat that? A witch? Me?" She cackled.

Michael glanced again at the bush where John had disappeared. "What were the charges?"

"I just told you: witchcraft," Mary said, her voice angry. "Are you deaf?"

Nibs grunted but offered nothing else, resigned to drawing in the dirt with his stick.

Michael's back stiffened. "No...what I mean is, that's not a real charge in Massachusetts...the last case was at the end of the nineteenth century, I believe."

"You calling me a liar?" Mary spat.

A hand gripped Michael's upper arm, making him flinch. Twins had sidled up to him.

"Now, now, Mary, dear. No need to get excited." He squeezed Michael's arm, then relaxed his hand, but he did not let go. "You're in pretty good shape, my friend. How old are you, exactly?"

"Twenty-eight." Michael hesitated. His anxiety grew thicker. He needed to retrieve John and get back into the parking lot and call an Uber. "Listen—"

"I remember twenty-eight," said Peter dreamily. "I always said I wouldn't live a life of regret, but that's my one. I should've started traveling while I was nineteen."

He kicked the edge of the fire with the toe of his boot. The flames sizzled.

"After all, if one is going to be trapped in one vessel for all eternity, one must select the encasement carefully."

Michael took two quick steps toward the bush, but Twins held his sleeve.

"John?" Michael's call sounded tiny and hollow. "*John?*"

Ignoring the outburst, Peter walked over to Michael, looking him over like a target, then slowly grabbed the Irish cap off of Michael's head and placed it on his own.

"All four of us have been traveling for quite some time. Mary's been out the longest, then me, then Nibs and Twins. But even when we weren't a team, we were the same: we all discovered at some point the secret to a very, very long life." He touched the cap lightly and smiled. "I like to think of us as the Found Boys."

Michael swallowed. "Why is that?"

Twins moved his hand around Michael's back and gripped his opposite shoulder in an awkward side-hug, voice dropping in his ear. "Because we aren't *lost*. Just...misplaced."

He issued a hearty laugh and shook Michael back and forth like the two men were swaying in time to a musical tune.

Peter smiled. "You see, Peter Pan's boys...well, they wanted to remain young and carefree forever, but they never really zeroed in on how to sustain that youth, both in soul and body, without being trapped in one place. Never perfected a *game plan* for the long haul, I guess you'd say."

Michael looked at him, then toward the bush where John had disappeared, then to Nibs, who was still sketching aimlessly in the dirt, circles with plus symbols inside, an array of crosshairs over and over in the space of earth along the side of the campfire. Nibs looked up from his work and stared at Michael. His face was blank, an executioner's mask.

Michael pushed Twins away and ran sideways around Peter and up the embankment where his partner had disappeared. He stumbled but caught himself, reaching the edge of the overgrowth.

"Watch your step there, mate. Lots of bottles and jagged rocks around to trip you," Peter said.

A round of laughter followed.

Sure enough, as soon as Michael entered the brush, his foot caught on something hard and sturdy, and his body propelled forward, into the bush, then onto the wet ground. A searing pain shot into his ankle, and when Michael tried to pull his foot forward, he found that it had been caught under an exposed root. From under the lowest branches, the campfire glowed with the four killers surrounding it.

When he spread an arm to lever himself to stand, his hand brushed something soft and familiar. He ran his fingers along the object, trying to identify it. Hair. John's hair. Searching for his partner's face, he encountered something wet and warm and sticky dripping onto the cold earth instead. His eyes adjusted, making out the fresh gunshot at his partner's temple.

The four no longer surrounded the campfire.

Hands gripped his legs, and Michael was being pulled backward.

Nibs rolled Michael onto his back. Mary leaned forward and unbuttoned his dress shirt, exposing his goose-bumped flesh to the moonlight.

When a scalpel flashed in Peter's hands, the Found Boys waited with great anticipation for their leader to free the life force from Michael's body so that they might devour it.

And Michael squeezed his eyes shut, praying it would be quick.

THE THICKENING

THEY CALLED IT THE Thickening.

Originally, the media tried on a number of monikers, attempting to incorporate the disease's unfortunate first benefactor, Trevor Davison, a hip-hop artist who rose to fame purely through self-produced YouTube videos and guerilla-style social media bombing. Davison was only twenty-four when the first symptoms appeared. He displayed episodes of confusion, started missing appointments, even had to halt recording sessions because he couldn't remember the words to his own song. His entourage chalked it up to drugs, maybe a bit of day-drinking. His girlfriend attributed it to stress. *He must have overextended himself.*

But his mother Joanna? She recognized that it had to be something organic.

The doctors rendered a hesitant diagnosis of early-onset Alzheimer's disease, but they were perplexed. Davison was showing other signs atypical of Alzheimer's patients. For one, his symptoms had come on all of a sudden and in full force: One day he was focused, energetic, and articulate, the next, he was confused, lethargic, and garbling even the simplest of sentences. In addition, Davison would have cursory moments of clarity; he'd speak lucidly to others for hours on end, but within the conversation, he'd spontaneously drift off, sometimes breaking his locution in mid-word. An hour or so later, he'd become intelligible again, but the coherence never lasted more than a day. And unlike in Alzheimer's, there seemed no rhyme or reason to when his communication breakdown would begin; there was no so-called "sundowning" as the afternoon stretched into evening.

Trevor, and those who were diagnosed after him, simply slowed; their communication abilities congealed like viscous liquids—*thickened*. The affected became toys who'd been played with too long or smartphones that were too out of date to accept the most recent software upgrade: they glitched, they did not respond to commands, and soon, they would stop working altogether.

Joanna's documentation of her son's progression transpired accidentally. As his first fan turned tour manager and public relations director, she had always carefully chronicled his every creation from his first notions of prose to the final, sample-woven track. Soon, she had armed herself with five separate cell phones with the most advanced photo and video capabilities and quickly became an expert in rapid image editing, and when his YouTube follower number reached one million, she hired three assistants to film, edit, and post twenty hours of each day in shifts.

"Jesus, Ma—" Trevor held his hand backwards over his face like he was shielding himself from the glare of a searchlight. "I'm eating breakfast, fah Christ's sake." With his free arm, he shoveled a heaping spoonful of sugary cereal into his mouth, the sloppy overflow of milk dripping down his chin and onto his tank top.

Joanna held the camera steady. "T, your fans are watching. They want to know everything about you. Don't leave them hangin'!"

And with this, her son put down his arm, quickly wiped the milk from his face and chest, and smiled brightly into the lens. He closed his eyes and began to sing a cappella, resting his palm on his stomach to feel his own breath.

Social media junkies bathed in Davison's Instagram, Facebook, Twitter, and TikTok updates, and when his Periscope recordings expanded to a minimum of eight hours per day, he sometimes attracted an audience of fifty thousand, often nudging out the White House in popularity during times of peace.

And then, during one of Trevor's live recording sessions, his mind began to skip, an ancient LP record traced by a dull needle. And Joanna continued to film.

· · · • · • · • · · ·

Miriam Cavanaugh had worked her whole career at the Centers for Disease Control and Prevention.

Originally from Springfield, Massachusetts, she had earned a full scholarship to Penn State, and though she completed her doctoral work back in the Commonwealth at MIT, she found herself pulled southward again when the government agency wooed her, desiring her expertise in the domestic transference of communicable diseases. It had taken some resolve to adjust to Atlanta's sweltering summers, but by the time she had settled into permanent housing and delivered a son, her body had acclimated.

It was on a Monday that she sat at her desk in the lab and reviewed the most recent spinal tap samples from patients exhibiting symptoms of the mysterious brain disorder that had been slowly devouring the nation. A number of the newest cases appeared much milder than the older, better known ones. The President himself, for example, had contracted the affliction, though it didn't prevent him from powering through the fog to send regular, often disjointed and nonsensical tweets to his devout followers.

Miriam could not determine why any of this was so. The easiest—and most desirable— explanation was that the disease was simply disappearing as quickly as it arrived.

At first, Davison's Dementia, as Miriam nicknamed it—The Thickening seemed too much like a B-movie title to her—had appeared to afflict celebrities, movie stars, and recording artists almost exclusively. Upon further inspection, however, it seemed to correlate with how large of a digital footprint the affected individual possessed. The more Google hits a patient gleaned within a simple web search, the more severe and quickly his or her dissension was into unintelligible rambling.

"Sounds like we need a social scientist here, not a microbiologist," her lab mate Bridget joked when the research group met to analyze the lack of a disease transference trail. Her colleagues laughed, and Bridget turned to face Miriam. "Speaking of which, how is David?" she asked.

Miriam thought she saw a bit of a wink in her eye above the woman's wide smile.

She grinned slyly back at her but said nothing.

Her son was a graduate student in anthropology, and he had returned home the previous week to spend some time with friends and with her before the next semester began. David was darkly handsome with high cheekbones, and people—even those in solidly cemented relationships like Bridget—salivated over him. But Miriam was fiercely protective of her only child. He was still young and the last thing he needed was to be hunted, a big net thrown over his broad, athletic body, and dragged kicking and screaming into the chains of commitment.

Anthony, another member of the group, was saying something, but Miriam had been too lost in her own thoughts to have been listening. "I'm sorry—what was that?" she stammered, embarrassed at her distraction.

Anthony buttoned and unbuttoned the cuff on his left sleeve. "We were saying that nowhere in our initial findings does it suggest that screen viewing time has any effect on the disease: neither its infection nor its progression." He rubbed his palms together. "The symptoms seem to be limited to those who are the subjects of online activity—photographs, videos, and the like—those being watched, not the watchers themselves."

"No direct contact transmission," added Bridget. "It's not passed through physical contact nor through bodily fluids. No indirect contact either: animals and insects appear to be unaffected, and there's nothing connecting it to water, food source, or air contaminants either, at least at this point."

Miriam tapped her jaw with her finger. "We're still looking at the spinal fluid transmutation. The viscosity is markedly different in patients showing symptoms—"

"But it's still unclear if the thickening happens all at once or is progressive," Bridget added quickly. "If the fluid shows signs of exposure to the virus or mutation or..."

"We don't even know if it IS a virus," Miriam pointed out. "We haven't isolated one. Not in the bloodstream, not in spinal fluid, nowhere as of yet." She paused. "And god, I hate that term, *thickening*. It makes the body sound like a bouillabaisse."

Anthony began typing frantically on his iPad and the notes appeared on the projected board behind him. "So, it's all suspect-but-not-prove as of now. We know there's a change in spinal fluid consistency. We know patients exhibit changes in thought processes, speech patterns, and states of consciousness."

"And there's some sort of connection to social media presence..." Bridget added.

"Suspect, can't prove. Connection, maybe. Causation? Unclear."

Miriam raised her voice. "So, why is it dissipating?"

The three were silent for a minute. Miriam continued. "Why, after such a flourishing of new cases for months, are we seeing a dramatic dip in infections? Why is the disease waning in some while it continues to spike in others?"

Again, the room fell to a hush. "Schadenfreude phenomenon?" Anthony said and emitted a low chuckle.

"Come again?"

"If it's true that the disease strikes patients based on their social media presence, maybe people are too busy watching the celebrities die to post their own updates, photographs, and videos," he said somberly. "There's nothing more entertaining than watching someone self-destruct."

• • • • • • • • • •

Joanna knew better than to put down the camera. In the early 1990s, she'd joined friends on a coastal pilgrimage to the Pacific Northwest. The

Seattle music scene was raging, and her friend Marlene played a mean bass and dated a decent-looking drummer named George, and by some serendipitous accident, they'd befriended a guitarist they called FlapJack who owned the kind of windowless van Joanna thought only belonged to predatory pedophiles and government surveillance groups.

On their journey up the coast, they'd stopped in Los Angeles and the four piled into a roach-friendly hotel for a few hours of shuteye. Joanna, who'd slept most of the day curled up around a beaten-up amp that rubbed raw the skin along her upper arm, was not tired, so she curiously ventured out alone in West Hollywood, hoping to ferret out a cheap drink or a free show.

As she neared a well-known bar that hosted the talent from the L.A. rock scene on the Sunset Strip, she spied a circle of onlookers, their mouths wide as two paramedics rushed to the aid of a collapsed patron on the sidewalk nearby. It wasn't until she had reached the crowd that she recognized the victim; the last time she had seen his face, it had been twenty feet wide and she'd dumped half her bag of popcorn onto a new pair of shorts, staining them with slippery, butter-flavored oil.

As the medical team hoisted the actor's lifeless body onto a stretcher, Joanna scanned the crowd. A man stood statue-like, holding a camera at his waist, its lens pointed at the ground. He hadn't taken one shot. Later, when Joanna stumbled upon an article about the fatal drug overdose, she spied a short blurb from the photographer. He stated that he hadn't taken any pictures out of respect for the performer's family.

"What an idiot," Joanna said, and she tossed the magazine in the trash.

· · • ● • ● • • ·

Miriam pushed her work shoes off without bothering to untie the laces, stripped down to her underwear, and stepped into a pair of running pants. She grabbed a t-shirt that had been draped over the back of a nearby chair and sniffed it. It was a few days past clean, but she didn't plan on seeing anyone that night, so she pulled it over her head and padded into the great room. There was still some Scotch in the crystal decanter her co-workers had bought her for a housewarming present many years back. She'd never gotten the gist of pouring liquor into special containers for display purposes, but she admitted, utilizing the vessel made her feel a bit more sophisticated when she drank alone.

She flopped onto her worn sofa and tucked her feet under her thighs. After flipping mindlessly through a series of sports commentary, home shopping, and crime reenactment shows, she finally settled on a softly-lit cooking program. The host, a grandfatherly-looking man with a beard too long to be sanitary for food preparation, stirred something methodically in a large chrome pot on a burner.

"There's nothing more delicious and satisfying on a cold fall evening than a dinner flavored with savory meat stock," he said, staring flatly into the camera. "While you may reduce a large pot of homemade stock reduced down to a *demi-glace*, or, even further, to a *glace de viande*, it is of the utmost importance that you do not simmer for an extended amount of time, or the aromatic texture will evaporate along with much of the liquid content.

"Similarly, thickening into a sauce will intensify flavor and create a more appealing texture. However, if you reduce your succulent stock too long, its flavor will flatten, and attempting to revive the sauce by adding water will be fruitless. The damage is already done."

The man paused and drew his wooden spoon up from the pot and brought the tip to his mouth. As he slowly parted his lips to taste the concoction, David's voice materialized behind Miriam, startling her.

"Sounds delightful," he said, pouring a bottle of water into a glass. He rubbed the inside of his ear and squinted at the television. "Since when do you watch cooking shows?"

"Since when do I cook?" quipped Miriam.

David walked to the front of the sofa and sat down hard next to his mother. He always did that: practically falling into chairs with such force, one would think his body was made of solid lead.

Miriam turned to look at her son. "Do you have an Instagram account? Or a Facebook?"

He smiled conspiratorially and sipped his drink before responding. "Why? Are you planning on following me?"

She ignored his playfulness. "What about a TikTok account? Do you make YouTube videos?"

David smiled. "No, I don't have any of those things. No Twitter either, which is sometimes a disadvantage because a lot of people only communicate through their social media accounts these days. I miss a party invite or a big announcement because I am out of the loop."

"So, then, why don't you have them? The accounts?"

David thought for a moment. "Honestly, first it was because you scared the bejesus out of me about what potential college admission counselors and then desirable employers might find out." He laughed. "Not that I'm living some sort of wild, secret life or anything. But I don't know...I guess I'm comfortable just living life as I see it. Maybe I'm behind the times. There have been plenty of cultures who shunned movies and photography."

"In this day and age? I find it hard to believe anyone could avoid cameras these days," said Miriam.

"Yes, well, there have always been slightly ominous connotations associated with recording a person's likeness. The Amish dissuade photography for religious reasons. If a person consents to being photographed, he or she is allowing a graven image to be created, and that is a sinful action. When interest in photography began to build in the mid 1800s, superstitions sprang up, such as in a picture of three people, the person in the middle would be the first to die."

David paused to finish the rest of the water in his glass.

"And, of course, there are the Kayapo of the Amazon. In their native language, the phrase *akaron kaba* translates to both 'take a photograph' and 'steal one's soul.'"

He paused again, staring at his mother without expression.

"I don't think that was accidental, do you?"

· · · · ● · ● · · ·

Joanna pawed the screen of her Smartphone awkwardly with her index finger, the long, polished nail scraping the edge with every swipe, making a squeaking sound. On the muted television above the microwave, a 24-hour news station featured an interview with a representative from the CDC as a ticker scrolled excitedly along the bottom of the screen: *Apple releases newest iPhone model...NASDAQ in third day of steady decline...sudden deaths of Singer sisters reinvigorates lipstick line*, the last notation referencing a pair of tabloid celebrities who had become famous simply by starring in their family's vacuous reality series and launching their own line of lip plumpers and butt padding. Joanna owned three tubes of the former; she didn't need the latter.

When the camera's eye gazed upon the scientist from the CDC, a caption below her image read *Government agency discourages people from participating in social media*. Joanna rolled her eyes and with some effort, managed to hit the MUTE button on the remote control and the sound roared to life.

"Are you telling the American public to stay off of Facebook?" asked the interviewer incredulously.

"We're saying, stop filming yourself and posting the images online, at least until we have a better idea of what is happening here. For your own health and safety," answered Miriam. "You can visit as many social media sites as you wish."

The interviewer crossed his arms over his chest. "But without someone to watch, what's the point of going online?"

Joanna hit the POWER button on the remote and the screen image sucked itself into a tiny glittering spark and turned black. Still clutching her phone, she walked down the hall and into the guest room. The lighting was dim, and although it was the middle of the day, all of the window shades were pulled. She flicked the switch on the wall just inside the doorway and paused as her eyes adjusted.

In the bed, nearly motionless, lay her son. His eyes twitched and followed her as Joanna walked to the side of the mattress where his body was completely prostrated. She rested her phone on the nightstand, grabbed Trevor's shoulders, and awkwardly pulled him upward so that he was half-sitting, half leaning on the stack of pillows propped against the headboard.

"How's my superstar today?" she asked him.

Without waiting for a response, she grabbed her phone and opened the camera, then connected to the live feed. As she pointed the lens at her son, a distorted response emanated from his mouth.

"Meeeee," Trevor said. "Ma...no, please," he continued, a few wisps of clarity breaking free. "No...more," he pleaded. "Me...no..."

His voice drifted off and he turned his head away from the phone five feet from his face.

"T, your fans want to know how you're doing." Joanna's disembodied voice wafted from behind the electronic eye. "They are anxious for you to recover and go back on tour, my love. Tell them how much they mean to you," his mother commanded.

"Me..." Trevor's voice was only a whisper. "Me. Meee..." he repeated, still looking in the other direction.

Joanna could see a trickle of drool sliding down the side of his mouth, and she reached out and officiously wiped it away, hoping the fans hadn't noticed. Her touch seemed to set into motion a shiver that began in her son's mouth and wound its way down his neck and intensified as it reached his spine. Trevor began to buck and seize, his body flailing back and forth; his head struck the wooden headboard repeatedly, the sound of a baseball struck by a bat over and over, a home-run hit on instant replay.

Joanna did not move. She watched as her son thrashed about for a full minute then was perfectly still. As life leaked from him, his eyes glazed and emptied their memories, and his mouth slacked into a rubber mask, one religiously bleached tooth peering out from behind parted lips.

Joanna was still holding the camera. She hadn't tilted it even an inch.

She swiped her finger sideways and looked at Trevor's video feed. She watched, mesmerized, as his follower numbers doubled, then tripled. The wide expanse of universe had witnessed her only child's violent escape from it. Countless viewers would replay the clip in their feeds, his immolation to immortality.

Joanna sat down on the bed softly next to Trevor, taking great care not to jostle his soft body, and settled into a comfortable position. Then, she turned the camera to focus on her own face.

She cleared her throat, smiled prettily into the gaping black hole of the lens, and welcomed her captive audience.

WENDIGO

PENNY SURREPTITIOUSLY GLANCED AT her watch: it was only six o'clock. It was late winter, and the dying sunlight drizzled languidly through the window. A half-naked maple tree danced drunkenly on the lawn outside. Penny could hear the shrieks of children playing somewhere nearby. These were children from the neighboring homes that stayed warm and toasty from October through April and bundled themselves in blankets of fresh, green lawns from May through September.

She herself lived in a poor but eerily quiet district of the city. The nearest house was a good ten-minute walk down the road; she never thought to draw her curtains at night, although the draftiness forced her to cover her windows with plastic sheeting each year, making her feel like a strange bug being slowly cocooned. Once upon a time, Penny had ambitions of wealth, but those were soon dashed, and it was just as well.

It wasn't that Brian Shea was a difficult patient. He was generally agreeable, fought her only on the rare occasion that he was under the weather or cranky, and most nights, he was perfectly content to lie in bed, staring blankly at the television on his bureau, binge-watching a comedy series or police procedural without any conversation. That was the hardest part of her job, as far as Penny was concerned: keeping the mindless chatter going day after day. But Brian kept to himself more often than not, and she had grown relatively comfortable to the silence that grew between them each evening as the sun set.

As a licensed nurse, Penny would have gleaned a more lucrative salary had she selected a position in a hospital or physician's practice, but working as a caretaker provided her with a more tranquil schedule and much less paperwork. Her last client had been a woman in her eighties named Stella Lewandowski. Stella had a mild case of dementia, and Penny had worked the day shift then, eight in the morning until five at night, escaping the worst of her client's confusion just as the sun began to disappear and her relief arrived to take over. Penny had her own demons at home, and an overnight run seemed like a good opportunity to refocus them, so when Stella finally passed—her frail, powdery body discovered in an awkward clump on the floor next to the bed one stormy afternoon—Penny specifically requested an evening shift for her next placement, and her tour with Brian began.

Brian Shea was atypical of her standard clientele. A robust man in his early forties, he was broad-shouldered and athletic with a handsome, square jaw, and he worked as a systems analyst for a financial planning agency in the city. After a bizarre snowboarding accident while on holiday in Glen Shee a month ago, Brian had been frustrated to learn he'd be bedridden at home for at least ten weeks with two broken legs and a fractured wrist. He was a lifelong bachelor and, with no family to care for him full-time, he'd hired a nurse to tend to him during the days while he telecommuted to work, often wearing a custom-tailored dress shirt and tie over a pair of boxer shorts to engage in corporate Skype meetings in front of his laptop's webcam.

It wasn't until the night terrors began that Brian decided to hire an overnight nurse to stay with him.

The first one had happened out of the blue. He awoke disorientated, gasping for breath as he stared at the blue digital numbers on his alarm clock. Two o'clock. His sheets were soaked with sweat, and the skin on his back felt chafed and tender from lying in the quickly cooling wetness. There was a loud pounding on the door in the kitchen as Brian blinked furiously, trying to recall where he was and what had happened. The room was dark, darker than he could ever remember it being. It was only when he tried to climb out of bed that he remembered the two casts weighing down the lower half of his body.

"Fuck!" he cried out in frustration. The knocking stopped. A moment later, Brian's cell phone rang, the illuminated screen casting an alien glow over his nightstand. He grabbed the phone and tapped the green AN-SWER icon. "Hello?"

"Mr. Shea? Brian? It's Jade from next door," said a small voice. "I...we heard you screaming and...and I just wanted to check that you were al-right," she explained. "I'm sorry if I startled you. I know it's very late."

Screaming?

He hadn't remembered screaming, but now that he was speaking out loud, his throat felt raw.

"Yes," he began, "yes, Jade, I'm fine. Just a nightmare, I suppose."

Jade was quiet, and for a moment, Brian wondered if she'd hung up. Then she said, "Oh, alright...I was just concerned because...well, with three broken bones, you can never be too careful, you know, about the possibility of a fat embolism." Her voice drifted away from the phone at the end, like she was falling backwards, away from the receiver.

"I'm sorry, what was that?" Brian asked. "A *fat* embolism?"

"Yes, well, my uncle, he broke his femur once, falling off of a ladder. It was a pretty bad break, too: the doctors weren't sure if they'd have to put a few pins in it to keep it together." Brian could hear her swallow. "Basically, when you break a major bone, a piece of bone marrow fat can escape and float into the bloodstream. In extreme cases, it can kill you, but before that, there are all sorts of nasty symptoms. One day, my uncle had no idea who we were—started screaming just like we heard you doing, and well, I know you are alone here at night and pretty much trapped in bed." Brian blinked his eyes, his vision slowly adjusting to the darkness. "It's important to be a good neighbor," he heard Jade say finally.

Brian blinked again. He could make out the shape of his legs, useless tree trunks wrapped in white gauze under the blankets, his feet two pointy lumps a few inches from the edge of the mattress.

"Thank you, Jade," he said finally. "I'm fine. Thank you for checking."

He clicked the red END CALL icon without waiting for her to say goodbye.

Brian looked in the direction of the window next to the bed. A long sliver of brightness peeked out from the slits of pane visible on each side of the drawn shade. He heard the house quietly shudder as it settled and braced itself against the late February wind gusts. Snippets of the dream he'd experienced just moments earlier flashed in front of his eyes. There had been snow, he was certain of that: a lot of snow. He saw the side of a mountain. He had been sitting—no, *lying* on some sort of narrow plateau in the middle of nowhere. Bright, new snow covered everything in sight, tickling the tops of the pine trees in the distance; spreading like warm butter across the empty foot or so of space in front of him.

He could not see what was beyond the cliff's edge, but he had felt a sense of fear.

Was that what had made him scream?

Something had happened on that cliff...but what?

He couldn't remember. After the sudden wakes and the soaked sheets and the intermittent calls from Jade continued for a week straight, he made up his mind to hire a night nurse. If it was some sort of medical issue, a fatty embolism or whatever Jade had mentioned, there would be someone there to help him, and even if it weren't, at least he wouldn't have to lie in cold, wet sheets for hours until the day shift nurse arrived.

A reticent, pale young woman named Penelope began work two nights later. She asked Brian to call her Penny. Her smile was warm and her manner pleasant, but his nightmares remained.

· · · ● · ● · ● · · ·

Penny rubbed the cuticle bed of each individual finger and took a deep breath. Brian was an easy patient all right, but the nights were getting longer and longer. There were only so many episodes of *Law and Order* she could watch in one evening. Her patient subscribed to the maximum number of cable channels, yet only wanted to watch the same one, night after night.

Once Brian was asleep, she could sneak away to his guest bedroom next door and take a long nap. The biggest advantage of taking care of a man with two broken legs was it was a near certainty he wouldn't be creeping over to assault her while she slept. He was pretty much cemented in place. Even with assistance, Brian had difficulty moving his awkward body. On the multiple instances when she had changed his sweat-soaked sheets, it took her nearly an hour to alternately roll and pull his torso over and away from her, though she had been getting better at it. He was cumbersome, but not impossible to adjust. Left to his own devices, however, he'd be trapped on the bed indefinitely.

When her eyes drifted from the television set back to her patient, she jumped to discover he had been staring at her. For how long, she didn't know.

"Are you all right?" she asked him. "Do you need anything?"

He continued to look at her blankly for a long second, then he responded flatly, "Tell me a story about your other jobs, your other patients." He smiled at her. "You must have some creepy tales, working the graveyard shift and all. Though I expect they don't like you to use that term," he winked.

Penny snorted, then felt her cheeks flush.

She smiled self-consciously. "Not particularly. You're my first overnight patient," she said. "I used to work days. Not a lot of things creeping around in the daylight."

They were both quiet for a moment.

Then, Brian continued. "I used to be terribly afraid of the dark as child. My mum put a nightlight in the bathroom to placate me, but even then..." His voice drifted off and he turned at looked at the television screen, lost in thought. "It's funny: I remember being fifteen and still needing that light. I had just read Stephen King's *The Shining* and the woman in the bathtub, she scared the bejesus out of me. I could see the edge of our standing shower from my bed, you know, and something about the eerie glow of the nightlight on that frosted vinyl curtain... I don't know. It just made the whole thing worse. I didn't really grow out of it until I went away to school, and even then, I'd be up most of the night in the dorm anyway, studying or whatever. I never really slept in the dark until I got my own place. I don't know that I ever got used to it." He looked back at Penny, then nodded at the heavy black flashlight standing on his nightstand. "Silly, right?"

Penny looked down at her hands. It wasn't silly at all to her, but she wasn't about to share her personal issues with a patient. She couldn't tell him that it was the darkness that had pushed her to take the overnight shift in the first place.

She didn't know how to explain that there were some things that night-lights and visiting nurses couldn't scare away.

· · • · • · • · • ·

The ritual happened every night, without fail.

It wasn't enough for Penny to check under the bed.

No, she had to slowly open the closet door, push the cramped dresses and blouses aside, and peer cautiously around the back wall, aiming her flashlight at the corner. She'd mistake the indecipherable shadows of her dowdy clothing making odd shapes as monsters if she didn't look long and hard. He wasn't there.

Next, she walked to the other side of her bed, the two feet of space where she had sandwiched her nightstand, and the yellow beam of light flickered along the wisps of dust on the hardwood floor.

No one.

As an extra precaution, she lifted the bed skirt on this side of the mattress, squatted from a safe distance, and looked. The space appeared empty, but just as Penny clicked the switch to OFF, she swore she saw a flash of grey moving. She quickly slid the switch to ON and checked again. She bent forward and silently crept closer to the bed frame to investigate, all the while holding the light in front of her like an acolyte's offering.

There it was: a scraggly pile of grey matter, ancient and crumpled, a mummified hand with its fingernails jammed into its palm.

As she stared at it, trying to get a better look, it shook ever so slightly. Penny flinched, her hand lost its grip on the flashlight, sending its cheap plastic casing to the hard floor, and the illumination died with a sharp crack. Shrinking backward and half crab-walking back to the foot of the bed, she scrambled to her feet and once she was righted, grabbed the lamp from the nightstand, shucked the shade from its top, and pulled the light to the floor to shine the naked bulb under the bed. The grey hand was not a hand at all, but a clump of pet hair and dust bunny, and as Penny waved the light closer, its feathery ends waved in the resulting breeze.

She was alone, at least for that night, but she was certain he'd be back.

Six months earlier she had developed a terrible cough, one that kept her up for hours at night and prevented her from reaching deep sleep. Her throat felt like she had gargled glass, but much worse than the pain was the lethargy that resulted from her restlessness. As she lay in bed, tapping her phone screen to play along with a monotonous puzzle app in the hope of lulling her exhausted mind back to sleep, she could hear the far-away ticking of the battery-operated clock in the kitchen. The room was dark, and the brightness of her screen blinded Penny from seeing anything more than two feet in front of her.

She coughed into her shoulder, wincing as the hot sting seared her throat. Her eyes watered.

Tick-tick-tick, cough.

Tick-tick, cough.

Tick-tick-tick—

She sat up in bed, letting the glowing screen drop face-down into her lap. There was another sound, something under the ticking. She pawed her nightstand, trying to reach the switch on the small lamp, but in her frantic attempt to turn on the light, she knocked it out of her arm's reach. Cursing, she felt along her thighs for her phone.

Tick-tick-tick-tick...inhale, exhale.

There it was again. This time, Penny was sure she had heard it. Under the metallic clicking of the clock was a warm sound, a heavy sound: the sound of someone breathing hard.

Penny pressed the HOME button on her phone and slid her finger up the screen to turn on her flashlight. Slowly, she aimed the beam at the wall closest to her, then tilted the screen sideways to scan the entire room. Shadows danced in the crude illumination but Penny spotted no face, no hulking body, no ominous form lurking in her room. She held her breath. *Tick-tick-tick*...the clock continued on, relentless and unmoved by Penny's panic. She continued to hold her breath, convinced that if she could be as silent as death, she'd prove to herself that she'd been hearing things.

Her flashlight stopped on the open door to the hallway. The door was not flush to the wall behind it. In fact, it was pushed away from the wall about six inches, noticeably narrowing the doorway. Penny could see the dark outline of the arm to her heavy flannel bathrobe that hung behind the door. It was a thick robe, but the door was pushed forward much further than it should have been.

Penny crouched forward, resting her weight on her left hand while keeping the phone's light steady in her right. She kept her eyes trained on the arm of the bathrobe, trying to convince herself that no, it hadn't just moved. No, it really was her bathrobe; it was definitely not the arm of a man-like creature standing just behind the door, waiting and watching her as she slept.

Inhale. Exhale.

The sound was coming from behind the door. She leaned further forward, trying to glean a better look at the silhouette. Slowly, she shifted her weight and slid sideways to position herself on the edge of the mattress. She was so close to the door, she could almost reach out and touch its knob. If she could leap from the bed in one swift movement, a one-two step on the balls of her feet, she could propel herself out of the bedroom before he could reach out from the shadows and snatch her back inside, pull her back behind the door with him.

With the precision of a predatory cat, Penny stretched her legs to touch the cold wood floor with her toes. Ever so slowly, she relaxed her feet to place her soles fully on the ground and concentrated her strength in her thighs and left arm. Taking a final deep breath, she pushed herself from the bed and dashed from the room, breaking into a full sprint as soon as she was upright. Just before she was out of reach of the bed, she felt the stroke of bony fingers caress her right shoulder; her whole body flinched, and she dropped her phone and heard it sail under the bed as she rushed down the hall toward the front room. She continued to run until she was out of the house and had climbed into her car, locked the doors, and curled up in the back seat.

Long after the sun had resumed its place in the sky, she returned to the house. Her phone had been placed face-up on the nightstand. The cover was cracked.

· · · ● · ● · ● · ·

Brian snapped his fingers. "Earth to Penelope? Anyone home?"

She shook her head slightly and forced a smile on her face. "I'm so sorry—I got lost in thought for a bit there. Please forgive me," she said to her patient and rose to stretch her legs. "What do you say we play a board game? Some cards maybe? Enough of this television for now," she said, snatching the remote from its constant presence next to Brian's hip.

Brian grabbed for the controller at the same time, and the collision of their hands pushed the small box off the mattress and onto the floor. Penny crouched to retrieve it, her knees making dry cracking noises as she sunk into a squat and placed her hand on the bedspread to steady herself. Brian stared at her hand on the edge of the bed.

Snow, a plateau of snow.

He once again saw the side of the mountain from his dream. The snow had been everywhere, a carpet of white bunting rolled out along the cliff where he sat. It spread to the very edge of the cliff where... where the hand appeared. The image materialized, the rest of the nightmare finally clear. A gaunt, decomposing hand reaching up from below, stretching toward

Brian, reaching to use his leg... for leverage? To pull itself up? No. Brian shivered and finally understood. The creature that belonged to the hand wasn't climbing onto the plateau: it was reaching to pull Brian down with it. In the final seconds before he had awoken screaming in his sweat-soaked bed, the monster had thrust itself over the rock face and onto Brian. The last image in his memory was of its ashen face, its wet, black eyes staring straight into his while the gaping maw of a mouth, awash with jagged yellow teeth, opened wide to attach itself to his flesh.

Brian placed his hand over Penny's and squeezed. "Could I have a glass of water, please? I feel a bit sick," he said. "Perhaps cards later, yeah?"

Penny stood up and placed the remote on the nightstand. "Of course. Give me a minute." She smoothed her pants and walked down the narrow hallway to the kitchen. She touched the switch on the wall as she entered, and the room glowed with light. The luminescence twinkled off of the stainless-steel appliances, glass cabinet doors, and chrome hardware; it danced along the immaculate marble countertops and over the tops of the ivory silk accent curtains. Penny opened the door above the wide double basin sink and removed a short tumbler. It was Irish crystal, like all of Brian's drinkware.

Penny had learned early on that although her patient lived in a mod-est-sized house, its furnishings were indicative of the utmost affluence.

As she was filling the glass with water, a loud rapping sounded from the door behind her. Without invitation, a tall woman with long, dark hair opened the door a foot and stuck her head inside.

"Hi," she said, not venturing further from the mudroom. "I'm Jade; I live next door. I'm sorry to barge in like this..."

She seemed to be waiting for Penny to coax her inside, but Brian had made no mention of a friend nearby, and it seemed inappropriate to allow a stranger into her client's home without his permission.

"Do you mind if I check with Mr. Shea?" said Penny with as much authority as she could muster. She cemented her feet in place and kept her eyes focused on the woman. Her dead stare seemed to communicate her uneasiness, as Jade pulled her head back into the foyer and shut the door softly.

"Of course," she said as it closed. "I'll wait right here."

Penny wanted to lock the deadbolt before leaving the kitchen, but the woman seemed harmless enough, so Penny walked briskly down the hall to the bedroom. She found her patient asleep, bright images from the television blinking quietly like soft lightning flashes about the room. She left the heavy glass of water on the nightstand next to the flashlight.

Returning to the kitchen, she glanced at her watch again.

Less than an hour had passed.

More out of boredom than anything else, she opened the kitchen door, a wide smile plastered across her face, and asked the woman to come inside.

Jade the neighbor was taller than Penny, but she was wearing platform boots that added at least three inches in height. Their soles must be made of rubber or some other soft material, Penny thought, as when the woman walked across the tile floor, she glided soundlessly, like a ghost. "Mr. Shea is asleep, but please, have a seat," Penny said, gesturing to the breakfast bar in the center of the room.

Jade climbed effortlessly onto the chair and rested her elbows on the marble top.

"So, how is Brian doing? I've stopped over now and again, just to check on him. Poor guy: he's rather imprisoned here, isn't he? Like an animal in a hunter's trap," she said, a small laugh dancing in her throat.

"Yes, I suppose," said Penny. There was something about the woman's familiarity that made her nervous. "It's very kind of you to check on his welfare. You live next door, you say?"

Jade drummed her fingers on the countertop. "Yes, in the house right there."

She gestured toward the far wall. There was no window in the vicinity, so when Penny turned to look in the indicated direction, she found herself staring at the refrigerator.

"Brian gave us a bit of a scare early on: did he tell you?" Jade continued. "Frightful nightmares. Screamed like you wouldn't believe: my dad and I heard him all the way in our house, and with all of the windows closed!" She touched her lips lightly with the tip of her finger. "The sound scared me something awful, to be honest. I've had a few bad dreams myself after hearing those shrieks." She looked down at the rings adorning her fingers, then back up at Penny. "I don't scare easily. I'm a writer, actually. Jade Wren." She offered her hand to the nurse and Penny shook it but said nothing. Jade continued as if she had. "Mostly horror. Fiction. A few commissioned research pieces here and there, just to pay the bills, but I like writing the dark stuff, really." She paused. "But Brian's screeching: it was visceral, you know?"

Penny smiled, unsure of what to say. She didn't want to breach patient confidentiality, and the woman's intentions were unclear. Jade didn't seem to be in any hurry to complete her business and leave.

"I apologize that Mr. Shea is unavailable. Perhaps you could try back in the morning?" she asked, hoping to guide the woman along her way.

At the same time, she was slightly grateful for the fresh company, so when Jade began to slide sideways from the chair and walked back toward the door, Penny felt a pang of regret at not having cultivated the conversation further.

"No worries," said Jade. "If he wakes up, let him know I stopped by." She waved slightly with her right hand, then pulled the door open and disappeared behind it.

Alone again, Penny walked to the door and ceremoniously turned the deadbolt. She hadn't remembered leaving it unlocked after she arrived—Brian had given her a key on the day she was hired—but it must have slipped her mind. She checked on her patient; he was still sleeping, quietly snoring with his mouth slightly agape, and she soundlessly clicked the button on the remote control to turn off the television.

She had nothing to occupy her time until Brian needed her again, and it was too early for her to nap in the guest room, so she took out her phone and typed *Jade Wren* into the internet search bar. Multiple images of young women, most of them making those duck faces that always irritated Penny, lined up in her search results, followed by a White Pages directory page, a Facebook link, a LinkedIn profile, and a strange YouTube video of a blonde child lip-synching to a 1980s pop single in German. She clicked on each of these pages but did not find the neighbor.

She changed her search to *Jade Wren horror* and was more successful. On an online retailer's page of Jade's books, she flipped through excerpts from an encyclopedia-like book of fables and legends Wren had titled *The Things that Go Bump in the Night*.

When she landed on one entry in particular, the Algonquin legend of the wendigo, she stopped to read the summary.

Out of the corner of her eye, Penny saw a grey shape sail down the hallway. She turned toward it quickly but it disappeared. *A figment of my imagination*, she thought. *That's all it is.* She laughed to herself and placed her cell phone in her back pocket, then thought better of it, remembering the smashed cover months earlier. She placed the phone delicately on the countertop and walked cautiously down the hallway toward Brian's bedroom.

Her patient was awake but groggy. He blinked at Penny. His body trembled a bit and his eyes grew wide. "What time is it?" he asked quickly.

Penny looked at her watch. "Almost eight. Still early. Are you hungry?" She glanced at the glass on the nightstand; all of the ice had melted. "More water?"

Brain's eyes darted about the room. In the dead quiet, the house creaked and shivered. "It's so quiet in the winter," Brian finally said. "All that snow. Too quiet, I think. Don't you agree?"

Penny sat on the edge of the bed and placed her hand on her patient's arm. They were both still, and then flinched simultaneously. Under the sound of the floorboards and baseboards and pipes readjusting, there was another noise. It was subtle, and when Brian looked to the nurse to see if she, too, had heard it, he was disquieted to find her countenance empty.

Inhale. Exhale.

Brian's eyes darted about the room, then he motioned with his head toward the closet. "It's in there," he whispered, his eyes wide and his expression feverish. "There's someone in the closet."

Penny scanned his face. He reminded her of her brother when he was a boy. He, too, had night terrors, and their mother worked second shift, so while on babysitting duty, she'd often encounter his fearful cries just when she herself was drifting off to dreamland. Each time he'd awaken,

Penny would stroke her brother's forehead and try to soothe him back to sleep, but for what seemed like an hour, his pupils stayed wide as saucers: a tiny boy on a terrifying acid trip. The scariest part for Penny, though, was what her brother would say, over and over. He insisted to Penny that the monsters of his nightmares were real.

"It's okay, Brian," Penny said. She rubbed his forearm slowly, up and down. "It was a nightmare. Here: drink some water." She brought the glass to his lips but he shooed it away.

"It wasn't a fucking nightmare," he replied. Penny could see the beads of sweat pooling in the folds on his forehead. "There's someone in the closet. Stop patronizing me and get a weapon." He frowned at her, snatched the flashlight from his nightstand, and nodded twice at the closet door. His voice now a whisper, he added, "Quick: there's a baton under the bed, near the headboard on this side."

Penny frowned. "A baton?"

"Yes, yes, a policeman's baton," said Brian quickly. "My father was a cop, and after he retired, my mom used to keep it in her car... in case of emergencies."

Penny knelt down, her bony knees pressing into the hardwood floorboards. She leaned her head under the box spring and looked.

"Just grab it, okay?" Brian called frantically. "It's right there, under the bed. Grab it."

Penny continued to look under the bed, saying nothing.

Brian tried to pull himself toward the edge of the bed. He managed to lean over far enough so that he could see the back of Penny's head. Her face was hidden by the bed linens.

"What's taking you so long?"

Finally, Penny reemerged clutching a black wooden bat about a foot in length with a short handle at a right angle to its base. She pushed herself up to a standing position once more and walked slowly but firmly toward the closet. Clenching the base of the bat with her right hand, she placed her left hand on the doorknob.

After taking a long and deep breath, Penny turned the knob clockwise and flung the door open wide.

Behind her, Brian shined his flashlight into the recesses of the walk-in closet. There was no one. Penny inched her way into the storage space, pushing suit jackets and dress shirts aside with the tip of her baton. Still nothing. Penny exited the closet and shut the door tightly behind her. She placed her hands on her hips and stared at her patient.

"I need you to lie back down and relax, okay?" she said softly. "I will put the TV back on and set the sleep timer."

"You heard it breathing just as I did," Brian insisted. "You know something was here."

Penny exhaled audibly. "I know no such thing. You had a terrible dream and it colored your perception. I know it seemed real, but we talked about this: that's what night terrors are. You hired me to get you through them." She pressed her open palm against the sheet near his back. It didn't feel damp. "Would you like me to change the sheets?"

Her patient scowled and looked away, toward the blank television screen.

"No. Thank you," he said curtly.

He picked up the remote from the nightstand and tapped the ON button.

Penny sat on the edge of the bed and placed her hand on Brian's forehead. She stroked his hair back gently, like a lover, and after a long moment, he closed his eyes. Disjointed pieces of dialogue from a 1990s sitcom drifted from the television speakers.

Penny waited. She methodically counted to twenty in her head and slowed her own excited breathing. She walked carefully around the bed, pulling out the tuck of the bottom sheet with her hand. When she had freed the sheet from its tethers, she returned to where she had been standing when they heard the breathing noise.

Then, without batting an eyelash, she grasped the bottom sheet with both hands and pulled it violently towards her, bringing her patient toward the edge of the mattress. She let go of the sheet, grabbed Brian's forearm and thigh, and rolled his body as hard as she could, sending him toppling onto the hard floor.

Stunned, Brian looked up at her. "Penny? What are you doing? Help m—"

Before he could complete his sentence, Penny shoved the patient halfway under the bed. She watched as the thin, grey claw of a hand reached out from under the bed and wrapped its long, pointed fingers around Brian's upper arm.

As Brian began to scream, the creature yanked its prey closer to its waiting mouth and began to feed.

Penny smiled.

Perhaps she would request a day shift for her next rotation.

At least for a little while, she was safe from the darkness.

Runaround Sue

We all loved Sue, even if her name wasn't Sue, but Vivian, or Sandra, or even MaryAnn.

To us, they were all Sues, and we cherished them like the fragile china dolls that they were.

Loved them, that is, until we caught sight of a chip or a scratch, something that ruined their resale value. Then, we traded them in for brand new models—a side-slab Lincoln Continental to replace the yawning Mark V, for instance—and everything was as it should have been again.

It was 1961, and the world was a young man's oyster.

Bill, Chuck, Francis, and I were those young men, and proud members of The Lodge. The place didn't need a specific affiliation. Folks around town knew there was only one men's club—and it was The Lodge. No religious or fraternal ornamentation necessary. The Lodge was, first and foremost, for stretching our masculine legs: shooting the shit, drinking to excess, and escaping on weekend-long fishing trips and stag parties (even though no one had any plans to catch trout or get married). Inevitably, these extended periods of time saturated in Y chromosomes led to occasional grudge exchanges about the womenfolk.

Chuck, we learned, suspected that his latest girlfriend had a wandering eye. We hadn't met Chuck's new doll, as no one fraternized outside of The Lodge, but we listened eagerly just the same. After all, what affected one brother, affected us all, one of the older members once explained. We presented Chuck with open ears of detached empathy then encouraged him to kick the girl to the curb forthwith. After the third bottle of whiskey was empty, we bade each other goodnight, and Chuck poured himself behind the wheel of his Thunderbird with the intent of stopping by ol' Susie's house on the way home.

He never made it.

Our first assumption was that he'd died in a one-car accident, dizzily wrapped his Ford four-seater around a tree or skidded off the interstate. Instead, his car was discovered parked neatly in a shopping plaza lot, the headlights off but the engine running, a pair of women's panties, still warm, hanging from the rearview mirror. Chuck was still warm as well, but cooling quickly. I suppose that's what happens when your chest cavity is carved open and most of your blood supply has poured forward from the gaping maw and onto your blue and white vinyl upholstery. Chuck's rib cage had been sawed through with a sharp serrated blade, his heart sliced nearly in two, a clean split right between the ventricles and the halves turned to expose the organ's meaty pulp like a peeled orange divvied into neat segments.

We gathered at The Lodge after the Saturday funeral mass, our ties already halfway off before we exited the church. Bill was halfway in the bag as well before beers were passed, his shaky hand repeatedly sliding a silver flask from the inside of his suit jacket to his lips and back again in an attempt to chase a Friday night hangover with hair of the dog.

"Don't bring up Chuck again," he moaned, draining the last of the flask's contents into his mouth.

"We just buried him, Billy," I said. "How could we not bring up Chuck?"

"Up chuck!" Francis guffawed. "Don't up chuck! You get it?" He slapped his knee with one hand while accepting a pint of suds with the other.

Bill leaned forward and rubbed small circles into his temples with his middle and forefingers. "It sure sounded like his Susie was playing back seat bingo with other guys. I told him: just move on, don't bother with a goodbye. But he had to confront her."

"It was just dumb bad luck," I said. "You're talking about a skirt. Chuck was murdered. By someone with surgical experience, likely. That alone eliminates the possibility of a doll as the culprit."

"Speaking of luck," Francis interjected, licking the white foam of his draft from his upper lip, "'landlord's on my back about the rent. You two cleaned me out last weekend."

"Ain't that a bite," Bill droned monotonously.

"Front me a bill and let's play a few hands," Francis offered pleadingly.

I stood up and stretched. "You're on," I said.

It was the last time we'd talk about Chuck. His name disappeared down the rabbit hole of ancient memory and never resurfaced, even after the next Lodge brother turned up on the coroner's table the very next month.

· · · · ● · ● · · ·

"Wise up, Daddy-o."

Francis raised an eyebrow but kept his focus on the cards in his hand as he tossed this bit of advice in the kitty in lieu of an ante.

"How's that?" Bill asked, consolidating his cards into a small pile in his palm. "You know something I don't?"

Francis wiggled the end of the Pall Mall around his mouth with his tongue. "All I'm saying is, any girl with that kind of tight social calendar ain't filling it with choir practices and sewing circles."

"Sewing circle? What in God's name is that?" I asked, tossing a chip into the center of the table.

Bill chewed his bottom lip thoughtfully, then took a long swing of beer. "We're together every Saturday night like clockwork. Tomorrow, we're supposed to go to the drive-in: *Snow White and the Three Stooges* is playing."

Francis added his chip to mine, shooting Bill a long, hard stare as the plastic coins made a clicking sound upon impact.

"What do you think she is doing the other six days of the week, champ?"

I'll never know if he found out. No one will. By the time the drive-in emptied out and the exhausted projectionist ventured into the dark lot to investigate why the lonely green Dodge Dart remained still hours after the final credits rolled, Bill's corpse already had begun to stiffen. He lay on his right side, half-naked, his head cradled against the passenger-side door, the silver window crank handle frozen in a mid-stroke of his hair. Like Chuck's, Bill's chest cavity had been torn open, but in the latter's case, a roughly squarish hole had been sawed out, leaving a wet, pulpy window where his heart had once been.

"What do you think the killer did with it?" Francis leaned over to stage whisper to me just as the preacher was leading the mourners in a final prayer for "eternal life" over the casket.

I thought Francis was talking about the eternal life.

I wasn't overly concerned about the eerie similarity between Chuck's and Bill's demises. Perhaps, by some stretch of the imagination, they'd managed to be grifted by a femme fatale, someone akin to Barbara Stanwyck's character in *Double Indemnity* or maybe even one of those dames in *Diabolique*, but I was perfectly safe. I made it a point to never date the same Sue twice. It boggled my mind why anyone would amuse oneself with the same toy repeatedly when there was a world of playthings available for the taking. I was simply quicker than my fellow Lodge members to discover the flaws in my dolls and return them to the sales floor, sometimes with the plastic display box still unopened.

Francis' uncouth commentary earned him a black-veiled bouquet of stern, shaming faces, which he heeded mostly unnoticed. I glanced about the crowd apologetically, absorbing the rebuke on behalf of my Lodge brother, when my eyes locked with the one pair not crushed by a frown. Not far below, a slight smile curled up from her bright red lips.

A new Sue.

This one wore a figure-hugging black dress with a white pinstripe up the side, like someone had dipped his finger in chalk and gently caressed her body from knee to shoulder. Her black hair was neatly gathered at the curve of her neck, but its soft waves along her face reflected nearly blue in the hazy sunlight. It made me want to touch it, to feel if it was as smooth as it appeared in its controlled cascade of abalone.

As friends and family embraced one another and offered tear-filled expressions of grief, I made a bee-line toward the white pinstripe squiggling away. "Pardon me, Miss?" I called out, my charisma heavily stocked and ready for a blinding assault.

The white line bent into an S-curve as Sue twisted her torso to look back at me. She raised one thin, black eyebrow but said nothing.

I quickened my pace and shimmied my expression into a countenance of sympathy. "I wanted to extend my condolences for your loss," I said—earnest but with my most sensitive-sounding lilt.

Sue's expression did not change, but her brow relaxed. "Thank you," she said. The slight upturned grin reappeared. "How did you know Bill?" she asked.

"The Lodge," I explained. "You?"

"Same," she replied without missing a beat. Then, to my surprise, she winked and turned back toward the direction she was going.

I double stepped to appear at her side. "Would you like to have a cup of coffee?" I offered. "Talk about it?"

She eyed me with a sly sideways glance but continued walking. "I have to catch a plane, unfortunately. Perhaps another time."

"A plane? Any place interesting?"

"Las Vegas," Sue said. "I'm seeing Frankie Avalon at the Sands."

I managed to slide my body in front of her, forcing Sue to stop and look at me.

"Are you a Nevada native?"

She rested her hand on her hip, the tips of her fingernails delicately tapping at the white pinstripe.

"Oh no, I simply like to travel. And the Strip is gorgeous at night: a billion lights against a pitch-black desert sky."

Her eyes twinkled as she said this, and I felt a strange sensation in my chest, once I hadn't experienced before. It felt like a tickle, or perhaps a moth batting its wings against the inside of my ribcage.

I wanted this doll for my collection.

"May I call you when you return?" I asked.

I put on my shades and watched her shimmy to a large black Cadillac rag top and climb inside. As her engine roared to life, Francis appeared beside me, nudging my rib cage with his elbow.

"Now there's a snake I have to rattle," he commented, watching the car drive away.

I held up the scrap of paper on which she'd written her digits.

"Maybe after I give her a twirl," I said as we loped toward my blue Bel Air and headed back to The Lodge.

· · · · ● · ● · · · ·

I waited a week to call Sue, but she did not answer her phone until nearly two weeks after that.

She agreed to meet me at Salvatore's downtown at eight o'clock. The place was jumping when I pulled in, and I was forced to park in the only spot available, beside the dumpster at the back of the property.

I waited at the bar for an hour.

Two hours.

When the minute hand drifted toward the three-hour mark, I paid my tab and collected my hat from the coat-check girl. Steaming, I marched back to my car, climbed inside, and shut the door. I had tossed my fedora into the back and was running a comb through my hair when I heard a soft knock on the passenger window. I looked over to find Sue standing on the other side of the door, her porcelain face half-hidden in shadow.

I fingered the lock and she let herself in.

"Fancy meeting you here," she said, her red lips curled into the familiar half-smile.

"Fancy is right," I replied flatly. She was cloaked in an oversized wool coat, unbuttoned. A slim, dark skirt peeked out from below its hem. The interior immediately filled with the smell of her, a spicy, heady scent that reminded me of rich chocolate. "I was just about the leave."

She turned to face me, head-on. "I wasn't very hungry anyway," she said.

"Oh no?" I asked, cocking an eyebrow but feeling the last vestige of anger slip from my voice.

Sue slid slowly my way, arched her back slightly, and shrugged off her bulky wrap, letting it fall to the floor in a high clump in front of the pedals. With her left hand, she stroked the side of my face, her eyes fixed on mine, then drifting downward to gaze intently at my mouth, my neck, and up to my ear. Softly, but with firm intention, she leaned forward and pressed her lips to my cheek, backward to the edge of my sideburn, backward still to my lobe. Her breath was light, playful, and like a tropical ocean wave. Her upper body draped itself suddenly atop mine. I felt a rush of warmth surge through me as her left arm encircled my torso and she pressed her firm breasts against me.

I clasped my hands to her back, felt her spine lean and stretch through her thin, soft sweater, and we entangled ourselves, first gently, teasingly, and then resolute, urgent. The windows fogged, sealing us in relative privacy in the darkness of the lot.

When the last winks of excitement had evaporated, she reached down to her coat pocket to fish us a couple of smokes. She pushed her belongings toward the passenger side of the foot well and sat backwards as I felt around the pile of shed clothing to find my Zippo. I struck it once to ignite the flame and blinked rapidly in the sudden illumination.

Sue's smooth, pale skin glowed in the flickers of firelight, but it was the glint of the bone saw that immediately caught my eye. Her lips curled slightly upward at one corner, and the lighter fell from my hands as with both hands, she jammed the tip of the blade into the center of my chest before I could react. She pulled the weapon out and struck again, and again, until shadows of fuzzy dark splatter flashed onto the ceiling, over the brown herringbone upholstery, and onto the dim hourglass shape straddling my waist. Heat gushed from the quickly expanding wound and poured downward to the valley of my neck, and I struck my arms toward Sue in a panic. It was over before it began. I choked, sputtering and drowning in my own blood.

Sue loved me, loved all of us dearly—and more passionately—than any other doll had.

But she put me down without a second thought.

And everything was as it should have been again.

THE CAVE

SARA WAS THANKFUL SHE wasn't claustrophobic.

The entrance to the cave, nearly imperceptible to passersby, was too constricted for Sadie, her companion on this hike. And despite numerous attempts, the yellow Labrador was not able to contort her meaty body through the passage, which, for about two feet, narrowed so severely that Sara had to turn sideways and force the thickest part of her torso, her modest chest, between the rock walls and say a quick prayer that she wouldn't get stuck.

Sure, it occurred to Sara briefly that she might experience the same difficulty on the exit, but she'd left a red signal flag planted firmly in front of the entrance as insurance, just as she'd watched Maria do on their last exploration, and the canteen was nearly full, so the thought did not linger.

The Mount Holyoke Range was a haven for Pioneer Valley hikers, an intertwining of traprock mountains nearly ten miles long that dissected Western Massachusetts from east to west as its pinnacles loomed over the Amherst area from more than 1000 feet in the clouds. In the spring and summer, the lush peaks were covered in a pointillism of greens and browns; in the winter, they transformed into vast oceans of grey and white waves frozen in the icy landscape. It was fall now, Sara's favorite season, when leaf peepers from all over the Northeast traveled by the thousands to the region and drove lazily down routes 47 and 116 surrounded by tapestries of fiery foliage.

There were others who were drawn to this place for reasons other than its beauty, though. Sara first heard of the legend in her Topics in History course which, that semester, focused on the Cold War in Massachusetts. In the middle of the twentieth century, a nearby Air Force base established a top secret subterranean bunker at the base of one of the mountains of the range. Its purpose, primarily, was to provide sanctuary for high ranking officials in the event of a nuclear attack, and the clandestine retreat, its main entrance well concealed by the heavy brush, included both a command center and living quarters with decontamination showers and food and water that could, in theory, sustain a team of men for more than three months.

The walls, Professor Rice said, were constructed of steel three feet thick and were therefore soundproof, and because residents of the town were prohibited from visiting the facility, rumors spread of top secret experiments being conducted beneath the mountain's veneer.

After the fall of the Berlin Wall, the military abandoned the bunker and a local college repurposed part of the space as a book depository, sealing off the War Room and a number of the isolated chambers. At the same time, Bare Mountain's steep incline began to attract those local hikers looking for a challenge. Their payoff, if they completed the ascent, was an unparalleled view of the valley from more than 1,000 feet, but it required the explorers to scramble and strain up much of the rocky terrain in order to reach the top. One hapless depository employee, a senior at the neighboring University of Massachusetts named Heather Mounce, went exploring after work one afternoon and became trapped under debris when part of an inset near the bottom of the mountain collapsed. Mounce's body was never recovered, and local folklore theorized that she had burrowed her way deeper into the mountain and remained sealed but alive in one of the uninhabited spaces of the bunker.

She was remembering the images Professor Rice had projected onto the screen—low-ceilinged rooms filled with Cold War-era fixtures and ancient technology; barren, buried dormitories and underground kitchenettes—when the sudden sawbuzz of the blender, the metallic gears grinding ice into pulverized slush, drew Sara back to her friends' discussion. They were sitting in Rao's Coffee Shop: Sara, Maria, and two other women from the History class, as they did every Thursday afternoon, and were discussing the professor's recent lecture with morbid intensity. As Sara refocused her attention, her eyes fell on Maria, who was staring at her girlfriend with irritation, keenly aware that she'd been drifting off. Sara shifted in her seat uncomfortably.

"Seriously, though," Lynn repeated. "How long can a person go without food?"

Vickie tipped her coffee cup like a news reporter interviewing a wayward man-on-the-street with an obnoxiously large microphone. "Well, that depends on whether she had water. Without water, three days, tops. True?"

"You're talking about Heather, right?" Sara broke in, then realized, with some shame, that she'd been daydreaming when this point had been established.

If they noticed her embarrassment, the other two women made no show of it.

"Yeah, but let's say she had some water," Lynn went on. "Eventually, she needs food. Starvation is one of the worst ways to die." She paused, then turned toward Maria and added without irony, "Make sure you pack a handful of protein bars Saturday."

Before Sara could open her mouth to comment, Vickie jumped in. "What's Saturday? Special trip?"

Maria stretched her arm around Sara's shoulder and squeezed. "In honor of Rice's creepiest anecdote to date, I'm taking this girl for her first hike of Bare Mountain."

Vickie took a healthy swig from her cup. "Ugh: don't plan on doing much Sunday, then. My calves were killing me for days after. It's pretty steep. And watch your ankles."

"Yeah, I—" Sara began, but Maria cut her off.

"I'll probably bring her up the slower trail, the one past the quarry." She removed her arm from Sara's back and began to tap on the table with her fingers. "I mean, Sadie's climbed the main trail with me no problem, but this is only Sara's third climb."

She glanced at her girlfriend, patting the top of her head with her voice like one might do to a small child.

"Well, you'll likely have the area pretty much to yourself. It's supposed to be chilly. Overcast, too," said Lynn. "But definitely bring those Powerbars, unless you're itching to end up an addition to Rice's Prezi."

Vickie folded her fingers together and rested her chin in them. "'You plan to look for the secret chambers? There has to be at least five or six that are still there, right, if Amherst only rehabbed half of the original facility for the depository."

"I'm sure all of the original entrances and escape hatches were buried when the bunker was closed, but I've seen a few rifts in the rock off the main path. I'm thinking one of them might be disguising a way in...you know, things have to have shifted over the years," said Maria.

Vickie grinned at Sara. "You must be so excited!" she said.

Before her girlfriend could silence her, Sara said, "I am," and raised her arm to scratch at the shoulder where Maria's hand had rested just moments before.

· · · · • · • · • · ·

But two days later, Sara woke to find Maria already absent from the bed they shared and sitting at the kitchen table they often repurposed as a desk, furiously tapping away on her MacBook.

Before she could utter a *good morning*, Maria said, "I have to rewrite my paper for Sarat's seminar. I emailed it last week but somehow it didn't go through, and fuck if I can't find it anywhere on here." Her eyes didn't move from the screen. "At least my sources were still bookmarked, and his T.A. told me if I got it in by five, he wouldn't penalize me."

Sara paused. "We're not hiking today, then, I gather."

She glanced out of the window above the sink. The sky was clear but silvery-blue. It reminded Sara of the days she spent raking leaves as a child.

Maria emitted a small sigh and stopped typing. "Oh, god—I completely forgot. I'm sorry." She rubbed her eyes and finally turned them on Sara. "Maybe next weekend, yeah?"

Sara told herself that she hadn't meant to be purposefully duplicitous, but when she asked Maria if she could borrow her car to take Sadie to the Farmers' Market on the town green, she waited until she was on the porch to tug on her hiking boots. Maria had already gathered their gear in a duffle the night they returned home from the coffee shop, so it wasn't as if she had snuck around the apartment, gathering materials in a clandestine manner, but admittedly, she grabbed two bottles of water from the refrigerator to fill the canteen instead of using the sink where she would have been in full view of Maria.

Now, an hour later, as she felt the fabric of her shirt snag on a tiny crest of stone, lengthen and thin, then spring back with an audible smack against her ribcage, Sara slid the last of her body from the constrictive rock foyer and pulled her shoulders back to stretch her body tall again. She was standing on a shallow plateau with nothing immediately visible over her head. She had made it inside the mountain at last.

Sadie barked a plaintive protest from outside. "It's okay, Say," Sara called back.

The dog paced anxiously back and forth in front of the entrance, alternately hiding then revealing Sara's slim view of the dirt and sky outside. From this angle, she could no longer see her signal flag nor the travel water bowl she had set firmly in the ground, but she paid that no mind: she had allotted herself a few hours to explore. That would leave her more than enough time to hike back down to the road with Sadie and return to the apartment before sundown.

"Stop your fretting," she added. "Besides, you're liable to knock my flag down if you keep walking back and forth like that."

She opened her hands wide and stretched her fingers inside of the gloves, then pulled her flashlight from the holster on her waist and clicked the dial to turn it on. The entranceway poured a slender slice of light onto the rock where she was standing, but she was hesitant to move more than a few inches without having a better understanding of the terrain. Fumbling on her belt for Maria's nylon head strap, she watched the beam from the torch dance along the stony ground beneath her. Once she had mounted the light onto her forehead, she adjusted the dial and dimmed the beam slightly; as long as she kept the output level to medium, she should have a solid three-hour block of light.

On her second and most recent hike with Maria, she had misjudged her timing and found herself heading home in near to complete darkness, with only the narrow beam of her girlfriend's headlight leading the way for both of them. To add insult to injury, earlier that same day, she had insisted on holding her lamp even with her shoulder as she walked, a stance that Maria said reminded her of how television police officers interrogated drivers from the sides of vehicles. When Sara took an unfortunate stumble, she watched the ball of brightness tumble far ahead of her down a thickly wooded mountainside, then spent the next half hour climbing carefully down after it, refusing to acknowledge Maria's smug expression for at least an hour following.

Sara began her investigation with the area nearest to her feet and swept her gaze slowly below her. She was perched on a shallow plateau—a long ridge, really—that jutted suddenly into gaping darkness. As she quickly turned to look around in a 360-degree angle, the cave's interior gradually revealed itself to be a massive chamber about thirty feet wide and forty from floor to ceiling. It reminded her, vaguely, of one of her stuffy college lecture halls with cathedral ceilings and drab, earth-toned decor.

She edged forward slightly. From the ridge where she stood to the cave bottom was about three stories. Sara felt her stomach plummet sickly into the lowest part of her abdomen: had she not been cautious when she first made it out of the foyer, she might have slipped right off of the edge of the plateau.

Maybe that's what happened to good ol' Heather, she thought. *Maybe I'll stumble across her broken and mummified body. Gross.*

She leaned forward a bit further and tilted her chin to her chest to refocus the beam. It was difficult to make out the terrain of the floor, but it appeared rough and uneven in some parts and shiny and slick in others.

Were mummified remains shiny?

She didn't think so.

She turned her head back to the wall to the right of the narrow gap where she had entered. Approximately twelve feet over and a bit closer to the ground, there appeared to be a large opening with another plateau similar to Sara's. However, the expanse of wall between the two entrances looked darker than the rock in the rest of the cave, a deep charcoal granite with ribbon grooves and smooth dimples, and in some places, Sara was certain it was damp with either a thin layer of running water or thick condensation.

She walked carefully toward the wall and stretched her hand as far along it as she could, feeling the pit of her stomach shift above the gaping maw of blackness below. The rock was indeed wet; she stepped backward and wiped the slimy film from her palm onto her thigh. Water must be dribbling from somewhere: it would be too slippery to scale sideways.

She pointed her gaze back over the edge. First, she could make her way to the very bottom, and then she could climb back up to the other ridge. She felt inside her waist pouch for her chalk. She had never free climbed, but she'd watched Maria do it, sometimes without ropes or safety gear of any kind, and Maria had been generous with her unsolicited explanations of every move. Her girlfriend depicted each of her adventures in rock climbing like it was some sort of superhuman feat, but how hard would it be, really? Sara thought. She was in good shape: when the weather cooperated, she ran three miles nearly every weekday, and she had good arm strength from years of Pilates and push-ups. She could use Maria's gear to belay herself down to the floor then free climb up the other side, and perhaps the other opening would provide a more comfortable exit. If not, she could always clamber back up the way she descended: it would be as simple as climbing the ropes in high school gym class.

She pulled a spring-loaded camming device from the pouch on her waist and scanned the plateau floor for a crack or hole. Fastening the cam to a tree or even the outside of the cave would have been a better choice, but Sara had not imagined that the descent would be so painfully steep—or high, for that matter—and it was too late now. When she finally managed to locate a small pocket that seemed promising, she wedged the cam's axel into the crack just as Maria taught her, released the grip, and felt the trigger spring to life, firmly anchoring the device to the rock face.

See that? she thought. *Piece of cake.*

She attached a carabiner and ran a sling of rope through it, attached one end to her harness, then shifted her stance to keep the wall behind her before testing the hold.

Sadie's muffled bark again echoed from just outside of the chamber entrance.

"Take a load off, girl," Sara called back. "You wouldn't want to be in here with me: trust me on this one."

The rope appeared secure, and Sara ran her hands over her pouch, harness, and headlamp in a subconscious attempt to check that she was ready for the dangerous venture. "Remember our deal, Sadie," she said loudly. "If I'm not home for dinner, go tell the sheriff that Timmy fell in the well." Sadie did not respond, likely having thrown in the towel and curled up in the sun for her afternoon nap.

Sara threw the expanse of rope over the edge of the ridge, and turning her body so that her face pointed toward the entrance, leaned back into her harness and stepped slowly backward over the side. She felt her heart race and a pang of fear slap her chest. Images of the rope snapping, the nut releasing, and the rope sliding weightlessly from her waist flashed through her vision, blurring her rationale for a moment. *You're going to die.* The thought was as clear as if Maria herself had spoken it aloud in her ear. She closed her eyes and inhaled as slowly as she could, counting the seconds. *One... two... three... fo—* and exhaled at a similar pace, pushing her stomach muscles into her spine. *Five... six... seven...* She tried to picture the release of breath wringing her body of carbon monoxide like it was a deep red sponge.

When the panic had passed, she opened her eyes once more. She was only a few feet down the wall. She could easily climb up, unhook her equipment, shimmy back through the passageway, and hike home with Sadie. She had seen the inside of the mountain: what else *was* there, really? She already had a story to tell the women, and this time, Maria would not be able to interject her patronizing narrative.

She steeled her shoulders, then slowly moved her right leg back up the cliff side. As she did so, her knee jostled the canteen sitting in the pouch attached to her belt, and Sara felt the water in the canister slosh around slightly. She pulled her body upward, then slid her other leg up the wall, trying to fix her weight on the small notch in the rock, but her boot missed the edge, and Sara's foot slid clumsily down the wall. In a moment of panic, Sara overcompensated and pulled her body closer to the rock, and when her right leg folded toward her torso, it nudged the canteen holster upward, spilling its contents up and out of the pouch. The canteen tumbled downward into the darkness below and landed with a soft thump.

It had been the previous March when Maria brought her home with her to meet her family for the first time. They had been dating for only a few months, but the relationship seemed firmly planted on the long-distance track, and when Maria's grandfather passed away, Sara accompanied her partner home for the services. It had been her grandfather—Grampy—who'd taken Maria on her first hike as a child, Maria confided, and taught her everything she knew about climbing, so as her boisterous cousins snatched silver heirlooms and first-edition hardcovers from the patriarch's sprawling Victorian the day after the funeral, Maria walked straight into the garage, grabbed the canteen from a shelf, and left with Sara for the airport without a single goodbye.

Sara craned her neck downward and looked at her waist, hoping she'd only imagined the canteen's departure. She hadn't. Maria would never forgive her; she had no choice but to go after the item. With this thought, she straightened her legs, then bent them in unison and pushed back against the wall to jump backwards, belaying her way further down into the cave.

The entire descent took less than thirty minutes, not because the distance had been shorter than Sara first estimated but because most of the time, Sara did not pause to think between jumps. Once the top of the plateau disappeared from sight, the expanse of darkness in her peripheral vision seemed to close around her. She concentrated on keeping her face forward, centering the breadth of light on the cave wall and scanning the surface for finger pockets and edges to aid in her later ascent should she need them.

Halfway down, Sara felt a rush of air swoop past behind her. The hairs on the back of her neck tingled and a shiver shimmied down her spine.

A bird, she reassured herself. *That's all. A bird got lost and is flying around, trying to find its way back outside.*

Still, the sensation threw off her rhythm, and she paused in her jumping and rested her feet on a shallow ridge. Her body relaxed, pulling her face against the wall. The rock was cold and dry against her cheek. The light from her headlamp reflected off of the smooth stone, temporarily blinding her. Reflexively, she pulled her face away and angled her head toward the ground, and it was then that she got a clearer view of the cave floor. It was covered in some sort of wet foliage: leaves, perhaps? She would find out soon enough. Less than fifteen feet from the ground remained.

She blinked rapidly to refocus her attention, then turned her head back toward the cave wall. As she did so, however, a dark shadow scurried along the floor at the farthest edge of her vision. Sara's head snapped back toward the floor. Her eyes were playing tricks: there was nothing there but a black carpet of wet leaves.

She turned her head back to the wall again, this time shutting her eyes as she did so. When she faced the stone once more, she opened her eyes, pushed back, and jumped once, twice—

It was on that third push that the rope, possibly frayed from straining against the sharp edge of the plateau above, snapped and gave way. Sara's feet touched the cave wall, her toes and heels making full contact for a long second, and then gravity reached its greedy hand up from the earth and yanked the back of her harness hard.

She felt her body fall and tried to right herself to keep from landing on her tailbone. She attempted to position herself to drop and curl instantly into a roll, but instead, she misjudged the distance remaining and landed squarely on her right foot. A sharp stab of pain shot from her ankle and paralyzed her leg, and Sara crumpled onto her side and into the thick covering of wet debris on the floor, her face immediately half-buried in a glob of what felt like mulch soaked in dirty rainwater. The smell and feel of the muck wasn't leaves exactly, but it reminded Sara of the kind of ground cover she sometimes encountered while running alongside a stream in the woods, especially after a cold autumn rain. It smelled musty and dank: a sickly-sweet scent of decay.

She rolled onto her back and concentrated on her breathing. The throbbing in her leg coupled with the growing strange aroma and sensation of wetness soaking into her clothing was making her slightly nauseous.

Jesus, Sara, she thought. *Keep your shit together.*

"You want to end up like Heather?"

This last sentence she spoke out loud, the sound of her voice ricocheting off the walls then suddenly silenced as if it had been smothered by the muck. The beam on her flashlight remained strong but projected onto emptiness, the ceiling of the cave a faraway blank canvas.

Slowly, Sara sat up and pointed her headlamp in the direction of the other plateau. She could roll up the rest of the rope and repair what she could later; in the meantime, if the other wall contained better outcroppings and footholds, she might be able to climb back up without too much strain on her injured ankle. She pushed herself carefully first onto her knees and then onto her left foot. Holding onto the nearby wall as best she could, she gingerly stood up straight and shifted part of her weight to her right foot. The sharp pain was still there, but nothing seemed broken, only sprained.

She slowly swept the headlamp's light from side to side, then over toward the other plateau. Several yards ahead, a clump of light gray cloth peeked strangely from a lumpy pile of debris. It was a shirt of some kind, with faded maroon lettering barely visible under the grime. Sara thought of the socks and occasional pair of panties she passed on her runs through the woods. She always assumed the clothing had been discarded during romantic trysts, but she doubted anyone was rolling around down here. At least, not by choice.

Finally, her luck was changing: the canteen was only a few tentative hops away, and Sara retrieved it successfully, wiping the brown liquid from its exterior before replacing it—securely, this time, she hoped—in the pouch at her waist.

The distance to the other wall was less than fifteen feet, but it seemed to take Sara an eternity to make the journey. With her footing compromised, she was loath to rush and possibly injure herself further. Besides, every two steps, her feet would become buried in a larger piling of the wet debris, which, she soon learned, sometimes contained large, hard pieces that tripped her.

Branches, most likely.

But who was dragging three-foot tree branches into an abandoned chasm?

Sara didn't have the energy to consider this question too closely. She didn't care what was in the muck; she only wanted to maneuver through it and begin the surely painful ascent before she lost her stamina completely. The stench of the decaying leaves—and likely, of animals lost to misadventure, she was growing to believe—was becoming stronger by the minute. She needed to get away from it, far away from it, and fast.

The wall on this side of the cave was rockier, and already, Sara felt a resurgence of hope when she scanned the face for a suitable path. She began by placing her left foot on a notch a foot up from the floor and followed by gripping a deep indentation a few inches above her head with both hands. Keeping most of her weight on her left foot, she gently aligned her right foot in a wide slit nearly even with her left.

Even as she attempted to push off from her right foot, she knew it would be fruitless. Her body rebelled and her leg shuddered in pain. Her ascent would be slow but steady, alternating her weight from her left leg to her hands; she had to treat the right leg not as a muscle or lever but as a piece of gear she was lugging along.

Halfway through the journey, Sara's hands began to shake as she pulled herself upwards. Her body was shutting down, piece by piece. The sweat that had previously run over her brow and into her eyes had long since cooled and dried, her body shifting into conservation mode and quickly dehydrating. She thought of the water in the canteen at her belt but knew she could not risk removing her hands from the rock wall to retrieve it.

Twice, she shut her eyes and felt herself nearly pass out from exhaustion.

When her hands gripped the top of the wall at last, she no longer cared about the pain and shoved herself upward with both feet to fold her torso onto the edge of the plateau. She remained in this prone position even after her legs swung sideways and her body slid away from the edge and firmly onto the ridge.

After a moment, Sara stretched her neck to look forward. She was facing the wet wall of the cave; the one barrier that separated her from the outside, from freedom and escape, was less than two feet away from her. The beam from the headlamp illuminated the opening she'd spotted from the other plateau; now that she was closer, she was relieved to see that indeed, it was much wider than the foyer through which she had contorted her body upon arrival. In fact, if pushed up with her arms, she could crawl to the hole, if only she weren't so tired, so very, very tired.

It was Sadie's bark, much farther away than it had been previously but just as insistent, that woke Sara. She wasn't sure how much time had passed, but her fingertips were raw and her head pounded, and although her right leg still ached, she pushed herself up to a slouching but standing position and hobbled, half dead, toward the cave opening. Before she could step inside, however, a figure appeared in front of her.

Sara reached her right hand to her face and rubbed her eyes, feeling the grime paint streaks of filth along her face. She pulled the flashlight from her head mount and aimed it at the figure, expecting to reveal that it was nothing but a trick of her mind. Instead, it bathed the pale, gaunt body of what appeared to be a human in a full spotlight. However, what Sara could see of its face appeared almost blue, as if it had been previously submerged in icy water. Its dark hair hung in mats and clumps around the shoulders. Two wet black eyes, the irises swallowed by dilated pupils long ago, glinted in the artificial illumination, but the ghoul didn't flinch or react to the unusual brightness except to contort its mouth into a snarl. What few teeth it displayed were sharpened into pointed shards.

In the sterile echo of the cave, the growl that originated from deep within its throat sounded feral and urgent.

And wet.

Sara stumbled backwards in horror, almost toppling off the ridge, but stepped hard on her right foot to regain her balance. In an instance of darkest comedy, her body reacted to the shot of fresh agony and tripped her again, and this time, she tumbled sideways off the cliff. Even before the white-hot pain seared through the left side of her body, she heard the bones in her left arm and thigh snap upon impact with the floor, and although she had held tight to the flashlight the whole way down, the light extinguished as soon as the lamp hit the ground. Without thinking, Sara weakly shook the case with her right hand and a faint beam began to strobe along the wet clumps of debris surrounding her.

It was only as her head sank deeper into the mulch-like material that she again spotted the light gray patch of sweatshirt half-buried in the pile closest to her; this time, she saw what her foot had stumbled over. Her eyes traveled along what was left of Heather Mounce's decomposed corpse until they stopped on the single strand of long, blonde hair atop it. It was only a patch. Most of the co-ed's head had been gnawed away, her eye sockets empty and ghastly, her nose a wet clump of half-digested meat, the bite marks still visible in what mummified flesh remained. It took her last bit of strength to move the flashlight sideways, but when she saw and finally understood, she wished she had simply closed her eyes and let go.

It hadn't been mulch at all, at least not the kind Sara had seen before. It hadn't been decomposing leaves and branches. But three decades of dead faunae—and the occasional lithe but unlucky explorer—in various stages of rot could easily be mistaken for moldering vegetation…especially on the deep floor of a nearly inaccessible and long-forgotten cavern.

She felt only a rush of air above her.

She didn't hear a sound.

And then the hungry cave inhabitant was upon her, a string of drool dripping from its open mouth and into Sara's ear.

Fear No Drowning

Jamie didn't want to drown.

Bludgeoning, stabbing—hell, even strangling—were preferable ways to die.

He had felt this way since he was a kid, and thus avoided bodies of water as much as was humanly possible. He selected a college in the Southwest, far from any lake; he did his residency in a hospital hundreds of miles from any whiff of the sea. When he confessed his fear of the water to a college girlfriend, her only reply was to quote scripture in a sing-songy voice. *He who is damned to hang need fear no drowning.* Jamie dumped her, and her patronizing smile, at a keg party the next evening. By the close of his twenties, he became a master at dishing out a smorgasbord of excuses why he could not join friends and lovers on seaside holiday.

Then, Ulie came, and there he was, living in a beachfront summer rental year-round, the rocky shore standing guard against the angry Atlantic in his backyard.

Truth be told, it was Molly, Ulie's mother, who arrived first. They met at a casino: Jamie on a bachelors' weekend with a bunch of men from work he barely knew, Molly at a bridesmaids' retreat with her best friends from college. They spent one drunken encounter together then exchanged phone numbers with the unspoken intention of never using them, so when his screen lit up a year later, displaying her name, he nearly ignored the call.

It was Molly's father, informing him. Head-on collision with a drunk driver; no warning, no wait time. One day here, next day gone. Jamie had seen plenty of them on his rotation in the emergency room: dead on arrival, harvest what's salvageable.

Molly had moved back with her parents in Maine soon after her best friend's wedding. Eight months later, she gave birth to a son, a healthy, ten-fingered, ten-toed baby she named Ulysses, a nod to her favorite author and the semester she spent abroad in Ireland. "She always liked Joyce, wanted to pursue a doctorate in Irish studies and write her dissertation on his work," Molly's father said, his voice gravelly—the typical stoic New Englander who kept his excitement tempered and his grief smothered. "She put her studies on hold to raise him." In the long silence that followed, Jamie imagined the man looking over at his infant grandchild, furrowing his brow.

So Jamie came. He gave notice at the hospital, packed his few belongings into his car, and drove north, holding his breath as the car crossed the wide, open bridge over the Piscataqua River and feeling the prickles of dread as the sedative smell of the ocean wafted through his car windows and vents.

The house belonged to the family and required only a few upgrades to make it hospitable year-round. Molly's father signed the deed over to Jamie; he need only put forth the annual taxes while the baby's grandparents lived an hour inland and would visit frequently. He accepted a position at an urgent care clinic in nearby Portland, a massive cut in pay.

It was his first look at Ulysses that convinced him.

He didn't look like Jamie, exactly, though the thick black hair and light eyes were surely his.

When Jamie looked into his son's face, he felt not recognition but a strange feeling of déjà vu, a sensation that very quickly, and permanently, turned to a previously unknown one of unselfish love.

· · • • · • • · · ·

The two settled into a quiet life, even as the harried tourists clogged the dirt road leading to the cottage with their family vehicles and trampled down the nearby public way to the beach each summer.

Ulysses, or Ulie, as his father called him, expanded and contracted like a strange fish, growing pudgy one year only to redistribute the extra mass as he lengthened the next. By the time he was fifteen, Ulie grew to be less than a head shorter than his father and his body settled on an athletic build that served him well both on the soccer field during games and in the Olympic-sized swimming pool during swim meets.

"She was always a strong swimmer," Molly's father remarked as he sat next to Jamie on the stands, the two of them occasionally knocking knees as they watched Ulie dart just beneath the surface of the water like a marlin. "Loved the water like it was her second home."

"He certainly didn't get it from me," Jamie admitted.

The old man's lips twitched subtly. "Landlubber, eh?" he said, more as a statement than a question. "You said as much when you first came here. Any reason for it?"

Jamie leaned back and tried to shift his weight on the disagreeable metal bench. "I grew up in Western Massachusetts and, every summer, my parents piled us into the station wagon and headed to the coast: Cape Cod, Rocky Neck, Misquamicut. It was a new place every year, so I'm not really sure where it happened, but one year—I must have been five or six at the most—I wandered down to the end of the dock to where the older kids were horsing around in the water."

Jamie swallowed. He felt the muscles in his back stiffen.

"You know how kids are. I must have thought, if they could play in the water there, so could I. I don't know what I was thinking, really. I just jumped in. No floatation device, no adult supervision, nothing."

"Did you know how to swim?"

"Dog-paddle. And a poor one at that," Jamie said.

He watched Ulie push himself from the water and climb onto the tile along the edge of the pool. He stumbled slightly, his legs seeming to liquefy for just a split-second, then he righted himself and walked toward the rest of his team.

"I watched him like a hawk, never let him swim alone," Jamie continued. "I still have nightmares of him wandering off in the middle of the night to jump into the ocean, even now."

Ulie raised a hand to his father and grandfather and filed with the rest of his team into the door marked Locker Room. Jamie nodded to his son in return.

Molly's father slapped his hands softly on his knees. "And so it goes," he said, and slowly rose to his feet to leave.

· • • ● • ● • • • ·

Even after many years living away from the city, Jamie marveled at the night sky. He sat on the back deck in the early darkness, a thick blanket insulating his torso against the wet chill of late April, and listened to the waves crash in the distance, the ocean beginning its gradual creep forward. The quick rap on the sliding glass door shook him from his thoughts.

"Hey," Ulie said, stepping outside.

Under his feet was a dusting of sand where the wind had blown it from the beach below. He walked over to the railing, leaving taps of footprints along the wood, and leaned his back against it. Jamie noticed he was limping a bit.

"Hey," Jamie said. He jutted his chin toward his son. "What's going on? You're favoring your left leg."

Ulie bit his lip, then bent over slightly to rub his thigh. "Just cramped. Coach says maybe it's dehydration." He paused. "I fell in the locker room."

Jamie sat forward in his chair. "You fell? Are you okay?"

Ulie looked down at his shoes, traced a short arc in the sand with his toe. "Yeah, yeah, it's no big deal, but…"

He didn't look up.

"But?" Jamie loosened the blanket. "Hey…" he softened his voice. "No secrets. We promised, yeah?"

The teenager straightened up and plopped into a nearby chaise lounge. His breath left faint trails of smoke in the air, but he didn't appear to be cold, not in the least. Adolescent boys, Jamie thought. They were powerhouses of energy and heat, like shiny new boilers on full power. He remembered being that young, invincible.

"Coach says I should talk to you about it, the falling," Ulie said. He furrowed his brow. "I didn't want to worry you. I know how you get."

Jamie pushed the blanket off of himself. "Wait—" he said, "have you fallen more than once?"

Ulie bit his lip again. "Maybe four or five times. Six?" He held his hand up to stop his father from scolding. "I've always been a klutz, you know that. It's just been in the last month or so. But with the cramping and stuff..." His voice trailed off.

"I'll call Dr. Denham in the morning," Jamie said. "No arguments."

Ulie bent forward and slapped his knees just as Jamie had seen his grandfather do that afternoon. "Okay."

He stood up and looked over at the faint outline of the surf below the trickle of bright stars beginning to dot the sky. He nodded his head toward the window at the corner of the house.

"I've been watching the water more and more lately. I used to think you were crazy, coming out here every night and staring out into space, but I think I'm starting to get it." He looked at his father. "Sometimes I think it's calling out to me."

He walked quietly back into the house and slid the glass door shut behind him.

Jamie began spending his evenings out on the deck when Ulie was just a toddler, more as a way to avoid turning on the noisy television that might wake the child, who was a fussy sleeper as it was.

Jamie considered it his progressive exposure therapy, though he rarely left the safety of the elevated deck except to accompany his son to make sandcastles or dip their toes in the surf. He learned to enjoy the feeling of the undertow as it swarmed around his ankles, dragging hundreds of stinging sand grains along his skin and pulling his feet deep into the wet earth, but he had never ventured further into the sea than that.

He thought back to that day, his plunge into the blue water at the end of the dock. His small body shooting downward until the soft mush of the ocean floor caught him and folded itself around his toes.

There had been...

No.

His memory played tricks on him, shuffled the images from his box of childhood and dealt a card out of order. He was confusing a flashback from a movie, or perhaps a television show, with what he had seen under the water.

But he *had* seen it, hadn't he?

A woman—but not so much a woman. A bird—a woman-bird—crouched in the sand in front of him, her giant maroon and green wings shiny like the scales of a coho salmon. Her legs—again, not legs at all but shriveled sticks covered in mottled skin—folded below her broad, human torso. Sea grasses undulated all around her like surrealist metronomes. She looked at Jamie then crooked one shoulder, opening her wing just the slightest bit as if to offer a swaddling nest where he could curl up and nap.

Around him, bits of shell and seaweed and sand suspended in the sea water danced. He felt an overwhelming urge to go to her, to touch the smoothness of her glossy pinions, to feel them surround his body in a feathery embrace.

Her eyes fixed on him, round pools of black swirled with abalone like the inside of a seashell turned to catch the light. Her mouth did not move, but she was saying something, something Jamie could not hear, though he leaned forward to try and listen. The creature tilted her head and began to stretch her neck toward him as if to kiss his cheek.

It was the sharp digging of fingers into his armpits that broke the spell, followed by the sensation of something powerful yanking him upwards. Jamie weightless, rising like a helium balloon toward the surface. He looked down at the woman-bird one last time, just long enough to see her mouth open, the thick rows of jagged white triangles frightfully snapping and chewing at the water where he once stood.

He was coughing. All around him, family members knelt like suppli-
cants, reaching out to touch his skin. His throat burned and when they
lifted him to his feet, his legs melted into jelly, pouring him back onto
the deck where he lay until someone (his father? his brother? he could
not remember) lifted him over their shoulders and dumped him onto the
family's blanket on the sand.

Jamie remembered all of it. Suddenly, it was as clear as if it had happened
in front of him just a moment before. He wrapped the coverlet back
around himself, feeling his shirt mop up the sweat that was pooling on his
back.

When he rose from the deck chair and slid open the door, he heard it:
the woman-bird's voice, finally breaking through the muffled wall of ocean
water and memory.

It called to him from nearly forty years earlier, its voice scratchy and
deep.

Just one word.

"Mine."

· · • •• • • •· ·

"So." Molly's father's voice did not change in pitch or volume. "What
did they say?"

Jamie moved the phone to his other ear and walked out onto the deck.
The early August sun was bright and clean with no clouds about to filter
it. Jamie looked around for his sunglasses.

"Charcot-Marie-Tooth disease," he said, wrestling the shades onto his
face with his free hand. "It's a progressive neuropathy—a kind of cousin
to muscular dystrophy. You know, the Jerry Lewis thing."

He could hear himself adapting his physician voice, the professionally
distanced cadence shaded with just a whisper of the palliative he reserved
for delivering bad news to a patient.

Irritatingly, it sounded a lot like the everyday intonation with which Molly's father spoke.

The line was quiet. Then, "And the prognosis?"

Jamie scanned the beach as he spoke. He could see Ulie lying on a bright blue towel a few yards from the water. He was staring blankly at the waves. "There's a progressive loss of muscle tissue, some loss of sensation—feeling—as the disease progresses." He felt his eyes tear and took a deep breath and exhaled quietly. "We can monitor it, stave off the progression, maybe, with regular exercise and nutrition."

He watched Ulie stand up and walk over to the water, stretch his legs into the surf.

After months of general practice physician visits without definitive answers, Jamie had secured an appointment with a specialist in Boston. They drove down to the city on the Friday before Ulie's sixteenth birthday for an electromyogram. Jamie tried to make a weekend of it, to lighten the solemnity by taking his son to a Sox game, but no boys of summer could have prepared them for the ordeal of the testing his son had endured. Jamie had to wrap his arms tightly around himself to keep from reaching out to comfort his son as the doctor first delivered a series of measured shocks to his arms and legs, then inserted a long needle into each major muscle to record its reactive activity. Less than a week later, the doctor called with the news.

Molly's father cleared his throat. "What can we do?"

There was an awkward, dead silence between the two men. Ulie stopped kicking at the water and suddenly dove into the waves, disappearing under the water only to resurface a second later. Jamie watched the boy's head tilt rhythmically back and forth as he swam a slow breaststroke parallel to the shore until he was halfway down the beach. Then he ducked under the water again and swam back the way he came.

"James?" Molly's father finally said.

"Nothing...for now," Jamie said. He swallowed. "It's going to be alright." He hung up the phone without saying goodbye.

• • • •●•●• • •

Jamie spent the next month reading every medical journal he could find on CMT. He met over lunch with colleagues at the clinic and networked himself into Zoom meetings with faraway colleagues of those colleagues. Ulie didn't have the foot drop or muscle atrophies typical to the disease. There were many subtypes of the disorder, for sure, and Jamie had no specialized training in neurology, but there was something digging at him in the corner of his mind, something that told him that everyone—he, the doctors, the technicians—had missed something.

Two weeks into his junior year, Ulie quit the soccer team. There was no discussion with Jamie regarding the matter, and Jamie did not push it, and the afternoons his son had previously spent at practice were replaced with long stretches of moping about the house, and more and more often, sitting on the deck alone, staring at the ocean.

Soon after, Jamie awoke in the middle of the night screaming, fragments of a vivid nightmare still fresh in his mind.

In the dream, Ulie stood on the deck, overlooking the ocean as the tide drifted inward. His wrists were bound firmly to the railing: thick sisal rope, its taut fibers digging into his skin and leaving red scratches and pock marks dusted with a fine layer of beach sand that had been carried by the wind. Behind him, the dark ocean swelled, its sinister water thickening like cooling gelatin, pouring itself along the barren stretch of sand. Jamie peered down to watch the sea envelop the bottom steps, and a figure appeared there, crouching in the water. It was the woman-bird from his childhood, her black eyes wet and round, staring up at him as she snapped her jaw menacingly at the open air. The creature began to wail, a low hum that quickly intensified to a high-pitched screech that made Jamie's breastbone shake in its timbre. He ran to his son and pressed his hands tightly on either side of the boy's head, trying desperately to block the sound from his ears, but as he did so, a pair of raptorial talons snaked around his legs and grabbed hold of Ulie's ankles.

"Dad?" Nightmare Ulie's eyes were wild and confused. "Dad?" he asked again, but before Jamie could answer, the woman-bird dug her claws into his calves and jerked them violently downward.

Jamie stood helplessly watching as the side of the deck gave way and fell backwards into the swirling water below, his son still anchored to its broken barrier.

When he awoke, Jamie sprang from his bed and immediately ran to the sliding glass door, then each window, and finally, the front door, checking and rechecking the locks.

Ulie appeared in the hallway, rubbing his bed-tousled hair. "What's going on?" he asked sleepily, but his father ignored him and continued to run his fingers along the edges of every possible access point.

Whatever was hunting his son, stealing him from Jamie, would not be allowed in without a fight.

· · · ● · ● · · · ·

After that fretful evening, Jamie began taking an over-the-counter sleep aid each night before bed. It staved off the bad dreams—at least, any memory of them—but the pills were a daily reminder of the frightful images still fresh in his mind.

It was only a month later that Jamie awoke disorientated from a deep sleep. It was the middle of the night and the house was silent save for the click and hum of the furnace turning on as it did from early October to the end of April. Halloween was still two weeks away, but the cold fronts always made an early sweep of the shoreline before branching inland as the season evolved. It wasn't the furnace that had stirred him.

His intuition prickling, Jamie swung his feet out of bed and walked out of his bedroom, not bothering to step into his slippers or wrap himself in a robe. He padded over to the sliding glass door and checked the lock. Secure. He cupped his hands on either side of his face to look out. There were fresh footprints in the wisps of sand along the deck: not the taps of shoe bottoms, but bare foot imprints, angled away from the house and toward the steps leading below.

Jamie turned and ran across the dark room, knocking over a dining chair with a clatter. He rushed blindly down the hallway and opened the door to Ulie's room and turned on the light.

His son was not in bed.

He wasn't anywhere in the room.

A soft breeze caressed Jamie's face.

The window was open, wide open, wide enough for his son to climb out.

Jamie rushed back to the sliding glass door, unlatched it, and pulled it open. He turned on the outside light, its brightness bathing the deck in a pool of mechanical brilliance. Indeed, the footprints began under Ulie's open window. Jamie followed them down the stairs to the beach and began to run across the sand, ignoring the stabs of pain as his bare feet dug into sharp rocks and broken mussel shells. The full moon hovered ominously above, reflecting off the water so that it appeared the dangerous color of a gas flame, a carpet of blue fire spouting and cresting pockets of white ash toward the shore.

"Ulie!" Jamie screamed, the crashing water determined to drown out his voice. "Ulysses!"

Jamie squinted, willing his eyes to adjust to the dim light. He scanned the sand; there were no footprints, but the tide was coming in and could have erased them.

"Ulie!" he called again, then, though he was unsure to whom he was asking, added, "Please?!"

In the water, just beyond where the waves began to grow, there was a dark shape. Jamie could barely make it out, was not certain if it truly was a shape or a trick of the eye, but no, yes, no, yes, yes yes it was a shape. It was his son, it had to be his son, was it his son?

"Ulie!" Jamie screamed at the shape, cupping his hands around his mouth like a megaphone. There was a faint cry. The shape seemed to jump, leap sideways. It bobbed beneath the water then reappeared. Another cry.

"I'm coming!" Jamie yelled and ran into the sea, toward the shape. Icy water seized his ankles, his calves, his knees, but he broke from its grasp, running until the water seemed to encase his legs in cement and the waves crashed onto his chest and onto his face. "Ulysses, I'm coming!" he cried again, then dove forward, into the oncoming wave, digging deep into muscle memory of his childhood to kick his feet, to scoop the water downward with his cupped hands, to push himself over the dark mountains of ocean moving quickly towards him.

Before long, he realized that he was in water over his head, that he could not stop paddling or kicking or he would sink to the bottom and drown. He imagined, for an instant, what would happen if the moon were to go dark, if a cloud were to cover the only winking of light.

Where is Ulie?

He felt his heart race and his breathing quicken. He was panicking. He spun his head rapidly to scan the surface of the water around him.

Where is Ulie? Where? Where?

He took a deep breath into his stomach and forced himself to slow its release, like he had taught himself in medical school to keep his mind from racing and the anxiety to swallow him whole.

Sure enough, on the last edge of exhale, the shape reappeared, just beyond the final wave. His son, flailing helplessly in the water in front of him, his arms pumping frantically on either side, saw his father in the water and sputtered a gasping cry.

"My legs," he stammered. "I can't...don't work."

Jamie took another deep breath and concentrated on paddling. The waves were calmer here, but he had to work to stay afloat.

"Can you float on your back?" he called.

Ulie turned and attempted to lie backwards but to Jamie's horror, sank immediately downward.

His head resurfaced. "No," answered Ulie flatly, spitting water from between chattering teeth.

Jamie paddled closer to his son. "Listen to me. I am going to try to get us to shore, but I am going to need you to help me as much as you can, do you understand?" he asked.

"Y-yes, yes," stammered Ulie. His lips shivered.

"Put your arm around my neck, but try not to choke me, okay?" Jamie said. "I need you to use your other arm to swim hard, to help push us forward and keep you afloat, too, okay?"

Jamie paddled next to his son, trying to position himself close enough for the boy to touch. Alarmingly, as soon as he was in reach, Ulie grasped onto his father in desperation, and the two sank under the water. In a panic, Jamie shook off his son's arms and kicked back up to the surface, gasping for air. Ulie's head reemerged as well, coughing.

He began to cry.

Jamie felt a visceral dividing within him: the adrenaline of self-preservation screamed within his mind, but the primal need to protect his son beat it mercilessly to a faraway whisper.

"Listen to me," Jamie yelled. "We are going to get back to shore, but I need you to listen to me and do what I say. Do you understand?" He raised his voice as sternly as possible. "Do you understand, Ulysses?"

"Yes," his son shuddered.

Slowly, carefully, the two pushed themselves, the three-armed, two-legged body, through the water and toward the dark beach, using the momentum of the waves to their advantage. Jamie kicked his legs furiously, feeling the last reserves of energy begin to leak from his muscles with every inch forward. Water sloshed over his eyes and he shook it away, but his vision grew cloudier. At last, when he was finally able to stand, he wrapped his arms under his son's knees and neck and carried him, just as he had when Ulysses was a toddler, to the shore until the two collapsed onto the dry sand.

Jamie turned to his son, grasping his face in his hand. "Ulysses? Are you okay?"

His son began to cry, sob in a manner Jamie had not seen him do since the boy was still a child. Instinctively, he rolled onto him and hugged him tightly, trying desperately to warm his son's shivering body with his own.

"It's okay. We made it. It's okay. Shhhh."

Ulie sniffled in his ear, a combination of snot and salt water. "I can't...my legs...I still can't feel them. Dad..."

Jamie pulled his head back to look into his son's eyes. "You're in shock. That's all," he whispered and stroked his son's hair. "Give yourself a minute. Let's just rest here for a beat. I don't think I could walk myself right now." He squinted at his son in the dim light and felt his stomach drop as he saw Ulie's expression change from exhaustion to fear.

"Dad?" he squeaked, looking over Jamie's shoulder and towards the water. They both felt the frigid caress of the incoming tide slithering around their bodies. Ulie's face collapsed into a sob as the boy shut his eyes tightly in sheer terror.

Jamie let go of his son and twisted his body to face the ocean. There, standing on the edge of the water, was the woman-bird. Water dripped from her iridescent wings. Her new, human legs were planted firmly in the surf, and she stretched her mouth into a terrible grin, the tips of her triangle teeth glinting like sparks in the moonlight.

Over the roar of the ocean, he heard her familiar hiss.

"Mine."

HAUNT

New sex—*STRANGE* sex—was the best sex of all.

Though he was circling middle-age, Michael was still quite handsome, even by younger standards, and so it was easy to find random strangers to take home and sleep with multiple days a week. Never the same woman, mind you—unless he was desperate, and even then, he was highly selective. The encounter, intimate yet impersonal, was as powerful of a stimulant as any drug. It kept him energized; perhaps, it even kept him young.

The only thing more enjoyable to Michael than new sex was his routine.

He liked having a schedule, one both he controlled and allowed to control him. Six days a week, he showered by eight, sat at his kitchen table in front of his laptop by nine, checked his email, read notes left by publishers and clients, then wrote until six, stopping only to make himself an afternoon pot of coffee. His friend Dave told him that the caffeine would act like an appetite suppressant, and Lord knows he wasn't doing his middle section any favors sitting stagnant in a chair for most of the day. At six-thirty, he watched the evening news while waiting for his dinner to be delivered or finish warming in the microwave. He paid special attention to the weather, though he was never quite sure why, as he rarely went out before sundown and never by foot. Uber and Lyft and the dwindling yellow cab services took him anywhere he needed to go, and besides, when he brought a woman back to his place, he had a built-in excuse not to drive her home. Everyone had a car service app on their phone these days; if they didn't, they were likely too old for Michael's liking and wouldn't have made it into the pool of possible hook-ups anyway.

Like most writers, he dreamed of scribing the great American novel—or at least, the great lucrative one—but freelancing paid the bills on his modest home and lifestyle, and as long as his hands could type and his brain continued to translate the cadence of his thoughts into euphonious sentences, he could sustain both of them without much of a sweat. He reviewed underground thrash shows for a regular column in an independent but slowly growing music magazine. He ghost-penned a memoir for a washed-up victims' rights attorney, a woman who claimed to have rubbed shoulders with celebrity chefs and aging 80s television stars. (He'd checked the dots on the i's on that liability clause twice, suspecting the woman was slightly unstable and weaving many of her anecdotes out of fairy threads.) He wrote movie pitches and travel brochures, magazine features and newsletter columns, encyclopedia articles and instruction manuals, and when his regular, paying gigs were caught up, he wrote his own short stories, quiet literary horror pieces with just enough gore to make a small press anthology grant him inclusion every now and then.

"I don't know where you come up with some of your stories, dude," Dave said, running the filter end of an American Spirit along his bottom lip.

Dave had tried vaping, but with the controversy over vapers' lung disease spreading like herpes at an after-prom party, he went back to good old-fashioned cancer sticks. The bars, even ones as sketchy as The Turtle, didn't let him light up inside, but feeling their presence along his mouth satiated the urge for the moment.

"Some of the things that happen in them?" Dave continued, bringing his fist in front of his own face then opened it. "BOOM! Blows my mind." He smiled, tapped the cigarette on the bar top. "You're a sick fuck, you know that? But I guess that's what sells these days."

Michael raised his two fingers to signal the bartender that he needed a refill. "Lady Inspiration, my friend," he replied. "She's a fickle bitch, but she's been kind to me over the past few years, so I try not to make any sudden moves."

Michael had read somewhere—probably in a Stephen King novel; Christ, he was always reading those books before bed, and the man never seemed to run out of ideas, the bastard—that a writer's motivation to create was like a ghost. It wasn't something he could call upon at will; it just appeared when it wanted to haunt him.

Dave nudged him with his elbow and lowered his voice. "Speaking of fickle bitches...you catch that redhead over by the juke?"

He motioned to the left with his eyes but did not turn his head. Michael leaned forward nonchalantly and gazed in the direction of his pupils. Sure enough, there was a woman standing next to the machine, its neon lights reflecting shimmering patterns on her skin and clothes like a kaleidoscope. Her hair was more auburn than red, but it was long with some curl throughout. Michael liked curly hair: his first serious girlfriend had been a brunette with tight ringlets down her back, tanned skin and light eyes—Jesus, she'd had a body he'd seen only in movies up to that point, and since, if he really thought of it. He still had the videos they'd taken on his laptop, and truth be told, he watched them now and again when the free porn sites became too tiresome, but he wasn't certain she would have been happy to know they still existed.

He took a long swig on his beer. "I prefer dark-haired women," Michael said. "Not only are there more of them to choose from, they tend to have shoulders that don't wither and peel after an hour in the sun." He nodded toward the jukebox. "Look at her. I can practically see her entire circulatory system through her skin."

Dave sputtered a laugh and slammed his empty glass onto the bar. "We all need a little color in our lives now and then, my friend. Besides, you know what they say about gingers." He leaned sideways toward his friend but didn't turn to face him. "They are fucking lunatics in the sack."

"Yeah, and out of it, too. That's all I need, some clingy chick calling my house at all hours of the day and night. No thanks."

But moments later, something made Michael turn his head and look at the woman again. This time, she was staring directly at him, fingering a charm on a gold chain around her neck with her head tilted slightly downward, forcing her eyes to widen and look up. Her mouth curved into a curious smile; she appeared to Michael like a doe transfixed, not by an oncoming car, but by a slowly approaching stranger holding a basket of gifts. When she saw Michael's acknowledgement, he swore he saw her wink.

"Where have you been, sexy?"

An arm, heavily perfumed, wrapped around his chest from behind. He turned sideways, more to loosen the interloper's embrace than to see to whom it belonged. With her short, dark hair, Gloria resembled Snow White; Michael almost expected a band of cartooned forest creatures to begin dancing about her when he'd fucked her the first time.

That was almost a year ago, and she'd returned to his house a few times since then.

A few more, and she'd be classified as dead to him.

New sex, strange sex, was good sex; comfortable, like an old shoe sex was not.

His sex life was one thing; routine was another.

They did not mix.

Still, Gloria smelled wonderful, a strange, soothing potpourri of piña coladas and home-baked treats. And it was getting late. He looked at the jukebox woman one more time. She was still looking at him, tracing her finger along the metallic glint on her collarbone.

"What do you say we get out of here?" he said to Gloria.

As they walked together toward the door, he kept his eyes forward, avoiding the jukebox woman's gaze even though he felt it pulling him like a magnet. When the car dropped him and Gloria at his house, they entered through his front door, the one that opened onto his living room, and before she could even reach for a light-switch, they devoured each other like animals. Best of all, before he passed out on the couch, she called for another cab and was gone.

In the morning, Michael awoke clear-headed and well-rested. Yet, when he sat down at his kitchen table in front of his laptop, he felt another sensation, one he hadn't experienced in years.

He could no longer write.

· · • • · • • · · ·

It had happened before, of course.

Sometimes, Michael would drink a bit more than he planned, perhaps on a nearly empty stomach—again, watching the waistline—and wake up with his face pressed against the cold bathroom tiles, the room both spinning on its axis and pressing his skull into a helmet three sizes too small. Other times, he'd travel home for a few days over holiday to visit with his family, the heavy plates of turkey soaked in gravy and drowning in starchy side dishes weighing his body down, making everything sluggish, including his brain.

After a day or two of recovery, the words would flow again, rushing from his mind like notes on a music sheet, his fingers tapping out the translation.

This time, however, the boomerang he'd thrown out into the wind had become lost somewhere, and it neither returned nor gave hint at where it had landed. He sat at his laptop for hours, writing, then rewriting the same sentence, over and over, until his head throbbed and he simply gave up.

· · • • · • • · · ·

Two months later, he wandered the Liquors 44 store, trailing Dave like a nervous child in an unfamiliar home.

"What d'ya think?" Dave asked, pulling a blue bottle of gin from the shelf and holding it for Michael's inspection. "Good for martinis? I figure, I bring this and a jar of olives, and pow! I'm covered for the hostess gift, yeah?"

Michael nodded weakly and let his eyes drift along the Christmas decorations draped merrily throughout the store. They seemed garish and obnoxious in the glare of the fluorescent overhead lighting, especially since it was still November. It seemed unfair to Thanksgiving somehow, to leapfrog over the holiday and barrel headlong into Santaland, but he supposed that's what the country did these days: everyone was always gazing ahead, looking past what was happening in the here and now. Plan, plan, plan.

"I wonder if they put up Thanksgiving decorations before Halloween," he said out loud.

"What?" Dave was replacing the blue bottle and taking a look at another. "Who the hell puts up Thanksgiving decorations?" He tapped the unlit cigarette shoved behind one ear and replaced the new bottle on the shelf. "Fuck it. I'll just bring a bottle of Kahlua and some cheap vodka. Black Russians for everyone."

He sauntered away and disappeared around the end cap display.

Michael stared at the bottles on the shelf in front of him until the labels seemed to blend together, one long ribbon of gold and green and black text sloshing back and forth in undulation. He hadn't written anything in nearly eight weeks, not one line. He had tried everything to create even a paragraph of literary merit: revisiting his notes, reading his favorite authors, even speaking aloud in stream-of-consciousness, and the words were there, the images he could see, but the sentences—the *stories*—they were trapped behind soundproof glass, beating ferociously with their fists but never making even a fissure.

And then, she was there. The jukebox woman, her neck wrapped tightly in a scarf and her auburn hair hidden mostly by a gray knitted cap. She stopped and peered at him from the next aisle over the smokestacks of clear and brown bottles.

He was certain it was her: since that night at the bar, he had been seeing her everywhere. He stopped at the grocery store, and there she was, sorting through the imported cheese. He stood in the line at the bank, and there she was, walking away from the teller, tucking her receipt in her jacket pocket. He rode in a cab, and there she was, walking down the street just blocks from his destination. Even at the club the previous week, where he did his best to take copious notes for the review piece he'd never begin, there she was, sitting at a table alone. Always touching her neck with one finger, always toying with her necklace.

She never approached him, though, and he, sinking deeper into the quicksands of depression and resignation, had no will to approach her.

They simply stared at one another like adversaries before a duel.

Michael blinked his eyes, hard. She was the closest she'd ever been. He could see the color of her eyes now: they were green, a graying green, the color of sun-bleached grass in an old photograph. If he stretched his arms, really reached as far as his arms would go, he could touch her, maybe even grab her. Grab her by the neck and shake her. Shake her and ask her why the hell she was following him everywhere.

He didn't. Instead, after a long minute, she broke her gaze and walked slowly away without saying anything.

Dave clapped Michael on the back. "We ready?" He held two bottles in his hand. "Let's get out of here. I gotta hit the road for Nancy's before rush hour. The Pike's gonna be a nightmare, it being a holiday week and all. You coming?"

Michael gazed down at his phone. There were two new emails in his inbox, both from clients. Each informed him that his lack of material as of late had forced them to contract elsewhere.

"Who's texting you? Is it that leggy number from Saturday? The one who kept talking about her gym habits?" Dave nudged him with his elbow.

Michael silenced his phone and shoved the cell back in his pocket.

"Yeah, you know me," he said weakly.

He followed his friend to the register and then to his car, speaking again only when he wished him a happy Thanksgiving and walked up the steps to his front door.

· · · ● · ● · · · ·

It had been easier than he thought to weasel out of Thanksgiving dinner with his family.

A few coughs and a well-timed FaceTime call placed moments after spending a half hour in an unvented bathroom, the shower turned as hot as it would go, and his mother agreed: Michael should stay home. Why risk getting everyone else sick, and besides, he needed to recover quickly: didn't he have that meeting with the Hollywood agent coming up? The weakness in his returning smile didn't need to be faked: *oh yeah, the agent meeting: I can't miss that.*

Except, of course, that the agent had canceled on him weeks earlier.

He tried to self-medicate himself on the couch, a bottle of bourbon and a glass full of ice by his side, but there was nothing worth watching on television. Every show he turned on only reminded him of his own lost story-telling ability. After an hour of channel-surfing, Michael made up his mind: The Turtle was open. He'd call a car to bring him there, maybe play some Keno and listen to the jukebox shuffle through a few 80s hair metal before stumbling home to bed.

And, she was there. Quite frankly, if she hadn't been, he would have been surprised. Why she wouldn't be spending the holiday with her own family never crossed his mind, but as the first football game of the day wrapped up, he made up his mind to approach and confront her. He had nothing left to lose.

As if on cue, the jukebox startled to life. Someone had selected a 90s riot grrrl tune, Kathleen Hanna or P.J. Harvey or another one of those women screaming that her lover wished he'd *never! never met her!* His target was dressed in green from head to toe, an ensemble Michael would have been happy to lampoon in a short story had she not looked curiously beautiful in it. As he slid into the barstool next to hers, he cleared his throat and racked his brain for a clever opening line. She beat him to the punch.

"Thought it was about time you tried to chase *me* for a while, huh?" she said, the same knowing grin he had been seeing for months, pursing her lips together and twinkling her eyes.

Michael nervously sipped his drink. "Yes," he stammered. "Apparently, the only place you haven't been of mine is my home. Unless you skulk around while I'm sleeping."

He only half-laughed at this, realizing the gravity of the statement as he spoke it. She did seem to be everywhere in his life; it might have been less bizarre to find her sitting uninvited in his kitchen one morning.

She fingered the gold charm around her neck. "Then why don't you remedy that?" The doe eyes again, staring him down amusingly.

Michael looked at his nearly empty glass. What *did* he have to lose? He was alone for the week, and he had nothing better to do. What was the worst this strange woman could do? Refuse to leave? He helped her with her coat, and the two shared a cab back to his house.

It had snowed the evening before—just a light dusting, but enough to make his front walk a bit slick. Most of the side entrance was covered by a porte-cochère, so the ground was free of debris. He took her hand and led her up the driveway, and they entered his home through the kitchen door.

His laptop was still propped up at the table; a mousepad, detached keyboard, and scraps of notes strewn nearby. She shook off her jacket and draped it on one of the chairs.

"You're a writer," she said.

Unlike the other women who he'd brought home, she didn't pose this as a question, but a statement.

Michael scratched his head. "Yeah, I guess."

He peeled his hooded sweatshirt from his torso and opened the freezer to look for an ice tray. He hadn't planned on company and would have to improvise. He might have a nice bottle of wine in his cellar somewhere, but he didn't even know this woman's name. And yet, it was Thanksgiving, and so—

She was sitting at his computer, staring at the screen. Somehow, she had unlocked his password-protected laptop and was reading his work, or, more accurately, his lack of work. The unfinished story, one he'd begun months earlier and never progressed further, was in front of her, and she was reading it. She was reading and her eyes danced. She was laughing. She was laughing at him, at his literary impotence, at his humiliation. At his failure.

Michael felt the last vestige of self-worth slip from the shelf of his mind and break.

He snatched her from the chair, wrapping his hands around her throat. Her sinewy muscles resisted his grasp, then acquiesced, folding into themselves; he could feel her windpipe flatten. He had read somewhere—likely in a bout of research for one of his horror stories—that it took up to three minutes for a victim to die of strangulation: one minute before they passed out and two more to finish the job.

He stared at her face and in his surprise, released his grip.

She wasn't scared.

She wasn't the least bit panicked.

As he choked her, she simply stared at him, those doe eyes beckoning him to continue.

Taunting him.

Baiting him.

She was amused by him.

If he couldn't scare the look off of her face, he'd simply make her face disappear. He began to strike her about the face. Over and over, he pummeled her: in the eyes until they swelled shut, in the nose until it crunched under his fist, and in the jaw until he felt pieces break free and rattle inside. He hit her until he felt the bones in his own hands shatter and rupture, and then he beat her further, his own agony driving him to punish her further. In his final blow, he felt the blood from his fingers, now just sticks of raw meat, pool with hers: one sticky puddle of pulp and bone fragments.

Her body went limp and slumped sideways onto the side of the table. In the overhead light, something glinted at her collarbone. Michael poked at the gold with what remained of his index finger and turned the charm over so he could read the inscription. It was only one word.

Muse.

Then he fell to his knees and sobbed.

ACKNOWLEDGMENTS

Thank you to Kevin Bell, who provided space, quiet, and support unconditionally; Louis Stephenson, who has been my invaluable sounding board for the past four years; Ruth Estabrook, Ann Michaels, Dylan Burakiewicz, Erin Zwirn, Doug Ford, Holly Rae Garcia, Missy Giroux, Ronald Malfi, and Zachary Hastings Hooper, who cheered for me even when I was crawling on my hands and knees to finish the race; Shawn Macomber, who championed this collection and steered it to calm seas; the strangers who bought my work and left lovely reviews, even though they had a wealth of other options and a shitload of other things to do; and Tom Morello.

Because he's Tom Morello. And not suing me.

As the muse once said to the author,
(even though you'll wish you never met her and you'll lick her injuries)
You're not rid of me.

Rebecca

ABOUT THE AUTHOR

Rebecca Rowland is the dark fiction author of two fiction collections, one novel, a handful of novellas, and too many short stories. She is also the editor of seven horror anthologies, and her speculative fiction, critical essays, and book reviews regularly appear in a variety of online and print venues. A New England native, Rebecca has lived all over Massachusetts and as a result, chooses to torture most of her characters there.

Follow her on Instagram:
@Rebecca_Rowland_books
For more information about her books and other writing projects,
please visit RowlandBooks.com